Stranger, Visitor, Foreigner, Guest

ELIZABETH PORTER

INDEPENDENT INNOVATIVE INTERNATIONAL

Published by Cinnamon Press,
Meirion House,
Tanygrisiau,
Blaenau Ffestiniog,
Gwynedd
LL41 3SU
www.cinnamonpress.com

The right of Elizabeth Porter to be identified as author of this work has been asserted by her in accordance with the Copyright, Designs and Patent Act, 1988. © 2015 Elizabeth Porter.
ISBN 978-1-909077-64-5
British Library Cataloguing in Publication Data. A CIP record for this book can be obtained from the British Library.
Designed and typeset in Garamond by Cinnamon Press. Cover design by Adam Craig © Adam Craig.

Cinnamon Press is represented by Inpress and by the Welsh Books Council in Wales.

Printed in Poland

The publisher acknowledges the support of the Welsh Books Council

Acknowledgements

I am very grateful to the Arts Council of Wales and to the Jerwood and Arvon Foundations for their support.
My heartfelt thanks also to Jane Blank, Candida Clark, Deborah Kay Davies, Helen Doyle, Jan Fortune, Marseli Kastuli, Alex Klaushofer, Perpetua Mano, Victoria Mushi, Cesilia Nangay, Molly Owens, Tamlyn Rabey, Jamie Rance, Norman Schwenk, Ruth Smith, Claire Syder, Joseph Tesha, Shelagh Weeks and Joe Wright.

In memory of

John Porter

1930 - 2013

Taking Notes at the Funeral

1992

I wished I could travel by dhow to Zanzibar, even though Lou had warned me, 'Nobody does it that way, dumb-ass, not unless they want to die young.' The dhow in the harbour at Dar Es Salaam looked calm and strong, rocking a little on the water, her patched sail twitching in the breeze while men loaded the hull with fish traps, bulging plastic sacks, cooking pots tied together by the handles. She seemed to promise the quiet crossing I longed for, and I needed to convince myself that Lou didn't necessarily know best; that I could still make my own decisions. 'Name your price,' I'd say to those guys, and they'd be glad to take me on board.

But I knew my dodgy knee wouldn't cope with the jump from the quayside, the sudden tilt of wood and water underfoot, so instead I shuffled with everyone else along the gangplank onto the ferry. I wasn't so different from the tourists, all of us pursuing our corny dream of the most romantic island in the world, according to the guidebooks, although the fat woman in front of me struggling with a crate full of live chickens was probably not thinking along those lines.

On deck I found a space for myself at the rail, intending to enjoy the view in peace, but it wasn't long before another backpacker, a girl, sidled up and stood just a little bit too close. 'Hi,' she said, 'I'm Susie.' Susie's hair was tightly braided in those cornrows which are not such a great idea on white women, and she asked way too many questions. Was I travelling alone? How long had I spent in Dar Es Salaam? First time on Zanzibar? What did I do for a living? Which I didn't mind because she was British, so 'I used to play baseball' meant nothing to her. But when I told her I was going to Zanzibar to visit my girlfriend she lost interest, and soon moved away.

Later, when the sea became choppy, I noticed several white people throwing up over the rail, Susie amongst them, her beaded braids swinging in her face. I fixed my gaze on the horizon and drank Coca-cola, its familiar zing just managing to distract my stomach from the motion and the smell of engine oil and chicken shit. But it didn't stop me from worrying about seeing Lou again, and imagining what it would be like to have sex with her tonight, after nine months apart. I'd tried to explain over the phone that my leg, although mending, was not exactly one hundred per cent; that I had problems with my balance, was still rebuilding my strength, and she'd just cackled down the line, 'Are you telling me you're *emasculated*, Sasha?' – and what could I do but laugh with her?

After a few hours, a band of low cloud in the distance became a land mass, and there was Zanzibar, waiting for us, the blurry outline steadily gaining definition, as if an invisible pencil were sketching in the minarets, the palm trees reaching up to the sky like children waving. I scanned the tiny figures on the quay and my spirits began to lift, even though Lou had said the ferry was so unpredictable she wouldn't bother coming to meet me.

As soon as I'd gone through customs I was mobbed by a pack of young dudes tapping my arm, offering me accommodation, guided tours and excellent exchange rates. A kid tugged the straps of my backpack. 'Come with me sir, I bring you to one very cheap room!'

'Thanks, but I already have a reservation at the Eastern Star.' I eased the pack off my shoulders so I could find Lou's directions. The boy grabbed it. 'You follow,' he said, and set off towards the Stone Town.

'Hey!' I yelled, 'I know where to go!' Then I laughed at myself for lying and began to jog after him. The streets of the Stone Town were very narrow, hardly more than alleys, and deserted apart from a few kids playing, their voices eerie against the hush. I saw a flash of colour somewhere above and looked up: a woman was leaning from a window, a yellow kanga over her hair, her face like a sunflower. She smiled at me, so I smiled back and hurried on. Eventually my guide led me to a dead end, where there was a house with a painted sign above the door, a lurid pink and gold sunburst. 'Eastern Star,' he said. I thanked him and tried to give him a hundred shillings but he waved the money away with a grin and disappeared down a gap between two buildings.

I knocked on the door several times. When I called, 'Hello?' my voice echoed against the stone. A little girl came out of the next house and said something in a shrill, important voice. 'Sorry,' I said. 'I don't understand.' She stood on tiptoe and pressed a button set into the wall. I heard a bell ringing somewhere deep inside the building.

The man who opened the door was tall, good looking, with a beard tapering to a point. He took one glance at my state-of-the-art rucksack with its pockets and fluorescent orange straps, then shook his head. 'I am sorry my friend, we have no vacancies at present.'

'But I've come to see Lou – she's expecting me.'

'Mama Lou?' His eyes widened. 'Then you must be Sasha.' He grasped my hand and shook it, and didn't let go. 'Welcome! We are very happy to meet you, Sasha. I am Fidelis John.'

The name that cropped up over and over again in Lou's letters: Fidelis, who'd given her a roof over her head, who'd welcomed her into his family, who'd fixed everything so she could fill her notebooks with the data that would turn into the thesis that would one day secure her tenure. 'Fidelis is my entrée,' she wrote early on. Now he stood before me, and he was not the wise, grey-haired elder I had imagined.

'Very pleased to meet you, Fidelis. Lou told me about you – this is your place, right?'

He was still holding my hand. 'Sure. I am the manager.' We went inside, past a bare wooden reception desk with three rows of pigeonholes for keys behind it, and up a staircase several flights to the top floor. On the landing there were two doors. 'The bathroom, and your bedroom. I think you will be pleased.'

The bedroom floor was painted red, worn and flaking in patches. There was a window covered by a wire mesh. Two single beds, wire hoops suspended above them and lumpy garlands of mosquito netting tucked up out of the way.

'Mama Lou has made this room very nice,' said Fidelis, indicating the cloths tacked up on the walls, batik pictures of women carrying baskets of fruit on their heads and babies on their backs. I went to the window, which looked straight across to the house opposite, close enough almost to reach out and touch. I tried to keep my voice casual. 'Where is Lou?'

'This morning she went to the shamba, that is our farm, with my sister Christina. It is high time they were coming home.'

There was something funny about his polite, old-fashioned English, which didn't seem to fit the way he looked. He was a big man, as big as me. I found it hard to tell his age – maybe early thirties? A few years older than me and Lou? *I am the manager*, he'd said, and I was conscious, as I often was these days, that here was someone with a job and responsibilities and a busy schedule, whereas I had none of these things.

'Perhaps you would like to rest?' he said. I was hungry, and a little disappointed that Lou wasn't here waiting for me, but above all I was tired. So after Fidelis left I stretched out on the bed beneath the bunched-up mosquito net.

It was dark when I woke up. For a moment I thought it must be the middle of the night, but it was only half past seven in the evening. I went to answer the knock at the door. A small boy said carefully, 'Please, let me bring you to Mama Lou.'

At last. And again, that lifting sensation, scary but hopeful, as if nine long, sad months were clouds about to float away. The boy led me downstairs, along a passage towards a muddle of noise, pots clattering, women and kids laughing. A spicy, meaty smell made me realise how hungry I was. He brought me to a yard where I had to screw up my eyes against the smoke from a charcoal stove. Then I saw Lou, sitting on an upright chair, legs splayed, shelling peas into a metal tray on her lap, her red hair longer than it used to be. But she was wearing what she always wore: a faded indigo T shirt, a long blue denim skirt, clumpy brown lace-up shoes. Only Lou could dress like that and get away with it. And when she noticed me and smiled, she looked beautiful. 'Hey!' she called, 'How're you doing?' – as if we'd been apart for no more than a couple of days.

'It's so good to see you.' I bent to kiss her but she ducked, took my hand and murmured, 'Not here, OK?' The women and kids were gathering round us. Lou spoke Swahili and I caught my own name; the women nodded and repeated, 'Ah, Sasha, Sasha,' as if I was the answer to a crucial question.

I sat down next to Lou on a lumpy sack, a little freaked out by that fluent Swahili. She looked so at home.

'I can't believe I'm here at last.'

'Neither can I. It's weird.' She grinned, then yawned. 'Christina and I have been working like maniacs at the shamba all day. I'm exhausted.'

'Lou, when do we eat? I didn't eat since midday …'

'Just let me finish these, then we'll find Fidelis.' She unzipped the last few pods with her thumbnail, flicking the peas into the tray. Christina, the young woman who seemed

9

to be in charge of this cooking operation, took the tray from Lou and we went through a narrow gate into another yard. Men were gathered round a table, watching Fidelis and another man play a game on a wooden board with two rows of neatly carved hollows and a set of small wooden balls. When Fidelis saw us he sat back, folded his hands behind his head and said, 'So! You have found Mama Lou at last. Have you been talking about old times?'

His retro English was too perfect; too quaint. He made it sound like we were friends, not lovers. I mumbled, 'We haven't had a chance to talk about anything yet … But I guess I'm very happy just to be here.'

Fidelis stroked his beard. 'It is not good to be alone for so long.'

'Too right,' said Lou briskly. 'Nine months is a hell of a stint for a long-distance relationship. Please, don't let us stop you guys carrying on with your game.'

So we sat around some more while they played. I was starving. A little girl sidled in and leaned against Fidelis, staring at me. When I said 'Hi,' she hid her face in his belly and everyone laughed, but he gave her a nudge and she peeped at me and whispered, 'Shikamo.'

'That's the greeting for an elder – now *you* have to say 'Marahaba'. Go on, say it!' Lou was waiting expectantly, but I couldn't get my tongue round the word, felt myself going red. The child hid her face again. Lou ran her hand over the little girl's hair. 'Never mind, Malaika.'

'It is very good that you are trying to speak Swahili,' said Fidelis. 'Mama Lou was so quick to learn, after only three months here she could be mistaken for a true Zanzibari.'

'Don't exaggerate,' Lou said. 'Anyway, I have to have the language for my work. Sasha's just here to relax.'

Fidelis won the game, there were hi-fives all round, and at last, allelujah, it was time to eat. We returned to the other yard where men were drinking beer and eating red beans and rice with their fingers. Someone handed me a beer, but it was food I wanted, the smoky smell of the rice making me drool. Women stood over a huge blackened pot on a charcoal stove, prodding the contents, arguing with each other. A girl served me a plastic dish piled high, and overwhelmed by the urge to stuff myself with carbs I dug straight in with my fingers, dropping grains of rice everywhere. A few minutes later the same girl discreetly brought me a spoon.

Through a half-open door I glimpsed someone small, hunched over a green plastic tub of steaming water. 'Who's that?'

'That's the dhobi, the guy who does the laundry,' Lou whispered. 'He's called Musa.'

'Doesn't he get to eat?'

'Maybe he already did. He has to finish the sheets so they can be hung out to dry first thing tomorrow morning.'

Musa seemed to be the only man doing any work, although the women were cooking, serving, washing the pots non-stop. For a few seconds Christina leaned against the wall and took a swig of orange soda from a bottle. The little kids were still milling around, but when one tot fell asleep in a corner Christina scooped him up into a cloth and tied him to her back, wedged another baby on her hip, snapped her fingers at a few more and led them away. I said to Fidelis, 'Your wife must be very strong.'

'Say again?'

'Your wife – carrying two kids at once like that. And she's been working all day too, Lou tells me.'

The men sitting nearest to us stopped eating, their fingers still clutching squashed-up balls of rice. An embarrassed silence gave way to some awkward chuckles and tongue clicking. Fidelis looked thoughtful, turned and murmured something to Lou, who rolled her eyes and groaned, 'Oh God! I am so sorry.'

It didn't make sense. 'Excuse me? Did I say something wrong?' But Fidelis, humming to himself, had wandered off to collect more beers from the crate.

'Christina's his *sister*. That's his wife, over there.' A slighter, paler-skinned young woman was stirring the pot on the stove.

'How was I to know?'

'Fidelis says he told you earlier. When he said I was at the shamba with her.'

'He did? Well, I – I didn't take it in, can you blame me? I just got here, you weren't around, I was trying to figure out what was going on...'

'Just... try to think before you speak, OK? Oh, look, it doesn't matter. Everyone knows you didn't mean any harm.'

'Thanks.' I felt stupid and angry; not a good combination.

'Don't be like that.' She took hold of my hand. 'Actually, Christina's getting married in two weeks' time, over on the East coast, and we're invited to the wedding, isn't that fantastic? A whole week of partying!'

'I thought we were going to the coast anyway, just you and me. You said you wanted us to have a proper holiday.'

'We will! We will too, but this will be special, the best fun!'

'With a bunch of people I don't know.'

'Oh but Sasha they will make you so welcome; they are such good, kind people.' She squeezed my hand, looking so happy I felt bad for being sour. 'Plus, this will be such an opportunity for me. For my research.'

I wished I'd paid more attention to the stuff in her letters. 'You've already been to weddings, you wrote me about them.'

'But this is different, it'll be my first Christian Muslim wedding. Besides, Fidelis will introduce us to all sorts of useful people.'

12

'I think I already met enough people tonight to last me,' I said. 'Lou, these three months I have with you – they're precious. After November I'll never see any of these guys again.'

'You're right, Sasha, this is a precious time. Why don't you just enjoy all the amazing experiences we can share here? Experiences you'll remember for the rest of your life.'

I wanted her to say: *Things must have been so bad for you, back home. I'm sorry.* I wanted her to say she'd missed me, and then I could say I'd missed her. But she didn't, and neither did I.

It was very late when we finally went upstairs to our room. I felt exhausted but wide awake, and nervous. I was rummaging in my backpack for my toothbrush when the electricity suddenly cut out. Lou lit a hurricane lamp, and frowned. 'This needs cleaning, just look at all this crap. We better keep the wick down low, OK? Otherwise the glass might shatter.' The lamp gave a feeble glow and the room was full of shadows. I put my hands on her waist, pulled her towards me. She tilted her chin against my chest.

'I've missed you,' I said at last.

'It's so great to have you here,' she murmured. Then she went up on her toes to kiss me, but it was a very quick kiss, and then she turned her cheek sideways and yawned. 'Sorry! You know, I'm so tired I could sleep for a week. You have the bed near the door, honey, and don't forget to tuck your net well in; those little bastards are biting.'

'Get up!' For a second I didn't recognise Lou's voice. My head was thick with sleep and the mosquito net was billowing above me. 'Get up, Sasha! We're going to Prison Island.'

'Why?' I moaned, hugging the pillow. 'What have I done?'

'Idiot! Wake *up*. You'll love it, the beach is fabulous.'

'Oh, Lou ... I thought today we could maybe just take a walk, around the Stone town ... couldn't we go to this island some other time?'

'Nope, we could not. Fidelis has arranged this especially for you, he's borrowing his brother's boat just for today. Come on, we mustn't keep him waiting!'

He was sitting on the harbour wall in a black T shirt and cut-off jeans, his hands resting on the muscular slabs of his thighs. 'Good morning!' he called. 'How did you sleep?'

I shook his hand warmly, to make up for being a grouch when Lou was so excited; more animated than I had ever seen her. She crowed, 'A day off! I haven't had a day off since July.'

'But I know you too well, Mama Lou. You won't be able to stop asking questions.'

'No questions today, Fidelis, I promise. Look, no notebook, no tape recorder. Just me.'

The beach was long and white and narrow like a bone. A mass of trees and vegetation hid the rest of the island from view. I felt smothered by the heat and took off my shirt. Lou told me to be careful not to burn. She was wearing a navy swimsuit and a blue and red kanga wrapped round her hips, a huge red flower swirling over her backside. We walked, Fidelis asking me questions about my family, life in the US, carefully avoiding anything to do with how I earned a living. My answers sounded cautious, as if I was talking about someone other than myself, a person I didn't know very well. I felt half relieved that Fidelis was being so tactful, half despondent at the thought of what Lou must have told him.

After a while Fidelis said, 'Here,' just as Lou said, 'Here we are. This place is fabulous for swimming,' and she untied the knot at her waist and let the cloth fall. Fidelis eased the black T shirt over the curve of his chest. We

14

swam. The water was warm, the waves pulsing gently. Fidelis lay on his back, eyes shut against the sun; Lou splashed water over me. I was mesmerised by her wet hair, the way it sprang into red-black ringlets with a life of their own. We swam and lazed for a long time, until hunger and a stray cloud over the sun drove us back to the beach. Fidelis jogged to the boat and returned with a picnic: chapattis, boiled eggs, fruit. Lou stroked a giant turtle, its scaly head flinching a little beneath her fingers. Fidelis laughed. 'Would you like to put him in the boat and take him home to be your pet?'

'Tanzanians think we're crazy, keeping animals in the house,' Lou explained, and with a pang I remembered Flo, my Labrador. Lou twisted on her side and said to Fidelis, 'You wouldn't let me keep one in your guest house. You'd complain about the turtle shit everywhere.'

'I would build you a small hut,' he said.

'For the turtle?'

'For the turtle and for you. I would come and visit you there. Sometimes.'

He grinned at her and she flung a handful of white sand at him, but he dodged so it spattered off his back. Then she pelted him and he put up his hands, laughing, until I blurted out, 'Lou, don't do that.'

'What's the problem?' She stared at me, and carried on staring until I looked away. Fidelis glanced at the sun and sighed. 'We must head for home. I have some business to do tonight.'

Business? I was glad. It meant I'd have Lou to myself.

Over the next few days I tried and failed to put Fidelis out of my mind, as Lou and I roamed the Stone Town together. She said it was fine to hold hands in public, although not to kiss; everyone in Tanzania held hands all the time, even the guys (I'd noticed), and she said how nice it was for her to be a tourist for a change. Partly I

15

welcomed, with an aching relief, the newness of it all; how different it was from home, but I also wanted it not to be strange any more, to know my way around the narrow streets that never seemed to lead me where they should. Lou made sure I saw all the sights: the Anglican Cathedral, the market, the palaces on the seafront that looked like wedding cakes and that we couldn't go inside because they were Government Offices. Why didn't they make a few bucks by letting tourists in? Because the Sultans built those palaces on the slave trade, she told me, so now they had been reclaimed for the nation. 'Power to the people,' I said, and she said, 'Sasha, for goodness' sake keep your voice down.'

Everywhere we went, people greeted Lou, calling, 'Hey, sister!' and catching hold of her free hand, and I was startled by how warmly she responded, hugging the women, talking with the men as if she had all the time in the world. They smiled at me and shook my hand too, and over and over again I heard, 'Mzungu, mzungu,' like a fly buzzing around my head. 'Does mzungu mean boyfriend?' I asked Lou.

'No, honey, it means white person.'

'Really? Isn't that a bit …?'

'Sasha, it's OK, it's fine. It's not like it's offensive. Actually, the literal translation is wanderer. That's what people thought white people were doing when they first came to East Africa, just wandering around. Kind of ironic when you think what they were really getting up to.'

Mzungu wasn't such a bad name, and all the staring and questions weren't so different from back home when Lou and I first started dating: the Alpha student and the baseball star, and Lou said, people are bound to be curious, it's human nature. Just be cool with it.

All through the Stone Town I tried to be cool, although my skin was slick with sweat, and I kept hold of Lou's hand, telling myself that she, at least, was still a very good reason for being alive. But every time we returned to the Eastern Star, there was Fidelis, going about his endless *business*, booking guests in, organising this or despatching that, soothing people, charming people, cuddling his little daughter Malaika on his lap, and especially at sunset when he sat in the yard outside his own living quarters, gently snapping his fingers to Bob Marley while the women prepared the evening meal – especially then, it felt inevitable that Lou would want to sleep apart from me, in her own bed by the window. Maybe she feels after all this time we need to take things slowly, I thought. Maybe she's right.

One evening Lou took me to the Forodhani gardens on the seafront, a wide, grassy area where crowds of people were buying food from stalls, drinking beer if they could afford it or 'local brew' if they couldn't, or simply strolling hand in hand like Lou and me. Someone switched on a battered old cassette player, filling the air with snaky, teasing, high-pitched music that Lou said was called Taarabu; people began to dance. It felt like everyone was having a good time, and above us the stars were linked in a web of light. Lou squeezed my hand. 'I've been saving this place for you, isn't it great?' We ate squid, and I burnt my lips gnawing maize cobs charred on braziers until the golden grains had puckered and blackened like tortoiseshell. Then I eased the pain with bottle after bottle of Tusker. Even though it was ten o'clock at night, small boys were playing on the quay, jumping in and out of the water, their bodies twisting in the air. From the crowd a group of men came walking towards us. Lou called, 'Fidelis!' and I thought, Oh shit, but Fidelis was already shaking my hand, insisting on buying me another beer.

His pals seemed to have disappeared amongst the crowds. The three of us sat on the edge of the quay, our feet dangling over the water. My head was spinning lightly and the sky swooped in a blaze of stars as I tipped the bottle into my mouth, the mineral tastes of glass and beer mingling on my tongue. The palm trees were black starfish, and beneath them the little kids were still diving and hauling themselves up, over and over. What time did they ever go to bed?

Another kid was standing next to us, a wooden tray suspended from a cord around his neck. On the tray were some shrivelled shapes. 'Feesh,' he said proudly. Lou and I lay on our backs and laughed. Fidelis gently tapped the boy on the shoulder. 'You, take this,' he said, and gave him a maize cob. The kid's face lit up, he breathed his thanks and slipped away into the crowd.

The alcohol was doing its work; I felt relaxed, more relaxed than I'd felt in several months, and Fidelis was my friend. 'Another beer, Fidelis?' He smiled slowly, but Lou shook her head. 'Time for bed, boys,' she said, took us both by the hand and led us home.

In our room, when I kissed her my burnt lips stung. The pain made me long for her. She murmured, 'Hurry up.' I went to the bathroom. As I was coming out, I looked down and saw Fidelis at the bottom of the stairwell, looking up. 'Goodnight, sleep well,' he called in English. Maybe his accent made the words seem loaded. I said, 'Goodnight, see you in the morning,' like a little kid to his father.

Behind the pale drift of the mosquito net Lou was naked on the bed, her legs drawn up and her arms around her knees. There was a smell of kerosene. She must have cleaned the hurricane lamp, because now a big flame leapt beneath the sheeny glass bell, the wick turned up as high as it could go. Lou laughed at me as I stared at her. 'Quick,' she said, 'come under the net.' But it was too late; I'd already been bitten.

The next morning I woke in a sweat and went straight to the bathroom to shower. Just when I was covered in lather, the feeble stream of water wilted, then petered out altogether, trickling across the floor towards the drain in the corner. I scurried after it, trying to scoop it up, but it was hopeless. My skin was slimy. Maybe they could spare me a bucket from the kitchen, just to rinse off. I wrapped a towel round my waist and was about to scoot downstairs when I heard a voice, and a thump, and another thump, and the voice again, angry. I looked over the banisters. At the bottom of the stairwell was Fidelis, and someone else, someone who wore on his head the neat white Muslim kufia. It was Musa, the dhobi, and Fidelis was slamming him against the wall, matching each slam with a snarl.

I didn't want to watch.

There was fear in the little man's eyes. Another vicious slam, and Musa's face twisted. Fidelis scowled and turned away. He said a word which I knew meant, 'Get out!' because I'd heard people use it to dogs.

Fidelis hadn't seen me. I grew hot with shame at the thought that Musa might have done. In the bedroom Lou was packing her bag for fieldwork.

'What is it with Fidelis and that little guy?'

'Who?'

'The guy who does the laundry – I just saw him and Fidelis, he was crazy, he was beating the crap out of him.'

She was selecting pens and notebooks. 'Who beat the crap out of who?'

'Oh, come on Lou. You know how small that guy is; it's like there's something wrong with him, some stunted growth thing, I don't know – I'm telling you, Fidelis was slamming him into that wall like he wanted to kill him.'

She frowned. 'Fidelis is one of the gentlest, kindest people I have ever – '

'That's not what I just saw. Jesus, I have to say something to him, I can't let this go – '

'You're his guest, remember?'

'I'm not. I'm *your* guest. You're paying him for this room.'

The soapy trails were drying on my skin. Lou turned away, began to adjust the buckle on her bag. 'You better not say anything, Sasha. You don't know what was going on. Look, I've been here eight months now, I know my way around and I know how often I've misunderstood situations. It's not my job to interfere. And it certainly isn't yours.' She picked up the bag and went to the door.

'I can't believe I'm hearing this.'

She sighed, turned back, placed her hands on my shoulders. 'Oh, Sasha. I know it's hard, and you're doing so well – but people do things differently here; they have different dynamics, and it's not for us to weigh in and tell them how to behave – God knows there's been enough of that in the past. You have to be with people for years and years before you can really begin to get an idea of why they behave the way they do.'

I tried to read her face, her green eyes that were pleading or pitying. 'Are you   telling me you intend to stay on Zanzibar for years?'

'You know I'm not. Even if I wanted to, I've only got funding for the next two years, and that's barely adequate.'

'I can pay my own way, Lou. Let me give you a contribution, why don't you? You know I have more than enough.'

'Don't be silly.'

'No really, let me pay for this room. Because I don't want to feel like I owe anything to Fidelis, and if I see him do anything like that ever again, I won't just stand there and say nothing.'

I listened for the slam of the heavy front door and then went to the window where I could watch her striding down the street, waving greetings to the neighbours rather than stop and become caught up in gossip. She was already late for her day's work, off-schedule. If I was back home now, I'd be like her – impatient to be out training, working on my fitness. But I was on Zanzibar, with a day full of nothing to do. The trails of dried soap were making my skin itch and I felt miserable, frustrated by Lou's inability to see anything wrong in what Fidelis had done.

With my towel round my waist I went downstairs to the yard where Christina and another woman were taking turns to pound maize in a huge mortar. The little girl Malaika slunk into the outhouse as soon as she saw me. 'Hey, Sasha! Hello brother! How's it going, what's your news?' I returned their greetings as best I could, then faltered in phrasebook Swahili: 'I beg water.' They roared, slapping their thighs, high-fiving each other. Malaika peeped round the door to see what all the fuss was about.

Christina went down on one knee, and put her hands either side of a bucket that was full to the brim with water. She hoisted it onto her head, then stood up and steadied herself, gazing at some invisible point on the wall, a muscle quivering in her neck. I'd seen women do this a hundred times; I felt mortified that Christina should be doing it for me. 'OK,' she said with a smile. 'Please come,' and I followed her upstairs, all the way bleating, 'No really, let me, please, I can carry it myself.'

After I'd washed off the soap I went to the trunk in the corner where Lou kept her work materials. Inside, amongst the camera equipment and tapes and files, there were stacks of exercise books with flimsy buff covers, the kind that schoolkids used, each one with its weird yet familiar heading in Lou's firm capitals: HARVEST. KINSHIP. SEXUAL BEHAVIOR. I flicked through one of the books. Lou's handwriting was fast and fluid, racing across the page, blurring here and there into a single horizontal line. How could she ever read this back to herself? There were figures, tables, names, Swahili words. I thought of the ring in my money belt, digging into my belly. Lou laughed at me for wearing that belt all the time. 'Trust people,' she said. 'Don't be such a tourist.' I thought of Chicago, where it was Fall, pictured myself running through scarlet leaves in the park with Flo at my heels. Maybe I should go home. Maybe I should stay here. Maybe I should go home, then return to Tanzania in the cool springtime and marry Lou at the summit of Kilimanjaro: just the kind of extreme ritual she'd like, provided my stupid, injured leg could get me up the mountain.

I lay on the bed for a while. Then I picked up SEXUAL BEHAVIOR again, poring over the scrawl. There was stuff about taboo relationships, and attitudes to AIDS and contraception in a multi-faith community, and the word I couldn't get out of my head was 'intrusive'. I imagined Lou asking questions, being shrewd, reading between the lines, getting under the skin. I lay on the bed for a few more hours, disgusted by my own resentfulness.

When the sun was high in the sky I went downstairs again, this time heading for the yard where all the laundry was done, and there I found Musa sitting on a stool, a tub of grey water in front of him, scrubbing sheets with a giant stick of soap and a stone. He nodded for me to sit down next to the wash tub. I asked him, as best I could, '*What is your news?*'

'*My news is good. Your news?*'

'*Very good.*' It didn't feel like a real conversation. I said in English, 'Are you OK?' and Musa shook his head, murmuring, '*I don't speak English.*'

I rubbed my shoulder, mimed pain. 'OK now?' Musa looked at me, but carried on with the laundry. I searched his face for some change, some sign of understanding. What did he feel? Angry, hurt, sad? Suspicious?'

When Lou came back at the end of the day she asked politely what I'd been doing.

'Just hanging out. You know.'

'Are you bored?'

'No. No, I love it here. It's great just to be with you, but… maybe I could come with you tomorrow?'

'Oh, Sasha, that's really difficult. People won't talk to me in the same way – I'm supposed to merge in, be a fly on the wall. Kind of impossible with you around. You're pretty unmissable.' She ran a fingertip along my jaw, kissed me.

'I feel useless. Everyone else is working so hard, they never stop. And I'm just sitting around all day. It's embarrassing. I hate feeling like this. I thought it was bad enough back home after the accident. Not being able to do anything.'

It was the first time I'd mentioned my injury. I hadn't meant to bring it up like this, and Lou seemed uncomfortable. She said, 'Look, so you can't walk backwards any more without falling over. It's not the end of the world. Sasha, you're twenty-nine. How many years did you have left, realistically? We discussed all this way back, before you got injured, remember, what we'd do after you stopped being able to play, and we agreed I should go abroad, and that's why I'm here now. Getting my career together, because without a PhD…'

Lou was right; of course she was right. But she didn't understand – would never understand – what it had been like to be the player who could make a crowd of thousands hold their breath; who could make them rise to their feet and cheer.

She carried on, briskly. 'Maybe you should get involved in some kind of project.'

'Like what?'

'Fidelis is building a house for his grandmother. You could help him.'

'I don't speak Swahili.'

'But his English is perfect. Anyway, you could *learn* some Swahili. He's a good teacher, look how quickly I've picked it up.'

'He taught you?'

'Yes. He's been a great help.'

'What's in it for him?'

'He just wants to make things easier for me. He's an intelligent man, he understands exactly why I'm here and what I'm trying to do.' She frowned. 'Which is perhaps more than I can say for you.'

It was cruel, and maybe there was more than a grain of truth in it. I'd never taken much interest in Lou's research, which had seemed to me so remote from the life I was living, she might as well have been studying another planet. I pushed that thought aside and carried on. 'How can you be friends with someone who – whose every move you're watching and, and *analysing* and writing down in your little notebooks, what kind of friendship is that?'

Lou looked surprised. 'What's wrong? You've never been like this before, Sasha, you know what I want to do with my life, I've explained it all to you – '

'Maybe not everything, Lou. There are some things I don't understand.'

'Is this about what you saw this morning? Because I can explain that, too. Musa was supposed to get charcoal yesterday but he didn't. Then this morning he went off to the mosque early, so there was no fire, so the kids didn't get their porridge before school because they couldn't boil the water. So that's why Fidelis was mad with Musa, and why there was a spare bucket of water left over for you.'

'Who told you that? Hell, can't I even use the bathroom in this place without everybody gets to hear about it?'

'Darling I know, I know what it's like to lose your privacy. It takes some getting used to, believe me. And you never really belong. The most you can hope for is to fit in.'

'Is that what you do, Lou? Do you fit in?'

'I think so, I hope so.' She was stroking my face again. 'But if I do, it's all down to Fidelis making me welcome in his family. Like he's made *you* welcome.'

The day of Christina's wedding came closer. I was the only man allowed to see the wedding dress – as far as I could make out, it was much the same as any other wedding dress the world over: white, shiny and tacky. Lou told me that for inter-religious marriages in this part of East Africa there was no preparation for 'conversion'; Christina would simply become a Muslim the moment she was married. I said, 'Doesn't that make a mockery of religion?' and Lou said, 'Sasha, what makes you think the Western way is the right way?' This annoyed me, and then I felt ashamed of being annoyed, and then I felt defensive.

The plan was for Christina, Fidelis, Lou and me to travel ahead to the eastern seaboard, and the rest of the family to follow after a few days. I tried to be pleased that they hadn't excluded me, had invited me to go for the whole shebang. Also, it would be good to be out of the Stone Town at last.

On the morning of our departure I woke early with a throbbing head. I winced at the prospect of the journey; Lou had warned me we'd be jolting around for hours in the back of a pickup. Don't be a wuss, I told myself. Come on, you're unfit, that's the trouble. I got up, pulled on my running shorts. Lou was still asleep as I let myself out and jogged along to the quay, a careful jog that didn't put too much strain on my knee. In the market place women were setting out their little pyramids of oranges, tomatoes and swollen green papayas; maybe it was the smell of faintly rotting fruit that dragged this heaviness into my limbs, my neck. The smell merged into hot lights that swam like fish before my eyes, and my legs, my once-so-valuable muscular legs were suddenly made of dough. I sank down amongst the jangling cries of the market women, *Hey, Sasha!* – and collapsed on the quay, *mzungu mzungu* droning in my ears as I forced myself up again, tottered back to the guest house, pausing every few steps to hug a cold stone wall, too feeble to answer the people who asked me what was wrong.

It was Siberia, where dreams were a multimedia experience and the cold took hold of your teeth and shook them up and down in your mouth. I crawled across the bedroom floor to the cupboard where Lou's clothes were stored. It would have been nice to curl up inside the cupboard, but the floor was too hard and surely Siberia could not be Siberia in bed with all Lou's clothes on top of me. Piles and piles of lovely blue clothes, smelling of Lou. If only I could keep my eyes focussed on these hot fish, I wouldn't freeze to death. But I had to throw up.

Musa found me draped over the toilet. 'Let me stay here,' I pleaded. For someone with such a small frame, he was strong. He hooked his hands under my armpits and gently dragged me back to the bedroom. Why was there an orange bucket by my bed? Orange was not a good colour, I was obliged to inform Musa. When he stripped away the sheet and the piles of clothes, I thought I'd better put up a fight – but I couldn't move a muscle.

'*Drink.*' Musa held a glass of water to my lips. It was so cool, so wonderfully cool, I began to cry, and the tears drizzled hot tears of shame down my chest like candle wax.

Later, a nun loomed at a giddy angle over the bed, a cheerful pink nun with white hair. 'Oh yes,' she beamed, 'this is a very sick young man.'

'I can't help my thoughts,' I mumbled. She said, 'Take these tablets and you'll soon be right as rain. Maybe just a little ringing in the ears, but it could be a lot worse than that, couldn't it!'

I had malaria for three days. From time to time Musa appeared with water and tablets that he made me swallow, and then with small meals: bowls of ugali which I picked at without making a fuss; some cool slices of mango. On the third day I could sit up in bed without keeling over, and Musa brought me a bowl of water and a cloth. For a moment I thought he was going to wash me, but he just mimed, wiping his own brow. I ran the cloth over my face. The cold water gave me courage and made me sad. I croaked, 'Mama Lou?'

Musa shook his head.

And she hadn't phoned – or if she had, there was nobody here who could tell me. I imagined her, flat out on a beach, defying the sun, her head full of kinship, the long involved conversations with Fidelis, the sharing of knowledge. Even so, I longed for her to return. Soon I would wake up and there she would be, silent for a change, holding a glass of water to my lips, her face expressing love, compassion, maybe even a little guilt.

On the fourth day I woke up hungry. Outside my window the sky was morning-glory blue and my ears had stopped ringing. I decided to go downstairs to see if I could beg something to eat, porridge perhaps, or bananas.

The yard was deserted, the charcoal in the stove grey and cold. 'Hello?' I called. 'It's me, Sasha. Is there any tea?'

One of the women came out of the house and took my hand. She was crying.

'What's wrong? Where is everyone?'

She led me to Musa's place. Just as we arrived he entered through the back gate, a bucket of water balanced on his head. The woman spoke to him, choking on her tears.

'OK,' said Musa. He put down the bucket. Then he went into his hut, coming out with a chair. '*Sit.*' I was bewildered. In my stomach was that shifting, shapeless feeling which means something is very, very wrong.

'*What is the problem?*' I managed to put the phrase together, but Musa shook his head. He gave me a scalding hot glass of tea, swirling with leaves. Feeling weak again, I added three spoons of sugar. Musa went away.

I waited half an hour until he returned with a boy in the white shirt and khaki shorts of the local secondary school. The boy was excited and nervous. 'He ask me to tell you that we are all in great sadness this morning because the little kid of Fidelis, she is dead.'

It didn't make sense; I must still be sick.

Malaika, the little girl, the shy one.

'Malaika? *Malaika?*'

The boy nodded. 'Yes, it is in the night and she is dead.'

'What happened?'

'She … ' The boy broke off and spoke rapidly to Musa. 'She has a fever and then she is very sick and they take her to the hospital but she is dead and they think this small kid, she is not having enough of water.'

'That's why she died? She was dehydrated?'

'Yes. Probably it is for this reason?'

'Does – does Fidelis know? Is he here?'

The boy looked uncertain. 'He has gone to the east coast. They have tried to make a telephone call but it did not work. But probably he knows. Yes, probably he knows.'

As he was about to leave I asked him, 'Would you say to Musa – what can I do to help?'

It was a Suzuki jeep, borrowed from I don't know where. They sent me to the market with the schoolboy to buy rice, goat meat and sugar, which he told me was for the meal after the funeral. 'It is customary.' Some of the market women tried to flirt with me – *Hey, Sasha, how come you got this nice car?* – but the boy murmured something and then they understood and went quiet. The morning passed quickly as I did one errand after another, ferrying the extended family to the market, the Anglican cathedral, and

28

finally the hospital. I couldn't look at the tiny coffin when they put it on the back seat. We returned to the Eastern Star and waited. I was dreading their arrival, but I wanted to be there. And when at last we heard the pickup, there was a surge of people to the yard gate. Then the sound of a man wailing. Fidelis burst into the yard, running through the crowd to his own quarters, one arm across his face. Lou stumbled after him, the dusty kanga unravelling from her waist and hampering her, and when she saw me she didn't stop running.

I found her later in our room, sitting on the bed, biting her nails. Had she been crying? Her eyes looked sombre, but not red.

'This is shit,' she said.

'How's Fidelis?'

'How do you think?' She began unpacking her bag, taking out little bundles of clothes and the notebooks. Clearly she didn't want to talk. It crossed my mind I could ask her why she hadn't stayed with me when I was so ill with malaria, but straightaway I felt disgusted with myself for having such a thought when Malaika was dead.

In the afternoon she told me to dress in the best clothes I had — a pair of chinos and a blue shirt. Lou wrapped her blue and red kanga round her waist, and another identical one over her head and shoulders. 'All the women have to cover their heads.' She looked so different, it was scary. We went downstairs to the rooms where Fidelis and his family lived. 'We have to speak to the family first,' said Lou, and I was glad she was taking charge, but the living room was full of men, and she murmured, 'I'll be outside,' and left me there. I felt awkward. Then Musa was at my elbow, steering me to join a line of people. We shuffled round the room. At the other end of the line, Fidelis was slumped the wrong way round on a wooden chair, leaning his arms on the back.

Next to him there was another chair, and on this, the tiny coffin.

The line moved very slowly. At last it was our turn. I watched as Musa shook Fidelis's hand and said, '*Very sorry.*'

Fidelis whispered, '*Thank you.*' His face sagged like the face of an old man. He had barely looked at Musa, but now, when I stood before him there was a flicker of something – gratitude? Pity? I had to stoop to take his hand, this man's hand which had held mine so many times before, but this time it was different, and now Fidelis held my hand in both his own, just for a second.

Then we were moving on towards the coffin. Perhaps Musa sensed me delaying, because he looked round and beckoned me over. We stood together, looking down at her. She lay on a folded white blanket, her eyelashes smooth fans on the curve of each cheek. They had dressed her in the shiny, lacy frock that she should have worn to Christina's wedding. She was the centre of attention now, as she had hardly ever been when she was alive, one of the swarm of kids getting under everyone's feet, being scolded, teased, loved. Now we saw her for who she really was, as if a mask had been removed that nobody knew she had been wearing.

Musa and I moved on, out of the room and into the clinging heat. Lou was talking to the women. When she saw me she asked, 'How was it?'

'It was... very sad. But it was the right thing to do.'

She nodded. 'Do you feel more foreign than ever? Because I do.'

She had found my thoughts, and again I was startled and felt a glimmer of hope that maybe things would turn out OK for us.

We walked to the cathedral, a slow, painful procession. At the door Lou muttered, 'I can't sit with you.' I thought, that's it, she's done with me – then I realised all the women were sitting to one side of the aisle and all the men the other. I sat by myself, but at the last minute Musa slipped in beside me.

The burial took place some miles away, on a patch of open land at the edge of a forest. The coffin was lowered into the grave, and the men took turns to cover it with earth. Malaika's mother wasn't there; I realised she hadn't been at the cathedral either. Fidelis stood apart from everyone else. The heat was suffocating, but he wore a long brown overcoat buttoned up to his neck. I stole a glance at Lou, her kanga still tightly drawn around her head, the vivid blue cloth making her look pale and strange. Her mouth was set in a straight line, and I wondered if she was trying not to cry. I also wondered why everyone was standing aside, looking at me, and then I realised a man was offering me the spade. Clumsily I dug into the bank of earth, cast a few clods onto the coffin. When it was covered, a woman knelt to place on the mound a spray of purple flowers.

Back at the guest house the women took themselves away again, leaving the men to sit in the living room with Fidelis. I watched with dread as they passed round a gourd full of something that stank of fermenting bananas. Just in time, two men arrived with a crate and they gave me a bottle of Tusker instead. I wished I could sit outside where the women were cooking. After a while a few of them came in, Lou amongst them, and when they opened a door into another room I saw more women, and Fidelis's wife, lying on a bed in a tangle of sheets. She was just a girl. The door closed.

When Lou came out again she was white.

A smiling woman said, 'Welcome,' and gave me a plate piled high with rice and spiced meat. I no longer felt like eating, but Musa took the decision for me. '*Eat*,' he said. The atmosphere in the room had changed, lightened, everyone eating and talking; somebody even laughed. Fidelis wasn't there.

After a quarter of an hour I went to find Lou. Time, now, for her to explain why she left me when I was so sick, like she did before, in America. Time to stop being a guest and a stranger, time for me to say what was on my mind. She wasn't in the yard. I asked Musa. 'Lou?' He shook his head. I couldn't see Fidelis either. I peered through the smoke in the cooking hut and huddled in the darkest corner were two figures; I pushed my way towards them and they were two old women, laughing. I ran, leaped over a sack of maize, not caring about the sudden pain in my knee, scattering chickens as the women called, '*Hey, Sasha! Come here, brother,*' but I ignored them, kept on running through the back door and into the guest house, the stone walls cold like slabs of ice against my hands as with the little strength I had left, I forced myself up the narrow staircase to our room.

When I burst in, first I saw the kangas, tossed on the floor. Lou, in her T shirt and knickers, was sitting cross-legged on the bed. She had her notebook and pen. She stared up at me without a word as I stood panting in the doorway. I looked round the room for someone else. Then I looked at her again, and began to realise.

'Lou, what are you doing?'

What do you *think* I'm doing?'

'How can you do this now? Today?'

'I have to.' Her pen was running out of ink and she scribbled impatiently in the margin. 'Otherwise I'll forget.'

'You should be downstairs.'

'Making notes where everyone can see me? That would be appalling.'

'Too late, Lou. *I* see you. Where's Fidelis?'

She looked blank. 'With the others, I guess.'

'Have you been with him?'

'What do you mean?'

32

I realised it no longer mattered, but I had to say it anyway, just to know.

'Have you been screwing him?'

There was a moment when I held her puzzled gaze. Then her expression changed to contempt, as she said, 'What do you take me for?' But it was when she looked down at her notebook and started to write again, that the feeling of loss rushed into me like a boat filling with water.

Because there was nowhere else to go, I went back downstairs. People were really letting their hair down now, laughter from the kitchen, some of the men passing a joint. Fidelis was with them, his eyes red. I would have liked to say something to him, perhaps just say I was sorry again. Then Lou came down, and the men called her into their circle.

Musa was raking out the soft grey ash from the bottom of the stove. 'I'm leaving.' Something in my tone or stance must have told him this, because he shook my hand, muttered a farewell, met my eye for one brief moment. 'Thanks for looking after me,' I said.

I stuffed my things in the backpack, then went to another guest house outside the Stone Town, where nobody knew me. I checked in for the night and was shown to my room by a bored, unfriendly girl. Empty except for a bed and a mosquito net, the room was painted all over, even the ceiling, in aquamarine gloss. I spent most of the night awake, not knowing that this weird, intense colour would always afterwards remind me how I fell out of love.

At sunrise the ocean was pulling steadily against the shore. The sky was a pure, washed blue. I stumbled a little from tiredness and the ache in my knee as I picked my way through the ropes and seaweed on the quay, but I kept going, kept moving towards the tall mast of the dhow, the trembling sail. An old man with grizzled hair and a bare,

scarred chest was hauling up nets for the day's work,
flinging them into the hull. It didn't take long for him to
understand what I wanted. 'Dar Es Salaam.' He nodded.
The other, younger fishermen called out, 'Welcome!' and
'Good morning brother!' and 'Where are you going?' I
jumped across the narrow strip of water into the dhow. As
I landed, my knee gave way and I fell flat on my face. They
were more shocked than I was, clicking their tongues and
sucking in their breath as they reached out to help me up,
but I tried to tell them it didn't matter; really, it didn't
matter at all.

House of Wonders

Dawn. Gulls weeping.

Our steamer nosing through the dhows, the jagged screen of their tall lateen sails hiding the island from us. A glimpse of a palace, glittering white. Men running to help me down the gangplank. I tried to refuse, but the solid ground made me stagger and clutch at their hands.

'Now you have sea legs when you need land legs,' said Father. 'Never mind, Lucy. We'll soon settle.'

We stood, arm in arm, while our English sailors sauntered away without a backward glance. One of them said to his friend, 'The stink of bloody Zanzibar don't never get any better, do it?'

The air already thick with warmth, brine, something vegetal and rank. Porters in long white garments bright as magnesium, lifting our boxes onto their heads. The sky a searing blue, the vacuum of light at its heart unbearable. My black gown soaking up the heat.

We waited. We did not know where we should go. Father pretended to be cheerful. 'That fellow Bertram must have forgotten we were coming on the *Madura*!' The porters set down our luggage, grumbled and paced around us.

'Perhaps it was a mistake to change our plans,' I said. 'Perhaps we should have gone straight to Africa after all.'

'Please, Lucy. You know we are *needed* here.' His face was glistening. A melting man. Could this really be my father?

When Bertram at last arrived, with no apology for being late, I wished we weren't reliant on his help. He was all handshakes and chuckles and 'Welcome to Zanzibar, sorry about the smell,' and 'This must be Miss Hemmings, ooh, won't Nurse Milton be pleased to see *you!* with a gleam in his eye that told me he was lying. He chivvied us through Customs, led us past the white palace, turned down a narrow alley, then another, then another, through streets that were mean and dark and confining, except now and again wherever a mound of rubble made space for sunlight boiling with dust motes. 'Oh yes, the hurricane; very nasty. All the IBEA people were safe, though. We make sure our houses are solidly built, don't you know? And this is the one we've got all nicely set up for you, Doctor!'

Our house. Our home. The door pocked with metal studs like a prison gate. A narrow flight of stairs to the first floor parlour. One armchair, one chaise longue. A gilded mirror reflecting the emptiness.

Another flight of stairs. The master bedroom, overlooking a courtyard where servants shall cook, do the laundry and, apparently, sleep. Across the landing, a smaller room above the street. My room. A travesty of a four-poster bed, ramshackle, the grey net bundled above it like a raincloud. 'I'm afraid the people make a dreadful racket,' Bertram remarked cheerfully. 'They're awake all hours, to and fro to their mosques and what-have-you. What's that, Doctor? Supper tonight? Oh, you've no servants yet. They won't start work until they've seen with their own eyes the white man who'll pay them! I shall round them up and bring them here in the morning. But tonight, his Excellency Mr. Kirk has invited you to dine at the Residence. He's holding a little reception for us British and a few of the Yankees. I dare say there'll be some young men pleased to meet Miss Lucy.' He winked. I was appalled.

But we had to eat, so I changed my creased black tarlatan for my creased black silk, and Bertram marched us through streets so narrow, we couldn't help but jostle against the people. Somewhere, not far away, there was a din: laughter, jangling bells and excited voices. I wondered what it was. Children swarmed towards us, stopped in their tracks, shrieked and then leapt at me, hands upraised as if they meant to hit me, but giggling and chattering in Swahili too fast for me to follow. 'What are they saying about me?'

Bertram sniggered. 'They've never seen a mzungu woman with ginger hair, Miss Hemmings. They want to touch it. Off you go, you little rascals! Shoo!'

I fumed at their insolence, and Bertram's, but I held my head high. Let them stare, I thought to myself, and then it was my turn to stare, for we rounded a corner and there before us was the source of that jangling racket: a parade, a full-blown parade, of ladies in scarlet and gold, pantaloons dripping with brocade and bells, bells at their ankles, bells at their wrists, and a vast lantern held up high, and masks on all their faces and mocking smiles beneath, and the scent of oiled hair and lamplight and roses, mingling with the sewage that everyone warned me is Zanzibar's constant stench.

'Oh damnation!' exclaimed Bertram. 'Begging your pardon Miss Lucy. We'll not get through this lot, let's take a detour.'

'Who are they? What are they doing?'

Father grasped my arm rather too tightly and said, 'Follow Mr. Bertram, Lucy, and don't look back. Don't look back!'

'Why ever not?' I said, looking back at that glorious bevy, but just as suddenly as they had appeared they were lost to sight, and here we were in another alley, with a vista of the sea before us, and soon we came to the seafront gardens, and the only reminder of that spectacle the crimson sun, sinking superbly beyond the horizon.

The British Consulate is a palace requisitioned quite recently from the Sultan – who, according to Bertram, claims he never liked it anyway. As we drew nearer, we saw a colonnaded verandah hung with lights, people strolling and laughing. 'Look,' he pointed at a woman riding towards the colonnade. 'There she goes, a-riding on her donkey!'

My heart jumped. At the colonnade the woman dismounted and tethered the animal. I had not expected to meet Martha Milton so soon.

When we entered the Residence there was no sign of her, but Mr. Kirk and the American Consul, Mr. Craig, were waiting to receive us. I curtsied to them, answered their polite enquiries about our journey, listened with pride as Father tried as best he could to acknowledge their thanks that he should have come to join them, 'to continue the great work that Sir Bartle Frere has begun.'

That *Livingstone* began, I thought to myself. True, Frere signed the treaty to end the slave trade, and stood over the Sultan until he signed too. But without Livingstone's efforts, none of you gentlemen would be in this fine palace now.

Father was of the same opinion, for he murmured politely and then moved into the drawing room. I would have followed him but Mr. Craig detained me. 'And what do you think of Zanzibar, Miss Hemmings?' Ridiculous question.

'I think it will be quite interesting, sir. But it's not Africa. It's just a small island, like Britain.'

'So young, and yet so blasé.' He and Mr. Kirk laughed, though more from puzzlement than unkindness. I hastened to explain.

'We were to have gone to Africa. We went to hear Livingstone's envoy address the Church Missionary Society in Newcastle, and he painted such a picture, of the savannah and the rabid rivers, and of the village that Livingstone has built on the Lake shore…'

But Mr. Kirk and Mr. Craig were looking beyond me, to the next arrivals. Subdued, I passed on to the drawing room. Father was standing at the fireplace, talking to an elderly gentleman in Episcopal purple. How astonishing to meet at last the Bishop, whose Swahili Grammar we have pored over for so many hundreds of hours, and whose letter arrived last June, asking Father whether, if he could no longer go to Africa, he might be willing to become Superintendent at the Sultan's hospital on Zanzibar.

And now the great man, saying, 'Your father tells me you are quite the scholar, Miss Hemmings; that your Swahili is better than his!'

'Any powers of intellect that I may possess, I owe to my father,' I replied modestly. 'And of course, learning a language is easy when you have such a magnificent Grammar.'

The Bishop smiled. 'Dr. Hemmings has a reputation that has spread as far as East Africa, and that is why I urged you to come here, in spite of your great loss. Your work is here, with the poor and the suffering. You were called to Zanzibar.'

I was too distracted to argue. A figure was approaching us through the florid merchants and their over-ornamented wives, towering above them, so stalwart, so pure in her plain blue gown of poplin. Her skin was red as an apple. I have never seen a lady such a hue. All around her head like a halo, her brown hair was pinned up in a perfect pompadour, and this was strange, for the pompadour is how fashionable ladies wear their hair, and yet this lady rides upon a donkey.

'Ah!' said the Bishop. 'And who better to help you answer the call than Nurse Milton?'

I searched her face, and my heart swelled.

So why did I take a step back when she held out her hands to me?

If she saw my hesitation, she didn't react to it. 'This must be dear Lucy!'

She spoke of her excitement when she heard I would be coming to join her 'in the great task'. She greeted Father warmly, compassionately. Then we were called in to dinner, and I cringe to remember what came next.

At first the conversation was bland, banal even, as Bertram and his IBEA cronies held forth on coconuts, sugar and the tonnage of gum copal they expect to harvest this year. I was so weary, my mind began to wander. Then I heard Father's voice, and his alone, as the entire company listened, avidly, to his theory of cholera: that the disease comes in waves, which can be anticipated and managed so as to avoid the rapid spread of infection. I was proud to see how eloquently he addressed them all, and how eager they were for his reassurances

Mrs. Craig, the American Consul's wife, sat opposite. She wore a necklace of creamy opals, veined with pale pink and blue. 'My dear,' she said to me across the table, 'I admire you both so much for coming here to do this noble, dangerous work. Your husband is so *brave* to tend the native sick…'

For a second I was confused – then I felt the full shame of it, and the embarrassment, the awful pity of Mr. Craig and the Bishop, and Martha Milton… Everyone, it seems, knew of our circumstances except for Mrs. Craig, whose smile sagged. In the silence, only Father's attempts at speech could be heard. 'I – oh – she – oh no, no…' Father, crimson, reduced again to misery. 'My wife was taken from us seven months ago. Otherwise we should have gone to Africa.'

Where I wished to be right now, in some mean mud hut. Not here in this too-splendid room reeking of roses.

Martha Milton saved us. 'Your Grace,' she said. 'Before Dr. Hemmings and his daughter go home tonight, would you show them the plans for the Cathedral? Mr. Bertram says they are such close neighbours, they must surely hear every hammer blow!' And everyone laughed, and the Bishop told us how the Cathedral is being built on the site of the old slave market, closed last June, and the altar was to be positioned where once the whipping post stood, as a glorious reminder of our victory over the slave trade.

Then it was time for the ladies to leave the table, and we went into the drawing room, my cheeks still burning. Mrs. Craig came up to me and tucked something into my hand. It was an ivory comb, frail as a leaf skeleton. 'Just fancy,' she said, with a tremor in her voice, 'this tiny little thing came from a mighty elephant! I think it will suit you, Miss Hemmings; you have such beautiful hair, like Mr. Rossetti's Beatrice.' I thanked her, promising to wear it, and saw how relieved she was to be forgiven for her mistake.

Martha Milton had observed us. As I waited at the coffee urn, the Nurse whispered to me, 'That was gracefully done, Lucy.' My heart lifted. 'But Lucy –' she fingered my black silk. 'If you must still mourn, you should wear white. Black absorbs heat, and the heat can drive us all insane.'

Was it a rebuke? My eyes prickled. 'I feel...'

'Yes, my dear? What is it you feel?'

'I feel I shall never belong here. Nobody believes a young English girl can be of any use on Zanzibar. It would have been different if we could have gone to Africa as we planned. If we could have worked with Livingstone, as my mother wanted...'

It was too painful. She allowed me a moment to compose myself. Then she said, 'There is a woman called Dora Manley who came out here with her husband, the Reverend Edward, just last July. I think Mrs. Craig confused you with her. Mrs. Manley is much younger than her husband, who I must say lacks your father's commanding presence. They live in the bush, and do the best they can with their little church. Lucy, there is no need to be faint-hearted. You will adapt to life here, and I shall teach you all my skills, all my knowledge.'

'Thank you, Miss Milton.'

'You must call me Nurse. And I shall send you one of my own best girls to be your maid, to care for you in your

41

new home. You shall not be alone.' Her voice was firm; her eyes were very blue; I felt comforted but at the same time oddly fearful. Fearful that I shall never be able to match Nurse Milton's achievements here and prove that I am, after all, worthwhile.

It is very late, but the street beneath my bedroom window is alive with candlelight and excited voices. Men saunter, hand in hand. A woman pours a pail of soapy water over her doorstep, and over the feet of another woman who screeches at her. People laugh. Bertram did not exaggerate the noise.

Nobody can see me sitting here in the darkness. Across the street, our neighbour's window glows. A lantern illuminates a divan, and a low table set with tiny glass tumblers. On the far wall, a looking glass returns my dark window, and my own face, faint, lonely as a ghost.

This morning I woke to a racket. My eyes still sticky with sleep, I groped beyond the gauze net for matches and candle, thinking I must have slept late, but the clock said: half past five. I crushed my face into the pillow, yearning to return to that dreamworld so far away from Zanzibar, but the voices and bells persisted, so I rose and went to the window where I saw the street below jammed with people: the confluence of two processions, filling the air with rills and rivulets of Arabic for ten minutes or more until a woman's high command rang out above the noise, and then one procession headed by the lantern began to move to the left, while the other swayed to the right, the jingling and clamour little by little diminishing. I hung out of the window to see the last of them as they disappeared round the corners of our street. The women at the tail end were drab, dressed only in black veils, cream tunics and trousers and sandals. Yet, they were every bit as joyful as those who wore scarlet and gold.

At breakfast Father said he had no idea who they were. Bertram arrived early, with a huddle of servants whom he addressed very loudly in English. We have a cook, an old man called Ibrahim who will not look at us when we talk to him, a laundry maid, Zeinab: a big, vigorous girl who will probably be very good at her job, and two other maids whose duties will be to clean the house and help Ibrahim and Zeinab. One of these is called Pili, the other's name I did not catch and I can't remember how to ask 'What is your name?' in Swahili so I shall have to look it up in the Bishop's book. We also have an askari who is even older than Ibrahim and who will sit at the foot of our stairs to repel invaders. He is armed with a panga, a cruel, broad blade which I doubt he would have the strength to wield.

I would have asked Bertram about the scarlet processions but he was eager for us to set off on what he grandly declared 'a tour of the island', talking all the while, and Father had many questions, such as how did the people dispose of their sewage, to which Bertram responded with a hooting laugh: 'Out the window, sir! Out the window!' It's true that the streets reek. As he hurried us along I had to be so careful where I put my feet, I could not form any sense of how this dark maze is constructed. The dwellings are tall stone houses like ours, or mean shacks; there is little difference between those ruined by the hurricane and the new ones built in their stead. When we found ourselves on the seafront it was a relief to be near that vast, diaphanous expanse, a promise of purity and calm, dhows drifting like distant angels, the prospect marred only by the grey men o' war skulking on the horizon, patrolling for slave ships. Bertram remarked that on a clear day you can see Africa; I peered and squinted, desperate for a glimpse – but although the sky above us was unblemished by a single cloud, I saw no trace of a coastline.

Then he hustled us into a carriage and away from the town, past IBEA plantations where curving lines of coconut palms are already rising again, in contrast to the wrecked Arab shambas, crisscrossed with felled, gargantuan trees; relics of the hurricane. To our left we saw people weeding, some waved as we passed. To our right, people sat dully by the roadside. When I asked why they were idle, Bertram explained they were the slaves of Arab plantation owners, who could not afford to replant their land. Last night the Bishop said the hurricane was in some ways a blessing, bringing many converts to the Mission. Perhaps it was a blessing for the IBEA too.

The carriage stopped in a clearing before a squat thatched hut. I thought maybe the driver had some business there – but Bertram said this was where the Reverend and Mrs. Manley lived. A white woman came running out, clutching a baby to her bosom with one hand and waving frantically with the other. How strange she looked, her fair hair straggling from its pins, her gown of yellow muslin filthy at the hem. The baby's fat legs were bent like a frog's. It was not reassuring to hear the woman screech: 'Thank God you've come! Thank God!' Her husband, rather older than she, emerged from the hut, his clerical collar standing out clearly beneath his pink face. I was appalled to remember how Father and I were mistaken for these people last night.

There was some discussion as to whether we should sit inside or out; I was intrigued to see how the Manleys lived, but the hut was so dark, it was a while before my eyes could make out the mean interior, its walls a ramshackle lattice of sticks and mud. In the darkest recesses, something rustled, eyes agleam. A picture of Jesus in a gold frame hung from a twig. The Manleys' sullen English nursemaid took the baby and deposited him on a rush mat. He alone was placid. The nursemaid brewed tea over a smoky fire, and then poured it into a teapot with a chipped lid. Tea was served in china cups without saucers. We sat on mats on the ground. I was marvelling at our surroundings, feeling both relieved and guilty that Father and I have been spared what we were assured was typical missionary accommodation, when something unpleasant happened.

'It is such a relief to have you here, Doctor,' Mrs. Manley was saying. 'For little George.'

'Is the child unwell?' Father asked.

'No, but when he is, you alone shall treat him. Nobody else is competent.'

'What about the excellent Nurse Milton? You are not so far from her Livingstone Dispensary.'

'That woman? That woman who rides around on a donkey like Jesus entering Jerusalem? Calling herself a nurse when she's no more a nurse than I am? Not if George was at death's door! I would rather hand him over to a native.'

The Reverend looked embarrassed at this intemperate outburst; Father looked astonished; Bertram sniggered. I said, 'Why do you hate her so much?' But the Reverend said, in a surprisingly steely voice, 'Dora, tell the girl to make more tea,' and Father said, 'I am impatient to see the hospital this afternoon,' and Dora Manley sniffed and went outside to find the servant. Perhaps living in 'the bush' has affected Mrs. Manley's head. I don't think I could live like that.

After our strange luncheon of bananas and breadfruit, the Manleys showed us their church and their little school where children and adults sat side by side, writing their names in the dust. The people sang a hymn: *There is a green hill far away*, which always made me cry before, with its plaintive tune and sad words, but today it sounded joyful, because they harmonized and added funny little grace notes to the end of each line, and clapped in time to the music. The Manleys promised to visit us in town. Father and the Reverend spoke of visiting the Sultan 'for the sake of goodwill.' I tried to catch Dora Manley's eye, but she wouldn't look at me.

On our journey back, slaves were still sitting idle while their free counterparts continued to labour in the fields just the other side of that long, dusty road. Was it wrong of me to revel in the beauty of the scene, the green saplings, their lines taut and spry, gradually shimmering into a distant heat haze like a melting green cloud? Don't these British farms represent the turning of the tide – the end of slavery?

Dinner, Ibrahim gave us to understand through waving his hands and shaking his head, would be delayed. While Bertram took Father to visit the hospital, I lay on my bed, too weary even to pull down the mosquito net as dusk darkened the room, until I was disturbed by the same hubbub I heard at dawn. I went to the window: there again were the two processions, jostling and milling in the street below. Then a male voice sounded above them, and every head tilted up and I saw the gold masks glittering like a nest of cunning birds, each one craning up to the window opposite mine. There was a man, with dark eyes and beard, his elbows resting on the sill, dressed in white and gold brocade, on his head a hat of tightly wound white fabric. He looked as if he were in a box at the theatre, and at the same time as if he should be performing in a play. We were so close, I could see his eyes dancing as he raised his hand to greet the women below, and one of them, bolder and gaudier than the rest, called out the only Arabic phrase I know: *Salaam aleikhum* – and then she seemed to challenge him with a stream of clattering words to which he responded with many solemn shakes of his head; mock-solemnity I could tell, for the women in the street were quite beside themselves with laughter, until suddenly he said something in a different tone, more abrupt, and in a ripple of scarlet and gold every masked face turned. To look at me. I slid down from my windowseat and crouched on the floor, my heart thumping, until I could hear that the processions had gone their separate ways. When I dared raise my head again, the room opposite was in darkness

What had I imagined? Mud, I suppose. A round mud hut with a bed in the middle of it. Mother leaning over the clean white sheets to tend our compliant patient.

When mother died I stopped picturing this scene.

And here I am, at the Livingstone Dispensary, a shed made of brick with a tin roof that glares in the sun. You can see it for miles around, because the dispensary stands in acres of barren land that nobody bothers to cultivate. Nearby, there is a sparse grove where Martha Milton tethers her donkey, and where we sit on mats to eat our midday meal. A path of beaten earth, which begins in the middle of nowhere and ends at the dispensary door, has been lined with white pebbles and jaunty orange marigolds that make my heart sink.

For our work, day after day after day, is all about making the best of things. Making the best of this dull landscape. Making the best of patients whose ailments always seem to entail viscous, malodorous substances – diarrhoea, suppurating sores, pus, phlegm, vomit. On my second day here I made my own emetic contribution, in the grove of trees where I had run, gagging and retching, from a child with a burn on the arm. It was humiliating, especially when Nurse Milton sent Mwanaidi to throw a bucket of sand over my mess.

'Next time you see a nasty burn like that, you won't be sick, because it won't be such a shock. And believe me, Lucy, you will see burns all the time – the people are so careless with fire.'

47

It is horribly clear that Nurse Milton has accepted me as her student out of kindness. I asked if I might teach at her orphan school instead. No, she said, her trained girls were very capable – two of her first pupils, now grown up, and who better to teach the children?

The tedium. The revulsion. The guilt that I cannot rejoice in this menial work. The frustration on seeing the same ailments day in, day out, as the weaklings queue at the back door with their 'Indian coins'.

Mwanaidi is deft and practical. Mwanaidi has an instinct for when people are going to be sick; always there with her bowl at the ready. And then she sings as she saunters to the rubbish pit. Mwanaidi came from the orphan school, so maybe she is grateful for the chance to tip out other people's vomit. At the end of every day Nurse Milton tests me on what I have observed, making me repeat each treatment step for step. Mwanaidi pretends to be busy but she is eavesdropping. Her eyes dance when Nurse shakes her head. 'No, Lucy, you have forgotten to swab the wound,' or '*Never* use ipecac for diarrhoea, Lucy. You might kill someone!'

And even at the end of the day the dreariness is not over, for here comes my chaperone to escort me home. Why has Martha Milton lumbered me with such a glum little wretch?

'Alicia, you are a very lucky girl to be working for Miss Lucy!' So Nurse told her when first she brought Alicia to our house, and yet my new maid looked terrified, peeping at me from beneath her black shela.

'Where does she come from?' Father asked.

'Nobody knows. I've had her since she was a babe-in-arms.'

'A foundling, then?'

'One of my best girls. Alicia can do plain sewing, and she speaks beautiful English. I thought to myself, Lucy *needs* Alicia. '

'But I want to practise my Swahili,' I objected.

'You can do that at work. At home you need to rest and allow Alicia to look after you.'

Is Martha Milton glad to be rid of this down-in-the-mouth?

'What's the matter, Alicia?' I said. 'Cat got your tongue?'

'Yes, mother.'

'I am not your mother!'

'She's translating *mama*,' said Martha Milton, 'which means *mother* and also *madam*. It's a common confusion.'

'You should call me Miss. Miss Lucy.'

'Yes, Missy Lucy.'

'*Miss.*'

'*Missy.*'

'Oh for heaven's sake!'

Father and Nurse Milton laughed. The first time I have seen Father laugh so heartily in many months. 'Remember, Lucy, in Swahili every word ends in a vowel; that's why you are a little Missy to Alicia.'

That first night, drifting off to sleep with my shutters ajar so that I would hear the procession if it should come at dawn, the door opened and in she slipped. I thought perhaps she was bringing up the fresh laundry, but through the mosquito net I saw her unroll a mat, slide it below my bed and crawl underneath.

'Alicia?'

'Yes mother?'

'Alicia, what are you doing under my bed?'

A pause. 'I am going to sleep, mother.'

'Under my bed?'

Another pause. 'Yes mother. If you like.'

'No, Alicia, I don't like! I don't like it one little bit! You will sleep in the courtyard with the other servants.'

'Yes mother.' She wriggled out, rolled up her mat, tucked it under her arm and left.

When I told Martha Milton about this bizarre behaviour she laughed until she cried. 'Bless the child! Bless the child!' I didn't know whether she meant me or Alicia. 'She must have thought that was her final duty of the day. Such devotion!'

'But why?'

Martha sighed. 'It's common practice, unfortunately, amongst Arab women and their slaves. Never mind.' She stood up, smoothed her pinafore. 'Alicia will do exactly as you say, Lucy. Now, please bring me the ipecac and squill.'

I wondered how Alicia should know about the bizarre habits of Arab ladies, if she has spent her entire life in the orphanage. But I suppose people gossip on a small island. And perhaps one day, she will tell me more about those ladies, and satisfy my curiosity.

September 1873

Today I nearly killed a baby.

'Hold the fort, will you, Lucy dear?' Nurse said when I arrived at work. 'I have to go to Mzimbazi to see a man with a gangrenous amputation.' I was too proud to tell her I was afraid I wouldn't manage on my own, but she guessed, because she said, 'Don't be alarmed! Mwanaidi will help you.' Sly Mwanaidi, who can't wait to see me trip up. Well, she had her satisfaction today.

All morning we were quiet, just the usual cases wincing and whimpering at our door with their diarrhoea and infected sores. By noon the last patient had gone away and I was in the store-room having a little rest when Mwanaidi, her eyes gleaming with spite, announced that two very sick babies were in need of treatment and one of them was a mzungu.

They were lying side by side on the truckle bed. The white baby was George Manley, covered in pustules that gave his skin the look of a gouged-open pawpaw with seeds floating in rubescent flesh. The native baby was brown, but his eyes, when I pulled back the lids, were yellow. His thin cries were scarcely audible through George's screams. I felt revulsion – and panic. Mrs. Manley and her Essex nursemaid gabbled: 'What is wrong with him? Do you know? Do you know what it is? Have you seen this before? You can help him, can't you? It came on very sudden, he was fine yesterday, he's been playing all morning in the shade and then he took ill. Oh, I can't bear to hear him crying like this, it's too pitiful. What are you going to do, Lucy? Why, oh why isn't that wretched Milton woman here?'

The mother of the native baby stood to one side, twisting in her fingers a corner of the orange cloth she wore.

In case of fever, the temperature must be brought down. I laid my hands on the babies' stomachs: hot loaves, straight from the oven. Then I scrutinized my palms as if they might show me which child had the higher temperature.

'What are you doing, Lucy? Why are you looking at your hands like that?'

I took sponges soaked in tepid water and gave one to the native mother, who attended mutely to her infant as I tried to soothe George's burning brow – poor George, it must have hurt him when I touched those blisters, for his wails got louder and louder. The other baby had not a mark on his smooth brown body. All the time I kept talking in a low, hurried voice, saying nothing intelligent but hoping to appear as if I knew what I was doing: 'There there, hush now, we'll make you better by and by, there now, hush, we'll help you' – and it was a lie, yet another lie, for I had no idea what was wrong with these babies.

The door opened, sending a blade of light across the truckle bed, and I nearly wept to see Martha Milton.

'Whatever's the matter? Is this little George? Hello George, my sweet dumpling!' She might have been cooing over him at a tea party. Then she saw the other infant, curled against his mother's thin breast. She spoke to the woman in Swahili and listened keenly to the reply. She crossed the room, selected one key from the great bundle at her waist, unlocked the cupboard and took out a phial of powder. This she mixed in a flagon with boiled water from the stone jar. The sight of the grains spinning round and round in the water seemed to calm us all, even George, as if our fear was dissolving too. She took the native baby in the crook of her arm and spooned a little of the mixture into his puckered mouth. Her face was grave. Droplets spattered her bodice but she paid no heed and carried on until he had taken all the liquid. She spoke again to the mother, who curtsied, swaddled the child tightly in another orange cloth and tied him on her back. Then, to our surprise, the mother darted forward to embrace Martha Milton, tears squeezing from the corners of her eyes. Nurse accepted the embrace for a few seconds, before gently disengaging herself and leading the woman to the door. As she left, all my anxiety finally subsided and I too wanted to fall upon Martha Milton's bosom, thank her a thousand times, beg her to tell me that I am forgiven for the sins she knows about, and those she does not.

She turned to George, plucked him up from the truckle bed and sat him on the edge of the table, his fat knees bulging sideways. 'Now then, young man, where have you been playing?'

The nursemaid was sulky. 'I watched him the whole time, I never took my eyes off of him. I never let no-one else touch him, there wasn't no other little ones playing nearby – '

'Yes, dear, but *where* was George?'

'Under that big tree behind the Reverend's house, ma'am. I thought it would be nice and shady for him. And then when I come to take him in for his milk, he was busting out all over with them horrible blisters, poor little lamb!'

Martha Milton's lips twitched. 'Oh George,' she said, giving his stomach a prod. 'Have you been eating caterpillars?'

Mrs. Manley fainted. As soon as she hit the earthen floor she came round, but couldn't get up again, so the nursemaid and I had to put our hands under her armpits and hoick her into a chair. Martha Milton, meanwhile, was anointing George with a smelly pink lotion. Its coolness must have pleased him, for he left off screaming and contemplated our exertions with his usual benign expression. 'Yes,' she said, with some relish, 'those big brown caterpillars with the black spots on their hairy backs. Ugh! George, how could you?'

At last Mrs. Manley took George away, alternately thanking us and berating the maid. I couldn't help but think how she had changed her tune, because she, too, embraced the Nurse as she left, with no sign of her earlier virulent mistrust. Oh yes; Martha Milton was her saviour now. I skulked in the laundry room, humiliated, angry with myself, for shouldn't I have been content that the babies were cured, their mothers overjoyed? But I could not shake off the sense of failure, heavy as a winter cloak, oppressing me with the truth that if those babies had been left to my feeble devices, one of them might have died. How I yearned to be like *her*: calm, capable, wise. There is not a single Zanzibari, however resentful towards the British, who yet would not declare his admiration for 'Mama Martha'. The people do not respect me. They do not call me 'Mama Lucy', just 'mzungu'. I think they wonder why I have come to Zanzibar: so young, so white, so exceedingly useless.

In this wretched frame of mind I was scrubbing pus from the sheet when Martha Milton came to find me, holding aloft my traveller's medical kit which I thought I had hidden cleverly at the back of the store cupboard. 'Good old Burroughs and Wellcome!' she sang out. 'Where would we be without them, Lucy?'

For shame and the nervous strain of what had happened, I broke down and wept as noisily as George, wailing that I should never have come, that Father and I should have stayed in England, that everything would be different if only Mother were still alive. She tried to comfort me but I couldn't stop. Eventually she held my face in her hands and said, 'Lucy, Lucy, you must listen to me, listen to what I am going to tell you ...' and by and by her steady, speedwell-blue gaze drew me out of my misery, and I needed to wipe my nose, and the mundane task of searching for a handkerchief made me feel silly, so I stopped crying.

'Lucy, do you remember what Livingstone said?' Her voice was exultant. It made me shiver. 'Do you remember his words to those of us who have chosen to follow him? Do you remember?'

I was embarrassed by her intensity, but of course I remembered Livingstone's words very well. '*You do not know what you can do until you try.*'

'Just so. The trying is what matters, Lucy. Sometimes we fail, but if we *try* and fail, we have done God's work. Today, you have really *tried.*'

I wasn't convinced. An incompetent can hardly be pleasing in God's eyes. When Alicia arrived to take me home, Martha Milton murmured a few words to her in Swahili which I could not catch, but I thought my maid looked at me pityingly, which I found very difficult to bear on our dusty walk back to the Stone town.

Obsessions never come to any good, Father says, perhaps wondering whether he truly did hear the call to Zanzibar. But surely it isn't wrong to pursue colour and mystery? The joy of cobalt, vermilion, gold, a white portico, bright as heaven, a ripple of strange words? Ever since our first night, I had been possessed by the image of that dusk procession, longed to know where they were going, and why, and whether it would be possible for a pale English girl to join them.

It is not the obsession that is wrong – it is the sins committed to satisfy the obsession.

The shela was easy to make: I had packed my black funeral shawl, and told myself Mother would be pleased to know of its new use – Mother, who yearned for Africa, for adventure, for the unknown. I thought of borrowing a calico tunic and trousers from the courtyard washing line, but servants are there at every hour, watching and gossiping. So I asked Martha Milton if I might take home some mending from her orphan school. 'You are very considerate, Lucy,' she said. For shame, I darned those holes with exquisite stitches. Then I folded the clothes away inside my trunk, and waited.

Every morning for six days I woke radiantly, fearfully, to an imperative carillon in the street below – which proved to be nothing but the clang of iron buckets, accompanied by sighs and grumbles from our neighbours on their way to draw water. On the seventh day I slept, until Alicia brought me tea. On the eighth day bells jangled at the fringes of my dream – then I was awake with a jolt, and I darted to the window to see the procession already rounding the corner. I pulled on the trousers and tunic, fastened the shawl over my head, crept downstairs, hovered for a moment beside the snoring askari, sneaked to the courtyard, where, in semi-darkness, I could just make out ghostly shapes of servants moving about their business. Alicia washes her sandals every night, then she props them against a wall to dry. My hand shot out, I hooked my finger through the two leather thongs and they were mine. Trembling for guilt and fear of interception, I slunk past the askari once more, nudged open the front door, and out into the throng. Scarlet! Aquamarine! Cyclamen pink! Orange, crimson, violet and gold. I drank colour; breathed colour, sang colour as the princesses streamed past me. Clutching the black shawl over my face I twisted my hips this way and that to cleave my path through the jostling crowd. My calico lendings were so light, I felt so free, I could have flown into the air. But I stayed earthbound, revelling in my anonymity within this throng, all their attention on the princesses, smiles sly below scarlet silk masks, black corkscrew curls shining with oil, bobbing as they embraced each other, their voices high and exuberant.

Someone bumped against me and my shawl slipped. A man pointed to my toes, curling like pale shrimps, and then he looked into my eyes. 'Mzungu!' he said incredulously. 'Mzungu!' A surge thrust us forward, the procession swelling up the narrow street, and he lost interest, calling out to a young boy ahead of us. My heart was pounding. On and on, our swaying, linear waltz, all of us craning to see those fine ladies, dripping with gold, bells at their ankles, bells at their wrists, leading us, marching and jangling, heaven knows where.

The sky was already faded to indigo, flecked with watery stars. I had no idea of our destination; we could have been wandering around and around those secretive streets purely for the joy of vermilion parade and raucous song. I was compelled to follow. The indigo sky broadened. The sea confronted us with a warning glitter. Still the procession streamed on, along the promenade, past the Customs House, through Forodhani gardens towards the vast iron gates of the Beit al-Sahel. There, at last, the crowds fragmented like flotsam as the gates opened to receive the crimson princesses, and my fellow hangers-on began to break away, a little crestfallen, as if, like me, they had no desire to return to their humdrum lives.

Daylight. I scuttled into the warren of streets and soon realised how foolish I had been: one stone alley looks the same as any other. Rapidly I walked, vulnerable now without the crowd swirling around me, head down to hide my blue eyes. At a shop I half-recognised I turned right, and a few minutes later, to my dismay, I found myself on the seafront again. Back I went into the maze; I would not let it defeat me. A boy, eight or nine years old, was setting out a tray with oranges. 'Take me to the English doctor's house,' I said to him, as boldly as I could. He stared, as if I were naked. I tried again, in perfect Swahili. 'Do you understand?' He hung his head, but I caught him smirking. He must have known our house, for everybody in the Stone Town knows Father. Biting back my anger I hurried on.

The air became pungent with coffee. On a street corner some men were gathered around a brazier, drinking from tiny cups like thimbles. How I longed for a draught of that hot black syrup! One man tipped his head back to drain his cup, then, as he half-turned and bent to put the cup down on the ground, I recognised my neighbour, that man I had seen in the window across the street. Please, please let him lead me safely home before Father discovers I am gone! He bade his companions 'Kwa heri' and set off at a fast pace, so that I stumbled behind him in the flapping calico trousers, still clutching my shawl, and once the tip of my sandal caught in a crack in the uneven pavement and I tripped and fell, grazing my hands. A woman called out in sympathy: *Oh, sorry mama!* I thought I should be discovered – but the man did not so much as glance back. Neither did he pause until he reached his house and I, with a stitch in my side, leaned against our blessed familiar wall, pressing my cheek into the cool stone.

'So, you like dressing up?' From his dark hallway he smiled at me. Then the door closed and he was gone.

I bolted into our house, past the askari who was still asleep, up the stairs to my room. First I slammed shut the shutters, then, with fingers that shook so I could hardly undo the ties, I exchanged my light, loose clothes for stockings that clung to my skin, a dull mauve gown, button boots. Too late to return Alicia's sandals; the courtyard would be full of prying servants all day. I put them under my bed and went down to the dining-room.

Father was already at the breakfast table, reading a month-old copy of the Times. 'Good morning Lucy.' His voice was as usual, kind and warm. The newspaper was propped against the pot of Keelwell's marmalade that we brought with us all the way from Tynemouth. Both of us are tacitly reluctant to spread any on our toast, for when it is finished, we will have lost another memento of home.

I was enjoying my porridge when raised voices in the courtyard startled us, and we went to the window. Alicia and Zeinab were screeching into each other's faces while Ibrahim the cook tried to put himself between them, bellowing to no avail. Who would have guessed Alicia could make so much noise? The other servants were laughing heartily, but when Father called down, 'What on earth is going on?' these spectators leapt back and became very busy. Zeinab continued to berate Alicia, who burst into tears and covered her face.

I began to guess what had happened.

Father summoned all three upstairs. Zeinab speaks no English at all, and Alicia was incoherent with weeping, so Ibrahim took it upon himself to explain, 'Alicia, she say Zeinab she thief shoe.'

'Alicia,' I said, 'are you looking for your sandals? You left them upstairs. Yes, you did! I found them and put them in my room for safekeeping. Go and see for yourself.'

Her eyes were brimming with bewildered tears as she left the room. When she returned a few minutes later with the sandals she looked resentful – or perhaps my guilt made me imagine so. Zeinab tossed her head and muttered. Ibrahim told her to hold her tongue.

'Well, Alicia,' said Father. 'It appears your accusation was false. It is a very serious matter, you know, to accuse someone of theft. You must be more careful in future. Now, I think you owe Zeinab an apology.'

Alicia hung her head and whispered. Ibrahim helpfully translated, 'She say Zeinab, she thief shoe and then hide in house.'

'Oh, I don't think so,' I said, shocked by my own easy mendacity. 'Zeinab would have no reason to come upstairs to the top landing. Perhaps Alicia took her sandals off when her feet were tired, and forgot to put them back on again.'

Alicia made a grudging apology, which Zeinab grudgingly accepted. Ibrahim chivvied the girls downstairs, leaving us to finish our breakfast in peace. I confess, I felt ashamed. And unsettled. There was another matter on my mind.

'Father, have you ever spoken to that gentleman who lives across the way?'

Father shook out his newspaper. 'What gentleman?'

'The … the one who sometimes wears a grey frock coat.'

'Ah, that Arab. He has been introduced to me, yes, at the hospital. I don't remember his name, but he's the Sultan's Khatib.'

'What does that mean?'

'Means he thinks himself quite important. Fellow's a secretary, it's his job to attend to all the Sultan's written business; to arrange travel to the mainland; to supervise the household administration. The Bishop has had many dealings with him, especially since the treaty, and seems to regard him favourably. But you know the Bishop, Lucy. Never has a bad word to say about anyone. More than anyone else, he wants this treaty to last.'

All day long I worked hard at the dispensary to atone for my waywardness, and all the time, while engaged in the usual menial tasks, I wondered why my neighbour the Khatib should have brought me safely home without giving any indication that he knew of his follower.

The next day my right foot began to hurt. At first, I ignored the discomfort. But it grew.

Throb. Throb. Throb. Liar. Liar. Liar.

I hid it from Alicia when she came to chaperone me home. I forced myself to walk without hobbling and I did not wince.

But Alicia is uncanny. She came, long after I should have been asleep, to my room. If she knocked I did not hear her. She found me sitting on the edge of the bed in my nightgown, my right foot tucked up over my left knee, trying by lamplight to see whether the thing on my sole was really a black spot the size of a farthing, or just an ingrained lump of dirt. When I scratched it, the pain made me whimper. Then some tiny movement in the doorway made me look up, and there was Alicia, witness to my pokings and proddings. 'What is this?' I snapped.

'Funza,' she whispered. I was none the wiser. 'Excuse,' she said, and left. I wanted to call after her, Please help me! but she soon returned, with a jug of water and a needle. She struck a match, her sombre features suddenly leaping into life, her oval eyes glowing. She held the needle in the flame until the silver blackened. 'What are you going to do?' She sat on the bed next to me; I was too scared to protest.

Then she took my foot in her small brown hand – 'No!' I exclaimed, but she gripped me hard and in a panic I levered myself up off the bed, crying, 'Let go of me you stupid girl! How *dare* you?' Then I overbalanced and fell backwards onto the mattress. Wriggling onto my elbows, heart beating with fright, I watched as she narrowed her eyes the better to see the needle, and brought it steadily down, down. She slipped the point just under the surface of my skin, on the edge of that dread black mark. Very, very delicately, she began to scrape. There was no pain, no spurt of blood; not one tiny red bead. My breathing slowed. She drew out the needle, bearing its freight of minuscule, translucent eggs. For the first time ever, Alicia looked me in the eye. 'Better now,' she said. She began to probe again, and this time I did not resist.

In the morning Father unwittingly made everything clear.

'What does funza mean, Father?'

'Funza? That's the native name for the jigger. A wretched little creature that lives in the dust, looking for an opportunity to burrow under human skin. Then it lays its eggs and before you know where you are, your flesh is infected with its maggots. Extremely nasty. I'm sure Nurse Milton will have seen thousands of cases, Lucy. The trick, apparently, is to get the eggs out from under the skin before they hatch, with a needle and a steady hand. But rest assured, the fiendish thing can't penetrate stout leather boots. That's why we don't wear sandals like the natives.'

Today, on our way back from the dispensary, we walked along the sea front. 'Alicia, let's sit down for a while.'

We found a bench in the Forodhani gardens. Behind us the Sultan's palace glittered with hundreds of tiny lamps; ahead, more powerful than all the lamps in the world, the sun sank into the darkening sea. Doubtless Alicia did not understand why I wanted to remain outside at dusk, when the mosquitoes are at their most malevolent and the streets swarm with shadows, but she said nothing, seemingly absorbed in her own thoughts, gazing at some distant point on the horizon, undistracted by the urchins who played around us, or the dhows preparing for their lonely night voyages.

'Alicia,' I began. 'I am afraid I have deceived you.'

I told her everything. The parade we saw on our very first day here. My curiosity (and the intense tedium of my work at the dispensary). How carefully I assembled my costume. How I stole her sandals. She looked startled, then thoughtful. Didn't say a word. I continued, told her every last detail, how much I had loved being part of that living ribbon of colour, until the moment when I realised I didn't know my way home – and how that was at once frightening and thrilling. I even told her about our neighbour the Khatib.

'And so now you know, Alicia,' I concluded, 'how I came by my jigger. It serves me right for stealing your sandals. Do you think I'm very wicked?'

I expected her to say, 'Of course not, Missy Lucy!' But Alicia was still contemplating the darkening sea, with her head slightly on one side and her eyes limpid.

'I don't understand ...' She frowned. 'I don't understand why you wanted to dress like a slave.'

Hadn't I explained all that? 'Because I wanted to join in, I wanted to see what happened, where the princesses were going.'

'They were going home. To the Beit al-Sahel.'

'Well ...yes. But I wanted to be part of it all, Alicia, you can't imagine how glorious it was! The colours they wore! Everyone so excited, it was like a wonderful carnival!'

'But mother, you could have knocked on the door of the Beit al-Sahel and asked the princesses to join in their parade.'

Was she being deliberately obtuse?

'Could I?

'You are a mzungu, mother. You can go wherever you like.'

'Not everywhere, Alicia. Not to Africa.'

'Why do you want to go to Africa, mother?'

'Because … because we were called to Africa, to work with Dr. Livingstone. That is where I am meant to be. That is where we should be right now, but …'

'But your mama died, so you came to Zanzibar instead.'

I nodded, tears falling. Maybe she couldn't see them in the dark.

'One day, mother, you will go to Africa. You will go.'

'How can you be so certain, Alicia?'

'Because you are a mzungu.' She twisted round to face me. 'Mother, may I come with you?'

Her eyes were alight, and alert, and earnest. 'I should so much like to meet Dr. Livingstone again.'

'Again, Alicia?'

'Yes, mother. Dr. Livingstone came to the orphanage, and gave me my Bible for being Best Girl.'

'You *met* Livingstone?'

'I shook his hand, mother.'

She settled back again, gazing out to the ocean. 'He is such a good man. I am so happy, mother, that you want to work with Dr. Livingstone. You can take me with you and we can both help him.'

Well…! 'So, Alicia, you would not mind leaving Zanzibar, your birthplace, to travel overseas and live and work so far from home?'

'Not my birthplace, mother. Africa is my birthplace.'

'But …Nurse Milton brought you up from a babe in arms.'

'No, mother. Four years old. Fourteen years ago.'

'You were four years old when you came to the orphanage?'

'Yes, mother. A man brought me, I think he was a priest. I remember that day very well. It was raining. I remember the sound of the rain on the roof, *tatatatatatata*! And Nurse, she gave me some clothes to wear. Because my clothes from Africa were not good.'

'But your name? She gave you your name, Alicia?'

'No mother, I brought my name with me. The name mama gave me.'

I could hardly believe it – that Alicia should have shaken his hand, that she should want to come with me to Africa… that Martha Milton should have lied to me…

No, that was a mistake. Hundreds of children must have passed through Martha Milton's orphan school, she can't be expected to remember every arrival.

But never mind how Alicia came to Zanzibar; something has changed between us. I think she has forgiven me. And I think she is my ally. Perhaps, one day, she and I will go to Africa together.

October 1873

Sometimes I feel I cannot tolerate any more strange sights – for, beautiful or horrific, everything is strange here on Zanzibar. Today, the strangest sight of all, yet I don't know why it has unsettled me so much.

This morning I arrived early at the dispensary with Alisha. The window shutters of the little laundry room were open; I could hear splashing water and thought it must be Mwanaidi.

But it was the Nurse. It was Martha Milton, wearing only her petticoat. No bodice. Nothing at all, above her waist.

She was leaning over a basin, washing herself.

What shocked me first was the contrast between the worn russet skin of her face and neck, and the whiteness below.

The sight of her breasts wasn't shocking. Haven't I seen a hundred Zanzibari women, suckling their babies on the street?

No, it was the way she washed herself. Sluicing those breasts, white and glistening like two peeled pears. How tenderly she trickled the water over them.

I took Alicia's hand and drew her on, past the laundry room, to the main entrance. She piped, 'I will come back later, mother,' and I said, 'I'm not your mother,' and she said, 'No, mother,' and off she went. I busied myself amongst the medicines until the Nurse entered, her striped gown fastened, her apron tied, and we opened the doors to begin our day's work. Her servant overslept this morning and failed to draw water, so that's why she came to wash at the dispensary instead. Later she sent Mwanaidi to the well. 'Don't worry, Lucy,' she smiled, as Mwanaidi stalked off with a bucket on her head. 'That is one task I shall never ask you to perform. It would be quite unfair to ask you to do what only a native girl can.'

All I could think was, *I have seen your breasts*.

Her face may be sun-reddened, and her hands worn with hard work, but I know her breasts are white and full and beautiful. Just like any other woman's.

I tried hard not to, but I couldn't help picturing those breasts this evening when she came to our house for supper. She was a kind guest, complimenting me on the 'little homely touches' she claimed to observe in our drawing-room, (although I don't see what's so homely about a few cushions and a posy-vase of wilting frangipani blossoms), and she never once complained about Ibrahim's tough goat meat. After supper had been cleared, she remained sitting at the table while Father brought out our chess set – Martha Milton wants to learn chess so she can teach her girls at the Orphanage. 'It will be a far more stimulating pastime than their incessant singing and dancing.'

I sat in a corner with my book, thinking uncharitable thoughts about her obtuseness, because really she was very slow, and kept confusing knights with bishops and moving pawns two squares instead of one. Even Father, who is such a patient teacher, became frustrated at one point and exclaimed, 'No, no, no, you can't do that!' – putting out his hand to stop hers as she tried, for the umpteenth time, to move the knight diagonally. She blushed, and so did he.

November 1873

Alicia *is* uncanny. 'You could have knocked on the door …' she had said, when I confessed how much I wanted to go inside the Beit al Sahel.

And then our invitation from the Sultan arrived.

Such a day. Such an escape.

Instead of that dusty path to the dispensary, walking through the iron gates of the palace! And Father *did* knock on the vast door, and once inside, I could have danced across the chequered marble floor for the joy of being on holiday, of glorious escape from drudgery, as our party waited in the entrance hall below the vast double staircase, while our gifts for the Sultan were carried in. Mr. Bertram swore when the porters cracked one end of an enormous parcel against the newel post at the foot of the stairs. I was pleased to share with everyone the new word I have learned: *shaghalabhagala*, which means a mess and a muddle, and the Bishop congratulated me on my command of idiom although Father murmured, 'Lucy, manners.' But the only people present were slaves. How odd that we should be requested to sit on a row of rather hard chairs, as if for a photograph, by slaves – the very people whose fettered existence we are here to condemn.

Some while later, the Sultan and his entourage entered, all dressed in long white and gold coats, and crimson waistcoats, the Sultan's most ornate of all. He was shorter than I had expected, his stature and outline reminding me of our Queen, except for his long, untamed beard. He smiled at us, but his eyes were chips of granite. How strange, to be entertained by the man whose hand signed the treaty without which Father and I would not be here.

When our neighbour the Khatib stepped forward and began to interpret, I kept my eyes down as I had been instructed, but I listened to his voice shifting from Arabic to English and back to Arabic again, with such smoothness that I couldn't be sure whether I really had heard him say my name. Mrs. Manley and I were beckoned up to curtsey to the Sultan, George wriggling and grumbling against his mother's bosom. Then Father, the Bishop, Bertram, Mr. Manley, were ushered one way, and we ladies were taken aside by a tall plump gentleman who led us up the curving flight of stairs and through a door into a long, high room with many windows. There was an overpowering scent of roses. Between each window were shelves crammed with china and glassware; stacks of plates; teetering towers of cups; battalions of champagne flutes. At the far end of the room twenty or so ladies were lounging on velvet cushions; they did not rise when we entered, but by nods and smiles they invited us to join them. As we walked the length of the crimson carpet, the rose-fug made me giddy. They motioned us to sit on straight-backed chairs, placed to one side of a dais where a particularly magnificent lady sprawled. I was a little disappointed that nobody wore the red and gold finery of their dawn and dusk carnival; even so, they were extravagantly dressed in embroidered tunics and pantaloons. Mrs. Manley and I looked so dowdy in comparison – but the ladies had eyes only for George, gathering round him to prod and stroke his fat little cheek, cooing just as English women do; uttering rattling cries which had nothing English about them at all. Our rotund gentleman with the high voice interpreted their questions for us. Is it a boy or a girl? How old? Does he, in the European fashion, suck milk from his own mother's breast? Mrs. Manley flinched at this, but I answered for her. They served us tea in tiny gold-rimmed glasses that burned my fingers as I sipped, the black liquid scorching my tongue with a heady flavour of mint and cardamom. Mrs. Manley's tea remained untouched while she grappled with George, who grew increasingly restless and bad-tempered. Then, the lady on the dais pointed to him, mimed a cradling gesture, and held out her arms beseechingly.

'Oh dear. Oh dear, do you think I ought?' Mrs. Manley whispered.

'Why not?' I replied.

Forcing a smile, she passed George to the lady, who slipped her gloved hand beneath his head, and her companions sighed in unison, their dark eyes soft and adoring. The princess walked across to the open window (Mrs. Manley writhed on her chair) and held the baby up, and whatever he saw must have delighted him, for he began to gurgle and laugh, which made everyone else laugh too.

The time passed pleasantly as we sipped mint tea, admired jewels and gaudy necklaces and each other's clothes. Mrs. Manley embarrassed me with her questions, making no attempt to lower her voice even though the fat man could understand: 'Are these *really* all the Sultan's wives? It's disgusting, yet see how well they get on with each other. Why's that one sitting higher than the rest? Do you think she's the favourite? Do you think the others mind?' And all the time, her eyes were flitting back and forth as George was passed from lap to lap. But they could not, or would not, let him be still, and he suddenly produced a loud belch, then vomited: a stream of white curdy stuff gushing down his chin and spattering the amethyst pantaloons of the unlucky lady who happened to be dandling him. She held him at arms' length while her companions laughed merrily; a slave stepped forward, picked up George and glided away, the baby's startled face peeping over her shoulder. Mrs. Manley leapt up, but I laid my hand on her arm. 'We mustn't do anything to offend our hosts. Think of our Cathedral.' I hoped she would be shamed into behaving herself, and she sat down again, quivering. More tea was poured. Then two little children ran in, two pretty little girls, and while the ladies were distracted by their chatter Mrs. Manley whispered, 'Oh please Lucy, I can't bear it, what have they done with him?'

I looked round for the fat man but he had gone, which gave me an idea. 'The nursery can't be far from here.' By waving my hands around I made the princesses understand that we wished to leave the room. They looked somewhat surprised, but I rocked an invisible baby in my arms, pointed to Mrs. Manley, glumly drew a finger down my cheek, one of the ladies said, *Ah!* and spoke to a slave, who took us outside to the landing. I said quickly, 'You go that way and I'll go this' – then off I ran, up that magnificent staircase. I didn't look back when she called after me, 'Lucy, where are you going? Please don't leave me!' but a woman emerged from another room with a squawking bundle in her arms, and Mrs. Manley shrieked, 'George!'

As I sped away up one side of the double staircase, the great door of the harem swung shut behind them, its echo thrumming across the space. When it ceased to resound, the air seemed cooler, sharper than before, clear of the cloying rose perfume. I paused, leaning on the balustrade. Above my head a chandelier hung, huge and complex, like a crystal pomegranate. Beautiful. But I didn't have time to stand and admire it, if I was to explore the palace while I had my freedom.

Slaves did not seem to notice me as I darted past them. Going through an archway, I found myself at the beginning of a corridor, the walls emblazoned with swirls of black and gold. An ebony elephant stood sentinel, and I stroked his smooth trunk.

What was I looking for?

The sounds of the palace became more and more subdued. I stopped at the end of the black and gold corridor and listened for voices, but there were none. I was alone. It was frightening, and thrilling. In the near-silence, a fragrance of leather and sandalwood drifted from a room ahead of me, the door slightly ajar. I entered a library, the walls lined from floor to ceiling with Morocco-bound books. A desk stood before the window, the inkwell full, a pen lying across a sheet of paper covered with writing, not the elegant hooks and curlicues of Arabic, but our own Roman script: a neat hand, the letters evenly formed and slanting purposefully to the right. The document appeared to be a shopping list, with sums tallied and totalled after each item. These were accounts of expenditure from a voyage to America: cloth, guns, several clocks, a musical box, a typewriter, and at the very end:

$1 – ? I cannot remember, perhaps beer for the ship's captain

As I pondered this list and who might have itemised it so meticulously, a mild voice said, 'What are you doing?'

I whirled round. Our neighbour the Khatib was standing in the doorway.

What *was* I doing, creeping around the Sultan's palace like a thief?

Too late, now, to quell my unbearable curiosity. Too late for regret. Yet his face was calm, not angry. So I told him the truth. Almost.

'Forgive me, sir, I became lost while looking for Mrs. Manley's baby.'

'In this library? Can European babies read?'

'No, sir. Although the mother of this one perhaps fancies that it soon will.'

He laughed. 'I suppose you could not ask the slaves to take you to the nursery, for they have no English and you have no Swahili.'

'But I do speak Swahili! I have been studying the language for almost a year now, and speak it very well!'

Then he laughed again, and spoke a stream of words, observing me all the time, knowing I couldn't understand.

'Well,' I said. 'Now you are trying to catch me out.'

'That wasn't my intention. But perhaps you should practise your Swahili a little with me?'

Impossible to tell whether the smile on his lips was friendly or mocking.

'It's alright, thank you,' I replied. 'I shall return to the harem and see if the baby has been found.'

But he remained standing between me and the door. It came into my mind how ridiculous I must have looked that morning, in my calico tunic. Not knowing what else to do, I attempted to make conversation. 'Is – is the Sultan pleased with his gifts?'

'Oh yes, especially the clock. The mechanism is very fine. It can tell the seconds, as well as the minutes and hours. And the casing is of rosewood inlaid with gold. But perhaps you have seen it for yourself?'

'I have not. It was all packaged up this afternoon when we arrived.'

'Then let me show it to you.'

It was a relief to leave that secluded library. He led me back down the corridor, pointing out this knick-knack and that, until we emerged again onto the staircase. We descended to the ground floor, slaves passing us with averted eyes. I found their absence of interest disquieting. On the chequered marble stood a grandmother clock, a little over my height, similar to the one we had in Tynemouth. It ticked loudly. I scrutinized its yellow face:

71

the Roman numerals neat black incisions in the brass. A screw in the centre of the face had the look of a nose. Three more screws made the eyes and mouth. There were three hands: one for the hour, one for the minutes, and one that whirred round busily counting the seconds. Engraved on the face in copperplate script was a name I knew well: *French & Co.*

'Seventeen minutes past five of the clock,' the Khatib declared.

A compliment seemed required. 'It's very fine.'

He nodded. His face was thoughtful, almost grave, with no sign of the earlier mischief. 'In my own house I have a clock such as this,' he said, 'although not quite so splendid. I have spent many hours studying it, wondering at the transformation of seconds into minutes, minutes into hours, hours into days; marvelling that there is nothing I can do to make this process come to an end, for even if I were to take a hammer to my beautiful clock and pound it into many tiny pieces, time would continue.'

With his fingernail he traced over the glass case the whirring of the second hand on its inexorable journey. 'Listen. We can hear time as it passes.' His finger left a faint smear on the glass. 'You look sad. Does it distress you to see how little control we have over the short span of our lives?'

I stammered, 'No, no, it's just - we had a clock like this at home. When my mother died it became mine. Only we had to leave it behind.'

'In England.'

Tears were forming in my eyes. I turned away from him, to prevent more questions.

He said gently, 'I know what it is to lose a mother, and to leave a homeland.'

When I had composed myself he asked, 'Have you seen the Sultan's new chess set, which your Queen has so generously presented to him?' He led me to a console table where the chess set had been unpacked and arranged ready for play. But the white bishop and knight were in each other's places, so I switched them round.

'Are you familiar with this game?'

'Of course! My father and I play most evenings – but to pit yourself always against the same opponent is tedious, so I am teaching my maid to play too.'

'And do you always win?'

Did he think me arrogant? 'Well … father is a masterly player,' I conceded, 'but sometimes I outwit him. He says that is the greatest satisfaction of all: to be beaten by one's own pupil.'

'And the maid?'

'She has not beaten me yet. Maybe one day I shall know that bittersweet satisfaction.'

'That day shall never come.' It was glib, as compliments usually are. 'Now, it is high time you were returning to the princesses. They will be worried; it is too easy for a foreigner to become lost in the Beit al Sahel.'

'Please don't concern yourself, sir,' I said. 'I have an excellent sense of direction, as you know …' and with this bold reference to the morning when he had led me home, I ran up the staircase to the harem without once looking back.

The ladies hadn't missed me. Mrs. Manley was sitting on the dais, propped against cushions next to the large princess, George slumbering on her lap, with the younger ladies disposed around them gazing adoringly as at a Madonna and Child, while the older women were chatting to each other, humming dreamily or playing with the two little girls. I thought Mrs. Manley might have expressed admiration at my independence, or at least shown some interest in where I had been, but she had eyes only for George. A short while later we were summoned to leave. The gentlemen of our party were waiting in the entrance hall. There was no sign of the Khatib.

*

Once outside the palace gates, nobody seemed to know what we should do next. It was evening, but still warm, and the harsh glare of daylight had given way to a softer glow from a translucent, emerald sky. Far above us the first shadows of night were gathering. I wished I could tell them all of my adventure, and yet, at the same time, I wanted to keep it secret.

Mrs. Manley gulped the air. 'I never dreamed I should be glad to breathe the stench of Zanzibar, but anything is better than those sickly roses!'

How she exaggerates, I thought, although I could feel my own head clearing now we were in the open. Then she frowned, held up a finger. 'Listen. Did I hear a mosquito?' She bundled George under her veil; he immediately took a fat fistful of netting and stuffed it into his mouth. 'We must go home straight away, before George gets bitten.' Her husband looked as if he would prefer to stay and enjoy the evening, but they took their leave of us, hurrying away into the maze of streets. Father, the Bishop, Mr. Bertram, seemed subdued; almost crestfallen. 'Let us take a stroll in the Custom House gardens,' suggested the Bishop, as if he were trying to change an unspoken subject.

Away from the Palace, wandering amongst the ordinary people, the Bishop and Father became more talkative. Their meeting had been a success; all agreed they should invite the Sultan and his household to the ceremony on Christmas Day, when Sir Bartle Frere is to lay the foundation stone of our Cathedral. How, I mused, could it be the foundation stone when the Cathedral is already half-built? And what did the Bishop mean by the Sultan's household? The princesses? Their scarlet and gold, swirling up that sober nave? That would be an extraordinary sight.

I looked back at the façade of the Palace, glittering with hundreds of lanterns. The topmost storey was in darkness, apart from one window where a single light seemed to burn more fiercely than all the rest.

Bertram was watching me. 'Small island a bit more agreeable to you now, Miss Hemmings?'

'Mr. Bertram,' I blurted, 'When Europeans first come to Africa, to the mainland, how shall they begin to make the journey inland? How do they know which route to follow? And by what means? And who will supply them with food along the way?'

Bertram looked surprised, as well he might, because I'd never tried to engage him in conversation before.

'Since you ask,' he said, 'there's a man at Saadani, a native, actually, but a good one. Fellow by the name of Bwana Heri. You couldn't do better than trust him to find you somewhere to stay, and then the bullock wagons, the barter cloth for your food, and he knows all the porters, good and bad. Many times he's helped members of your London Missionary Society – but are you going on a journey, Miss Hemmings?'

Father was still in deep discussion with the Bishop. 'One day,' I said, 'Father and I will join Dr. Livingstone at Ujiji. One day soon.'

'And what will Nurse Milton do then, poor thing? How will she cope without you?'

I flushed. 'Nurse Milton has no need of my help.'

'You know what, Miss Hemmings? You're quite right there. That one knows exactly what she's doing.'

If Martha Milton had the slightest desire to know what the interior of the Palace was like, she would have marched in there herself. So she told me, as we knelt side by side at the washtub.

'Oh yes, I was invited. Edward Manley begged me to chaperone Dora, because she's scared of Arabs. But I declined, of course.'

Why would anyone turn down the chance to see how the Sultan lives? A painful thought occurred to me. 'So I was invited to accompany Mrs. Manley instead?'

'Exactly. Although it would have been better if neither of you had gone into that vile place.' She scrubbed and scrubbed as if she meant to punish the demijohn in her hands.

It was a bitter disappointment to learn that I had been included in the party purely for Mrs. Manley's sake.

'Then maybe you would have done better to accept,' I burst out, 'and protect *me*, if you were so worried about me going.'

Soap bubbles frothed in the tub.

'Not even for you, Lucy, would I accept the hospitality of Sultan Barghash. I'd rather die.'

'But … he signed the treaty. He has committed himself to ending slavery, and we should support him, not shun him!'

'Paper and ink, Lucy, paper and ink. Barghash sees the Men o' War out there, patrolling the ocean. He signed because he has no choice other than to appear to comply. But do you really think an Arab's word is his bond?'

That sneer was more than I could bear. 'What about the Bishop? What about my Father? Do you accuse them of colluding with the Sultan?'

She put down the demijohn and turned to look at me, and her eyes were so blue, so cold, I was scared into silence. 'How dare you suggest,' she said quietly, 'that I might doubt your Father's honesty? It's a momentous task, persuading the Arabs to relinquish centuries of wickedness. I am fortunate – you and I are fortunate – that we needn't take part in such diplomatic manoeuvres. Let the men do whatever they must do. And if anyone can teach by his shining example, it's your father, John Hemmings. He has the respect of everyone on this wretched island. I myself hold him in the highest esteem.'

She appeared to have forgotten her work, her hands still. Then she gave herself a little shake, and attacked the demijohn again.

Something was wrong. I decided to risk her anger again. 'And how do you regard *me*? Do you believe I'm wicked for wanting to know our neighbours better, for wanting to understand how they live? Do you really believe I should come half way round the globe and walk past them with my nose in the air?'

She placed the demi-john on the draining board and seized my hands. Her fingers were wet and smelled of carbolic. It was all I could do not to pull away. I made myself look into those speedwell eyes.

'Why did you come here, Lucy? Did you come here to do God's work? Or to wander around palaces, marvelling at ill-gotten wealth?'

'I came here to work with Dr. Livingstone.'

She tightened her grip. 'And so you shall,' she said evenly, 'when you are ready.'

I nodded, said I understood she had meant no slight to Father, and should I prepare some more saline solution or launder the sheets? And she replied she would be very grateful if I would attend to both of those tasks. Which I did, while gulping with the effort of breathing, of *being alive*, in the face of her anger.

But when I arrived home, the day took such a turn for the better! Father was in the drawing room, reading a note written on gilt-edged paper and looking perplexed. 'Most bizarre. This is a letter from the Sultan, Lucy, asking whether I would agree to your teaching the princesses chess once a week. He says, *Since there is no time like the present* – I can't imagine where he got that phrase from – *would she kindly start on Monday at five?* The nerve of the man! It's out of the question, of course.'

I spoke sharply, without allowing myself to hesitate. 'But why shouldn't I? Think of the good will, Father. Think how offended they will be if we refuse.'

Father opened his mouth and then shut it. I knew what he was thinking. He was thinking of the Sultan's wealth, which could fund iron bedsteads for the hospital, and consignments of medicines.

I took advantage. 'Alicia will come with me. It will just be a matter of my leaving the dispensary half an hour early. I'm sure Nurse Milton will consent to that, if *you* ask her. I'm sure she'll be pleased to hear the princesses want to exercise their brains for a change.'

How could he refuse, when he has been giving Martha Milton chess lessons for over a month now? And even though Alicia dared to question our new arrangement (*Why must we go there?*) one look from me was enough to make her bite her lip and mumble, 'Excuse me, mother,' which I think meant 'I'm sorry', rather than 'Please don't make me go'.

Christmas Day 1873

I woke as a little child wakes, with a startle and a thrill to the music of a joyous carillon ringing in our Lord's birth – just for a moment. Then I went to the window and gazed, wistfully, upon the princesses, jangling their bells, celebrating their brief freedom.

At ten, we set out for the Cathedral. My only shawl was the enveloping heat; I wore lace gloves, and yet my fingers chafed on the handle of my parasol, and the leather binding of my missal became sticky as I clutched it. Father ambled, took his hat off, waved it around as a fan, put it on, took it off again. Poor Father feels the heat even more than I do. 'I'd rather be at work,' he murmured, to himself I think – but then we heard: 'Dr. Hemmings! Lucy!' and the clip-clop of hooves echoing on stone, and there she was, illuminated at the end of an alley, in a gown of the same ferocious blue as the sky, and a huge straw hat tied, unusually for her, with pink ribbons. Father brightened as he moved towards her. I could not help saying, 'But Nurse, I thought you were going to open the dispensary today as normal?'

Ignoring me, she dismounted and spoke to Father. 'Have you met Sir Bartle Frere before?'

So I had offended her again. I am becoming inured to her dissatisfaction, but I didn't have time to ponder her change of mind before we arrived at the Cathedral. It's a magnificent building, a fitting testament to the generosity of our English benefactors. A pity the sandstone bricks are the colour of dried blood.

Inside, the cool descended like a blessing. How strange to see those pews filled with Arabs, all politely facing the altar they do not believe in, some looking rather ill at ease, others bizarrely at home, lolling in their pews, admiring the cross-stitched hassocks which Martha Milton's mission girls have been making.

Up in the organ loft, an invisible musician began the first hymn – I was curious to see whether the Arabs would stand – some did, some didn't. We sang. Then the workmen in clean green aprons made a respectful semicircle and the Bishop presented our honoured guest with a trowel and a hod. Poor sweltering Sir Bartle spread the grey cement, thick as butter, then set the stone in place.

It was a shock to me that Sir Bartle began his speech by thanking Sultan Barghash. Does the parent thank the child after whipping it? I'm not sure Barghash understood the speech, because nobody seemed to be interpreting for him. When we Christians processed to the altar, I wondered what the Arabs made of our Eucharistic feast. Has anyone explained to them how we partake of Christ's body and his blood? One bearded gentleman in a long, white garment tried to join the line of communicants; the Bishop's face betrayed a flicker of amusement, then he whispered to his young African acolyte, who led the gentleman aside.

On my way back from the altar I scanned the Arab ranks, but the Khatib wasn't there, and as I sat down between Martha Milton and Father I was surprised by my disappointment.

But later, my spirits rose. My spirits soared.

Ibrahim can now roast a fowl quite decently, and Father looked happier than he has been for months as he carved the bird, poured wine, proposed a toast 'to the future'. Martha Milton contributed a plum pudding, sent from Surrey by her aunt. There was an ugly scene in the courtyard when the maids almost came to blows over the best way to cook it; Zeinab insisted it should be fried in oil; Pili wanted to chop it up and stew it with spinach. We left the pudding bubbling safely in a pot of water while Alicia ran to the dispensary to collect the bottle of brandy Martha Milton had forgotten. When she returned I asked, 'May Alicia watch?'

'Of course she may,' Father said, and doused the pudding in brandy, then set a match to it. How we all laughed when Alicia gasped at the blue flames and clapped her hands to her face in horror: 'It is spoilt!'

'I shall keep you a piece to taste,' I said, 'then you shall see it isn't spoilt at all. It will be such a treat!'

'Don't be disappointed, Lucy,' Martha Milton warned. 'European food tends to disagree with the native stomach.'

After our meal I went down to the courtyard with the slice of pudding, and Alicia licked her lips and ate up every last scrap.

When I returned to the parlour, Father and Martha Milton were sitting side by side on the sofa, contemplating a large parcel wrapped in silver tissue on the rug before them. It was as if they were afraid to touch it. 'A gift?' I said. 'Where did that come from?'

The room smelled of roses.

'It was delivered just now,' said Father. 'It's for you.'

'For me?'

Father's earlier jolly mood had gone. Martha Milton was silent, her face blank.

'There's a note.' He appeared reluctant to pass it to me, but the name on the folded cream paper was mine, in a hand I recognised. I read the brief note aloud with tremulous pleasure. 'The Sultan wishes to thank Miss Hemmings for teaching the princesses chess.'

A tiny grunt from Martha Milton's pursed lips: *pah!*

'Shall I open it now?' I knelt on the rug and folded back layer after layer of silver tissue paper, until at last was revealed a house – a miniature palace – of rosewood, inlaid with mother of pearl in an intricate, interlocking design that could have been stars or moons or crosses. The roof had a gold catch. I unlatched it, and inside was – a chess set! Such a marvel of craftsmanship! A minuscule fretwork of lace at the white queen's neck; the black queen adorned with a filigree train; knights with teeth bared in tiny, terrifying grins; every pawn different in some delightful detail: an eye patch, an ivory scowl, a clenched fist the size of a pinhead.

For a few minutes I was lost, entranced, wanting only to explore and marvel over each perfect piece. Then I noticed their silence. Something dared me to provoke them. 'How kind of the Sultan.'

Father said, 'I suppose we must accept it.'

'Of course I must! It would be terribly rude to refuse such a magnificent gift.'

'Don't you think this has gone far enough?' said Martha Milton.

And Father, my Father the Doctor, my lionhearted Father whom everyone respects and obeys, looked miserable and confused. I hated her for that.

January 1874

Martha Milton never wears any ornament. For her, clothing is utilitarian: she dresses in plain cotton gowns without frills or lace, in order to be able to treat her patients briskly and efficiently. She wears no flowers, no pearls, not even a mourning brooch. She fastens her pompadour with simple pins. Her eyes are her only beauty.

In a dark corner of the dispensary a child is raving. He twists on the rough woven mat, his little limbs flipping and twitching as if tortured by volts of electricity. She bends low over him, and a coral necklace swings from the hollow at her throat. It is cleverly designed so the heaviness of the middle bead holds the necklace in place and prevents the clasp from slewing round to the front. She shakes the thermometer and smoothes the child's brow. When she stands up again, the pink coral glows above the plain white collar of her gown.

I'm finding it hard to breathe. She asks me what is the matter. It is all I can do to shake my head. I want to ask who gave her the necklace, but I'm too scared of the answer. I say I need air, and run down the marigold path. She calls after me, 'Lucy, dear, are you unwell?'

I have written my letter of thanks to the Sultan. I pored over it for hours in my darkening window, adding a word here, amending a phrase there, wasting our precious paper, just to make that letter sound exactly as I wanted: grateful, touched, intrigued. I tore it up, considered allowing the fragments to flutter down like white petals upon the dingy street – but I was scared that some urchin might gather my broken words and piece them together again. Now then, I told myself sternly, let this be the one, and I took another fresh sheet and wrote the letter, blotted it, folded it, addressed the envelope. I gave it to Alicia with instructions to deliver it straight away.

Alicia says, 'Why must I, mother?'

Sometimes she does this: questions me as though my authority over her means nothing at all; as though she knows some truth which I am not party to. 'Alicia, are you refusing to obey me?'

Her eyes burn with a candour that hurts me because I feel my own lack of it. 'Mother,' she says, 'I am afraid to go into the Palace on my own.'

What is there to be afraid of? Perhaps it reminds her of her past life, before she was redeemed. But she's safe now. I tell her to hurry along to the Palace with my letter, and be sure that it is delivered to him in person.

An hour later she comes creeping back. She will admit only that she gave it to him. No, there was no response.

I tell myself that the Nurse's coral necklace must be a token of thanks for her hard work. Gratitude, even, that she has been my mentor these six months. He is so dear, so grateful. I only wish he could extend his thankfulness to the Sultanate, without whose benevolence, after all, our lives here on Zanzibar would not be possible.

The island seems very small. The sea used to calm me; now, it is a constant reminder of how far away we are from Africa.

I stand before Father's desk. 'When shall we go to join Livingstone? We've been here for nearly six months. I am a good nurse, everybody says so, the people thank me. I should be useful to Livingstone now. Surely it is time to leave?'

He tries, poor Father, to answer me. 'Lucy, our work here is going so well...'

'But is it needed? Are we needed here as much as Livingstone needs us at the Lake?'

'You are quite right.' There is a light in his eyes, a hopeful excitement I have not seen since Tynemouth. 'You are wise, Lucy.' Too much flattery. 'You feel just as *we* do.'

We?

'We should work wherever we may find the poorest of the poor, wherever the suffering is greatest. Wherever people still live in darkness, ignorant of Christ.'

'Yes Father, I know.'

'Soon, Lucy. Soon we will leave the Stone town. No, I cannot tell you any more just yet, so please, ask no more questions. Only have faith that God has a purpose for you. For us all.' He looks exalted, as if nothing terrifies him, not even death.

And this evening, playing chess with Alicia, when I asked her if she thought Father changed, her eyes narrowed, giving her face a shrewdness that frightened me. 'It is not for me to say,' she replied.

'That means yes! You see a change, as I do. Why has he changed, Alicia?'

'Please mother, do not ask. Do not ask again.'

I was afraid if I pressed her, she would tell me a truth I did not want to hear.

'Promise me,' I said, taking her thin wrists between my fingers. 'Promise me you will never leave me.'

'I promise,' she whispered, her hands trembling like caught birds.

It is Sunday afternoon. They are sitting side by side on the sofa. There is no chess set on the table. The pupil is looking at the master as if *she* were his superior: that fond, indulgent pride. She has never been humble. She smiles, her apple cheeks glow. Father is rather less radiant. 'Lucy,' he says. 'I have happy news.'

'What do you mean?' But I already understand.

'Martha and I are to marry.'

'You can't.'

His face twists. She rises, still smiling, comes towards me holding out her hand as if to calm a small animal. 'Lucy, I shall be your mother now –'

'Don't say that!'

'Lucy!'

She retreats, her pompadour puffed up all round her face like the hood of a cobra. Her eyes harden. 'Nothing will change, Lucy, after your Father and I are married. You shall still live with us, of course, so that we may look after you and guide you. You shall carry on with your nursing, and you shall help us to meet our new challenge.'

'Father, how can you? How can you betray Mother?'

'Lucy, Lucy, nothing will change. Except that we are to leave this house and move to Nungwe, where we shall start a new mission, and you shall help us continue Doctor Livingstone's great work. Just as you have always longed to do.'

'Where's Nungwe? Is it on the Lake?'

'It is on the Eastern seaboard of Zanzibar.'

I confront her. 'You planned all this, didn't you? You set your sights on the widower as soon as he arrived – no; before, when you heard he was coming. You decided he should rescue you from spinsterhood.'

She flinches, he cries, 'Lucy, please!' but they cannot stop me; I know the truth. 'Doctor Livingstone was wrong. You do not care at all for the people. You are not here for the glory of God. You yearn to be admired. You are greedy for worship. You thought it would be enough to come here, do what you have done, oh, I cannot deny how well you have nursed the people, but every minute of every day you have basked in their need, and it is no longer enough to have the wretched sick standing at your door every morning, begging for your help. No, you must have my Father as well, to flatter you all the time and tell you what a wonderful nurse you are, what a remarkable woman. You wanted to be a legend; well, I cannot deny you have achieved that ambition with your deft fingers and your stupid donkey, but now you want marriage too, because you're getting old, and when you return to England you will need a home. Yes!' I am curiously pleased with myself for fathoming her. 'Father will save you from the indignity of poverty in England, where no-one will care who you are or what you have done.' And I smile into the face of the snake, and she sits down, her face averted. Never, never will she forgive me for this humiliation.

It's too late. Father stands between us. He says, 'I think you had better leave us, Lucy,' and he looks so sad. I go to my room, lie on the bed and weep into the pillow so they can't hear me.

Many hours later, at dusk, the bedroom door opened a fraction. 'Drink, mother.' Alicia passed me a glass of water and left. I took a few sips, lit the lamp, then went to the open window and waited. When he appeared, I did not slither down. I let him see me cry, the tears rolling heavily, silently down my face. He observed me for some time, without showing any sign of being moved. Then he unlatched the casement, opened the window wide and settled himself with his forearms on the sill, just a few feet away from me.

'You remind me of Miza Miza, sitting there, as still as a statue, except for the tears that roll down your face.'

I put my fingertips to my eyes and smoothed the tears away, although more came falling.

'Good. Now you are no longer a statue. She was too sad, Miza Miza.'

'Whoever she was, she couldn't be more unhappy than I.'

'You are wrong. Would you like to hear her story?'

I didn't reply. But he told me the story anyway.

'Once, long ago, when Kizimkazi was the foremost city on Zanzibar, there was a merchant who prospered and was so pleased with his life that he decided he could afford to take another wife: some young, beautiful wife befitting his success. So he went to a village where the maidens were said to be the fairest on all Zanzibar, and he passed from house to house, calling, *Hodi! Hodi!* And maiden after maiden would come to the door and he would shake his head and move on, until at last, at the poorest house in the village, he glimpsed through the mean doorway someone sitting in the corner, and he entered, and asked for a lamp to be brought, and when he saw her face in the light of the lamp she was more beautiful than any woman he had ever seen before, and her name was Miza. So he returned with Miza to Kizimkazi, and the wedding celebrations lasted for a fortnight. And the only one present at the feast who did not rejoice was his other wife, who was older and no longer so beautiful. And in her heart the first wife was very jealous of Miza. But she hid her jealousy, waiting for her time.

'Now, every day the two wives went to draw water together, and because Miza was a newcomer to Kizimkazi the older wife showed her all the places where water was plentiful. One day she said, *Miza, today we shall draw our water from the spring in the cave.* And Miza was afraid. Because other women had warned her that you must never call anyone by their name in that cave, for if you did, they would be turned to stone.

'The two wives went to the cave. Inside it was dark, and cold, the walls streaming with water. Because she knew the path, the older woman went first and Miza followed her into the darkness. Then the older wife turned and called, *Miza! Miza! Here is where we must draw water.*

And Miza began to weep, for she knew what must happen to her now. She said, *If this is your will, then so be it. May you go in peace.* And then her lips ceased to move, and her feet, and her arms, and her head, for she had become stone. Only her eyes were still wet with tears that streamed down her face.

When the merchant heard that his beautiful young wife had been turned to stone, he rushed to the cave with his followers, and beat his hands against the stone statue imploring her to live again, and they prayed and tried to appease their gods with gifts of goat's milk. The stone statue wept for seven days and seven nights, and after that Miza wept no more. But she still stands there today, in the cave at Kizimkazi, and the people of her village go there every year to remember her.'

For a while, neither of us spoke. At last he said, 'I have made you more unhappy.'

'No, sir,' I replied. 'No, you could not make me unhappier than I am now.' Such passion in my voice, I astonished myself.

He, too, seemed moved. 'I was wrong. You are not like Miza Miza at all. You shall never surrender to sorrow. But what is it you want instead?'

'Mother.' A whisper at my door. Alicia, hovering on the landing, looking over her shoulder down the stairs, a dish of scrambled eggs in her hand.

When I turned back to the window, he had gone.

'Please, mother, you must eat.'

I am not such a fool as to starve. Alicia watched me eat with the same morose, withdrawn expression she wore when first she came here. I knew she dreaded the collapse of this household, the loss of her own position which must surely follow. I pitied her, and as the raucous noise of the street began to die down, so did my passion, leaving me smarting with shame. Martha Milton is not wicked. She has saved countless lives. The people worship her because she heals them; her motives do not matter. It only matters that she cannot, must not, become my mother.

This morning I woke from a dream of myself: a distant figure, walking alone on a vast plain with nothing between the sun and the earth but me. And although I was so far away from myself, I could feel that I had a parched throat, and no prospect of anything to drink unless I turned back.

On waking, I thought of being cold stone, washed with tears, washed with goat's milk. Then I imagined the heat of Africa. The only choice.

I came down to breakfast meek and mild. 'Forgive me,' I whispered. And because my Father is a good, kind man, he forgave me straight away. 'Lucy,' he said, taking me in his arms, 'Think what the three of us will achieve together!'

It was easy to lie while he couldn't see my face. 'Yes,' I said. 'You are right, of course. Let me go to the Palace today as usual, so as not to disappoint the Sultan.'

So he allowed me to go to the Beit al Sahel, where to her great delight the princess Zemzem beat me hollow, because I was not concentrating. When the lesson was over Alicia and I took the upper staircase and made our way down the Indian corridor to the library. The open door framed the Khatib, writing on a long scroll, its curled end tapping at the carpet like an angry finger. Alicia was too scared to go in. 'Wait here, then,' I said, 'and keep watch.'

I knocked and entered. For several seconds he did not look up from the scroll. When at last he did, he was frowning, and my courage faltered.

'Sir,' I began, too loudly. 'Are you able to help me arrange a journey? I need a boat to take me to Saadani.'

I didn't really believe my confidence would fool him – but I hoped, so much, that he would help. For a little while he continued to look at me. Then his gaze dropped to the ink glittering blackly on the scroll. From a drawer he took a square of pale blue blotting paper, and pressed it down. Then he turned the blotting paper over, scrutinizing the backwards-script.

'A boat.'

'I must sail to Saadani.'

'Must you?'

He took up his pen, scarlet with a gold nib, and held it poised. 'Why do you ask for my help?'

'Because … I have heard that you make such arrangements. And Mr. Bertram has told me of a certain Bwana Heri, who helps people with further travel once they are in Saadani.' I thought I sounded insouciant, well-informed, with my airy mention of Bwana Heri. I dreaded the Khatib would say, *Does your father know?* But instead he asked, with an odd detachment, 'Do you wish to go home?'

'What do you mean? This is my home now. I want to *leave* home.'

'Well, where shall you live?'

'I'm going to Lake Tanganyika, to work with Dr. Livingstone.' Still I did not cry. There is a bitter satisfaction to be found in the restraint of tears.

He looked down, and drew a neat, firm line under a word in the middle of the page. 'Livingstone is at Ujiji. It is very far. How will you get there?'

'Oh, I'm sure Bwana Heri will help me. I've made plans, other travellers have advised me. But first of all, sir, I must have my passage to the mainland and for that I depend on your help.'

He raised his eyebrows.

'I have money,' I faltered, conscious of the blood rushing to my face.

'Of course you do.' Now he was tapping his forefinger gently against his teeth, while he gazed, not at me, but at the bookshelves behind me. 'It is impossible – '

'Oh, please don't say that!'

'I say, it is impossible for me to help you straight away. In a few days, perhaps.'

A few days? Only a few days left with Father?

'You are surprised. You are nervous. Do you really want to go?'

'Yes. Yes, I am quite determined. I can't stay on Zanzibar.'

Alicia stumbled down the corridor, almost tripping on the stairs, hurrying ahead, whereas usually she keeps a humble distance behind me. Outside, I told her I wanted to sit for a while on a bench in the Customs House gardens.

'Alicia, we are going on a journey.'

'To Nungwe?'

So even she knew of their plans.

'No, not to Nungwe.'

She gave a sigh and a smile, seemed to stretch a little, as a cat stretches in the warmth. She was glad we weren't going with them. How little I knew about her. I let her enjoy a long moment of relief, then said, 'We are going to Africa, where we shall work with Dr. Livingstone. Perhaps he will remember you.'

Her eyes widened. 'Africa, Mother?'

Fearful though I was, I wanted to laugh. 'Yes, to Africa! Saadani first, then we shall join a caravan to the Lake.'

'Mama Lucy,' she said, 'Does your father know?'

'Alicia, you must help me. You must run many errands for me, these next few days' – my voice trembled – 'you must gather our possessions, but *secretly*, and when the time comes for us to leave, you must force me to go through with it, even if I tell you I have changed my mind, do you understand? *Do you understand?*

'Yes, mother.'

The truth is, I do not know whether Alicia wants to accompany me.

The truth is, she has no choice. She has no friends. No family. She has nobody but me. She must come with me, or else endure the meanest poverty, for who will employ her after I have gone?

This waiting is so painful.

When I work alongside her at the dispensary, *yes Nurse, of course, Nurse*, pretending to atone for my outburst, my mind is writhing with the duplicity of it all, and at home in the evenings we all three sit at the supper table, and talk about our day's work, and she mistrusts me but cannot identify why, and Father is incredulous but dare not allow himself to be delighted with my transformation, for it is too soon, too inexplicable, and I am too good an actress, so good an actress that it hurts my head and makes me weary, and I long to throw my arms around him and confess, but I can't.

Alicia has proved her loyalty, packing the green canvas bag this evening when I could not gather my thoughts together, let alone my possessions. To my surprise, she packed the chess set; too heavy, I objected, but she insisted that it would be useful to me one day.

Once you move, you can't go back.

That final game lasted for hours, hunched over the board, Father's hand hovering in the lamplight, the familiar ridges and crimps of his veins, each white, translucent knuckle, those dear fingers that have stroked my hair and wiped my tears away.

In three swift moves, the game was mine. 'Lucy! However did you think of that?' His face: astonished, then so pleased with my ingenuity that I almost sobbed. All these lies have sharpened my brain.

Then, at last, he kissed me goodnight. The embrace was agony to me, for it was no more intense than usual; I could not show him how tenderly I felt.

Alicia woke me with her hand over my mouth.

The canvas bag hissed as we dragged it out from beneath the bed. I dressed. She went before me down the stairs: silent, black, a confident shadow. I tried to follow her quietly, but every step, every swish of silk or calico seemed too loud. On the last stair I slipped, and the askari stirred in his sleep. She pressed me against the wall, her arms spread, her body telling me to remain still. We waited.

The door felt so heavy. Outside, for once, the street was empty, the people all at prayer. In the porch she halted me again, drew from her sleeve a veil, hung it over my face, took my hand and led me away. And soon men began to spill from the mosques and I realised this was part of the plan: if many people were on the streets, two hurrying figures would not be noticed.

When we approached the landing stage opposite the palace I peered at the boats bobbing in the darkness, but she pulled me on, further and further along the waterfront. On and on we hastened, and I had a stitch in my side and gasped, 'Stop, just for a moment,' but she would not let me, saying, 'You must hurry, they won't wait for you!' Finally we came to a place where there was only one boat, alive with shadows leaping and contracting in the moonlight. 'This is for you,' she said. I was afraid. A man came to hand me in. It was too dark to see his face. The dhow was swaying, threatening to tip me out. None of the sailors paid me any attention. As I staggered, the man nearest to me wrapped himself in a blanket and squatted down, puffing morosely on a cigarette. Alicia said, 'There's a cabin,' but it was narrow and dark as a grave, and I cried, 'Oh no, we must stay on deck with the men, Alicia, I can't lie in that terrible hole –'

'You must sleep.' The more I panicked, the calmer she became. Her voice was light. 'I think it is best, mother, if you lie down and sleep.' She tucked my shawl around me as if I were a child. Not meeting my eye. Then nimbly she leapt across the glittering black water, back onto the quay. 'Alicia!' I called, and struggled up, meaning to run after her, but the rocking of the dhow made me stumble to my knees in a stinking puddle on the deck. I saw her talking to a man. Who was he? It was too dark to see.

The sailors were uncoiling the rope from the mooring post. Frantic, I did not care who heard me and I called, 'Alicia! Please come now, you must come now!'

Across the water she turned to me and shook her head. I thought I saw tears in her eyes. She said something in Swahili, but she was talking to the man, and when he began to walk away, into the labyrinth of streets, she followed him.

The sailor hauled in the rope. 'You must wait!' I pleaded. 'We can't leave yet! That girl is coming with me; we must wait for her to come back.'

'No,' he said roughly. 'We go now.'

Each breath tore my chest as I gasped for air; the rope slithering along the deck like a python, rising and rising into a coil. 'Keep down,' he said to me as they hoisted the sail.

The dhow began to glide away, rocking steadily, easily now, as if it were relieved to be free. Above me the sail reached up into the blackness, eerie as ectoplasm. Below, the pulse of the waves pulled us further and further out to sea.

By sunrise, exhaustion had leached me of everything but loneliness. And, perhaps, a little courage, for as the faint coastline slowly gained in definition, I began to think what to do next; where I should go. If I could only find Bwana Heri at Saadani, I told myself, I should entrust him with the planning of my long journey to the Lake.

We ran aground on a sandbar, the dhow taking such a blow that seawater hit the deck with a vicious slap and sent me scrambling towards the stern. A man was rowing a small boat towards us. The Captain of the dhow leered. 'You give me money? Or you like to come back to Zanzibar now?' I fumbled in my bag, but the men were laughing and the Captain said, 'No, is a joke. No money to pay. You go with him,' and they lifted me over the side, and handed me into the boat. I thought to myself: soon I shall be in Africa. At last.

The man rowed as far as he could, until the keel of the boat caught on the sand, then he carried me ashore. 'You stay,' he said. The beach was white and bare. A line of palm trees stretched as far as the eye could see. I wondered what lay beyond those palms, and how long it would be before I could summon up the courage to explore. But for now, exhausted, I wanted only to sit on the beach and await whatever might happen next.

The heat became stronger. I put up my parasol. Soon, people began to appear, wandering along the sand, bending now and then to pick up a scrap of driftwood, a shell. A small crowd of women and children gathered around me, giggling and tutting and shaking their heads. I wanted to cry, but instead I wished them good morning in Swahili. They returned my greeting, delighted. One of the women went away, beyond the palms and returned a few minutes later with tea for me in a china cup without a saucer. Again I almost cried, for her kindness, but I drank the tea, which was black and warm and sweet. I was very glad of it.

Around noon, I heaved my canvas bag a little further up the beach to the shade of a coconut palm, and sat there, and waited. There was much activity on the beach; men dragging fishing nets to and from the dhows, women cooking on little fires amongst the stones; children collecting coconuts or scavenging through the rubbish.

There were more boats than at Zanzibar. I had not known Saadani was so busy.

A portly man approached, motioning me to come with him. He took up my bag, swinging it onto his head, and led me along the beach towards the area where men were loading dhows, then turned left up a broad path on an incline towards the town. It was nothing like Zanzibar. Some streets were wide, the houses low, square and white with long verandas and porches. Here and there amongst these grand dwellings were round mud huts with roofs of thatch. There were shops, where dark-skinned men who looked neither Arab nor African chatted to each other or leaned on their counters gazing into the distance. Further on were grander, taller houses, and to one of these my guide brought me. I thought: this must be where Bwana Heri lives.

An African woman opened the door. She led me through a hall, and another room, and then across a courtyard where there were orange trees, and into a sunny room with three long windows looking onto a garden of pink and white roses. There was a low table set with platters of chicken, eggs and fruit: amber slices of mango and the red jewels of a pomegranate. I ate until I was no longer hungry. How kind of Bwana Heri, I thought. Then waited, for an hour, while a grandmother clock ticked.

It was a great shock to me when the Khatib came in, saying, 'Good afternoon. How was your journey?'

I could not speak.

'Has the cat got your tongue?' he said gently.

'Is this Bwana Heri's house?' Even as I asked the question, I was beginning to know the answer.

'No.' He sat down next to me. 'It's mine.'

'But – but you did not tell me you had a house in Saadani.'

'But, but, Lucy, this is not Saadani. This is Sinamani.'

96

'Sinamani?' It was not a name I had heard before. I was confused, and a little frightened. 'I asked you to help me travel to Saadani.'

'If you are planning a journey to the interior, the road from here is better, less dangerous. And you are most welcome to stay here in my house while you are waiting for your American cloth and your beads to be sent from Zanzibar.'

'Cloth? Beads?'

He raised his eyebrows. 'Your currency, Lucy. Your *hongo*.'

It was a word I had heard from Zanzibari, sometimes even European businessmen, but I had never wondered what it meant until now. It seems that chiefs will demand *hongo*, payment for the privilege of crossing their territory. The Khatib told me what I should need. Eight hundred and thirty-four miles to the Lake: so, he calculated, three hundred bolts of American cloth and at least two dozen pounds of the brightly coloured glass beads that are so precious here.

'I thought I could just travel with one of the caravans. I didn't know I would have to pay.' How stupid I sounded, how plaintive.

He was still gentle. 'I'm afraid you would be a dreadful danger to any caravan, even one of mine. I'm afraid if the chiefs saw a mzungu woman, they would know she was rich, and that she must make abundant payment to them.'

'But I'm not rich! We came with the Mission; everything we have has been bought for us by the London Missionary Society, by good people in England who raised the money to send us here … I mean, to Zanzibar.'

'Then perhaps you should write to the London Missionary Society and ask them to send you some American cloth, post-haste.'

'I can't do that.'

I was beginning to be angry. I did not want to be angry, not here, in his house, my only shelter. But why had he misled me? Then I remembered, with a creeping shame, how I had deflected his concerns with my remarks about Mr. Bertram and my familiarity with 'other travellers'. My airy claim to have 'plans'; the implication – no, the assertion – that all I required was my passage from Zanzibar.

He was waiting for me to speak.

'What shall I do?'

'There are choices. You have money – Indian coins, yes? You could buy American cloth and beads from our merchants here in Sinamani.'

I made myself look at him. I made myself speak steadily. 'I don't have enough money.'

'Then, of course, you could go back to Zanzibar.'

'Impossible!'

'It is a dreadful thing, Lucy, for a parent and a child to be estranged.'

'I'll write to Father. He'll be proud when he knows what I am doing. You must understand how very much he wanted to join Dr. Livingstone in his work. We would have gone to Ujiji, you see, if …'

'If?'

A whisper. 'If my mother had not died.'

'So he has lost his wife, and now his daughter too.'

He was testing me, testing my resolve – my cruelty. But the Khatib didn't understand how much I hated Martha Milton. 'I can't go back to Zanzibar, I can't. But … perhaps, if I can help Dr. Livingstone in his great work, then one day Father and I will see each other again, and he will forgive me…'

The Khatib had the look of someone trying to solve a problem at chess. He made no attempt to comfort me, which I was glad of, for comfort would have been unbearable. But it was a great relief when at last he said, 'There may be another way. There is a mission, north of this town. I don't think it can be your London Missionary Society, for these people are not from England, but from France and Germany and Alsace. But it is my perception that they are good people, these Spiritan Brothers, and they never turn away anybody who is in need. Why don't you go to them? Perhaps they could take you to Ujiji. Perhaps, even, they could help to bring about a reconciliation with your Father.'

'Please, please sir, take me to them.'

What an abject sight I must have been, my face tear-stained, my clothes crumpled and soiled with saltwater, rivulets of sand in every pleat and fold.

'It is evening. Should you like to sleep first?'

I told him I should like to sleep more than anything. And a servant came, and led me to a chamber where there was a bowl and a pitcher of warm water, and a bed carved from rosewood, made up with white linen. I took off my clothes, washed, and lay down under the sheet in my petticoat. As I was falling asleep I think I wondered why the Khatib had not told me, when I asked for his help on Zanzibar, that the dhow would bring me to Sinamani.

I woke this morning to rapturous sunlight, followed hard by the memory of loss, twisting inside me as it has done only once before in my life, in England. I let the pain come, and then the pain was engulfed by my new freedom, as a wave washes over the sand without erasing it.

In the garden room the table was set with a breakfast of eggs and bananas. For two hours I waited for the Khatib to come, and I wondered and wondered about those Spiritan Brothers. I never had much to do with Catholics before. Then I went to find a servant and asked, 'Where is the Khatib? Could you please take me to him?' but she appeared ignorant, so I roamed the house, a little nervously, looking for him – and at last found him in the garden, standing with a young man who bowed his head when he saw me, and moved away, his left leg dragging behind him.

'Thank you very much for your hospitality,' I told the Khatib, 'but I should like to go to the Mission now.'

Distracted, he replied, 'I am sorry. Today I am unable to take you there, because I have business.'

'Oh, but couldn't a servant –'

'Do you speak German?'

'Well, my French is almost fluent – '

'Then you will be able to talk with some of the brothers, but for the Abbé, German is essential. I myself am on very good terms with the Abbé, and I shall be able to express your wishes to him. Now, I shall arrange some amusement for you today, and perhaps tomorrow we shall go.'

I was taken to a balcony on the upper storey. There was a white wrought-iron chair with a scrolled back where I sat, looking out over the sea, and the sands milling with people. There was no exhilaration, such as you find on an English beach; none of that breeziness, that cheery, bracing freedom. These people moved with grim purpose, shouting urgently to each other. Only the sea was calm. Sequins of sunlight danced across my vision: *dart! stab! vanish!* as I strained to focus on the level line of the horizon.

And then a servant came onto the balcony with my chess set.

I have played chess against myself for many days. Once or twice the Khatib has joined me. He is a great strategist, and I take pleasure, when he observes how I favour my Queen's knight, in feeling that he knows my mind.

During these games I have not liked to ask again when he will take me to the Mission, although I cannot help wondering what is the reason for the delay.

And why Father hasn't come to look for me.

This blazing sky is unlike any February I have ever seen, but I calculate that it *is* February. It *must* be February. In May, I shall be eighteen years old.

I have not seen the Khatib for… seven days?

Today, when I asked the servant if he had returned, she nodded, and I made her take me to him. He was sitting at a desk littered with papers. I was nervous.

'The Mission?' He *had* forgotten. He was shuffling the papers, not reading them. 'Very well,' he said, 'I shall take you there myself, today.'

'I am a nuisance.'

He shook his head, but did not smile. 'We are proud of our hospitality to foreigners.'

True, he has been hospitable. The servants have looked after me well. But this has been such a strange time of waiting, and never in my life have I felt so completely ignorant of what is going on.

It was a relief to leave the house. The sun was already high as we walked through the streets, past the curious Hindi merchants, into the market place where women squatted with their tiny pots of oil, calling after the Khatib: 'Bwana! Bwana! …' lunging for the coins he threw. We went on, past the mud huts surrounded by steaming piles of rubbish. Only a dog ran after us as we left the town, its skinny flanks a-tremble, its eyes crazed, and although I was a little afraid of the wretched animal I was sorry when the Khatib hurled a stone at it, sending it yelping away.

We walked along the coastal path. To our right: the sea, to our left: Africa, an endless expanse of grass and scrub and palms. I shivered at the vastness.

'Where is this Mission, sir? Where are you taking me?'

He pointed to a distant tower. 'The church,' he said. Since I arrived in Sinamani I haven't prayed. Too late to pray now for Father's forgiveness.

We turned away from the sea, down a long, sandy avenue planted on either side with saplings, each one protected by cylinders of wood and wire. Mean-mouthed goats loitered, eyeing the young green leaves. A long way ahead of us the church tower rose, stark and white, and I felt inexplicably afraid.

There were people at the base of the tower. I could not tell whether they were European or African. They were moving towards us. Did they know we were coming? Perhaps the Khatib had informed them.

The white men wore black soutanes; the Africans, loin cloths. We moved towards each other slowly, a sombre galliard. At the head of the procession a white-bearded priest bore a crucifix. They did not shoulder the coffin, as my uncles did for mother. It was borne on a canvas sling, strung from poles that the men gripped, almost as men pull a boat up the beach. Four white Brothers. Two Africans. The coffin swaying between the sweet young trees.

Closer we came. The Khatib was frowning. 'What has happened here?' he said. The Africans who walked at the front of the coffin were gaunt, their faces hollow, as if their souls had been sucked out of them. Along their arms great corded veins stretched. One of the bearers was a grizzled old man. They should not have given him such a burden.

Why should a coffin be borne *away* from church and graveyard? Why carry a coffin to the sea?

I would have remained standing in their path, but the Khatib drew me aside. The cortège halted. The Abbé rested his crucifix on the dry ground. The Khatib spoke to him in German, and the Abbé replied. I strained to glean some words from the stream of unfamiliar language.

I heard a name. Livingstone.

'No! It can't be!'

The Khatib turned to me, and on his face pity and curiosity were combined. 'Lucy, you must be calm.' His hand was on my arm but I shook him off and ran to the

102

Abbé. 'You are lying! You are lying! This is not Livingstone! Livingstone is at the Lake, he is doing God's work there, I am to serve with him …'

Somebody was pulling me back. The Abbé was speaking to me, although I couldn't hear his words for my own rage and the Khatib urging me to be calm. 'Lucy. Lucy, do you understand where they are taking the body? The British Consul on Zanzibar will receive it. Then they will arrange the passage to England. You could go too. If that is what you want, the ship could stop here, and you could return to your real home.'

I was crying. My tears made dark marks in the dust. The Brothers were hitting out at the goats who dashed across their path. The old African said something in a language I did not recognise. The pallbearers took up their burden and moved on. I tried to run after them. The Khatib dragged me down, right down to the ground and the dust and the goat dung. Then he sat down next to me.

The Khatib and I remained, while the goats wandered around us and the procession continued on its way. We watched them dwindle to a series of black dots, dancing in the heat haze. I had never seen the Khatib's face so close before: the set of his brow, the curved mouth, the traces of silver in his beard. I waited for him to ask, *So what will you do? Where will you go?* But he stood up, brushing the dust from his coat, and said, 'There's no point in sitting here with the goats all day.' We walked into the Mission compound, deserted except for a solitary African boy, sweeping the dust with a broom made of twigs. The Khatib spoke to him in Swahili, asking him when Livingstone's body had arrived. I entered the church. It was very dark. On the ground before the altar was a black velvet cloth that still bore in its nap the imprint of the coffin. Frangipani blossoms were scattered over it like stars. I knelt, said a prayer for Livingstone and Father, and for myself, and for

Alicia too, since she has been much on my mind. Then I went outside, blinking at the sunlight.

'Will you stay here?' the Khatib said. 'This boy tells me there is a room for guests in the Sisters' house. They would look after you.'

'I called the Abbé a liar. I can't stay here. Besides, the Navy men will have told the Spiritans how I ran away and brought shame on my father. I can't stay here.'

'Then where?'

And that is how I came to live in this house as the Khatib's guest. I try not to reflect on how astonishing this is. Often he is absent, for he has a great deal of business, but on those rare nights when he is home we play chess, and he tells me about the Sultan, whose health is failing, and about the red sandstone Cathedral rising against the sky. I have never asked whether people speak of me, and he never mentions my father. Neither do we discuss how long I shall remain here in Sinamani, nor how I shall ever manage to leave.

Sometimes, as I scan the beach from my balcony, I believe I have seen the Khatib hurrying towards the sea when a dhow is arriving. I have no wish to go down to the beach myself. It still shames me: the memory of that morning when I sat in the sun, not knowing where I was or what I should do, while people stared and murmured and fingered my parasol, my foolishness plain to all.

So I spend my days on this balcony, studying its wrought-iron tracery of leaves. The iron burns red-hot in the daytime, but at night it is cool and I cling to it until the pattern makes angry ridges in my flesh.

I have become familiar with the rhythm of this household: the languid weeks when the Khatib is away, the taut anticipation of his return. Last night I remained on the balcony long after darkness made sea and shore invisible, listening to the waves' sad recitation. I stroked the chess pieces: the carved runnels of the knight's mane, the pawn's smooth skull, the rook's tiny battlements. All day the servants had been expecting their master, the house echoing with the slap slap slap of their sandals as they ran about their duties, the air edged with excitement and nervousness. At last I heard on the stairs behind me the footsteps I had been waiting for.

'Why do you sit alone in the dark?'

'There is nowhere else. Father has not come to look for me. Livingstone is dead. I have no family. I am completely dependent on your kindness, sir.'

He did not try to contradict me. He did not demur at my ungracious acknowledgement of his charity. Instead, he came to stand at the balcony rail, gazing over the invisible sea. 'I know what it is to be abandoned. When I was six years old, my mother died, and within a month my father too had died of grief. I was alone, except for my uncle, who took me away to Muscat. I remember the journey well. I was so excited to be going to that great city, never once imagining how difficult it would be to live with my cousins, who had no time for me and resented me for being younger than they, and yet better at my school books. So I studied, resolving that one day I should see the world. And I came to Zanzibar and was employed by the last Sultan, who sent me on a ship to London to do business for him there.'

I pictured the Khatib, walking down those grey streets in the cold rain, and I felt sorry for him. 'What did you think of London, sir?'

'It made me realise how little I knew about the world.'

'Should you have liked to live there?'

'No. How could I abandon my family? There were too many people to care for.'

I thought: he has a wife, somewhere, and children. Perhaps two wives. An Arab takes no more than two, unless

105

he is the Sultan. I summoned all my courage to say, 'Am I a burden to you, sir? Do I dishonour you by remaining in this house?'

He took my hand, and it was like a sudden pain, yet his skin was as warm as mine, our fingers slotting easily together. He did not answer my question.

Neither did he release my hand. Whose grip was firmer? I think we held each other with equal strength.

The corridor was too narrow for us to walk side by side. I followed him, when I could have turned away. I could have gone, even then, to the Mission. Instead I walked behind him, my heart beating twice for every step we took. As he opened the door to his chamber he took my hand again, and that gave me courage. We stood on the threshold, before a bed like my own, only grander, with scrolls carved at the head and four fluted columns supporting the mosquito net.

There was a scattering of sand on the floor. Beneath my bare feet I could feel every single grain.

When I woke, the dark square of sky through the window was still flecked with stars. He lay beneath a sheet; I was uncovered and naked. I studied his face. Oval lids, fringed with fine black lashes. Contoured cheekbones, sloping nose, pitted with pores. His mouth, ruddy and moist within the complex dark mass of his beard.

Strange how a sleeper can feel that he is being watched, and wake. At the first flutter of his eyelids, a rush of tenderness surprised me. He lay, looking up at the cloudy netting above us. Then he said, 'Can't you sleep?'

'I slept, but I have been awake for a while.'

'Should you prefer your own bed?'

I felt perhaps he was sending me away. So I rose and put on my petticoat. My legs ached as I walked down the corridor in the moonlight. I opened the door to my room.

Then I saw something on the floor, sticking out from under the bed.

A small brown hand.

I stifled a scream. Alicia scrambled out and cowered before me, her hair all sandy and awry. She looked older, the skin under her eyes pouched and dark, as if she had been wrenched from the deep slumber that only comes when you can no longer bear to be awake. 'Thank God,' I cried over and over as we clung to each other, but she could not speak. She held me so tight her fingernails pierced through the cambric petticoat into my flesh. In those precious seconds I forgot myself, forgot everyone but Alicia, overwhelmed with love and joy and shame and awe that she should have searched for me until she found me. The pain of her grip persisted in my shoulders even after she had released me and taken my hands instead to cover them with kisses. I remember the soft fall of her hair over my arms and wrists, and how I buried my face in her hair and was safe there. Until I felt her warm tears.

'What has happened?'

Her mouth was quivering. I held her as tightly as she had held me, with my hands on her shoulders. 'Alicia, please tell me what has happened.'

She whispered, so faintly I could hardly hear, 'It was fever…'

'Is my father dead?' It was not courage that made me ask so boldly. I spoke because I could not bear to be ignorant any longer. But at the same time it was a rare kindness on my part, since she needed only to reply: *Yes*.

She was still shivering. I wrapped her in my shawl, and we lay down on the bed, drawing the sheet over us. At last, when her sobs had quietened, she told me how my father died. She did not know the date. 'After Livingstone?' I asked.

'Yes. Soon after.'

And surely Father wondered if I knew of Livingstone's death. When I disappeared, Martha Milton told him not to go looking for me. Let her find her own way back, she said. Better Lucy should learn her limitations for herself. She'll get as far as Saadani and then that man Heri will explain how things are, and she will be very frightened and he will bring her home to us.

How did Alicia come to hear these brutal words? Because Mr. Bertram reported them to her, when she went to him and begged him to find me.

Alicia was dismissed on that very first morning. While Father ran down to the quay, Martha Milton bawled at her. 'Where has she gone? Who is she with? *Alone?* You little fool!' While I was sitting on the beach at Sinamani, Alicia was bundling up her few belongings, with only the jeers of the other servants to bid her farewell.

Father called for me in his typhoid delirium, my name the last word he spoke before he died. This, Alicia did hear directly from Martha Milton, who sought her out to say, 'See how you have killed him.'

Beneath the cotton sheet I held Alicia's hand more tightly. 'So she buried my Father.'

'She could not bury him,' Alicia said, 'because that same day she became ill. She died too.'

Sinamani is a traveller's town, the streets designed for the purpose of channelling strangers inexorably towards the sea. People may stare at the mzungu girl as she walks through the market place with her maid, but they have no more interest in her than in the porters from foreign tribes who pass through the Caravanserai, or the Brothers in their black soutanes, bartering and chatting amicably with Muslim and Christian alike. 'Kabila gani?' one old woman asked me. *What tribe?* Then to Alicia: 'And you, kabila gani?' As if the only difference between us were the colour of our skin.

Alicia insists we go for a walk every day; we should breathe fresh sea air to keep up our spirits. We sit on the beach in companionable silence, watching the *dart! stab! vanish!* of sunlight on water.

I shall never see Father again.

The loss is agony, compared to which my own self-inflicted disgrace is nothing at all. Nothing and yet everything. There is now an agreement between the Khatib and myself which ensures, at least, that Alicia and I have food and shelter. I wish there were some other way, not for my sake, but for hers, since she has told me something which sickens me whenever I think of it; something which, once disclosed, made perfect, terrible sense.

'Why did you leave me?' I asked her, as we walked along the shore. 'Why did you run back that night, on the quay? Who detained you?'

She stood still, her eyes wide. 'You didn't know? I thought you had agreed with him ...'

For a moment I was stupid, trying to understand what she meant.

'The Khatib? Why should the Khatib call you back?'

'For his payment,' she said.

And that was the worst moment of all.

Ahead of us, men are preparing for a voyage. It is high tide, so they must push and drag their boat down the beach, groaning and cursing, churning up the smooth brown sand. At last, the dhow finds its own element, sways, then glides fast and serene, as if the water sets it free. They hoist the sail. It is an angry ghost, crackling in the wind, rearing up against the luminous blue sky.

If the Child Cries

At seven in the morning they hoisted the sail while I hunkered down between my backpack and a slimy coil of rope, mentally checking off the contents of my money belt: passport, visa, dollars, traveller's cheques, a wad of Tanzanian shillings, a ruby and diamond ring, a Yellow Fever vaccination certificate, some smudgy, baffling forms that Immigration had given me to fill in on my arrival.

A return ticket.

Not an option.

From my lowly position I couldn't see Zanzibar as we left the shore. I didn't crane my neck to catch a last, wistful glimpse of those dinky minarets and towers, those palm trees dwindling. When the dhow began to dip and rock I trailed my hand in the water, thinking of Lou, and of Fidelis, whose child was lying beneath a mound of purple flowers. But I didn't feel what I should have felt. That's what happens when you stop loving somebody; the pain makes you forget that it's the dead who hurt us most of all.

I stared at the horizon until the sun began to burn my face, then rummaged in my backpack for a cap. The old man clicked his tongue and pointed to the sky, shaking his head as if the sun were a disgrace. A young guy handed me a plastic beaker of water. He had gaps in his top front teeth, and his grey T shirt had more holes in it than cloth. I was wary of his water but I drank it, so as not to hurt his feelings.

It was hours before land came in sight, spoiling my perfect horizon. OK, I thought, closing my eyes against the dazzle of light and sea. Go to Dar. Lose yourself for a while. My eyelids twitched as the sun tried to pry them open.

In the harbour was the same ferry I had boarded just three weeks earlier. 'How much do I owe you?' I asked the old man. He asked for two hundred shillings, a fraction of the ferry fare. Then the young guy came over, pointed to my baseball cap and to his own head. 'You give me, please?'

'Sure,' I said. 'You're welcome.' He put the cap on straight away. Some of the men had already clambered onto the quay, and one reached down for me to pass him my backpack. I put my hands flat on the concrete, braced my good leg against the wall and hauled myself up. When I stood, the other knee gave a sudden twinge that made me stagger. The old man said, 'You are sick?'

'It's OK. I'm fine.' We shook hands. I thought about giving him more money, but didn't want to patronise him.

When I looked round, some ass-hole had stolen my backpack.

While I cursed and raged, the young guy with gap-teeth said, 'I will find that thief!' and ran into the crowds of ferry passengers and ticket touts, darting this way and that until he disappeared up a side street. Soon he came back, crestfallen, empty-handed. I wished I hadn't given him my cap. Now all I had was the clothes I stood up in.

At the police station a skinny cop took down my details, and a fat cop with a moustache and a huge belly told me, 'You should not have trusted those sailors,' although I insisted they were not to blame. 'What are you?' he sneered. 'Some kind of bush lawyer? Kindly do not waste my time, sir.'

Once out in the street, I realised I didn't even know where the US embassy was, and that my Lonely Planet guide, which might have told me, was even now being thumbed by thieves eager to read up on the best place to book a safari. I started walking down Samora Machel Avenue. It was late afternoon. The banks were closing, grilles were coming down on store-fronts, office workers in smart clothes were going home, weaving among people who were less smartly dressed, or even in rags, just standing, watching, thinking. In a back street I found a second-hand clothes market which gave no sign of closing for the night. A man showed me some items which he thought might be my size: a red T shirt with a motorbike on it and 'Altrincham All-stars Cyclocross' in flaking gold letters; a pair of fake black Levis; blue jeans with no label; a blue cotton shirt. I forced myself to ask my assistant if he had any underpants for sale. He did. A little group of onlookers began to swell, people encouraging me to choose this pair or that. Going against public opinion I declined some leopard print Y fronts and bought two pairs of boxers, black and dark blue. The whole trousseau set me back three dollars. 'They're robbing you,' a man said pityingly as I left.

Now it was almost six, the streets streaming with people, people squeezing onto buses that were all too full, warm air echoing with hoarse, unfaltering cries: *Kisutu! Kisutu! Morogoro Morogoro Morogoro! Hurry up hurry up hurry up!* I stood for a moment against a wall, eyes closed, listening to the diesel roar, the manic jangle of car horns, fists thumping against the metal flanks of buses, place names floating and echoing: *Mikocheni Mikocheni Mikocheni...* A light touch on my arm made me jump, ready to fight off the next bandit. It was a young woman, her eyes soft with concern. 'Are you sick?'

'I need a hotel.'

I followed her directions to the New Africa, checked into the cheapest available room, stripped off, lay down and let the air-conditioned blankness numb my brain for a while. Later, I showered, put on the blue shirt and fake Levis and went down to the dining-room, full of couples, noisy groups and families, every one of them white. I left the hotel and cut across Sokoine Drive. Nobody around. It wasn't yet eight o'clock. Samora Avenue stretched ahead of me into a warm, secretive blackness. In the afternoon it had seemed Dar Es Salaam's main artery with its mixture of flashy airline offices, banks made of sheeny marble, stores selling tourist crap, dusty street stalls, trays of secondhand paperbacks. Now, the only signs of life were from night watchmen, sometimes huddled outside a bank or a bureau de change, playing chequers, sometimes alone, slumped on camp stools. I had to find somewhere to eat – if, on this main street in Tanzania's biggest city, there was anywhere open.

On the point of turning back to the hotel, I saw a red and white striped awning, a pot palm and a blackboard menu. There were no diners in 'The Rendezvous' except myself, which suited me fine. The Asian manageress, in her long turquoise beaded gown, recommended Tilapia and rice, which is what three waiters brought me, and the fourth brought a tray with a single, ice-cold bottle of Tusker. But it wasn't long before the place filled up with a party of adults and squealing kids, all hugging and kissing the manageress, and tables were pushed together until I found myself dining on the edge of an extended family to which I did not belong. A little kid in a highchair stuffed his cheeks with fries, then blew one in my direction. It landed on the table, brushing damply against my hand.

Two white men walked in. One was almost bald, the other was dark, thin-faced, sallow. Both wore African batik shirts that screamed *Look at me! I belong here.* They stood in the doorway, frowning until their gaze settled on the two empty seats at my table. I hoped they'd leave. But the waiter was bringing them over with a sweet smile. 'I think you will not mind if they join you,' he said.

The bald man held out his hand. 'Hi. Inge.'

'Heinrich,' said the other one. Their accents were hard to place. European was all I could tell.

I began to eat, which gave Inge the chance to tell me he was an agriculturalist from Trondheim and that Heinrich, who was German, lived in the Serengeti where he was researching the mating habits of hyenas. 'Heinrich spends all day and all night watching hyenas screwing. He thinks it is the best job in the world.'

'Oh yeah?' I said, through a mouthful of fish. 'Part of some Save the Hyena conservation campaign?'

Heinrich raised his eyebrows. 'No. Part of a cross-disciplinary study on gender roles within the animal kingdom.'

'Gender roles?' It sounded like the kind of crap Lou was into.

'Yes. The hyena is particularly interesting. The female's clitoris is so large, it functions almost like a penis.'

'Right,' I said, and then, '*What* did you say?'

He told me again. Inge looked thoughtful. 'So what brings you to Dar Es Salaam, Sasha?'

Before I could answer Heinrich said, 'Are you a tourist?'

His tone riled me. 'No. I've been visiting my girlfriend on Zanzibar.'

'She lives there?'

'Yes.' Why wasn't the look on my face enough to put them off?

'You are lucky,' said Heinrich. 'That is one hell of a place to have a girlfriend.'

'We just split up.'

'Too bad.' He drank from his beer bottle.

Inge was working hard to find something to say. 'I guess you won't want to spend long in Dar, the armpit of Africa.'

'Seems OK to me.'

'I'm waiting for spares for that pile of shit my employers call a tractor. Today I sat in the Massey Ferguson offices for three hours. The manager knows when the parts will be in, they tell me. Where is the manager? He has gone to pray. When will he back? Soon, soon, soon. Three hours later…'
Inge shrugged.

The waiter came and they ordered a dish consisting of bananas and goat meat. Something sour had got into me: I said it sounded gross.

Heinrich said, 'It's good. You should try it. But you are American. I guess you'll soon be on your way home.'

Smug ass-hole. 'No, I'm staying. I have three months left on my visa. Can you recommend some place I should go? Not a safari, thanks. Animals don't do it for me.'

Heinrich kept smiling.

'You want a beach?' said Inge. 'You could do a lot worse than Sinamani. Isn't that right, Heinrich?'

The smile faded.

It was midnight when we left the restaurant, the last customers. Even the huge family had gone, their smallest kid bawling and rubbing his eyes. Why had we stayed so long? Because Heinrich and Inge talked and talked and talked. They talked about Tanzania: how they loved this country even though it drove them crazy, sometimes even drove them to despair. Several times they said, 'There's no infrastructure, that's the problem.' They talked about how there was no point getting frustrated with the way things were, you just had to go with the flow because 'Africans see time differently'. I thought that was hypocritical of Inge, given how he'd been bitching about the three hour wait in the tractor office. But I didn't say anything. Instead, I half listened, all the time my mind on this small coastal town Inge had said I must visit. 'It's one weird place, but the beach is amazing, and no wazungu seem to know it's there. You'd have that beach pretty much to yourself, I think.'

Heinrich asked the waiter for the check.

Outside, the night was still warm. We shook hands. As I walked away, Heinrich called after me, 'What happened to your leg?'

*

115

I hit town like the Pope, on hands and knees with my nose in the Sinamani dust. The steep steps of the bus had been too much for me, my head still pounding with the diesel roar and fumes of a three hour journey. But I kept my grip on the strap of the blue nylon hold-all I'd bought from a street vendor that morning, and my new friend John Simba was the first to hook his hands under my arms and lever me up. For a small guy, he was strong. You could tell from his face that he was tough, too, and when he said, 'Let us drink tea,' I didn't argue, because John Simba was, in his own words, 'Headmaster,' and he was wearing a smart grey Kaunda suit buttoned up to the neck, while I was wearing second-hand fake Levis. I had been the first passenger on the bus, and when this man ignored all the other empty seats and came to sit next to me it freaked me out, until I noticed that's what everyone did: all the seats filling up two by two until the bus was full.

We sat in the Alpha Motel, a café overlooking the bus station, and a girl brought a battered kettle of warm water and a sliver of grey soap to wash the dust from our hands. 'Shikamo mwalimu!' She bobbed a curtsey to John Simba, who told me, 'That girl failed the Form Two examination three times. But at least she has a job. So. What brings you to Sinamani?'

The beach? It did not seem like a good answer. I told him I'd heard the town was old and of historic importance and … kind of interesting, so I thought I'd check it out.

That didn't fool him. 'Ya,' he said, putting his fingertips together. 'Once Sinamani was important. But now it is a backwater. The council have let this town go to rack and ruin, my friend. It is high time they did some work to restore it, and bring in more tourists like yourself. And those tourists would bring in foreign exchange! Ya!' He nodded vigorously. 'Foreign exchange. Jobs for these lazy young students I teach. Better conditions for the people.

Then maybe they would work harder, if they had an incentive.'

Outside, in the bus square, the people were strolling calmly past. John Simba continued, 'Where I come from, in Moshi – do you know Moshi? Will you climb Kilimanjaro? No? – the Chagga people are very hardworking and they have a much better life. Fruits, crops, cash crops, because they know how to make money. You know, we have a joke. A Chagga guy is lying unconscious on the operating table. The surgeon drops the scissors and the Chagga immediately sits up and says, 'That money is mine!'

I laughed. It was impossible to dislike him; he was too solid, too frank – too kind, since after all there was nothing in it for him, helping this klutz who couldn't walk down three steps without falling over, and who clearly had matters other than history on his mind. Most of all I liked John Simba because he didn't press me for details of my job, my marital status, my damaged leg. I asked him how come he'd left Moshi for Sinamani, and he replied that he'd been posted here (like a soldier might be posted to the Gulf); then he said he couldn't resign because his wife was expecting twins, who would swell their family to eight. 'Anyway,' he added, 'because I am headmaster I can get credit everywhere – like this,' and he called the girl with the kettle, spoke to her in Swahili. She nodded. John turned to me. 'OK Sasha. Let's go.'

We crossed the square, and the place seemed drenched in sudden silence – the roar of the engines, the haggling touts, all muffled and far away, although they were only yards behind us. 'You must go to the Bahari Beach hotel,' John told me. 'It is the only place for tourists.' We shook hands. 'You are welcome to my school and my home,' he said. 'While you are in Sinamani you should come and meet my wife.' But I knew he was just being polite.

Off the main dirt road there were wide tracks of fine, peppery grey sand. The sky was grey-white with a dull glow,

117

as if the sun must be pulsing away somewhere behind it. I lay down on a patch of sandy grass, watching the shifting clouds for a while, the way they seemed to travel and travel and never get anywhere. A man on a bike rode slowly by. 'Are you sick?' he asked.

Soon afterwards a goat came over and stuck its sneering face in mine, so I got up. No sign of the sea. Like the sun, it had to be there somewhere.

The town felt exposed. The sandy paths were straight and crisscrossed each other at crazy angles. There were shops and breezeblock houses with corrugated iron roofs, but also some older, stone houses, their carved wooden doors as fancy as anything I'd seen on Zanzibar. People clustered outside their homes, girls combing or braiding each other's hair, teasing out the thick black strands, twisting and tucking and twiddling as they sang. Men leaning against walls with their arms folded and their eyes closed; men playing bao; men working at sewing machines. One man was showing a girl a bolt of bright blue shiny cloth, shaking it out with a flourish so it rippled and shimmered over the table and down the steps of his little shop. The girl, who wore glasses, scooped up the blue cloth and as it flowed over her arms she beamed, perhaps imagining herself in the dress he'd make for her. He looked happy too; he knew he'd made a sale.

They saw me staring. 'Welcome!' the girl said. I smiled and walked on. She called after me, 'Where are you going?'

The Agip garage, its tin sign creaking in a feeble breeze, men hanging around with empty cans. A low building, just a roof with supporting pillars, where small children squirmed and fidgeted and snuggled together while they chanted the Koran. Then, a sandy triangle between three paths, and a structure that puzzled me: a wedge of grimy white limestone, my height, with one tiny window and a padlocked door. A giant sugar cube, left out in the rain. A hunk of mouldy cheese. It might have fallen from the moon. Close by was something else strange: a huge chequer board, five foot by five, its black and white squares set into the ground. Two men sat either side, legs splayed, playing chequers with bottle tops. I remembered Fidelis, hunched over his bao.

Well, I told myself breezily, this seemed like a nice place, where someone provided the locals with facilities for outdoor board games. I walked on, and must have gone round in a circle, because soon I found myself outside the Agip garage again. 'You have returned,' observed one of the men. When I asked for directions to the sea, an old woman said in flawless English, 'Take the road ahead and go straight on, straight on as far as you can. That is where you will find the sea.'

I followed the path until, through the trees, I glimpsed at last a diamond of subtle blue-grey, the view obstructed by more buildings of dull limestone, angular and blocky like a giant's teeth. Fortifications? Somebody's palace? The path took me right up to one of these buildings, home to some official maybe. But the limestone was mottled with grubby mould, the windows gleamed raggedly with broken glass, and a huge rusting hulk of metal lay out front like the kind of modern art Lou always found so fascinating. No, I thought, this was a ruin. Nobody could live here any more. And then, as I followed the path round the side, I saw one window high up, with a pink curtain twitching in the breeze, a pot of red flowers, and a bicycle sticking out from the open door.

A loud clanking came from further along the path, then voices, then an army of kids in navy and white. School was out. Some girls were smirking and giggling at me so I said, 'Hi,' which made them double up with laughter, until I asked how I could get to the Bahari Beach hotel. They became very important, and led me down towards the sea as they quizzed me – what was my name? Where was I from? Why had I come here? Would I be their penfriend?

At last they pointed to a narrow track, said goodbye and meandered away, arms around each other's waists, leaving me to approach the Bahari on my own.

It was not the glossy hotel I had been expecting. There was a cluster of single storey round buildings with conical roofs of plaited leaves. Further away, small white huts. The beach. The sea. Boats drifting. Heat haze slowing everything down. Beyond the clattering of palm fronds in the breeze, a deep silence.

Look, I said to myself. There's no big hurry. There's no hurry at all. Stay for a while. Lie low. It'll be OK.

Skinny Edison, white shirt, black bow tie, was the only person on duty at Reception. Straight away we were on first name terms. I checked in for three weeks, which seemed an embarrassingly long time for a lone traveller, and he looked at my sagging nylon holdall. 'Any more luggages, Sasha?' He winced and clicked his tongue when I explained about the backpack. Then he showed me to a hut, almost filled by a sturdy wooden bed with white sheets and mosquito net. No glass in the window, just a coarse wire mesh. A wooden cupboard with roughly carved elephants dancing across the doors. 'This'll do fine,' I said.

The showers were in a block that recalled some of the crappier ballparks I have played. That didn't bother me. All I wanted was somewhere simple. A place where I knew nobody and nobody knew me. No Americans, no Westerners with their obsessions, grievances, relationships.

Edison offered to bring hot water but I refused, preferring to stand under the cold shower to sluice the grime from my body; the dust that had sifted in through my shirt and the fake Levis and the second-hand boxers. After the shower I felt great, but I couldn't look in a mirror because there were no mirrors at the Bahari Beach hotel. Lou would have approved.

Steps led down to the beach through a garden planted with purple flowers. I sat on a low stone ledge, digging my toes into the white sand, burying my feet up to the ankles. My legs were rooted in the beach now. I thought, this is what you've always wanted, what you've been craving for years: time to do nothing. This is it. Here you are.

Humans are supposed to have a fundamental need to know and to be known. I have wondered about that other need: to be completely anonymous. Maybe that's why we sit and stare at the sea, reminding ourselves that although the earth we live on may be visible and obvious, there are other possibilities. As I sat on the stone ledge I remembered the dipping wooden hull of the dhow, and the vast, silent privacy below. I thought about the littleness of most lives: injuries, failures, possessions that continue to be ours for years after we have lost them, or the things we can't help longing for, like a length of blue cloth. I didn't want Lou back, not the Lou I left sitting cross-legged on a bed surrounded by notebooks. But to be hauled out of myself and into somebody else's life – yes, maybe that was what I wanted next.

A small boy approached, held out a tray of eggs. I shook my head. 'No thanks.'

'Why?' he asked shyly.

'Because I'm not hungry right now.'

He wandered off, humming to himself. Despite the weird, subdued atmosphere, the beach was a highway, couples and kids and old men all passing by, sauntering with a half weary, half content end-of-the-day aimlessness in their step. A young dude in a bright yellow T shirt and wrap-around shades was picking his way through the seaweed, searching for something. Further north along the beach there was a row of six pointed columns, twice the height of a man. Giant's pencils. People were dragging fishing-boats up the sand, flanking each boat as if they were encouraging the ocean through the last stages of an amazing multiple birth.

Edison was sitting near me on the ledge.

'How is it?' he said.

'It's beautiful.'

He nodded, frowning slightly, as if he were trying to work out what to say, and the problem was more than just translation. 'Yes,' he said at last. 'Very beautiful. This is what everybody says who comes here.'

'So what about you, Edison? Do you think it's beautiful?'

'Of course. You know, on some days, it is possible to see Zanzibar.'

A gull cried overhead. The pearly sky began to darken.

'Perhaps,' said Edison, 'you would like to drink a beer before your meal?'

He led me back through the garden to a curved, open bar on a low platform between the guest rooms and the beach steps. Wooden statues of devils and warriors with furious faces stood around the platform. They were all the height of children, and seemed a strange welcome for tourists. Perhaps they'd put everyone else off, because that night I was the only guest at the Bahari. When it was dark, I went to sit at a table beneath a woven palm shade. On the ground near my chair was an empty coke bottle with a mosquito coil balanced on top. The coil gleamed as it burned, turning from dull green to black, and smelling of joss sticks. The sea was invisible, only the sigh of the waves giving its presence away.

A young waitress called Maria brought me fish and rice. It felt weird to be served on my own, like some sad, lonely king. While I ate, Maria and Edison were talking quietly at the bar. They left a decent interval before she came to enquire, in her soft voice, whether I would have another beer. I sat for a long time in the warm, sighing dark, and if I did think of Lou, I thought about my blank future too.

It never occurred to me that the hotel staff might be waiting for me to go to bed so they could all go home. In the end it was long past eleven, and the watchman had already wrapped himself in a blanket and settled in a wicker chair near the bar. I said goodnight to him, and to Edison and Maria, and locked myself in the white room with the dancing elephants.

I got up late. Under the palm shade someone had laid a breakfast of pawpaw doused in lime juice, mango, sliced for my convenience, lightly scrambled eggs and a large thermos of instant coffee. The ocean was almost too bright to look at, changing every second from water to platinum. Fishermen were already bringing in their first catch of the day. A man in a green kanzu was walking towards the hotel steps, singing loudly; on his head, a basket with silver fishtails flopping over the sides. He headed straight for me, still singing, and dumped the basket on my breakfast table, the smell of fish swamping my coffee. He talked non-stop, and seemed to have some kind of axe to grind, hands on hips, tutting and gabbling as if I could understand every word. Out of the corner of my eye I could see the Bahari staff watching and laughing. Eventually Edison came across and said, 'Good morning, Sasha.' I thought he was going to send the man on his way – but instead they shook hands and fish-guy began to pull his catch from the basket, fanning out the plump silver bodies along the wall for Edison to admire.

That morning I walked along the beach for miles, staring at the sunlight on the ocean until I got black blobs before my eyes. I walked as far as a rocky outcrop where the water slewed around a series of linked pools. A boy picked through the flotsam until he found a single sodden Nike trainer. He tipped it upside down and a stream of water rasped on the rocks, then he strolled away, dangling the trainer by its lace. What would he do with it?

As I returned to the hotel Edison came jogging across the sand towards me. 'Sasha. How was your walk?'

'Great.'

'The manager has asked me to warn you that this beach is very dangerous.'

'No kidding? Underwater currents? I didn't swim yet, but actually I'm pretty strong – '

'Not the sea. The people. There are many robbers on this beach and if they see you are carrying anything, they will take it. They will take your watch' – he pointed to my Rolex. 'Sometimes they have beaten people, or even stabbed them with knives.'

I was surprised; the coast of Tanzania was mainly Muslim, and hadn't Lou told me Muslims were law-abiding?

Edison laughed. 'Here, we have Muslim thieves and Christian thieves and Seventh Day Adventist thieves; thieves of every faith and denomination. There was a certain girl, she was here just last month, I think she was from America too, maybe you know her? No? She was walking along the beach, at night, on her own, and some guys, they robbed her. They took everything, even her shoes!'

'That's terrible.' I scrapped my plans for a midnight stroll.

'Yeah,' he grinned. 'Even her shoes. There are some very, very bad people around. You must be careful Sasha.'

Fired up by Edison's scaremongering, I decided to take a walk around this town of bandits. But it was so still, so quiet, even the market place was subdued, and the women called out to me listlessly, as if they had no hope that I would buy their mangoes and bananas. On Main Street where the houses were tall and old, a little girl in a too-long tartan dress was drawing with a stick in the dust. Her smooth round head and light skin made her look more Arab than African. She held her skirt up as she danced over to me. 'Sid! Sid!'

'I'm not Sid, I'm Sasha.' Her face fell. I wandered on, peering through doors and windows into shadowy living-spaces where people moved and murmured and laughed. One or two smiled out at me and said, 'Karibu!' But they didn't really expect me to go into their homes.

From time to time vehicles ripped through the silence of Main Street in a whirl of dust; glossy Land Cruisers, chunky jeeps, all with some foreign government's logo on the side. Usually they were driven by a lone white person.

In between my slow circuits of the town I spent most of the day in cafés, nursing one warm Coca Cola after another, not daring to ask for a glass of water in case it should make me sick. One day, soon, I would follow the ocean path out of town. But today was too hot, and Edison's warnings spooked me. They say big men are more likely to get attacked. What if people figured out the pregnant lump under my T shirt was actually a money belt with a ruby ring inside? What if they kicked my bad leg, got me down on the ground and tore the clothes off me? What if they stole my shoes?

A broad, cobbled road sloped down towards the sea. At the bottom was a two storey building, semi-derelict, some kind of warehouse. Through the open door I could see rows of sacks slumped like corpses in a makeshift morgue. A boy was carrying a sack on his head, the rough hessian bulk sagging over his shoulders. It was hard to imagine the weight his neck was bearing. From a tiny hole in one corner of the sack, grains trickled. Perhaps he didn't know, or didn't care. Or perhaps he cared but did not dare stop the dogged momentum that kept him walking with that hideous weight until at last he could dump his sack in the warehouse with all the others.

Outside the building, set into a low wall facing the sea, was that row of giant's pencils I had noticed the previous evening. Now, up close, each column was as thick as a man, built from flaking brown bricks and shaped to a point at the top. Maybe they were for mooring dhows. A little further down, even more baffling, there was a grid arrangement of around thirty smaller pillars, squat grey stone, waist high, each one topped with an iron stem supporting a shallow, rusty iron dish. Remembering the chequer board I wondered if they might be for some other kind of game – some giant variation on bao, the players walking from pillar to pillar to place a ball in the dish.

As I began to walk back towards the town, my left knee aching from the effort of going uphill, a white pickup was coming down, slowly, because the driver was having a conversation through the window with some kids trotting alongside. The driver was a white man with a bushy, slightly ridiculous black beard. There were two passengers next to him. A white woman, beautiful, face like a Madonna. The other passenger, I was surprised and irritated to see, was Heinrich. He mustn't see me, I thought, and took a step backwards out of their way. The pain was instant and vicious: my knee buckled, I lurched and stumbled into a little girl who was carrying a full bucket of water on her head.

When I recall it now, I picture the bucket slipping over her forehead, spilling a wave into the air, a wave she caught the brunt of as she reached out to try to steady the bucket, too late, impossible, the thing already rolling and clattering on the cobbles, leaving her drenched, her ragged blouse sticking to her chest. People swarmed towards us. She looked shocked, embarrassed. Was she twelve years old? Older, I think now, since the bucket was big, and Tanzanian children look younger than they really are.

'What the fuck did you do that for?'

It was a shrill English voice. The woman scrambled out of the pickup, marched over, stood with her hands on her skinny hips, a scowl on her lovely face.

'I'm sorry,' I said. 'It was an accident.'

'Of all the stupid, careless …!' She could barely get her words out. 'Do you realise how far she's walked to get that water?' She turned to the girl, said something in fast Swahili. The girl muttered a reply.

'It's an hour's round trip for her and thanks to *you*, you *idiot*, she's got to start all over again. And look at her, she's soaking!'

'Now wait a minute,' I said, but the man with the beard cut in. 'It's OK, Jules, I'll give her a lift to the standpipe.' He said a few words to the girl and she smiled and thanked him.

Heinrich said, 'So you decided to visit Sinamani after all.'

The woman looked disgusted. 'Do you *know* him?' She sounded like she pitied anyone unlucky enough to have any contact with me.

'We met in Dar. He's a tourist,' Heinrich said, and then, to me, 'Tanzanians are very poor, you know. Many have no water in their houses. Children must walk a long way to fetch water.'

'Hey, come on now,' I said. 'How ignorant do you think I am? Look, it was an accident, OK?' I fumbled in my pocket for a note, which I offered to the girl. 'Sorry for the inconvenience.'

'How *dare* you patronise her?' The screech increased by several decibels. 'Five hundred poxy shillings and you think that makes it all right?'

'Never mind, Jules.' The man with the beard put his hand on her shoulder and drew her gently towards the pickup. 'Come on, if we go now we'll be home by dark.' He looked back at me, and mouthed, *Sorry*.

'I'm sorry,' I said. Heinrich helped the girl climb into the open back of the pickup where she sat hugging her empty bucket. The woman didn't look at me again, but I looked, couldn't help looking, at the curve of her slim thighs under the thin orange material of her skirt, the way her hair hung

127

glossily down her back, and I knew that shouldn't make me feel any worse about the accident, but it did.

They drove away, leaving me with the crowd of Tanzanians. Nobody screeched, nobody sneered. But they were talking about me, so I held up my hands, said, 'Sorry.' And some of them nodded and shrugged. One grinned. 'I think the doctor, she has a lot of anger with you.'

'She's a doctor?'

'Yes, Doctor Juliet. She is a saint.'

'She would be.' Then I walked back along the beach, where perhaps I'd get mugged and thrown into the sea for dead.

After breakfast the next day, still smarting at the memory, I went to sit on the beach wall to watch the sea. Soon a man wearing a red fez joined me. He had a lined, wistful face and spoke English so fast it was hard to follow him as he went through the usual interrogation – where was I from? Was I married? What did I think of Tanzania? But at some point, I couldn't tell when, the focus shifted and he began to mention various one-time world leaders, casually, as if they were personal acquaintances of his. I caught the names Nixon, Kruschev, Indira Ghandi, and, inevitably, Mwalimu Nyerere –

'And Mwalimu Nyerere was taught by an Englishman, Mr. Edward Pemberton. Do you know Mr. Edward Pemberton?'

'I'm afraid not.'

'Mr. Edward Pemberton is a very very very big friend of mine. One day I will go to see him in England.'

He fell silent then, but we sat peacefully together while he contemplated his dream and I brooded over the ticking off I'd had from that woman.

What I needed was to go for a run. I said goodbye to my friend with the fez, then remembered that thanks to the asshole who stole my backpack in Dar, I had no sneakers other than the ones I wore every day, and no shorts. OK, I would run in my boxers. Edison looked alarmed when I jogged past him, and dubious when I held out my bare arms and empty hands. 'If anyone tries to steal my underpants…' I joked. He laughed uneasily. I was sorry to worry him, but I went anyway, jogging down the beach alongside the platinum sea until I reached the rocks. I found a fragment of glass, smooth and frosted like a sugared almond, and sat on a rock with my treasure, thinking how good it was to be far away from everyone who knew me. What would happen if someone at home got sick, my mom, say, and they called the Eastern Star? I imagined Fidelis on the phone. 'He is not here. He has gone. We do not know where.' How upset they'd all be. 'What do you *mean, gone?*'

Soon I'd call home. But I wouldn't let them talk about Lou. I'd say, 'It's over. I'm staying here for a while.'

Or I'd just write a letter to my brother Carl.

For now, I could spend a whole day on my own, on the beach, doing whatever I liked. I walked in the sea, tried to steady my gaze against that cruel glitter while the water dragged around my ankles. 'This is good,' I told myself. 'This is as good as it gets. I am completely free.'

I turned away from the sea, and walked back to the Bahari. There's a limit to how long you can spend on a beach by yourself.

Edison looked relieved to see me fully dressed again. I told him I would like to visit John Simba; he gave me directions to the secondary school and I set off along the path. As I approached I could see three figures, one very short, two tall, standing amongst some trees next to a huge mound of freshly-dug earth. John Simba with, I guessed, two of his students. They looked in their late teens, or even older, but they wore white shirts and navy shorts like little kids, and they were leaning on spades, exhausted, while he ranted at them, stabbing the ground with his stick.

Suddenly he raised the stick, barked an order, they held out their hands and he whacked them good and hard. I changed my mind about going over to say hello. They didn't see me as I slunk away, past the limestone ruins, down Main Street past the Post Office and the shops with their sparse shelves of Blueband margarine, long grey sticks of soap, garish plastic key fobs.

On to the coastal path. 'Be careful!' a man called. 'There are many robbers!' But I saw nobody at all. To my right, the ocean, to my left, farmland and bush. Everywhere swimming in heat haze. Who, with any sense, would take a midday walk to nowhere in December, the hottest month of the year?

I decided to go as far as a distant line of trees, then come back. But the trees turned out to be a perfect avenue of mangoes, their dense leaves providing welcome shade, planted either side of a long straight road that led away from the sea and narrowed to a blur in the distance. All over the ground mangoes lay like pebbles, green ovals flushed with crimson, as curved and smooth as my glass jewel on the beach. I picked one up to fill my palm with its satiny weight, then bit into it, and the scent wafted out like a genie. I sat down against a tree trunk to eat, letting the juice spill over my chin, mingling with the sweat on my palms. I wolfed the fruit, gnawed the white fibrous stone, picked orange threads of flesh from my teeth.

There were giggles from behind the tree opposite – three little ragged kids watching me. 'Shikamo mzungu.' I began to walk down the avenue and they tagged along, muttering, sniggering, keeping their distance. So this was how I arrived at the Mission: with three children in tow, and mango stains all down my shirt. There was a sign on the gate: 'Welcome to the Order of the Spiritans. Welcome to the Church of Christ the Holy King.'

Inside the compound there was a church, and the sound of people singing. There's a tremor and a lilt to African singing that catches at your heart, no matter what you believe.

'Go and join the service.' I whipped round. An old white priest, long white beard, hurrying across the compound. 'And Livingstone's tower is over there,' he called, his accent middle-European. 'Don't miss it.'

The tower looked like it was all that remained of another, much older church. At its base the fragile mass of stone and decaying brick was hollowed out to form a dark, cave-like space. There was a plaque on the wall. 'In honour of Dr. David Livingstone, Anglican missionary and promoter of anti-slavery campaign. In honour of all who devoted their lives for the benefit of Africa.'

Stanley's sidekick, or was it the other way round? I dredged up memories of Elementary school and Mrs. Dempsey's history lessons. What seemed to have stuck was the tale of how the Doctor's body had been carried by his servants, Chuma and Sussi, for hundreds of miles to the coast. What colour had the corpse gone, my friends and I wondered. Had the servants been afraid to sleep next to it?

A jeep roared into the compound, swept to a halt in front of the church, and five African nuns got out, their wimples like huge white birds. They smoothed their sky blue skirts, shook hands with the driver and ran up the steps to a building with a sign saying 'Sisters' House'. After they'd gone, the compound was as quiet as before, apart from a voice chanting inside the church. I thought about going in, but I looked like some kind of deranged person, with juice stains all down my shirt. Besides, I wasn't in the right frame of mind. I decided to go back.

At the far end of that perfect mango avenue was the sea, and something white, something that quivered in the heat haze as I squinted to make out what it was. A cross, put there by someone who wanted to make their mark on this coastline. When I left the shade of the trees the heat flung itself on me like a blanket. I went right up to the cross on its high plinth set into the sand dunes. It was white marble, as white as the sand, and so hard, when I ran a finger down one edge it left a groove in my flesh. No plaque, no sign, nothing at all to say what it was for – but somebody knew exactly what they were doing. Somebody knew you couldn't turn from that church without seeing the cross every step of the way.

I dawdled along the path to town, wondering what I'd have for dinner: fish and rice or fish and fries? – thinking I could do with a Coke, when I heard the steady tssk tssk tssk of a bicycle. A bandit on a bike: yes, that could happen here. I wasn't going to look round. Let them stab me in the back. I heard the cyclist dismount, come up alongside me. It was that doctor woman. 'Hi,' she said, in her tight little British voice. 'I thought it was you.'

'Oh. Hello.'

Strands of her hair were sticking to her face. The bike she was pushing was one of the black Chinese monsters that everyone here seemed to ride. A huge sack was strapped to the luggage rack and plastic bags full of vegetables dangled from both handlebars. I would have offered to push the bike for her, but doubted she'd accept. 'Have you come from the Mission?' she asked.

'Yes.'

'I've just been to Mass. I didn't notice you there.'

'I didn't go inside the church.' Her small talk was making me suspicious.

'Sorry about yesterday.' *That* was more like it. But I was still angry.

'Do you make a habit of having a go at people?'

She flushed. 'Sometimes I can be a bit … a bit over the top. Even Sid says so. But … well, you do see an awful lot of tourists who haven't got a clue, have no idea what people's lives are like. How hard it is.' She waited for me to speak. 'I did say I was sorry.'

'And I said, it's OK. Thanks. Forget about it.' Suddenly, more than anything, I wanted to see her smile. 'What's with all the bags?'

'Father Johannes just gave me this sack of rice – we didn't have nearly enough for Friday.'

'Friday?'

And at last she smiled, incredulous. 'Christmas day. Don't tell me you didn't know?'

It was embarrassing to have forgotten. Humiliating to be spending Christmas alone, as perhaps she knew. How much else had Heinrich blabbed?

'It's too hot for Christmas.'

She laughed, brushing away a damp strand of hair.

'Can I push that bike for a while?'

She let me take the handlebars, and we walked on. I was glad it was a long way to town. I asked her, 'Don't you have a car?'

'Yes, a hospital jeep. But it's quicker to go by bike.'

'How can it be quicker?'

'Because of all the lifts. What happens is, if you have a car, you end up constantly giving people lifts. Like …'

'Like yesterday when you took that girl back to the well?'

'I didn't mean to harp on about it, but yes, that sort of thing happens all the time. Especially to me, being a doctor.'

She said it matter-of-factly. I had no idea, then, what it must be like to have people hammering on your door at all hours, totally dependent on your generosity. So I didn't really understand when she said, 'Sometimes it's easier just to hop on a bike. Anyway, I have to get back now. My shift starts at six. I can take a short cut to the hospital down here.'

She took the bike from me and turned it towards a track between the crops on our right, swung one leg over the crossbar, braced the other foot on the ground, paused, lopsided and beautiful. 'What's your name?'

'Sasha.'

'Well, Sasha,' she said, and hesitated. 'We – we always have a party at the hospital on Christmas Day. You'd be welcome to come. If you don't have any other plans. OK? Just come if you want to.'

She rode away, before I could answer.

Christmas day breakfast was a long time coming, because Edison was the only member of staff on duty. When I asked him if he got paid overtime, he laughed. There were more guests, a party of Scandinavian aid workers and their beautiful kids with soft, blonde hair like dandelion clocks. 'Merry Christmas!' they called. They were sorry for me.

Edison asked if I would require lunch. My pathetic pride in declaring that I had an invitation didn't last long. 'Ah yes, you are going to see Dr. Juliet.'

'How did you know that?'

'Oh, I think some fellow in town must have told me ...'

The road to the hospital was long and dull; for miles I saw nothing except bushes and sisal plants and heard only the sly bleating of goats. Eventually, a distant rumble turned into a Land Rover which zoomed past, then stopped. A white man, thin hair, sunburnt face, tired blue eyes, stuck his head out of the window and said, 'It's a long way to the hospital. Hop in.'

George Harvey was a British water engineer and a brilliant driver, slaloming around the potholes, swerving to avoid ruts. I asked him how he knew I was going to the hospital.

'Because there's not a lot else round here for a mzungu. Are you sick?'

'No. Not any more.'

'Just going to see Juliet, then.'

'Yes.'

He nodded, and for some reason I felt unsettled. 'She usually lays on a marvellous spread at Christmas.'

'Has she been there long?'

'Must be at least five years. She keeps renewing her contract. They'll send her home in a box.'

'And what about you? How long have you lived in Tanzania?'

'Fifteen years,' he said. 'It's a nice life for an expat. And no shortage of work, unfortunately, for people in my line.'

He stepped on the gas and we sailed over a hump in the road; his reactions were amazing. I wondered if he played sport. When the inevitable question came, and I told him what I used to do for a living, his eyes opened wide. 'Really? I saw the Red Sox beat the Yankees at Fenway in 1969. Unforgettable.'

'I know,' I said. 'I was there, with my dad.'

The hospital was a cluster of low, cream buildings with dark green corrugated iron roofs. I saw her face at a window, and soon after she came running out, calling, 'George, you're an angel!' She was wearing a green surgical gown, her hair tied back in a bouncy ponytail. George was tall, almost as tall as me, and Juliet stood on tiptoe to kiss him on the cheek. 'Are you staying?'

'No, no. Places to go, people to see.' He looked awkward, his scrawny arms dangling uselessly as she kissed him again.

'What a shame.' She took his hands for a moment. 'Still, thanks for bringing Sasha to me.'

'Enjoy the festivities.' He was already backing away, as if he couldn't wait to escape from her and her 'marvellous spread' and her good time.

I was sorry to see him drive away. In fact, I was panicking at the thought of this party.

'Well. You came.'

'I hope that's OK.' Maybe it was the hospital making me talk like some kind of sad loser. I always hated hospitals, even before my accident.

'Of course it's OK,' she said. 'The more the merrier. Come on, I'll show you round.'

We stood at the double doors of Ward One. What struck me was how nobody was tucked up in bed; instead, the patients were all lying exposed on top of their sheets. Fragile limbs like bundles of firewood. Faraway faces. Every bed with its little nativity scene of relatives gathered round.

Juliet said, 'We can cut through here.'

A woman was cleaning the floor, bent double, her butt sticking up in the air as she swung from side to side with her sopping brown cloth, leaving swathes of wet on the cement. I tried to walk lightly, but my sneakers left imprints all over her hard work. 'Sorry,' I murmured, but she just wiped her brow with her forearm, then went back to it.

'It's OK,' said Juliet. 'Aziza doesn't mind; it's her job.'

A young Tanzanian woman in a white coat marched down the central aisle, smiling, singing as she stroked a child's head, glancing at me. She looked familiar; I thought maybe I'd seen her somewhere around town.

I was glad when we went through the next set of double doors at the far end, and entered a courtyard. The Tanzanian flag hung from a central pole. Sitting under a flame tree, a man snoozed, bundled up in a filthy brown coat despite the heat. Tiny kids played, but kept their distance from him. We crossed the yard, through another door, along a footpath. They'd had a busy night, she said. Two births and an operation.

Beyond a grove of trees there were five small bungalows. Chickens pecked the dirt. Juliet pointed to one of the bungalows. 'My humble abode.' Hers was the biggest of the five. It had a veranda and tubs of flowers. Two black puppies came tumbling towards us. She bent down to let them lick her hands. 'Hello darlings.'

'What are they called?'

'Poppy and Lulu.'

'Cute names.'

She laughed. 'I'm afraid to everyone else they are Scud and Saddam.'

'Well, those names are less cute. Topical, though.'

'Grace, my assistant, can't understand why they've got names at all. A dog is not a human being, she says.'

I could have knelt by her side in the dirt playing with those pups for a long time – but from out of the house came laughter and the smell of cooking, and that whiny, sexy Taarabu music that drove me nuts on Zanzibar.

Juliet said drily, 'As you can hear, they didn't wait for us to begin the party.'

The tiny room was full of people, every seat taken by women in their best dresses, huge, flamboyant prints of fearsome flowers and psychedelic geometrics, kids on their laps, kids capering around, kids wiggling their hips to the music. There were men, too, somehow less of a presence. I scanned the room for Heinrich: not there. Good.

But there was a voice I recognised, grand and theatrical. 'Hello my friend, we meet again!' John Simba, sitting on a bench with four other guys like a row of substitutes. He did the introductions: on the end, with a green wool beanie, Mr Winston the telephone engineer – '*the* telephone engineer; there is only one' – next to him Sid, in baggy khaki shorts; in the middle John Simba himself with a gleam in his eye, looking more cheerful than any headmaster should; looking, in fact, drunk, although it was only just midday; then Babu, a wizened old man like a little tortoise in shirt and pants, and finally Juma, Babu's fresh-faced teenage grandson.

'Please, Sasha, sit with us!' It was ridiculous, there wasn't room, but John Simba grabbed my hand and pulled me down beside him.

'Hi,' said Sid, 'Have a beer.' I knew he'd never mention the accident with the girl and her water on the sea path, he was too nice. But as I thanked him, I wondered what he was to Juliet, this spacey-looking guy with his bushy beard and baggy pants.

She staggered out of the kitchen, lugging a huge pot full of rice. 'Dig in!' she gasped, and dashed back. The mamas got going with ladles and plates, and soon I was handed a plastic bowl full of pilau, by a tall girl in a blue dress, with a smile as perfect as a crescent moon.

'Do you remember me?' she said. How lovely her voice was, deep and velvet like a clarinet. She wore glasses.

'I saw you on the ward just now.'

'And before that?' Laughing, she spread out her silky blue skirt.

I remembered. 'In town. At the tailor's!'

'Are you admiring Grace's new frock?' Juliet glided past. 'Knock'em dead, Gracie.'

But Juliet was the most beautiful woman in the room, with her white blouse done up to the throat and her long orange skirt that clung to her neat hips.

'So, my friend. What are your impressions of Sinamani?' Maybe John Simba wasn't so drunk, since he looked steadily at me as he waited for my answer. I wanted to say the right thing. 'Well,' I said, remembering he'd called this place a backwater. 'It's peaceful.'

'That is because it is dying. A long, slow death. Bit by bit all the very splendid Arab buildings and German buildings, they are decaying and crumbling away, and one day there will be nothing left but these tin shacks where the people live who have nothing.' He sounded as if the town deserved to die.

'I hope that won't happen,' I said feebly.

He shrugged. 'Most probably it will. It is all down to our government.'

'You never know,' said Sid, 'maybe the government will turn it into a tourist paradise.'

'And what about the serpent?' John said. Just then his excitable friend in the green hat grabbed his hand and pulled him outside to look for beers, leaving me and Sid with a little more room. He told me about his job as diocesan pilot, flying the bishop up and down the coast in a light aircraft. Sometimes he helped the flying doctors, which sounded macho and heroic, and might, I figured, make him desirable to Juliet. When I asked him where he came from in England, he shook his head.

'My parents were missionaries. I was born in Kilimanjaro region, a place called Moshi.'

'Like me,' Grace put in. 'For my sins. But I came here, to Sinamani, so I could train to become a medical assistant.'

Sid laughed. 'Grace is a true Chagga girl. You know the Chagga? They're the most successful Tanzanian tribe, the best at making money.'

'So how come I don't have any?' said Grace.

I laughed along with everyone else, but the whole tribe thing made me uneasy, because I didn't understand it – this connection that wasn't family, wasn't nationality, but another kind of tie. Juliet, George Harvey, Sid – the same tribe? And what tribe was I? A little bit American, a little bit German, a hint of Jewish somewhere in the mix.

No. I lost my tribe the day my knee got mashed up.

The party went on all afternoon, a weird Christmas party with the heat so fierce, and outside the purple-blue jacaranda trees in full bloom. Juliet hardly sat still, serving everyone with pilau, darting to the crates of beer and soda, ordering the kids around in Swahili and sometimes exasperated English: 'No, no, no! Don't put it there, for crying out loud!' but only pretending to be mad at them. I stole glances at her sideboard, her shelves, spying for photographs, evidence of attachments – but the room was too crowded. From time to time she would perch somewhere to eat, scooping up rice with her fingers, never looking at me.

The old man Babu got up and Juma led him away. Was Babu tired? No, he was complaining that the beer was too cold. Mr. Winston rejoined me on the bench. 'Are you really the only telephone engineer in Sinamani?' I asked him.

'In the whole of Pwani Region, all along the coast.'

'He is a very successful fellow,' said John Simba. 'He knows how to mend telephones, and also how they can be prevented from working so that they *need* to be mended.'

'You better make sure you mend my phone before you go,' said Juliet. 'I want to call my mum.'

She sat down next to me. All the time she and Mr. Winston were arguing over the repair price, I was wishing he'd go away. Finally she seemed to really lose her temper – that indignant screech again. He stood, giggling and fanning himself with his green hat, then picked up his toolbag and left.

'Your Swahili is amazing,' I said to her. 'Have you lived here for a long time?' Not much of an opener, especially since I already knew the answer.

'Sometimes it feels like a long time.' She was running her finger along the gold chain at her throat. 'But it isn't, really. Not when you look at people like Sid and George.'

I decided she wanted me to probe further. 'What made you come here?'

'Oh … I was hacked off with England, did an elective in Namibia, fell in love with Africa, all the usual clichés, finished my training and applied here as soon as I saw the ad.'

Down by the Customs House she'd been so high and mighty. Here, in her own home, she was different, modest, nicer.

Then she got me.

'What caused your leg injury – you've damaged the posterior cruciate ligament, haven't you?'

'Is it so obvious?'

'To a doctor, yes. You wince when you step backwards, and that's a classic PCL injury symptom.' She bit her lip. 'I realise now, that's why you overbalanced that day, when we were down by the Customs house. I'm sorry. Again. I just wondered what happened to you; tell me to shut up and mind my own business if you like…'

Juliet was already backing away. I said, 'I don't mind you asking. It was a sports injury, about nine months ago.'

'Nine months? So you're taking time out from your job?'

'I have no job. Until this happened I was a baseball player.'

'Oh. Bad luck, then.' She looked stricken, perhaps regretting she'd asked. Usually I hated talking about my leg, but right now I just wanted her to stay and talk to me, no matter what.

'It's OK. Most people get injured, sooner or later. Besides, you can't play baseball for ever.'

This was what I'd coached myself to say. This wasn't the right place to say: *my life is in ruins*.

'What will you do instead?'

'I don't know. I need time to figure it all out.'

'Heinrich said you went to see your girlfriend on Zanzibar, but you split up.'

Thanks again Heinrich, you little shit, you fucker of hyenas. Inside I cringed at the thought of the two of them, discussing me, but I held it together and managed a shrug. 'I guess it was over anyway.'

'How did it happen? Your injury?'

'Oh, let's save that story for another time.'

Juliet nodded, apparently relieved. Because it meant we'd see each other again? Then Grace came with some urgent query from the kitchen, and off she went to sort it out. I was glad to see her go. 'I've got all the time in the world,' I thought. So I remained on the bench, and John Simba returned and talked to me about Sinamani, which was once, years ago, the grandest town in East Africa, until the Germans and the Arabs blew it to bits, and I half-listened, and then a small boy tripped over John's foot and landed on the cement floor with a thud and a wail.

'You! Stop that noise!' John hauled the kid up and sat him on his knee. 'It is your own fault. Greet our visitor!'

'Shikamo mzungu,' the kid sobbed.

'This is my lastborn, Gabriel. To hear him cry, you would not think his father's name was Simba, would you?' He gave Gabriel a little shake, not hard. 'I warned you but you would not listen. Sasha, we have a saying in Tanzania: If the child cries, give it a razor blade.'

'Good grief.'

'It means, if a person wants to do something dangerous, even though you know it will harm them, let them go ahead because then they will learn their lesson.' The kid wailed some more.

'How's your wife?' I asked. 'She's expecting twins, isn't she?'

'Yes. Soon there will be two more mouths to feed. Life is hard, my friend.'

Right on cue, Gabriel began to finger my Rolex.

'Be careful with that watch, Sasha. It is very valuable and people will try to steal it.'

Outside, the light was beginning to fail. Women were gathering up their children, their faces glistening with sweat and grease from the pilau. All the beer crates were empty. Babu tottered off with Juma at his elbow. Everyone was leaving. I joined the line of people waiting to shake Juliet's hand. She seemed tired, a little flushed. At last, she looked up at me and said, 'Thank you for coming.'

'I guess I should be on my way. Shouldn't I?'

'That rogue Winston is driving me home,' said John Simba behind me. 'He can give you a lift to your hotel.'

'It's OK, thanks,' I said. 'I like to walk.'

'I'll *sindikiza* you,' Juliet cut in, before John could insist. 'Do you know that word? It means to go with someone a little way on their journey. If you can hang on five minutes…'

Either she wasn't going to ask me to stay, or she wanted to wait until we had some privacy.

'You must come to the school.' John hoisted Gabriel onto his shoulders. 'Come and meet my wife. She is enormous!' He and Mr Winston wandered off down the path.

Juliet said, 'Won't be long,' but she was directing the clear-up operation, as if she wanted to get everyone and everything out of the way. I slotted empty bottles into crates and carried them out to the kitchen, scraped plastic bowls into the pig bucket, cleaned and lit the kerosene lamp.

'You don't have to do that,' she said shyly. 'The girls will see to it.'

'I don't want to be a useless tourist,' I said, and grinned at her.

'Touché.'

Quite a while later, she walked with me to the gate. Purple-blue jacaranda blossoms were scattered beneath our feet. Somewhere, a fire crackled; there was a faint smell of woodsmoke, the sound of families subsiding for the night.

She talked and talked, asking me if I'd enjoyed the pilau; how I'd met John Simba; what did I think of her house, was it embarrassing that it was so much bigger than all the other staff houses on the compound? I said I hadn't visited many Tanzanian homes, so… She wasn't listening. She prattled on and on, about the food, how the drink had run out too early, the complaining party guests, what a cheek! She's nervous, I thought. Nervous of me? I wanted to say to her: You're amazing. You *must* be amazing to make your

143

life here, helping sick Tanzanians when you could be earning so much more money back home. I wanted her to know that I admired her, but I couldn't think of a way to say it without sounding like a creep. Besides, a tiny, niggling part of me envied her: the camaraderie, that house full of friends, no commute to work, fresh food and plenty of helpers to cook it. The status, the respect, the affection. Don't be stupid, I told myself. Think of all the people she sees dying. The sick kids she can't help.

A man hurried past us, carrying a plastic bag full of blood.

She took a deep breath, then sighed. 'Your injury – you know, it's really not obvious at all. I wouldn't want you to feel self-conscious. Sorry if I was being nosy.'

'It's OK. I appreciated your interest.'

'And I'm sorry we haven't had much of a chance to talk. You could stay a bit longer if you like …'

But a girl was running through the trees towards us, and I'd been in Tanzania just long enough to know that nobody runs unless they have to. She was crying, 'Doctor! Doctor!'

'Oh bother.' Juliet took my hand and pressed it between hers. 'Are you still at the Bahari? I'm not working New Year's eve, emergencies permitting. Why don't I come over?'

She was already running away from me, running to meet the girl, relieved she'd made the move.

'You do that!' I called, and she half turned and gave me the loveliest smile.

The askari at the hospital gate glared at me, snapped something in Swahili. I shrugged. 'Sorry, I don't understand.' He shook his head, muttering, opened the gate and I set off on the long walk to town. Mr. Winston and John Simba passed in a pickup, hooting the horn. The back of the pickup was crammed with people, some balancing dangerously on the low sides. One of them yelled, 'Why are you walking? Where is your car?' and someone else sang, 'Beware robbers!'

I felt defiant, that Christmas night, daring bandits or demons to jump out from the spiky sisal plants that lined the road. Something hurt, and it wasn't my knee, but a niggling pain in my belly. I wished I'd left that ruby ring at the bottom of my backpack. For a while on Zanzibar it had lived snugly in a nest of underpants. I'd been meaning to tell Lou, knowing it would make her laugh. So why was it in my money belt now, rubbing against my flabby gut?

The darkness grew thicker as I walked further away from the hospital lights. I shivered. But it was the scraping, grating chant of the insects that spooked me.

I fumbled under my shirt, unzipped the money belt. In the dusk the ruby was black and opaque, the diamonds two specks of grit. I hooked the ring with my fingertip, then flipped it away and it went spinning into the bushes. Maybe it would lie there for ever, winking its one red eye at the snakes and lizards. Maybe a child in rags would find it and sell it to some kind, rich man who would give him the five thousand dollars that I had paid for it in Boston.

When someone knocked at my door the next morning I thought it must be Juliet. But they were two schoolgirls, peeping at my room, eyeing the towel round my waist, as they summoned up their very best English to tell me, 'Headmaster, he says, welcome to our school!'

School and I never did get on; I never was inclined to learn, perhaps because I'd been told from the age of four that all I really needed to concentrate on was the ball coming towards me at speed. I was done with school; knew everything there was to know about not learning – but just the appearance of John Simba's place shocked me into learning something else: the goats eating their way round the compound, the shabby buildings, the low, drab sheds,

145

one of them missing a roof. And this was supposed to give him status?

'How come you're still here when it's the vacation?' I asked the girls. They dissolved, could hardly get the words out for giggles.

'Punishment,' one spluttered at last.

They brought me to the staffroom: three walls of flaking green paint and a fourth taken up by a blackboard that was grey with the chalky ghosts of old messages: *Omary Juma will fetch extra water. Form IV shamba duty. Form II will repeat their geography examination.* A few teachers, all male, sat with clasped hands round a horseshoe arrangement of rickety tables. Julius Nyerere beamed toothily from a framed photo. 'Ah, my friend, welcome! Come and see the fruits of their labours!' John Simba, none the worse for the party, shook my hand.

Two young guys in uniform were standing near the blackboard. I recognised them: the ones he'd thrashed with a stick that day when I'd crept past. Proudly they held out a tattered, mud-stained sheet of paper torn from an exercise book. On top of it a disgusting object writhed, white and translucent.

'What the hell is that?'

Sniggers all round. 'That is the queen, my friend.'

I was none the wiser. John took pity on me, led me across the compound to the shed without a roof. The sign on the door said 'Library'. Inside were empty shelves. A desk stood near the door. He pushed it lightly and it wobbled. The fourth leg was missing, just a stump coated in a fine, reddish silt. I prodded it, and what should have been solid wood crumbled and dropped off.

'Termites are eating our school,' John said. It was almost funny, but I couldn't laugh. 'That is why I set those boys to dig up the queen, as a punishment for fighting. It is good if they can do something useful with their punishment, don't

146

you agree, Sasha? Yes? You think they've done a good job? Come and drink tea with us.'

The staff houses were similar to the classroom sheds, but smaller. Now I knew about the termites I noticed how some of the trees were ravaged: the gnawed branches like tormented limbs, some kind of Biblical warning. And yet John's wife Eluminata was pretty and calm, her huge belly graceful under a yellow kanga. Most of their living space was filled with Eluminata's girth and an over-sized sideboard with glass doors, which she unlocked to bring out china cups and saucers. I couldn't remember the last time I'd drunk from a china cup. While she made tea, John told me about the Inspectors who would come the following week and 'take our school to pieces.'

'Like the termites,' I said. Eluminata laughed. John did not.

'They will be very critical, ya. Only twelve students passed the Form Two examinations this year.'

'Out of how many?'

'Seventy four.'

And I thought I was dumb. Luckily the little boy Gabriel, lurking at the door, caught his father's attention and saved me from having to comment. 'Shikamo mzungu,' he whispered. Then he stretched up on the tips of his toes to lay his hand lightly on my head. I'd seen small children do this before, although never yet to me. The touch, I knew, was meant to show respect, but it felt more than that. It felt like a blessing.

'Good boy,' Eluminata said.

Next thing, while his parents were busy pouring the tea, he was unbuckling my watch.

'It's OK,' I said, when they noticed and started telling him off. 'He just wants to see how it works.' He brooded over the watch, his face full of longing, while I showed him the dials that set the time and date and opened the back so he could see the mechanism. Then, to his great delight I

147

fastened it round his wrist, and he held his puny arm up high to admire it dangling in the sunlight. 'Saa yangu,' he whispered. *My watch*. But Eluminata scooped it from him and John neatly planted the photo album on his lap before he could start to cry. 'Gabriel, where's Mama? Find Mama in this book.'

We spent half an hour identifying every relative, every schoolmate, every significant event in John's life and many not so significant. Then they insisted I eat rice and beans with them. I didn't make it back to the Bahari until gone four o'clock. 'Any visitors?' I asked Edison casually, but he shook his head.

She came, just as she had promised, on New Year's Eve. I was lying on my bed, writing an evasive letter home when a shadow passed in front of the mesh window. Seven seconds passed before she knocked on the door.

We went for a walk. 'This is a mystery tour,' she said. The path ran parallel to the beach, laced with bumpy tree roots, the sand silky, untrodden, as though people didn't come here very often. It was a narrow path. Juliet walked ahead of me, fast. Once she stumbled; I reached out to steady her, but managed to stop myself.

Neither of us said anything. At last we came to a clearing and a small cemetery, no more than twenty by thirty feet, surrounded by a low, rose-pink wall of faded brick, the mortar pale and crumbling. There were a few thin trees along the sea wall, their leaves limp in the heat.

'Here we are,' she said.

'You take me to the nicest places.'

There was a grubby white iron gate, spattered with a rash of rust. It creaked as she pushed it open.

'Sounds like the folks don't get many visitors.' If only I could shut up. If only she'd talk to me. She began to wander along the path between the graves. On each grave the name was German, and the same date: 1889, appeared over and over again. 'Did they all die in that war?'

'Almost all.' Her voice was hushed. 'Some of them would have had typhoid, or cholera, or malaria of course.' I don't know why she spoke so quietly. Maybe because she was telling me a story of disgrace. The headstones all leaned at crazy angles, as if they were flinching. Don't feel sorry for these guys, I told myself. They had no business to be here in the first place.

A freaky, faceless angel stood watch over a very small grave. *'Beate Schiller, 1884 - 1889.'* Juliet trailed her finger lightly over the angel. 'Poor little Beate.' She squatted down, and tugged at the sinewy creeper clambering over the gravestone.

'So do you come here often?' Again, I sounded like I was making some stupid joke, but that wasn't how I'd meant it.

'From time to time.' With a final sharp tug she pulled up the root of the creeper, twisted it round to form a noose of green leaves and threw it over the seawall, then rubbed her thumb and fingers together, flaking away the dirt.

'Why do you come here? It's a sad place.'

She hesitated. 'You'll laugh at me.'

'No I won't.'

'Alright. I'll trust you, Sasha. I come here to remind myself that wazungu are human. Because I don't like it when people go on and on about me and call me a saint, it makes me cringe, but sometimes, more often than I want, or possibly more often than necessary, I have to play God. So it's good to come down here to see the graves of all these dead white people, and remember that they died here, from bullets or bayonets or the shits or plain old malaria. They came here thinking they were going to rule the world, and look how they ended up.'

149

I wanted to reach out, draw her towards me. Instead I said, 'What about this little girl? Did she think she was going to rule the world?'

'Well, no. She couldn't help who her parents were.'

We were silent. She didn't look at me. I wanted to say something, tell her how much she touched me with her concern for this dead kid. But her face changed, became impish, and she said, 'Want to see a dead Englishwoman?'

That surprised me. The grave was at the boundary wall, in the corner most distant from the sea, as if whoever had buried her wanted to protect her from the waves. *Lucy Hemmings, born England, died Sinamani 1890*, was all the gravestone said.

'So what's her story?'

'I've no idea.' Juliet was subdued again. 'Perhaps she was a missionary.'

'But wouldn't she have been buried at the Mission?'

'True. On the other hand, I think the missionaries back then were mostly French. Oh, maybe she was a one-off, a bit of a maverick. An intrepid, saintly Englishwoman, just like me.'

She sat on the wall, swinging her legs above the grave. My shirt was plastered to my chest with sweat; her cream blouse was crisp and fresh. 'It is a bit weird, the way she's stuck in the corner, isn't it? It's like they weren't sure of the right thing to do with her. Maybe someone thought they should bury her with other Europeans and someone else thought, hmm, would she want to be with all these Germans? Oh, I don't know; maybe she was some hunky Kraut's mistress. Come on Sasha, don't look so miserable.'

Now it was her turn to be flippant. I went right up to her where she was sitting on the wall, so her face was level with mine, and I kissed her. After a while we were kissing so hard she nearly toppled backwards and she ducked her face away, but she laughed as she put her hands on my shoulders. 'Steady on!'

We walked back along the beach, hand in hand. 'You do realise,' she said, 'that this will be all round town tomorrow.'

'Is that a bad thing?'

'Maybe not for you, sunshine, but I'm the one who has to live at the epicentre of all the gossip, all the stories people tell about me.'

'What stories?' I asked, lightly.

'Believe me, you don't want to know.'

It didn't matter really; all that mattered was going to bed with her, without any soulful discussions before or afterwards. That's what I told myself. Still holding her hand, I picked up my key from Edison, who murmured reverently, 'Shikamo doctor,' and we strolled past a group of noisy whites ordering drinks at the bar. I saw how the men glanced at us, the flickers of interest, the envy.

I locked the door. Even so, we could hear voices the whole time; someone shouting in Swahili at the girls clattering their buckets as they cleaned the shower block; the up-and-down Scandinavian accents of the guests at the bar, Edison calling for water. Sometimes a shadow fell across the bed as someone walked right past the mesh window. Sometimes she stuffed her fist in her mouth to keep herself from laughing, bit down on her knuckles until teeth marks appeared in her peachy skin. I didn't laugh. I was too involved, and anyway, my leg was hurting.

We lay, watching the square of filtered light turn from white to silver and then darken as night fell. The voices carried on: Norwegians hell-bent on seeing the New Year in. We whispered to each other like kids hiding from our parents. We heard the scrape of the night watchman's chair, just yards away.

'Tell me about your accident,' she said.

The stadium was three-quarters full. It was a midseason game, one we were pretty sure to win, so I hadn't felt in advance the sick dread that plagued us all from time to time. All afternoon I had been resting in the sun, reading and re-reading a letter from Lou, who'd just gone to Zanzibar, wondering about our future. In the evening when I went out to bat I felt light and strong. There was no tension in the muscles, nothing to wreck my concentration. Everything was normal: the smell of hotdogs in a spicy wave from the crowd as the organ played faster and faster, whipping up the excitement, my buddy Tom Earnshaw grinning on second base, the friendly dip in the dirt beneath my feet as I took up my stance in the box, ready to swing.

It happened when I was stealing fourth – so near to home – my foot slid right underneath the base and got trapped so I couldn't twist out of the slide but fell with my leg jack-knifed underneath me, and the hard dirt tilting up to slam me in the face, and the crack from my leg like a gunshot. The amazing clarity of pain, held in a long, long moment, as full and pure and tremulous as a raindrop. Then everyone came running, and I could feel their footsteps, drumbeats on the tight skin of the field. I had flung out my arms trying to break the fall, which didn't work because my foot was trapped, and I still had my arms out, hugging the ground that was too hard, too flat. There was still the smell of hotdogs. Everything else was different – the low, agitated rumble from the crowd, my coach, gentle as I'd never heard him before, and my body, my poor dumb body, had changed for ever.

Her brown eyes looked straight into mine, all the time I was talking. When I was done, she sighed, and stroked my face.

I said, 'It happens to a lot of players. Better to go out when you're at your peak, like I was, than get old and slow and have everyone baying for you to be dropped.'

'Is it really over? Can't you play again?'

'Never in the Major League.'

'So what will you do instead?'

Stay here, I thought, stay here in Tanzania with you. I said, 'I don't know, yet. I aim to do something worthwhile with my life.'

The words sounded hollow, and she didn't come up with any suggestions. Why should she? Maybe I should have confessed that first, impulsive thought about us staying together.

'Well, good luck with that,' she said. Maybe she was thinking: all you've ever done is play baseball.

'Stay here tonight.'

'I can't. I'm working tomorrow morning. But I'm really hungry. Let's get something to eat.'

I suggested she slip out first and that I should follow a little later, but she said that was silly; there was no point being coy because everyone had seen us enter the hut and someone would have been timing us to see how long we had spent inside. So we walked out together, Juliet with her head held high, calling a greeting to the night watchman who jumped as he woke up.

Throughout dinner she was bright and chirpy, which bothered me. It seemed strange for her to be chatting away about emergency caesareans and how much she missed toast and marmalade, when earlier there had been no need for any words at all. Perhaps ever since I came here, perhaps even before Zanzibar, I had been craving the wordless company of someone who spoke my own language.

Once, she laid her hand on mine. 'You know what?' she said. 'I know you're not interested in lions and zebras and all that nature stuff – but really, you should take a trip to Ngorongoro to see the Crater. It is the most amazing place.'

'*This* is an amazing place.'

'To be honest, I sometimes think it's a bit of a dump. An historic dump, that's all. You don't want to just hang around here, not when there's so much else to see.'

'What about you? How long will you stay here? You seem pretty settled.'

Her hand was still on mine, and she stroked my fingers thoughtfully before she replied. 'Settled? In a way. But stay here for ever ...' She shook her head. 'No. I'd never belong here. Oh, I know what it must have looked like to you on Christmas day, open house, all those people drinking my beer, but ...sometimes I get lonely.'

Through such admissions, two people come to understand each other. Or, one turns away. I laced her fingers in mine and said, 'I'm asking you again. Please, stay here tonight.'

She said no, but maybe some other time, which was enough for me. And two nights later she came knocking at my door.

A week into January and the heat was so intense that to walk anywhere was torture. I decided to spend the afternoon on the beach. For Edison's sake I had taken to sunbathing in the same patch, within sight of the Bahari, although I always kept my eyes closed so people wouldn't try to talk to me. On that particular afternoon I listened to the soft shuffle of footsteps on sand growing closer and closer, until the footsteps stopped next to my head. Edison, I thought, you were right all along. But when I bravely opened my eyes I was looking up the tunnel legs of some baggy grey shorts.

'Sorry,' said Sid. 'Did I wake you?'

He sat down crosslegged with his bony knees sticking out and we talked for a while. Sid might have lived in Tanzania all his life, but he had seen the same movies I'd seen (he caught them in Nairobi), and he enjoyed baseball, which he sometimes watched on a friend's satellite TV. Talking to him, I didn't feel like a tourist.

'You must really like it here,' he said, 'to stay so long.'

'You said it yourself. It's paradise.' I nodded towards the white sweep of the beach, the sparkling ocean.

He smiled ruefully. 'Well ... there's more to it than that.'

I didn't know whether he meant the poverty, or crime, of which I'd yet to see any evidence, or perhaps Sinamani's history, although Sid didn't seem the type to get gloomy about events that happened a hundred years ago. So we sat in thoughtful, friendly silence until he said, 'I ought to be off ...' He stood up, brushing the sand from his clothes. 'Do you know the Alpha Motel? I'll be there this evening with John Simba, if you'd like to join us.'

The sky was flushed scarlet as I strolled into town, mightily pleased with myself for being invited back to the bar where I'd drunk coffee on my first day, no longer a stranger now, but a welcome guest. Music jangled from a ghetto blaster on the windowsill and two girls were dancing together on the porch. One of them was Grace, in her silky blue dress. I entered the bar with a glad, calm heart for the first time in many months. My body no longer seemed to let me down; the sun must have been working its magic because the pain had gone from my knee. Nobody had stared at me today, or asked why I was limping. John Simba and Sid were eating from a huge metal platter, dipping chunks of roast meat into a bowl of sauce. They called me over to join them, and the food was good. For an hour or so we talked about their jobs, about Sid's boss, the bishop; about Eluminata and her ever-increasing girth. John told us there had been an attempted robbery at the school, 'foiled,' he declared, by some Form One kids, including the worst-behaved boy in the school, a boy who had, until now, been heading for expulsion. It was a good story, a heart-warming story.

Then I went to find the bathroom.

There was a long corridor with doors opening off it, presumably bedrooms for guests, and then a courtyard where washing hung on several lines. The 'bathroom' was just a hole in a dark corner, with a faucet set low in the wall. I was out of there as soon as possible, dodging between the wet sheets to find my way back. At the end of the passage a door was ajar, laughter spilling from the crack of light. I thought it must be another entrance to the bar and opened the door.

But it was a very small room, with a very private party inside. The drinkers were crowded round a table, sharing plastic beakers of fermented banana brew. All were Tanzanian, except for Heinrich and Juliet. My stomach lurched. She was sitting on his lap, one arm around his neck.

She's sitting on his lap because there isn't enough room.

Straight away she said, 'Oh, hi.' Didn't even catch her breath. Heinrich said nothing.

'What are you doing here?' I said.

'Having a drink. Want to join us?' She looked me in the eye without blinking. His hands were round her waist and he stared at me too.

'Are you kidding?'

I don't know what the Tanzanians saw; just some too-tall mzungu glowering in the doorway, I guess. One man slurred a welcome, waving his plastic mug so the liquor slopped over the side. The rest scarcely looked up.

On Zanzibar I'd burst into the room expecting to find Lou and Fidelis. I'd been wrong. Here, in Sinamani, I was wrong again, but in a different way.

I stumbled back, crashing through the wet sheets in my hurry to find the corridor that led to the bar. John Simba said, 'My friend, what is the matter? You look as though you have seen a ghost.'

I ignored him. 'Heinrich and Juliet,' I said to Sid. 'They're here.'

He looked wary. 'Ye-es. They came in about half an hour ago.'

'They're in some kind of private party and she's sitting on his fucking lap.'

Sid hesitated. 'Well...' I wanted to put my fist right through his stupid beard.

'Did you know about her and me?'

'Well ... I thought perhaps there was something going on, maybe ...'

John Simba was studying the empty plate on the table.

'Why the hell didn't you say anything?'

Other men would have got mad at me. Sid said, 'Because I thought she might have told you herself. About Heinrich.'

'*Told* me?'

'Well, they've – they've been seeing each other for years. On and off, sort of thing. He's in the Serengeti for months on end with his, um, wife, and then he comes down here for a while and they kind of take up where they left off.' Sid's face was red. 'Sorry. You obviously didn't know.'

I turned to John Simba. 'I guess everyone else in town knows?'

He was sitting up very straight, very still. 'My friend,' he observed. 'You are angry. I'm sorry.'

'Yes. Yes, you're right, I am very angry. I have to go.'

I left, ignoring their protests, ignoring Grace who said, 'Sasha?' as I pushed past her on the veranda. Once I was on the dark path, someone blocked my way, scuttling ahead of me, low down and rapid. A man with no legs, propelling himself on a wooden board with wheels. I'd seen him around town before. Instead of taking the path, I walked straight down the narrow alleys between the shacks where people lived, ploughed over rough, sandy ground and scrambled down the bank onto the beach. The tide was beginning to go out, the waves dragging the darkness down and down. The saddest, most inevitable sound.

Next day, when I arrived at the hospital they told me she was busy.

'I'll wait.'

Back home they would have called the police: There's a guy hanging around the doctor's house – says he's not going until he's seen her. He's been there for hours. We're worried he may be kind of weird.

Here, they nodded and left the weirdo to it. In fact, some woman brought me a cup of tea. She greeted me by name, so she must have been at the Christmas party, although I didn't remember her.

When Juliet came through the trees and saw me on her doorstep she jumped, but recovered pretty fast. 'Afternoon,' she said. Just like the night before, as if I was someone she hardly knew. I didn't move, didn't speak. So she changed her tone. 'And what brings you here?'

'Are you ashamed of yourself?'

She folded her arms, leaned against the wall. 'I see. I get it. You had your nose put out of joint last night. Sorry, Sasha, but I go where I like, when I like, with whoever I like, I'm afraid, and if that upsets you, if you imagined you had some kind of claim on me, I must say I'm surprised. I thought you had more sense.'

'It doesn't matter that you and Heinrich screw each other when he's away from his wife. No, what upsets me, as you put it, is your deceitfulness, Juliet. It makes my skin crawl to think I've slept with you.'

That got to her. She took a step towards me. With her mouth set in a thin line, for the first time ever she looked ugly. 'For goodness sake, you and I did it *twice*. Did you think we were going to get married? What's your problem?'

'My problem is: I find you disgusting.'

She seemed about to cry. But then she relaxed, leaned back against the bungalow again, her palms spread against the rough walls. 'You know what this is about, Sasha. This is all about whatsername on Zanzibar. Sort yourself out, get over her, get a life.'

'You're right, it's connected with Lou. But it's not about her. You've put your finger on something that's been bugging me for a long time, something about white people and how confused they feel – hold on now, you said it yourself, let me remember – *I don't like being called a saint, it makes me cringe.* So next question, Juliet, what's it all about for *you*?' I stood up. 'Don't feel you have to answer straight away, because you perhaps don't know – you're perhaps a very confused girl. I suspect you *do* like being the saint, but that's too easy here, isn't it? So most of all, never mind what you said, Juliet, you like playing God. You like to think you can save African lives and treat white men like shit. That's the best kind of thrill, isn't it? The best of both worlds.'

'Oh fuck off!' she said, which pleased me, especially as I was already on my way.

Edison delicately pointed out that my reservation lasted until the following day, the eighth of January. The Bahari was expecting a large party of Danish aid workers. 'But if you are looking for other accommodations, Sasha, they have many vacancies at the Alpha Motel.'

While I was throwing my stuff into the holdall someone knocked at my door. I hoped it would be Juliet, come to say how sorry she was. It was Sid.

'Hello,' he said. 'I just came to say I'm sorry about last night.'

'You've nothing to be sorry for.'

'I should have said something earlier. I suppose it was a conflict of loyalties. I've known Juliet for years, ever since she first came here. And I do like her, although I don't like some of the things she does.'

His politeness made me wretched. I wondered how much he'd put up with. 'Did she ever do this to you?'

He flushed. 'No. No, we were never … I mean, we've always been friends. She isn't a bad person, you know, although I can understand you might not agree, just now.'

'I'm not sure I know what good and bad are any more.'

His gaze fell on the blue holdall, sagging around its miserable load. 'Are you going?'

I explained about the Danish aid workers. 'Edison recommended the Alpha Motel.'

'Oops,' he said, and in spite of everything I laughed. Then he laughed too. 'Look – if you like, come and stay at my place. You'd be doing me a favour. I have to go away next week, and it's not good to leave the house empty. There's some dodgy characters around. Honestly, karibu sana…'

There would have been no shame in refusing. It would have been easy just to catch the next plane home. I'd been away long enough; probably people wouldn't even have noticed I'd come back early. Probably they wouldn't have noticed me at all.

Sid's bungalow was on the outskirts of Sinamani, facing the ocean but a little way inland, in its own neat plot of grass and banana trees. The corrugated iron roof gleamed in the sun, the walls were pale grey. Marigolds were planted around the veranda, and there was a double wooden front door, not carved like the old doors in town, but plain and strong, built to resist burglars since Sid so often worked away.

Inside it was orderly, armchairs placed at neat right angles to a low wooden coffee table, copies of the Guardian Weekly stacked on a window sill, the kitchen sink empty and shining, and all the mugs and wooden cooking utensils hanging from hooks screwed into shelves. It surprised me that such a shambling, scruffy guy should live in such a clean home, until he told me that his housegirl, Zeituny, came in every morning.

The framed batiks on his walls, the carved ebony figures with inscrutable faces, were top quality, far better than anything I'd seen in the tourist shops. When I commented on them he scratched his head. 'Yes. Hmm. Sometimes I wonder why I've got them, though...'

Strangest of all was the absence of any trace of family, any personal life – no photos, no objects, no letters left lying around. No evidence of a girlfriend.

There was a silence hanging in the room. I didn't know what it meant, except it was something to do with me and Sid not wanting to intrude on each other. 'Listen,' I said, 'I really appreciate this, and if there's anything I can do to help out while I'm here, please just ask.'

'Actually there is. Tomorrow I fly to Arusha, but I promised John I'd give him a lift to Dar, to pick up some *mabati* – that's iron sheets – for his library roof. Could you drive him?'

When I arrived at the school, John was waiting with Mr. Winston the telephone engineer, who greeted me like his long-lost brother, and a kid in school uniform: 'Stephen Valentino our store-keeper.' Sid's Suzuki only had a single cabin. The four of us squeezed in. At first, every time my left elbow nudged against Mr. Winston's ribs I apologised, but he talked non-stop and didn't seem to notice the elbow or the apologies. I felt relieved to be going somewhere for a reason. Everyone was in a good mood, John cracking jokes in his awesome English about his wife having 'two buns in the oven'.

'Very unlucky,' Mr. Winston pronounced. 'Isn't it, Sasha? To have twins is very bad luck.'

'What is bad luck? It is an accident of birth.'

'Life is difficult,' Stephen Valentino sighed, wedged between his headmaster and Mr. Winston.

'Difficult? My young friend, you do not know the meaning of the word.'

'When will you return to America? So soon? That's a pity. Will you come back and bring me a multiple chicken roaster?'

'Wazungu like to come here. I would build a luxury tourist lodge. I would take them to Zanzibar for day trips.'

'Where will you find the money?'

'Perhaps I will have a Western sponsor who will help me.'

'Young wazungu, they like to live in tents like the Bedouin. A camp site is what you must build.'

'Don't you want to keep Sinamani like it is? Unspoilt and peaceful?'

'Peaceful? My friend, one hundred years ago this town was the capital of East Africa. Now it is dying.'

'Because of that war you told me about? That Arab war?'

'Because of poverty.'

'If I had a multiple chicken roaster I could start my own business.'

'The tourists stay away because they know it is not safe. They have heard this is a dangerous town of many thieves.'

'I've never felt in any danger here.'

'There was a mzungu woman, and she was been attacked on the beach when it is dark – '

'Don't you know any English? How are you going to pass the Form Four examination? You are an idiot.'

'And they say she was pregnant and they take everything she had.'

'Terrible, terrible. If I had a multiple chicken roaster I should need also a refrigeration unit for keeping the chickens before roasting, how much does a refrigeration unit cost in America?'

'Mr. Sasha, is it true that American women – '

'She was not from America, she was from England.'

'Yes! American!'

'You are confused in the head, my young friend. The dead English woman is buried in the German cemetery.'

'Yeah – how come?'

'They are useless, those people. A tourist lodge is safe. That is what white people want, to be safe, and that is what I shall build.'

'You cannot, you are a fool and you have no money.'

'Why is this road in such a state?'

'Ask the Pwani council.'

'Sasha, in Tanzania we have a saying: the drunk driver is he who drives in a straight line.'

By the time we reached Dar it was midday, and the air felt like molten lava. John Simba navigated me through the back streets to a store where he was to buy his sheets of corrugated iron. We passed several hardware stores along the way, but John said they were all too expensive. Mr. Winston suddenly asked me to stop, and he ducked out of the cabin and hurried away, leaving me wondering how we would ever find him again. It seemed we weren't to return directly after John had bought his *mabati*. The sheets were stacked in the back of the pickup and young Stephen Valentino was told to sit on top of the pile, 'to guard them.' The sun's rays were scoring into the metal.

'Won't he burn his butt off?' I objected.

'He is very tough,' said John. 'Let us take some lunch.'

All afternoon we trailed round the Kariakoo, a maze of streets clogged with dust, with trash, with sunlight. There were no tourist stores selling souvenirs. We drank tea, we drank soda, we inspected, but did not buy, various electrical items: a drill, a Baby Belling, a welding torch demonstrated by a man who didn't wear safety glasses and seemed to make a point of holding his face in the sparks. We drank tea in a café that had a sign over the door saying *A. Teashop.* We visited more places selling building materials (I didn't know why, since John often remarked that he didn't even have enough money to pay staff salaries), and I was introduced to business men in Kaunda suits, in white shirts and dark ties, in dreadlocks and a T shirt expressing support for Miss Iowa 1982. John Simba struck some deals: deals which began in English but always ended in Swahili. As evening drew on, the heat lessened and I grew uneasy, wondering if I should have left Sid's pickup with that school kid; wondering, too, what it would be like to drive back along the coast road riddled with pot holes in the pitch dark. I was relieved when we turned a corner and there was the pickup, with Stephen Valentino's silhouette hunched against the cabin. No sign of Mr. Winston. 'Do you think he'll be long?'

'He shall meet us at Kunduchi.' John was in an excellent mood. 'This is very good! We shall be able to repair our library before the inspectors come and the students will be able to study again. They will have nothing to complain about. Do you know, at the end of last term they sent me a deputation. "We have had no books and no meat for five weeks," they said.'

'What did you do?'

'I thrashed the leader for his insolence, and promised them rice with their beans at the weekend.'

As soon as we stopped for Winston, we were mobbed by an end-of-the-day crowd desperate to scramble on top of the precious mabati, but John stuck his head out the window and bellowed at them until they fell away, grumbling. People kept on trying to hitch all the way out of the city. Mr. Winston screamed at me to stop for one guy who he claimed was his *ndugu*, his relative, but John Simba refused, telling the man: 'You are too large, my friend.' We left the guy ruefully stroking his belly by the roadside. John finally relented for two scrawny little kids, I didn't even see them, would have driven past if he hadn't said angrily, 'Look at those boys! They should not be walking here at this time.' When he waved at them to join Stephen on his corrugated perch, their faces lit up as if we'd offered them velvet cushions.

An hour later, he asked me to drop them off. 'Their village is just a kilometre from Sinamani. They can walk the rest of the way.'

It was dark. 'Are we really almost home?'

'Ya, we are at the German cemetery. A journey of some five minutes from here, that is all.'

There was a racket behind us, shrill voices arguing. Stephen's face appeared at a crazy angle in the passenger window. He said, 'They are scared of ghosts. They say they do not want to walk from this place.'

'Ghosts do not exist,' John Simba scoffed. 'People like to scare themselves, that is all. People who are trying to evade their responsibilities in life.'

Mr. Winston asked slyly, 'Do you believe in ghosts, Mr. Sasha?'

'No.'

Only living ones. The thought came clear as water: I was haunted. Immediately I said, 'Where exactly do these kids live? I'm taking them home.'

The journey took another half hour. The kids, it was hinted to me, had lied about their address. Nobody was pleased. I drove doggedly, until the boys thumped on the cabin roof for me to stop. Even then, I waited until a door opened and the brief glow of lamplight revealed faces, arms drawing the children inside. Darkness again. No more talk. The main beam swept the road, a lunarscape.

When at last we arrived back in town, Mr. Winston, who had been snoring, woke up and asked to be dropped by the bus station. At the school I helped unload and carry the iron sheets to the shed where they were to be stored. John Simba thanked me profusely; I'd been forgiven for the detour.

'You're welcome,' I said. 'Guess I'll head back to Sid's.'

'Goodnight,' Stephen Valentino grinned. 'Be careful of ghosts.'

John Simba snorted. 'Ignore this young fool.'

A week later, for the third time in my life I woke and knew something was badly wrong with my body – my neck ached, my head ached and I couldn't lift it from the pillow; coloured fish darted across my field of vision. Sid was going away again, so I forced myself to get up. He was in the kitchen, and winced when he saw me. 'You're sick. Do you want me to take you to the hospital before I go?'

'No.'

'Look, you need to see a doctor. It doesn't have to be Juliet.'

'I said no.'

He shrugged. 'Don't let anyone borrow the Suzuki, but I'm leaving the keys on the hook by the door, in case you change your mind about going to the hospital.'

I went back to bed, heard the bishop's car arrive to take Sid away, and then my fever and I subsided into each other's tormenting company. At times throughout the day Zeituny would stand over me and shake her head, then tell me to drink more water. She came in again before she left, but I pretended to be asleep.

Did I sleep? When the blows on Sid's front door made the whole bungalow quiver I may have been dreaming, and maybe that's why they seemed too terrifying, at first, to answer. Long afterwards, John Simba told me that he banged on the door for several minutes, peered through the dark mesh at the bedroom window and saw my hulking

166

body beneath the bed clothes, thought perhaps I was dead. But he kept up the blows on the door because he had to, and I lay resentfully for a while, taking them as a personal insult. My head, however, seemed to approve of them in a pathetic, docile way, throbbing in harmony with the *Bam! Bam! Bam!*

A lucid flash: Sid might not be pleased to come home and find his door destroyed. So I got up, knowing it was the only way I'd stop that racket once and for all. John Simba was on the veranda. 'Sasha, I'm sorry to disturb you.' His voice was too light, too high. 'My wife is very sick. Please can you help us?'

'Excuse me?' I put my hand up against the doorframe so I could rest my head in the crook of my elbow. A sly whiff of sweat came from my armpit. He kept his eyes on mine.

'Sasha, please, you must drive us to the hospital. Sasha, we must go *now*. Do you understand?' It was strange to hear him giving orders, as if I were one of his students. My legs buckled. I staggered to a chair, sat down, and saw how he struggled between anger and panic.

'I'm sick too,' I said. 'I'm really sorry but … you have to ask someone else. I can't help you, John.'

'There is nobody else with a car.'

Bullshit. All those jeeps and pickups and Peugeots careering through the quiet streets of Sinamani, churning up the dust. Ah, but who owned them? Much later, he told me how he had been down to the Bahari where the Land Cruisers were parked up together like rhino at a water hole. Every single one belonged to a mzungu, and he hung around in the trees at the bottom of that track, working up courage to beg a white stranger for help, until Edison said, 'Go to Sid's.'

'I know Sid is away. Only you can help, Sasha.' Every time I looked up, there he was, staring right into my eyes.

'Sid said …' What had Sid said? Don't let anyone borrow the Suzuki? What was that supposed to mean?

167

'Sasha, you know my wife is expecting twins. She is in terrible pain. I am worried the babies will come too early.'

'I don't know where Sid left the car keys.' I began fumbling round the kitchen, bumping into obstacles: stove, water filter, table, chairs. In a basket full of vegetables I found an eggplant, cool and curved and smooth. I wanted to keep it in my palm, not drive miles through the bush to Juliet. John was hovering at my shoulder, reluctant to touch anything of Sid's. 'Are these the keys to his pickup?' He pointed to the hook on the wall.

'Yes, they are.' They dangled from my fingers, then dropped to the floor with a silly clatter. I stared as he bent to snatch them up.

'Please hurry,' he said, his voice still so calm.

Outside the moonlight made everything look pale and sick. I remember wondering if I could walk across the grass to the Suzuki, but I don't remember the walk itself, just stabbing at the door with one key, then another.

'Let me,' said John, but his fingers were shaking too. He opened the door and I lumbered into the driver's seat, slumped stupidly over the wheel as I listened to the frantic tapping at the passenger window. When I leaned across to let him in, my head whirled heavily.

'Sasha, please drive as fast as you can, *please*.' Even my stewed brain could tell he was trying not to sound rude. All the way across town he carried on talking: the babies weren't due for another month, then this afternoon she began to have pain, by evening the neighbours were saying, you must take her to the hospital. I wasn't bothered by this. My only concern was that every time I pressed my foot down on the gas my leg felt like it was taking a dip in outer space. But the nothingness beneath my feet was made up for by the road: a mean road, full of ruts and potholes, and I winced and whimpered all the way to the school, where I drove right past John's house. 'Stop!' he roared, forgetting to be polite.

Eluminata was on a chair in the doorway, swathed in kangas. Small children goggled at the dumb-ass behind the wheel as John and some women helped her into the cabin. She did not greet me, but sat between us, silent, gulping from time to time in such a way I could tell this was her way of coping with pain. With an effort I asked her, 'Are you OK?'

'Not good.'

I turned the key in the ignition, released the clutch too quickly and the Suzuki jolted and stalled. She cried out; John put his arm around her shoulders.

Into the lunarscape – were we delivering two small boys who were scared of ghosts? I had forgotten where the road led. Past the ruby ring. 'Please Sasha, drive quickly,' John muttered from time to time like a prayer, and that was fine because once my foot was down on the gas I was reluctant to lift it again. Too much effort. Truly, truly fine, while we were rushing down the straight dirt track, tyres walloping the ruts, in fact a great feeling, like flying, and then we came to the narrow bridge over the swamp, and we flew.

We flew over spires of sisal plants, dreaming into the starry sky.

A barrier. There must have been a barrier. Or maybe just the lurch in my belly as I realised we were going over. A downward tug of being out of control. Nothing but bodies, soft painful bodies knocking against me as the Suzuki rolled over the side of the bridge.

Who screamed?

It could have been me. My left knee a flare of pain.

A deeper groan, like a creature in distress.

In April after the rains, this bridge would span a torrent, they told me later. In January, it was a stinking morass of mud and weed.

As I sat on the bank, John dragged Eluminata up. She had been lying face down in the mud. He brought her up streaming, her kangas clinging to her like a peacock's bedraggled tail. Blue-grey, weird in the moonlight. She was crying. Tanzanians don't cry. Inside my head the cold pulse of fever. Maybe I was crying too.

We sat there, the three of us, John with his wet arms wrapped around his wife. How hot cold I felt. The sky, the scornful stars. Clear enough to see mosquitoes trailing their hair-thin legs behind them in the air, their whine inside my ear.

At dawn, a young kid swinging a bucket came over the bridge. He stood still for a moment, then walked hesitantly towards us, his eyes scared. John spoke to him, he turned and began to walk away. Then John shouted and the child ran.

Men arrived in a pickup. They lifted me into the back and I lay on some sacks that stank of animal fodder. I threw up a few times, and feebly tried to wipe away the streaks of vomit.

The hospital. Juliet running to help Eluminata tenderly out of the cabin. Eluminata gulping, gasping, the kangas around her black with blood. Me, hanging over the side of the pickup in case I puked again.

After John and Eluminata had been taken inside I lay on my own for some time, until a man in a stained white coat came back for me, and led me stumbling into a ward.

'Do you have any cuts?' he said coldly. He thrust a thermometer into my mouth. 'Lie on the bed.'

The sheet was tucked in too tight. I tried to pull it loose, then gave up and lay on top of the bed with my eyes closed.

A familiar voice said: 'So. Yet another little twat who thinks he's too *hard* to take malaria prophylactics.'

Juliet's face, suspended above mine at a slant, her hair looped behind her ears, her mouth talking, talking, talking. 'Don't you think we've got enough to do without over-indulged white men collapsing on our doorstep? Haven't

170

you done enough damage? Hey? Why don't you just go home and get out of our way?'

There was someone else the other side of the bed. Grace, taking my pulse. Calmly she wiped a damp cloth across my brow, like Musa did on Zanzibar. I just managed to hold back the tears.

The two women rolled me onto my side as if I was a baby, and Juliet jabbed a needle in my ass. Dimly I registered that this was humiliating.

The worst moment of all was not when I woke on that green bed to find John Simba sitting next to me, because the sight of him brought me pleasure. The worst came a second later, when I remembered. At first he didn't notice that I had woken. His eyes sagged with sadness. Then he saw my hand creep across the pillow, and he smiled.

'How do you feel? Let me get you some water.'

He took a blue plastic beaker from the windowsill, walked the length of the ward (why had they put me at the end, so far away from everyone?) and went out. He was gone for quite a while. I wondered if this was revenge: you want water? Well, you can't have any. But he came back. He must have been to some place where they kept a supply of filtered water for the weak bowels of white men. Again, a cup was held to my lips and again, helplessly, I drank. I knew what I had to say. 'I'm very sorry.' The croak let me down; I could just as well have been playing for sympathy.

He sighed, looked at his hands. 'Ya. My wife lost our kids.'

That was what he called them: that casual, throwaway word. He spoke again. 'It was God's will.'

I had no answer for that. Let him believe it, I thought. Or maybe he's trying to make me feel better.

'How is Eluminata?'

'She will be fine. Dr. Juliet says she can go home at the weekend.'

'That's good.' The awkwardness between us was thick as a sandbank.

Then he asked, 'When will you be leaving?'

'As soon as I can get a flight.'

His eyes widened. 'No! No, Sasha.' How come he sounded so reproachful? 'I meant, when will you be coming out of hospital?'

'I don't know. Soon, I guess. Whatever, I'll be heading back to the States. It's high time.' Now I was talking like a Tanzanian. Anything, rather than sound like someone who had no choices left.

How polite he was. How hard he tried to persuade me to stay, 'Just a little longer. Your family will want to hear that you had a good time in Tanzania.'

I said nothing.

'Although,' he faltered, 'of course they will be happy to see you. Your mother especially.'

But I knew that she would be unhappy to see my unhappiness, and that she would want to look after me, make sad promises that my leg would heal in time, be good as new, that I'd get over Lou, that these few months in Africa had been just a temporary obstacle to the sunny progress of my life. And it would be unbearable, because I would never be able to make her understand what a grave mistake I had made in coming here.

Later, Grace returned. For a few minutes she was a model professional, taking my pulse and temperature, writing notes. Then she sat on the end of the bed and said, in her lovely velvet voice, 'I hear you are leaving us.'

'Yeah. I have to go home.'

'Don't you like Tanzania?'

'Of course I do, I like Tanzania very much.'

'How can you like it if you want to go? I think you are a liar, Sasha.' She persisted delightfully. 'You don't like it here. Why not? What is wrong with us?'

I reached out to take her hand, and she let me cling on while I cried.

A grave mistake. But even so, I would miss the subdued streets, the platinum morning sands, the ocean's invisible presence at night. I would miss relentlessly cheerful music jangling from massive, ancient cassette players. I would miss the black, syrupy tea. I would even miss the constant chorus of kids murmuring or sniggering or calling out, *mzungu, mzungu* …

I can still picture myself, lying on that hospital bed, a white mound beneath a green sheet. I can picture Grace giving me a sip of water, and then a tablet, and then another sip of water. I know now, what was wrong with me was neither a knee injury nor malaria. It was the inability to see what was right under my stupid nose.

I didn't say goodbye to Juliet, just as I hadn't said goodbye to Lou. If I believed in closure and all that crap, I might have become convinced that this would screw me up even further. But walking away is no bad thing, if you can do it. Walking away in silence takes some courage. I think Sid appreciated that. When I told him, 'I have to go now. I've done enough damage,' he did not put up much of an argument.

'Sasha, it wasn't your fault. I'd have done the same as you, I can never say no to people.'

'But did you ever crash a car and cause two deaths?'

He looked away. 'You can't say that. What if you hadn't taken her? She might just as well have lost the twins at home, they've said so themselves.'

Sid was right. Even so, I couldn't stop remembering the way the mudsoaked, bloodsoaked cloths dragged around Eluminata's legs as she lay on that bank. And the memory kept turning into another: Zanzibar. A line of men moving slowly towards a chair. Malaika in her coffin. The mzungu who did not know what to say.

173

*

On the last morning, as I was getting into the bishop's jeep that Sid had borrowed to take me to the airport, a small figure came running, brandishing a cylinder of tightly rolled newspaper. And John Simba was smiling, a smile so full of kindness and regret, it made me despair. 'Sasha, this is for you. It is just a very small gift. You must come back to Tanzania. Next time, you will be our *mgeni*, and stay with me and my wife.'

I figured *mgeni* meant guest. But there was more to it than that.

Once the plane was in the air I unwrapped the parcel. A kanga, purple, yellow, pink and orange; the crazy colours of fever. I shook out the cloth to find the proverb at the bottom. *Mtoto akilie, mpe wembe.* If the child cries, give it a razor blade.

I sat back, wondering what had happened to those still-born babies. Did they get a funeral too? Surely, if an English woman could be buried in a corner of the German cemetery in Sinamani, there must be a resting-place somewhere for Eluminata's twins?

Blockhouse

On the day the Germans arrived, we dined on chicken and rice: the meat tender, the grains fragrant and steaming. Cook had done his work well. But as soon as our meal was over, I began to hunger for an apple. I saw the fruit clearly in my mind's eye, its stippled rosiness spreading from the stalk, deepening over the curve to crimson, then fading, merging into orange-yellow, then yellow-green, then palest translucent citrine around its puckered star-remnant of blossom. Just for an instant I tasted its tart juiciness on my tongue, until Alisha said, 'What's the matter, mama?' – and the precious flavour vanished. I tried to explain but it was useless; you cannot describe the taste of an apple to someone who has never even seen one.

The apple has stayed with me for months. I have imagined it on the tree, gently swaying from its branch, resting on my palm before I plucked it. I have imagined the apple sliced in half: two white hearts on a blue-flowered china plate that belonged to my grandmother. Whenever I bite into the heavy-scented flesh of a mango, that apple torments me. It will not go away, and neither will the Germans whom the Khatib calls 'our visitors'. Why do they unsettle me so much, when they are no different from Father Bauer who was born in Frankfurt, or Brother Josef from Köln? Why, for heaven's sake, should German soldiers remind me constantly of home?

At first it was a quiet, slow invasion. Alisha and I were sitting in the shade of the schoolhouse baraza, drinking our tea that is such a reward after a hot, frustrating afternoon's teaching, when the cup froze half way to my lips at the sight of two men, tall, thin and fair, walking unsteadily up

India street, bearing a stretcher on which lay a pile of rags. The men were like etiolated seedlings, badly in need of water and suffering from too much light. Their eyes were scanning the street, yet they did not notice me in my black buibui. As they passed by, the pile of rags moved, revealed a blonde head with wild, pale eyes, and a hand, feebly waving a sheaf of papers.

Alisha turned to me, astonished. 'Wazungu!'

I took a gulp of tea and scalded my throat. 'Well, yes. That much is obvious.'

'Do you know them, mama?'

'Don't be stupid. I haven't the faintest idea who they are.'

She nodded. 'If you had known them, you would have greeted each other.'

By nightfall the news was all around town: how this *Kapitassa*, young, German and very, very sick, had come to proclaim his new territories, signed away to him with illiterate crosses for the price of a few muskets; signed away to the *Docha stafrika gazella shafta*, as the people pronounce it. Soon afterwards the Germans erected noticeboards, blazoning their company's title across the town with promises of prosperity and success for Sinamani.

I came to this town when it was at its lowest ebb in the aftermath of cholera. Since then, I have seen it grow and flourish in its own way. The streets are narrow, though not so narrow as on Zanzibar, and they broaden as they approach the sea. All along India Street there are shops run by Hindi merchants, of whom Mr. Sewa Haji is the most prosperous and popular – it is thanks to him that we have desks and chairs at our school, and copy books for the children to practise their scrawl, and chalk for me, and a good supply of needle and thread for Alisha. 'You are my neighbours,' he said. 'I must look after my little neighbours.'

The children adore him, the youngest ones, as soon as they are dismissed, running to play in his compound and beg sweets. Sewa Haji's shop is at the big crossroads, opposite the market where we can buy goat meat, rice, salt, beaten copper pans, woven mats, and palm oil which is the pale orange hue of apricots, but a hundred times more pungent. Spiritan Brothers come from the Mission with fresh eggs to barter; even the Arabs are not above sending their slaves to sell mangoes and pomegranates from their gardens. Even the Khatib, when he has time, takes pleasure in scrutinizing each fruit as it ripens on the tree, selecting the best for our table, ordering the gardener to gather the rest for market. To market everyone comes, sooner or later, whether highborn or low: the Diwan himself and his fat, ambling wives, the Arabs, the Hindi shopkeepers, the Brothers, the native Swahili people, the freed slaves, the slaves and the slaves of the slaves. This is Sinamani: a raucous, slovenly hotchpotch of African and Arab, Muslim, Hindu and Christian, and although not all of these people are cordial to the mzungu woman who has lived all these years amongst them, there are plenty who welcome me for what I have tried to contribute to this town. Just as they have welcomed our German visitors; first, the company men, the Deutsch-Ostafrikanische Gesellschaft representatives, and now, the German soldiers.

Yesterday I saw one of the officers with his wife and his little girl; the child perhaps five years old, running around the marketplace, merry as could be. Her mother picked up a fan woven from palm leaves and wafted it over the child's hair: a nimbus white and fine as a dandelion clock. When they entered a tea-house I lingered in the shadows of the porch, wondering how they would manage to be served. They managed very easily. He spoke English to the Hindi proprietor: 'You have tea? You have coffee? Tea only?' His English not quite perfect, but so confident. 'No lemon? Then please, add plenty of sugar' – and in Swahili he urged the boy preparing their tea, '*Weka! Weka!*' and then they all smiled and murmured fondly as the little girl laughed to see the boy pouring her tea from one glass to another, back and forth, back and forth, to make it cool enough for her to drink. I wonder if that little girl misses apples.

I wonder if the wife, in her white lace soiled with red dust, misses elegant gowns and noble architecture. She must become accustomed to a new kind of beauty. I have learned to tolerate the extremes of life in the streets leading off this marketplace. The Arab houses are grand limestone constructions, each with its carved front door and shady baraza where visitors are entertained. But in amongst these houses are the shacks and steaming rubbish dumps of the Swahili people. This is how we coexist, rich and poor, side by intimate side. There is always music somewhere: nasal singing, the low confabulation of drums. I have come to like this music.

Wherever you may be in Sinamani, if you turn north you will be admonished by the Mission church tower, dark against the sky. The mango trees in Father Bauer's avenue have grown tall and vigorous, healthier than the Spiritans themselves, who die all the time, apart from the Abbé who seems immortal, and a few other stalwarts, dear Felicien among them. The Brothers are weaker than the Sisters, African and Indian nuns from Réunion, who wear habits of Morning Glory blue, and white wimples which, from a distance, look like the heads of strange birds. I love those blue habits. I seek colour wherever I can. Our garden, like all Arab gardens, is hidden within the heart of the tembe like a cache of jewels: roses are our rubies, heliotrope our amethysts, and the leaves of the camellia shine brighter than any emeralds. On my way to school in the morning I watch the native women going about their business wrapped in cloths of lime, scarlet, mustard yellow, and if only I could shed this black buibui I would gladly join them. At each day's end I revel in the molten carmine of sunset, until dark spots swim before my eyes and I have to look away.

On the shore, there is little colour. Everything is exposed against the null spectrum of dun, beige, white. Shouts and screams echo further down the beach. I do not look; I try not to listen. I fix my gaze on the sea, whose numbing repetitions seem to become the thundering of blood in my own head. And sometimes, when the sun is fierce, a million lights *dart*, *stab*, *vanish* on the waves, and terror drives me back to the town, where our 'visitors' are dismantling everything that has become familiar to me.

The urchins who scavenge on the rubbish tips for morsels of rotting food think the Germans figures of fun, fascinating diversions from the gross, random misfortune of their daily existence. They dart behind these tall blonde men, shout mzungu! and run away shrieking in fearful glee. To Bibi Hussein who sells onions at market, the Germans are customers, no different from Indian, Arab or Swahili. To the fishermen dragging their sea-battered dhows up the beach, these foreigners are stranger than the strangest fish that ever swam up from the depths of the ocean: mottled pink skin, scaly with sunburn; eyes, blue slivers squeezing out the light, or round, popping with surprise.

To anyone with power, the Germans are a threat.

The first blockhouse appeared overnight at the crossroads near our school. I wondered out loud, 'Why on earth have they left a big lump of limestone in the middle of the street?' Then Alisha, circling cautiously, discovered its door and the one small window. The blockhouse was big enough to hold one man, standing upright. Good luck to him, I said, trying to make light of my anxiety. As we walked on, we found the white, squat structures springing up all over town. 'Like mushrooms,' Alisha said.

They are the talk of the school. 'Have you seen the little houses, teacher?' my younger pupils clamoured. 'Are they for chickens? Do they have chickens in Germany?' The older ones showed off their knowledge. 'The Germans are going to hide in them and shoot us through the windows, *bam! bam! bam!*

'Don't be silly,' I scoffed, but of course that is exactly what the Germans meant to do, and they did it that very night, killing a slave who was unlucky enough or stupid enough to be walking towards a blockhouse with a rifle in his hand. I tried to make Felicien agree how outrageous it was. 'He wasn't even pointing it at anyone. Apparently he was using the thing as a walking-stick, and yet they killed him!'

Felicien said gravely that it was a warning. 'Haven't you heard about the new gun registration laws?'

I said, 'What do they think we're going to do, start a war? We should tell the Germans: we don't need to fight; you won't last.'

For they seem so pale and feeble, wilting in the heat. I could warn them: it will be much, much worse than this. They will come to know heat like a shroud: a winding sheet of heat that you must wear as you stumble along. To hear them talking to each other in their own peculiar tongue (sometimes so like Arabic, that ratchety choking at the back of the throat), you can tell they are excited, and uncertain, shocked by their own new-found power. They look around constantly: appraising, calculating. The other day I saw some of them walking down a narrow street, the narrowest street in Sinamani, and one spread his arms like an eagle extending his wings, and with his fingertips he prodded the buildings on either side of the street as if trying to push them over, and he said something, shaking his head, which made his companion snigger.

The rifle carried by that slave was of a type never seen before in Sinamani, with a rosewood stock in pristine condition, gleaming with oil. The man's blood gleamed too. People gathered around his corpse and peered at the blockhouse with its invisible sniper, but none dared approach. I know all this because the next morning some relatives of the dead man brought the rifle to our tembe. Alisha received it at the door. 'Why?' I demanded. 'What are we supposed to do with it? We don't want any Germans taking a pot shot at us, thank you!'

'They would never shoot *you*, mama.'

She's probably right. But it's galling to admit that I would be saved by the colour of my skin.

'Well anyway,' I said, 'I don't want the horrid thing near me. Clean it up, Alisha, and get the servants to hide it somewhere.'

When the Khatib comes back, I will ask him why the rifle has been brought to us. Perhaps it is because he is rich enough to afford the registration fee. It would not please him, paying money to the visitors, but on the other hand he might take some satisfaction in displaying his wealth, which has accrued considerably since he stopped working for the Sultan. When I first entered this house it was austere, with none of the rich furnishings and ornament that surrounded the Khatib in the Beit al Sahel. Over time our home has changed. Where once were plain floors and walls, now there are carpets (beaten daily to rid them of dust) and sandalwood chests, ivory statuettes of elephants and pouting boys, chandeliers, shelves laden with glass and china – it is a miniature House of Wonders, if stories from Zanzibar are to be believed.

I confess, I prefer emptiness. Sometimes I sit in the cool space of the garden room, breathe the scent of mimosa, enjoy the play of sunlight on leaves through the three arched windows. I sit there whenever I can, although even the garden room is no longer quite so peaceful now it contains Kasuku's cage. I hid there today, after I'd lost my temper with the kitchen boy. He was winnowing rice, jiggling the flat basket to and fro to make the chaff slip through the criss-cross weave, and at the same time gossiping over his shoulder with Cook, so he did not see three grains of rice fly up into the air and fall to the ground, and I shouted at him, 'Watch what you're doing!'

Then I whispered, 'My God. Three grains of rice. Has it come to this?'

The boy scrabbled in the dust to find the grains, glancing up at me and mumbling, 'Very sorry, very sorry mama.' He wasn't asking for forgiveness, he was showing sympathy for the wretched state I was in. The other servants had paused in their work, astounded by my outburst. Probably they wondered if I was going to beat him. I hope I shall never sink so low. But *three* grains of rice...

Of all the Khatib's gifts to me, Kasuku is the strangest. 'Now you shall never want for English conversation,' he told me kindly. But Kasuku must have learned her English from sailors, for she can be both aggressive – 'Break your head against the wall!' – and disconcertingly lewd, murmuring with a wink: 'I am a devil between the sheets.' She lives in the garden room, but I keep most of the gifts in my bedchamber. A necklace of intricate ivory beads, a jet bangle, from the south a Makonde carving of a tree whose trunk is a swarming mass of human figures clambering over each other, a needlecase made from the horn of a rhinoceros, a globe which the Khatib likes to spin and scrutinize. And fifteen chess sets, one for every year of our life together. Felicien couldn't believe it. 'Fifteen chess sets? Isn't one enough?'

'There'll be another next year, you'll see,' I said, then added slyly, 'If you're still here.' It was a nasty jibe, and unwarranted, for Felicien is not like the other Spiritans. Many die within a few months of their arrival, falling victim to blackwater fever, or tuberculosis or biliosis. But Felicien is strong. The first time I ever saw him he was in the marketplace, trying out his Swahili on the old woman who sells palm oil. Newly-arrived Spiritans usually wear an expression of constant alarm, as the reality of their vocation strikes in the form of dysentery, sending them hobbling for the bushes with their soutanes clutched close about their knees. But this young man had ruddy cheeks, glowing with health and pleasure as the bibi, overcome by his charm, made him a gift of three onions.

'Isn't his Swahili good!' Alisha marvelled. I said, 'He won't be grinning like that for long.'

A week later I was annoyed to find I could not command the attention of my pupils as I usually do. They were twisting in their seats to look out of the windows, giggling and muttering whenever I turned to the blackboard until at last I snapped, in English, 'Oh, for pity's sake, what's the matter with you all? Juma, do you have a crick in your neck?'

Juma is my outstanding student, always eager to learn. He looked guilty. 'It is the race, mama. We are all too excited about the race.'

'What race?'

'The obstacle race, mama, on the beach.'

At first I thought it must be some game they had concocted amongst themselves. Then I wondered where they got the word 'obstacle' from.

After I had dismissed the children, I happened to be taking a walk along the shore (sometimes I crave sea air after a stifling day in the schoolroom) when unfamiliar sounds began to drift towards me on the breeze: not shouts, not screams, but distant laughter, that came from a crowd swirling with activity like an ant's nest. As I drew closer I saw many children clamouring for the attention of the stocky, black-clad Spiritan. Sacks with the seams ripped apart had been tacked together loosely to form a long tunnel down which children were taking turns to wriggle –

the whole contraption looked like a snake swallowing a rat. Other children were running back and forth, scooping up water from a rockpool in coconut shells and pouring it into gourds. A third pair were skipping up and down two parallel hopscotch courts drawn in the sand.

Three sharp blasts on a whistle. The children stood stock-still. 'All change!' cried the Spiritan, and smooth as clockwork each group changed places with its neighbour. A truly ingenious obstacle race, planned to allow everyone to participate at once, not to mention the crowds of urchins, fishermen and old people gathered round to cheer them on.

'Welcome, mama!' Juma danced past me on the hopscotch court. 'Welcome to see our obstacle race!'

The Spiritan didn't notice me, too busy marshalling the children into orderly lines for the sack race, and glancing now and then at a large silver watch draped over a rock. Yes, you had better keep your eye on it or else it will be stolen.

Alisha, who was standing at the finishing line, didn't see me either, and I had to smile at her excitement. Then I tapped her smartly on the back. 'Alisha, haven't you got work to do?'

She turned to me, her face flushed. 'Oh, mama, Juma is so fast! Really, I think his team will win.'

'It's a shame I must spoil your fun,' I said, 'but I need you at home.'

Felicien is as perceptive as he is sturdy, so maybe he intuited my resentfulness. At any rate, he turned up a few days later at three o'clock, when I was tidying the schoolroom and wondering gloomily whether there was any hope of my pupils ever grasping that the plural of child is not 'childs'. I became aware of someone standing at the open door. 'Hodi?' he enquired, in the African way. 'I hope I'm not interrupting your work?' And his voice had the flat, homely, unmistakeable tones of Northern England. My face must have been a picture. He chuckled. 'Yes, I'm a Yorkshireman. Born but not entirely bred. Brother Felicien.' He held out his hand.

'What are you doing *here?*' Then I remembered my manners. 'Forgive me, Brother.'

'It's alright. I have the advantage; the children told me all about you. This is a grand little school you have here.' He was looking around, taking in the rickety desks, the blackboard covered in sums. Why had nobody told me about him? Perhaps because they did not know the significance. Perhaps because to them, he was just another mzungu Brother. Perhaps even the Khatib, who knows everyone, did not realise there was a Yorkshireman in Sinamani.

I collected my wits, invited him to sit. His solid body looked comical on the small chair. Comical, and poignant. Felicien has a round face, hazel eyes, black, curling hair. He doesn't look altogether English, but his father died before he was born and his mother was French. One day, when he was eight years old, an uncle took Felicien down to the carpenter's workshop, and the child planed a piece of wood perfectly – a natural talent. Then, to France, and school. His vocation came at fifteen: 'My great gift from God.' He always knew he would be a missionary, and come to Africa.

He didn't enquire about my background. I was grateful for his discretion, and embarrassed by it. Instead, he asked all about my little school and said, in his candid way, 'The children love it here; you're doing a fine job.' Then he surprised me. 'Could I help you sometimes? Help teach the children?'

'We are not a Christian establishment,' I replied. 'They are all Muslims, you know. We tell no Bible stories here. Besides, don't you have quite enough work at the Mission school?'

If he thought I was ungracious, he didn't show it. 'Oh yes!' he said. 'Plenty of work! But we Spiritans are your guests. The people of Sinamani have made us welcome, and it's good we should all help each other out. So I'd love to teach your lads a bit of carpentry now and then.'

Unnoticed by either of us, Alisha had come in. She clapped her hands and exclaimed, 'Wonderful! This is just what we were saying, mama, that our boys must learn to work with their hands.'

And so I bleated, 'You would be very welcome,' and he beamed, and said as soon as he had permission from Father Bauer he would return.

The prospect appalled me. I did not want this jolly Englishman coming to *my* school, that *I* had created. I did not want him delighting *my* children and filling their heads with such nonsense as obstacle races. I did not want him to remind me of England. Surely the Khatib would balk at a Christian Brother teaching our pupils? I tried to put out of my head his cordial friendship with Father Bauer, who would call to me across the marketplace, 'Please give my greetings to your husband!' Sometimes the Khatib even visited the Mission.

But neighbourliness was one thing, education quite another. He would soon put a stop to Felicien's plan.

'Excellent!' said the Khatib. 'Just what the children need! A craft of real use to them.'

I did my best to dissuade him. What if the children should neglect their reading and writing? What if they stole Brother Felicien's tools, for they would certainly try – but he was adamant. 'That young man,' he said, 'has already impressed the Sultan. We are fortunate to have him in Sinamani.'

It seems Sultan Seyyid Barghash, hearing reports of Felicien's skill, commissioned him to make a rosewood cabinet which so delighted the Sultan that he invited the young man to Zanzibar: an invitation which Felicien modestly and properly declined. The Khatib laughed when I said, 'But he's only been here five minutes!'

'Yes, and see how much he has achieved.'

So I had Felicien foisted upon me, and despite my determination to hate him, I couldn't. His success with the children caused me no jealousy, but pain, real pain, from the knowledge that I could never hope to secure their hearts as he did. His serenity was perplexing not only to me, but to all of us, since he neither feared death nor longed for home. Only once did I manage to unsettle him. He was clearing away the bent nails, sawdust and splinters after his lesson, when I asked him, 'What's your real name?' and in his surprise he dropped a handful of chippings.

'My *real* name?'

'Yes. I should like to know what you were called before you became Brother Felicien.'

He looked away. 'David. My name was David.'

'Were you sorry to lose it?'

'Oh no. That's all in the past. No, I don't miss anything. Why should I? This is where I'm supposed to be. My life is better here than ever it was in England.'

And he meant it. Felicien is never angry, or unkind, or unhappy. He swelters in his black soutane and laughs at the cruel sun; he tolerates my clumsy pupils with cheerful encouragement; he is tireless in visiting the sick, teaching, making simple chairs and tables for people who have not one stick of furniture to their name. He has learned Swahili, has picked up a smattering of Arabic, in French he is fluent, and he is the son of a Pocklington blacksmith.

I was with him yesterday when we witnessed something I have never seen before, something that disturbed me. On our way back from the house of a native woman who had fever, Felicien and I passed a group of women and girls returning from the freshwater stream, each with a full gourd balanced on her head, singing with their usual airy grace – then one girl tripped over a stone. As she struggled to regain her balance the gourd rocked once, twice, rolled off her head and her precious water filled the sunlight, rising, rising like a glimpse of angels' wings before it spattered on the sandy ground. The women shrieked in horror. 'Oops!' Felicien cried. She, drenched, began to weep for her long walk back to the stream. Felicien rushed over. 'Don't cry,' he said. 'We'll give you water at the Mission, then you won't have to walk all that way again. Don't cry.'

That is the difference between Felicien and me. To him, the disaster was simply an opportunity for kindness. To him there are no bad omens. But I have never before seen a woman spill water, not once in all my time in Africa. Sixteen years. Never once. And when that gourd wobbled and rolled and fell, losing its precious cargo, all I could think was: another sign.

Today we gave Kasuku her freedom. Alisha, who believes Kasuku is possessed by a demon, begged me not to do it, but Felicien and I teased her and jeered at her and eventually she agreed to help us. We were in the long, bare garden room where Kasuku spends her solitary hours, entertained only by her reflection in the mirror. At the far end of the room are three narrow, glassless arches that look out onto our jewel-garden. Late afternoon sun streams through these windows, casting ellipses of light on the floor, tormenting poor Kasuku with the radiance of freedom. Felicien said, 'You know what? If it weren't for those windows she could have a high old time in here.'

So Alisha stood on a chair and pinned muslin sheeting against the window frames, leaving no gaps for escape. I opened the cage door. For a moment, Kasuku paused, her eyes glittering with suspicion as if to say, 'Is this a trap?'

But when you've lived ten years in one prison, any other is preferable. She shrugged – shivered – and cast herself into the air, soaring up to the ceiling, Felicien whooping and whirling beneath her, Alisha shrieking in a pretence of fear, and down swooped Kasuku to thrust a fury of feathers at Alisha's face; the next instant up again, describing a parabola over our heads and, 'Go on, Kasuku!' I found myself shouting, 'Go on!' Then she noticed those incandescent arches of gauze and light. At the middle window she hovered, knowing there was no way out. So she veered away and skimmed another arc the length of the room, splattering vengeful blots beneath her as she went. A grey-green pellet hit Felicien's black soutane, but he cared nothing; this is a man who cradles typhoid patients in his arms and blesses them as they vomit. How we laughed and dodged Kasuku's missiles! How joyously we passed the long afternoon. How oblivious we were to the door opening, and the little servant girl slipping in. The child tugged Alisha's sleeve. 'He's back!'

Alisha and I froze. Felicien turned, puzzled. Only Kasuku continued her airborne capers.

'Impossible,' I snapped. 'He left only last week; it's impossible he should return so soon.' Alisha was already at the windows to pull the muslins down, but Felicien put out his hand to stop her – 'Don't! She'll fly out!' and he took something from the leather pouch on his belt. 'Kasuku, Kasuku,' he crooned, unfolding a scrap of paper, sprinkling sunflower seeds into his palm as he crossed the room to stand by the open cage door. Poor Kasuku didn't know which to choose: her freedom or her treat. She flew frantically from one end of the room to the other, hurled herself one last time at the window, and then plummeted down to the cage where he was swift to bundle her in and secure the catch. From behind the bars her scratchy little voice muttered, 'Damn you all to hell and back again!'

Alisha yanked down the muslins, one, two, three, scattering pins everywhere.

When the Khatib came in, we were standing by the open windows, breathing too heavily, and Kasuku was thrumming the bars of her cage with her talons. The Khatib did not acknowledge Felicien's presence. That made me more afraid. Alisha shuffled her feet. On the floor a pin rolled to and fro, to and fro.

'Welcome home, sir.'

He was frowning at the floor. 'What is this?'

The Khatib is a fastidious man who cannot even tolerate the fine sand that blows through his house from the shore. He repeated, 'What is this filth?'

Felicien said, 'It's easy enough cleaned up…'

A grey feather rocked down through the silence.

The Khatib addressed me. 'What has been happening here?'

'I let Kasuku out of her cage, just to take a little exercise. It's my fault. I'll make sure the mess is cleaned up straight away. Won't you go and rest?'

'You allowed the bird to defecate in my house?'

Looking at the knot of flesh between his gathered brows, I felt ashamed. He was weary. There was dust on the hem of his kanzu; he had walked a long way. Elsewhere in this house servants were heating water, preparing a meal, unrolling the prayer mat. I should have been waiting on the veranda to greet him.

He said, 'Must I wring that creature's neck?'

Felicien blurted, 'Don't!'

I winced. The Khatib is sensitive to language but I doubt even he can decipher the nuances of a foreign intonation. He turned to Felicien. 'Will you drink tea with us?'

Felicien was already sidling towards the door. 'No thank you… I ought to be on my way.' I couldn't look at him, but

190

I wonder whether he tried to catch my eye, to reassure himself that we would come to no harm.

And as soon as Felicien had gone, the Khatib turned to Alisha. 'Well? What are you waiting for?' He struck her a ringing blow across the shoulder that made her stagger. Then he, too, left us.

'Alisha, I'm sorry.'

She adjusted her veil, embarrassed. 'Mama, you must not apologise to me.'

'I'll get a cloth and clean up the mess myself.'

'No, mama. You mustn't do that either.'

'But I didn't listen when you told me not to let Kasuku out. It was foolish of me.'

'You weren't to know Bwana would come back.' She loked at me pityingly. 'Anyway, it wasn't Kasuku's mess that upset him. It's the Germans.'

Because of Kasuku I did not ask the Khatib about the rifle that had been brought to our house. I considered doing so when he visited me at night, as sometimes on these occasions he lets down his guard and talks with candour. But he was still angry, so I lay beneath him quietly, uttering soft cries only when I judged he wanted to hear my voice, and when he had finished he lay in silence for a minute, then rose and left the room. These days, he no longer summons me to his own chamber as he used to do in our first year together. He would send Alisha, always after I had fallen asleep, and she would rouse me with a whisper, 'He calls you, mama,' as proud as if *she* were the object of his desire. I asked her once why he always called me at the same time every month, and was amazed when she said it was the best time to conceive a child.

It seems a cruel mockery of my barrenness that the Swahili people should address me as 'mama'. The absence of a child has never been mentioned by the Khatib. Nor do we discuss what my husband does on his long safaris to the interior, safaris that seem over the years to have become both longer and more frequent, accompanying at first the caravans of Sultan Seyyid Barghash, and more recently those of other, unnamed merchants.

Once, the Khatib came to me straight upon his return. We did not even know of his arrival. I awoke to his fingertips brushing my face, and I felt great joy, soon followed by sadness because I was still in Africa. But I accepted him, and my sadness weakened a little, like spilt water. What the Khatib did not know, and what I had forgotten, was that Alisha lay in the space beneath my bed that night, as she always used to do whenever the Khatib was away from home. I forgot about her silent, listening presence beneath us. I did not remember her until morning, long after she must have risen and begun her day's duties, and then I was curious, wondering what she had thought, whether it gave her pleasure, or whether she lay there in terror in case she should sneeze or shift her position slightly, and be discovered. And what would the Khatib have done, if he had found her? Then I became fearful, imagining what might have happened, and vowed never to let her sleep beneath my bed again.

From my balcony I can see the German officer walking along the street. He walks briskly, with short steps. It is the gait of someone who pretends to be confident.

Instead of turning left towards the boma, he continues. He draws near. My heart begins to jump. He has yellow hair like a slick of butter down his forehead. It is the officer who was in the tea-house with his wife and child.

If he were to look up, he would see me standing on the balcony, but he does not look up. He gazes around, a frown on his damp face. I think of calling down, *Hello! I am so happy to meet you at last!* But I don't speak. Better he should seek me out.

A servant is sweeping sand from the baraza. I can hear the officer addressing him in good, grammatical Swahili; my pupils would do well to copy him. He asks the servant: 'Where is your master?' The servant replies with typical Swahili evasiveness: 'The master has gone away.'

'Where has he gone?'

'I don't know.'

'When will he return?'

'I don't know.'

'Are you lying to me?'

I shiver. 'No,' says the sweeper placidly. 'I am not lying to you.' The German paces back and forth a few times, still with that air of suppressed uncertainty.

'The mistress is here,' says the servant. 'She is a mzungu like you. Would you like to see her?'

'No. I wish to see your master only, do you understand?'

'I understand perfectly.'

'You will tell him that Udo Schiller called. As soon as he returns, you say my name, Udo Schiller, you understand?'

'Udo Schiller,' the servant parrots.

The German steps back from the baraza. I watch him walk all the way down the street, sweat spreading across the back of his shirt like a big dark bird. He's very angry about coming all this way for nothing. I'm sick with disappointment and humiliation. But what would I have said to him? What could he have said to me? I wonder how he perceives me. As a disgrace who is best avoided?

If he won't come to me, then I shall go to him.

They have tents, taut, squat and brown like turtles that have ambled up from the sea. These tents are mostly occupied by their infantry: Sudanese and Zulu soldiers. The Germans have already begun to build fortifications and also to dismantle Sinamani, knocking down the shacks and razing the rubbish heaps in the town centre. Their new buildings are of limestone, the biggest a boma with two crenellated

193

towers, sheer walls and no windows. It is rumoured that the windows are all on the inner, courtyard walls.

They have taken over the Customs House on the shore. Next to it they have constructed a grid of stone pedestals, high as a man's waist, each one topped with an iron bowl broad enough to hold a sack of grain, and below it a shallow, hollow ledge filled with water. The rats, who cannot climb beyond the water, dart around this stone garden mad with hunger and rage, unable to understand where their food has gone. It is, everyone grudgingly admits, a most ingenious solution to the problem of where to store surplus grain.

The Deutsch-Ostafrikanische Gesellschaft are better at trading than the Indians and the Arabs. Their caravans are well-equipped and move fast because the oxcarts are carefully maintained and the porters get a good meat ration. These Germans are rich men becoming even richer. They are at once resourceful and despicably casual.

I was walking up the broad road that leads from the Customs House to the town. Ahead of me, a Zulu porter hefted a sack onto his head too vigorously, a seam split and spewed out a multi-coloured cataract, hitting the road with a roar that surpassed even the waves: beads bowling down the cobblestones, people stumbling and swearing and leaping out of their way: a hurtling river, a thick, hissing python. It seems that while the Arabs store their beads on strings, the Germans bundle them into sacks any-old-how. The Zulu was shaking beads out of his clothes and hair like raindrops. Two German officers were leaning against a wall nearby. I held my breath, waiting for them to strike the porter, but they didn't move. They just laughed at the children who came running from every direction, shrieking and scrambling in their haste to scoop up bright handfuls of treasure.

Even now, days later, the Customs House road is veined with beads, red, blue, orange beads silting every crack and crevice, vivid against the drab stones. Beads crunch and shatter underfoot; I take a perverse pleasure in grinding them beneath my heel – they are not my property. To the Germans they are intrinsically worthless; just an easy way of bartering for ivory from the interior.

But my young pupils talk of nothing else. As soon as I dismiss them they run down to the shore and scour the dust for rich pickings. Today Juma sidled up to me with a clenched fist. 'Look.' He opened his palm to reveal a red kernel.

'Well now,' I said. 'Aren't you lucky! Is red your favourite colour?'

'Red ones are the best,' he said fervently. 'These are for you, mama.' The children have constructed their own hierarchy of colour: three yellow beads are worth one blue; two blue beads worth one red.

Some people have taken jobs with the German officers, who pay better wages. Others are angry with these turncoats. The Arab merchants are galled by the success of the German caravans; the Indian merchants see them as a useful source of provisions for their shops.

Rice, water, beads. Everything falling apart.

Felicien has asked if he may borrow Alisha – just for an afternoon. He wants her to visit a young orphan, a Christian child of ransomed slaves, and persuade the boy he should come to live at the Mission.

'What's that got to do with Alisha?'

'Well, the poor little lad won't come out from under his bed. The neighbours have tried coaxing him with food, but he won't budge.' Felicien's voice softened. 'I reckon Alisha might be the one to do it; she's so good with the little ones.' Then he added hastily, 'As you are, with those naughty older kids!'

I could have told him: they are scared of the mzungu. But instead I replied, 'Of course you must take Alisha. Let's hope the wretched child can be comforted.'

It pained me to see them depart together: two black-clad figures, one stocky, one slight. They hurried down the street, Felicien talking to Alisha all the time, and then he said something that made her laugh, and I found myself clutching the balcony rail. It was if someone else was inside my head, thinking wicked, jealous thoughts. I hate having such thoughts, but their friendship is so precious to me, I couldn't bear to lose them ...

I must be rational. Felicien is a celibate, and Alisha is long past marrying age now.

There were times when I feared somebody might take her as his wife; a time when I had to admit that men considered her lovely. Sideways glances in the street; an appraising twitch of the mouth. What was her secret? True, she had a reputation for gentleness. True, her skin glowed like a rose – but she was so shy, it was impossible to imagine her ever having two words to say to anyone other than our pupils or me.

Or the gardener. A young man, lame, who moved around our courtyard with a swaying, endearing gait. So quiet, he seemed to speak only to my husband, reporting what had flowered, what had failed; although in those days it seemed every plant thrived. I don't remember his name, just that he was even shyer than Alisha. Once, when she and I were sewing in the garden room, she happened to remark that she preferred yellow above all other colours – and six months later: yellow, yellow everywhere; mimosa, marigolds, roses, and the tallest sunflowers ever seen, astonishing us each day as they reached higher and higher, their faces beaming down on us. The gardener mumbled that the seeds could be crushed to make oil.

But the Khatib abhors yellow, so he dismissed our lame gardener. I was sorry for Alisha's distress, and for the garden too. Since then, it has not flourished in quite the same way. There are bare, sandy patches in between the plants. 'Bad soil,' says the old man who tends the garden now, and we all, even the Khatib, shrug and agree – all except Alisha, who says nothing.

I'm no longer fearful that Alisha will leave me, and I ought not to mind how she blossoms: visiting redeemed slaves in their villages, teaching in our school, helping Felicien with his charitable work. I ought to rejoice in her happiness. Once she said to me, 'You'll never dismiss me, will you mama?' clasping my hand, and I, overjoyed, promised that I never would, since she is my family now, and I have come to love her as my own.

What I am afraid of is that *I* must leave *her*. What will become of her? That depends whether the Khatib will suspect she helped me to escape, as she helped me once before. I shall leave him a letter to explain myself, and hope that will deflect his rage. Or perhaps, if war comes, he will understand all too well why I had to leave, and be glad that I am off his hands.

Never once has he offered me money for my passage to England. My conscience knows why I can never ask.

Women are forbidden to enter the Caravanserai. But there is nothing to prevent a woman from lingering amongst the nearby coconut palms along the sea path while a meeting takes place within; while the Diwan Bushiri harangues the Arabs gathered there, the Khatib amongst them, all of them men of status, all submitting meekly to the lash of Bushiri's tongue.

It became known late this afternoon that there was to be a meeting, when the streets and tea-houses were flooded with disgruntled Arab porters evicted from the Caravanserai, their haven. The Khatib announced he was going to sunset prayer and would not return home to eat. So, after my solitary meal, I put on my black buibui and walked in darkness towards the sea.

The Caravanserai stands in a grove of banana trees a little way from the sea path. It reminds us why we are here: we, who depend on the porters and traders who seek rest in this building; we who are carried on their shoulders. Without the Caravanserai and its trade, Sinamani would not exist. It is one of the largest buildings in Sinamani, but is not constructed in grand Arab style – there is no baraza and the door is of plain wood. The limestone walls are painted a thick, ochre yellow. In daylight these yellow walls glare through the slatted leaves of the banana trees. All through the night you can see the softer gleam of lamps in the windows, since a caravan may arrive at any time, and there is always a fire burning for those who are hungry, desperate to lay down their burdens and rest at their long journey's end – except tonight, when the porters must roam the streets, drunk on mbege or provoking each other with anxious gossip.

When the Diwan Bushiri and his men approached the Caravanserai I stepped back, although he could not have seen me in my hiding place. I met him once, some years ago, when he came to our house. He did not look at me then, nor did he acknowledge my presence by a single word. In truth, I was glad to be ignored. People fear and revere him; to many, he is known simply as 'The Pangani Arab' – as if they are too scared to speak his name.

Tonight, he was as I remembered him: short of stature, thickset, solid as a baobab. His eyes gleam black, like gouts of blood. His hair and beard are flecked with iron-grey. I remember at our house how he talked and talked, dominating the meal, his mouth frothing as he swore his eternal hatred of the Sultan, who would hang him if he should ever set foot on Zanzibar again, and I wondered why he should be saying all this in the presence of the Khatib, who was, at that time, still in the Sultan's employ.

Tonight, his venom was all for our German visitors. What fools we had been to let Carl Peters into Sinamani with his papers that Bushiri, of course, would have torn to shreds and scattered on the wind. But Peters would never dare set foot in Pangani. Bushiri ranted: What do I care for paper? What do I care for wazungu? What do I care? Thus he challenged his listeners to confront their own cowardice; his unspoken message: 'Fear *me*, for I fear nobody.'

And I did fear him, and at the same time I was afraid of what I knew to be true: that the Khatib no longer enjoys the Sultan's protection, and must therefore respect the will of this ferocious man.

What fools we were, Bushiri continued, to permit Europeans where only the Arab should ply his trade. See how we reap the fruits of our stupidity: the town crawling with soldiers, their vile defences everywhere like boils upon our skin.

He did not once mention what everyone knows: that Von Gravenreuth, the German commander, has ordered Bushiri to secede his plantation. But his voice was choked with outrage, and he only became calm as he began to announce his strategy.

I left, too scared to hear any more, wondering why Bushiri should convene this meeting so close to the very forces he is determined to overthrow. Hurrying along the sea path I tripped on a tree root, fell headlong, and cried out. Then I crouched, silent in the grass for ten minutes, convinced that those figures strolling on the moonlit beach must be Germans who would ask me what I was doing there, so that I should inadvertently betray the plotters, and would myself be betrayed.

*

I wore my mauve silk gown. It is dingy now, and the bodice sags. In Newcastle I would look absurd, sixteen years behind the fashion; here it doesn't matter. Nobody gave me more than a glance as I walked through Sinamani. I overheard one Swahili man say to his companion: 'There goes another German woman.'

Three Africans stood guard outside the boma. An officer came towards me, carrying his helmet under his arm, a pink welt across his forehead where the helmet had chafed. I recognised him, for he is well-known as the soldier who built the first block-house: his name is Von Wissmann.

I tried to sound bold. 'Do you speak English?' He shook his head.

'I want to see Udo Schiller.'

He held up his hand. 'Wait'.

For a long time I sat on a stone in the shade. Somewhere within those limestone walls a child was singing. When at last my butter-haired friend Schiller came out, he walked with the swagger of someone who enjoys being in a land where he is the foreigner. A long time ago I saw this confidence in Americans on Zanzibar, and more recently in Arabs visiting from Oman, but never so much as in this German officer.

'Hello,' he said. 'Are you English?'

'Sir, I am.' He looked me up and down, taking in the faded silk, the opal necklace at my throat. Of course, he had seen me before in the market, in buibui and gold hoop earrings. He saw through my attempt to dress as his ally. He must know my story. Everyone knows my story.

'Well now,' he said, 'What brings *you* to Sinamani?'

'Marriage.' Let him ask further if he dared.

His eyes opened wide. 'There is an Englishman living in this town?'

'No.' I gave the Khatib's name.

'Really? Can it be true?'

I nodded.

'But I have spoken with your… husband, on several occasions. I am afraid he has been less than helpful.'

'Then I am sorry.'

'No need to be sorry. Maybe you have some influence with him.'

'It is possible.'

'But first, madam' – he drew himself up, in a parody of good manners – 'how may I be of service to you?'

My mouth was dry. The speech, so many times rehearsed, died on my lips. 'I was wondering … I need to borrow money…'

For a moment, incredulous amusement flashed across his face. Then he composed himself. 'I see. How large a sum do you require?'

'Enough for my passage home.' He waited, gazing at me, taking in my wretchedness. 'I don't know the exact amount, a great deal, I should imagine …'

'Why do you ask me?' His face was watchful: he longed to know more, but could not let himself appear intrigued, for that would give me the upper hand.

'I do not ask you for your personal help, sir, but for your assistance as fellow Europeans.'

'Your husband is a wealthy man. Am I to understand he knows nothing of your intentions?'

'I cannot ask him. It is impossible.'

'Then you are making a most difficult request. The problem for us would not be the money; no, of that we have plenty and we could arrange for you also a chaperone. The problem is your husband. We should make him very angry, I am sure, if we were to assist you in this way without his knowledge. And we do not wish to anger our neighbours. It is very important that we should all live side by side, in peace.'

I wanted to cry, what about your guns? What about this boma, these hideous blockhouses? But I was reliant on his goodwill, so I had to be meek. 'My husband need never know.'

Schiller shook his head. 'I shall see what I can do. But I'm afraid I do not have much hope.' He pursed his lips, shrugged, enjoying his own performance. 'It is such a difficult situation; very awkward.'

'Please try.' My voice was shaking. Without looking him in the eye again, I hurried away down the sea path.

'Perhaps it is for all of us,' Alisha suggested, when the Germans set the giant chessboard in the ground at the crossroads. Alisha *wants* to understand. It must be bewildering to have served, all these years, a mzungu mistress, to believe she knew what to expect of Europeans, and then to have her expectations repeatedly shattered.

They are seducing our children. Time after time I have scolded my pupils: 'Don't hang around those soldiers, you make yourselves look stupid. Where's your loyalty?' But the little ones don't know what loyalty means, and the older children say, 'Yes mama,' look stricken, and can't resist sneaking off to the crossroads whenever possible. The Zulus and Sudanese box the children's ears if they are cheeky. The German officers give them sweets. No doubt some of these men have left children behind in Germany. Others are simply bored, and seek relief from the tedium of an African day. All are scheming for a future when they shall have total control, not only of this town, but of the whole country, and our children shall be their compliant labourers and maybe, one day, their infantry.

The giant chess pieces are hideous: rough-hewn, every flaw magnified. The knights bare their teeth unevenly. The pawns' faceted polls seem mutilated. Rumour has it they were made in a nearby village by a woodcarver famed for his fine detail, and the Germans are too stupid to see that he has insulted them with shoddy work. But although the pieces are ugly, their size ensures they are imposing. Now I

have felt their heaviness in my own hands, I can testify to
their power.

It was dusk. I walked down to the crossroads for no other
reason than I hoped to see Schiller, and I was not
disappointed. He, knowing I was watching him, turned and
smiled. 'Karibu!' he called, in the African way. 'Won't you
join us?'

I lingered, clinging to the safety of silence – he could
not be sure whether I was insolent or merely shy. The other
player, his subordinate, stepped back from the game and
began to realign the pieces. I dared not ignore the invitation
any longer. But I could have made an excuse and walked
away.

Slowly I approached the giant's board. He held out his
hand. 'A nice evening for a game of chess, isn't it? Come. I
hear you are a devilish good player.'

Who told him? He must have cherished that snippet of
small talk, waiting for his moment. Thank God, for once
we had no audience of children. At first only the other
officer watched as we played. The pieces were much, much
heavier than I had expected. As soon as I picked up a
bishop by the cross on its rough mitre, I had to put it down
again because the weight was too much for me. My
opponent said, 'You have to move him now.'

'I know the rules of chess.'

A lantern hung from a pole in the ground nearby. The
light hollowed his skin, giving him a feverish air. He was
intent on the game, and on me, looking up every now and
then to check I had not run away. When it was my turn to
move he watched me all the time. The marble squares had
been swept clear of sand, and felt slippery beneath my feet.

Shopkeepers were standing in doorways. A small group
gathered on Sewa Haji's baraza.

Who was supposed to win this game? Did he intend victory to be his: an emblem of his power? But how could he assume I would be no match for him?

Or maybe it was more complicated. Maybe I was to be the victor, so that I would feel more at ease with him, and more inclined to do whatever he wanted.

My queen took his ugly, gurning knight. He said, 'Where has your husband gone?' – his tone so careless, he might have been enquiring after a mutual acquaintance.

'I don't know, sir.' For once I was glad of my ignorance, glad at least *this* betrayal could be avoided. But the next question was more difficult, because I knew the answer.

'Does your husband associate with Bushiri bin Salim Al-Harthi?'

Yes or *no* would have sufficed. I said, 'That diwan is famous throughout the region, all along the coast.' Then I moved a pawn so stupidly that I left Schiller with no option but to take my bishop.

He asked only those two questions, which hovered in the dusk throughout our game. His subordinate strolled up and down within earshot, smiling at a clever move, clicking his tongue in sympathy when I lost my rook; when Schiller lost his second knight. Despite my anxieties, I willed myself to play the game of my life, forcing us into a stalemate that left both of us equally gracious, equally on guard.

'I enjoyed our game,' he said. Quite likely he meant it. 'When shall we play again?'

'In a week's time.' An expression flickered briefly across his face: something between impatience and resentment. Whatever disquiet he wanted me to feel, he thought I was not feeling, and this gave me heart – for surely he will need me to talk to him again, and the more we talk, the more he will be in my debt.

'Goodbye,' I said. 'Until next week.'

'Goodnight,' he replied, almost tenderly, as if he had already accepted his disappointment and forgiven me.

The shopkeepers remained at their windows, the shutters thrown open to the night. Lamplight tinged their faces. As I walked past the little crowd on Sewa Haji's baraza, I thought I heard one of them say, 'She'll be fucking him next.'

Alisha asked if she might go to the Mission to spend the day with 'her' orphan. I struggled with my jealousy, conquered it, gave permission, and after I had watched her disappear into the distance, some perverse impulse took me into the Khatib's own chamber, to the sandalwood chest at the foot of his bed. I lifted the lid. What I saw inside was no surprise. If I were less of a coward, I might have explored the contents thoroughly, but I could hear the slap slap slap of servants' feet as they padded around the house, and so I lowered the lid, and stole away to the garden room where I sat all morning.

And devilment drives me through the heat of the day, through the streets where the shopkeepers look at me differently now, past the house where, if I am not mistaken, Sewa Haji nods and smiles with embarrassment rather than warmth. I walk fast, meaning to reach my destination before I should change my mind. But first I must pass the Caravanserai.

A man sits on the ground, his back against the wall, legs stretched in front of him like brittle sticks. His skin is mottled with dust. Between his closed eyes, a deep-etched cleft of weariness. The kofia is slightly askew where his head lolls against the ochre wall. Does he sleep? Or is he reliving the encounters of his journey? Can he not quite relinquish the memory of swamps and barren ground and struggle? Even with his eyes shut, his face looks hard and angry. I hope he will not open his eyes.

For I have stopped, disquieted by the sight of marching figures in the distance, a tight cohort quite unlike the long straggle of a caravan. If the men of the Caravanserai have noticed, they do not show it, but continue about their business, resting, talking and arguing. A steady hubbub within; from time to time, a ripple of laughter. In the rough yard at the front, facing the sea, a man brews coffee in a tall conical pot on a hearth of stones. The smell is so strong, so rich, my mouth waters.

I could turn back, or I could call out, 'Look! See who is coming!' Or I could walk on to meet the marchers, and maybe Schiller will be amongst them.

The cohort is led by a single figure: Von Gravenreuth. By his side trots a black dog; behind the dog, four officers. Not Schiller. At a shouted order the cohort halts outside the Caravanserai. Another order and the formation of Zulu infantrymen turns, loosens like a wave breaking and like a wave they rush upon the Caravanserai, past the men with cups raised to their lips, past the one-time sleeper who is wide awake now, astounded, as a soldier trips over his outstretched legs and strikes him with the butt of his rifle, and into the building they pour, while Von Gravenreuth gazes out to sea as if he would prefer to be sitting on deck in the sun. The noise is colossal: Swahili porters shouting and cursing, their cries, the thwack of wood on bone, and other words, African words which I cannot understand. The infantry chase the porters out of the building into the front yard, guns held to their throats. An officer kicks over the coffee pot, which shoots out a dark stream, and a different smell assails me: coffee thickened with dust. Von Gravenreuth speaks in his rasping German, stopping abruptly after each sentence for his translator to convey the message to the livid men of the Caravanserai

That from this day on, the Caravanserai will be requisitioned. That it is to become a warehouse for German imports. That the Arabs' disgraceful trade of slavery must be extinguished – *kwisha!* – once and for all. Soon, he says, nothing will remain. You can be certain, if you try to continue with your vile, inhuman trade, we shall find you out, and all your efforts will be destroyed.

The men receive the speech in sullen silence, until Von Gravenreuth says they must leave Sinamani immediately, without their burdens which must remain inside. At this, a man expectorates an oyster of spittle onto the toe of an officer's boot. Von Gravenreuth unleashes his dog, and the porters scatter, running from its teeth, but they cannot run far because the soldiers will not let them, and the dog leaps and snarls and bites, one dog, fifty men, the hot, midday air churning with wrath and shame and hatred. I have seen enough.

I found Alisha in the garden room at her sewing. 'He is so happy now!' she sang out when she saw me, her face glowing with compassion, and perhaps also a little pride. 'So settled at the Mission!'

'Haven't you heard? Don't you know what has been happening today, at the Caravanserai?'

Her needlework slipped to the floor. 'What is it, mama?'

How I relished my power to destroy her tranquillity. 'Yes,' I said. 'Another outrage. They have taken over the Caravanserai. Oh, they'll find nothing there, of course. No guns, no weapons.' (I noted how she trembled a little.) 'But that is not all: they mean to stamp out our independent trade, take what is ours for themselves. We should be afraid of what they may do next.'

In the evening I walked past the Caravanserai again, on my way to play chess. The building was dark. No lamplight in the windows, no laughter, no smell of cooking food. Only two Zulu infantrymen on guard at the door, and the drooping, slatted branches of the banana trees clattering in the weak breeze.

Further inland, at the crossroads, there was no breeze at all. The air was sultry. I slipped off my sandals, desiring cool marble beneath my feet. I wondered if Schiller might mention what had happened, to test my opinion. But his pleasant greeting acknowledged nothing, and only when my queen was poised to take his bishop did he unnerve me by asking why the Khatib was so often away from home, and did I know where he was now, and I had to declare I did not.

'Then let me tell you.'

I dropped the queen. She rocked and rattled on her wooden base.

'I saw him just today, on the beach at Pangani. You are surprised? You thought he was far from home?'

'Business takes him all over the coastal region, and beyond.'

'What business does he do, exactly?'

'Trading. Like yourselves, he brings goods from the interior to the coast. Commodities such as ivory – '

'And what does he import?'

I spoke carefully. 'Sometimes large parcels are brought to our tembe. I'm not sure what they contain.'

'He doesn't tell you?'

'I don't ask.'

'Are they heavy, these parcels?'

'Would you expect me to lift them?'

'You see your servants lift them. Do they struggle? Do they stagger?'

I bowed my head. 'Yes. The parcels seem to be very heavy.'

We had ceased all pretence of playing chess, the game suspended, pieces strewn across the board, static, waiting for our hands to give them life.

'I could find out what is in those parcels,' I said. 'If you should like to know.'

It was a dreadful risk: the Hindi shopkeepers gathered silently at their windows, and any one of them might have picked up enough English, on their travels or from Sewa Haji, to understand me.

'I should like to know very much.'

'It won't be easy for me to find out.'

'But I shall appreciate your efforts.'

That night again I played him into a stalemate. He kissed my hand, said he looked forward to seeing me next week.

And now the Khatib is home, he makes no mention of the desolate Caravanserai, and there is no sign of him going on another safari. I have wondered how I am to play chess with Schiller, let alone go snooping and spying inside this house. But it shall be done.

I was sitting at the long glass in my bedroom, Alisha behind me with the hairbrush: stroking, stroking, stroking the glinting skeins to make them spring like sparks from the fire, and when the placid rhythm had calmed us both, I said, 'Alisha, soon you must keep watch for me.' Her face fell. Perhaps she remembered the last time I told her to be my spy, on Zanzibar. I explained what I wanted her to do, but not why I wanted to look in the chest.

'You don't need to look,' she said. 'I know what's in there.'

My face in the glass: ludicrous surprise. 'You know?'

'We all know. All the servants had to know, so we should not make a mistake and tell somebody. As I am telling you now.' She looked ashamed.

'But who told you?'

'The Khatib, mama.'

'Why should he tell all of you, and not me?'

'Perhaps he thought you would be afraid.'

There was pity in her voice. For my vulnerability? Or because I have been an idiot?

Two choices. Tell her the truth. Promise to take her with me. Believe with all my heart that the Germans will pity her plight and allow her to accompany me.

Or, I could frighten her into doing what I wanted. I said, 'You don't keep secrets from me. Remember you have a roof over your head thanks to me. If it weren't for me, you'd be a street girl at anyone's mercy.'

'Yes, mama.' Her face closed. She listened to what she must do.

They were wrapped in yellow American cloth. They smelled of oil and the wooden stocks looked alive, glossy, like horses' limbs. There was a bulging pouch of bullets. In a smaller parcel were pistols, which my pupils call *mtoto bunduki* – 'baby guns'. Like nestlings they clustered together, the barrel eyes dark. I began to count.

As I reached fifty, footsteps sounded in the passage. There would be just time to finish. Fifty-three, fifty-four, fifty-five – I hurriedly swaddled the guns in their cloth, closed the lid, then turned, expecting to see Alisha at the door. It was the kitchen boy. He tried not to smile, but his eyes were gleeful as he glanced at the tell-tale corner of cloth hanging out from beneath the lid.

'What is it?'

'Cook says to inform you there is no salt.'

'Well, go to market and buy some more.'

'Cook says, there is no money.'

'For goodness' sake, borrow some! Steal some, prepare the food without salt, but stop bothering me with requests you know I cannot grant!'

'It wasn't a request, mama. It was just information.' He bowed and left me quivering with anger, and fear of the whispers and sniggers in the kitchen that will soon reach the Khatib's ears.

How did that boy get past Alisha?

I marched down the corridor, found her lying on a mat asleep, or feigning sleep, grabbed a handful of her long black hair and yanked her to her feet. They must have heard the screams on Zanzibar.

When at last my rage had run out, she continued to beg forgiveness. 'I was tired, I was tired,' she repeated. 'I'm sorry, I'm sorry, I'm sorry. I would never betray you, mama, I love you, I love you more than my own dead mama.' There was a whine in her voice I had never heard before. Whether contrived or genuine, it was hateful to me. And I was hateful to myself, for allowing myself to be caught out by the kitchen boy; for preparing to betray the Khatib, who has given me shelter these fifteen years, for causing such pain to Alisha in her body and, soon, in her heart. It is a matter of survival. But that does not ease my conscience one little bit.

Alisha wept for hours, in her little room next to mine. That was no comfort to me, since I could cry too when I think that betrayal is a disease that has infected all of us in this town, and is spreading, and will destroy millions.

I saw sickness everywhere tonight as I hurried through the streets. The white buildings, blunt as leprous limbs. The Caravanserai: blackened, blinded. A dog scavenging on a fly-ridden rubbish dump. When it saw me it slunk into the shadows, not waiting to find out whether I would be kind or cruel.

I did not need to introduce myself at the boma. The guards saw me, and one of them went inside. 'Wait,' he said.

I waited and waited, until the thick, plain door swung open, and Schiller came out. I could tell he did not want to see me, so I spoke before he could send me away.

'Fifty-five.'

He dashed his hand distractedly across his brow. 'Is that all? No more?'

Is that all? Surely, surely he could not be disappointed? 'I counted them, but I was seen by one of the servants. Please, please, you must help me now. It will not be long before he finds out...' Gabbling, I noticed his brow was stippled with sweat, even though the evening air was cool. 'You must understand,' I said, 'I am in danger.'

'Yes,' he repeated, 'you are in danger.' It seemed the desultory parroting of someone who is powerless to speak for himself.

'Please,' I hissed, 'keep your promise.'

'You have no chaperone. It is not possible – '

'My maid.' In that instant I forgave Alisha. 'Just give me enough money for my maid and myself to travel to Saadani, and there we shall board the steamship and you shall never hear of me again, but please, sir, do this for me if you have any pity left in you for an Englishwoman.'

He blinked, looked around, said, 'It shall be arranged. Stand at the crossroads tomorrow evening. Someone shall meet you there. You shall be given the package you require.'

'Tomorrow evening, sir? But my husband is at home, what if he should hear that I have betrayed him – these people, you know the native people gossip terribly, they are not to be trusted ...'

He shook his head, backing away. 'We had an agreement and I shall honour it. Tomorrow evening. Now, you must excuse me, for my daughter is very sick.'

Light woke me this morning, sharp and bright as a blade. Lying in bed, I turned my face towards its warmth. The same sun shines over Europe, neither so close, nor so fierce, and yet it is the very same sun. Some things will never change. So be calm.

But I wondered how I could wait these few remaining hours until I should feel that packet in my hand, hear the crackle of paper.

'Hodi.' A voice at my door. The smirking kitchen boy, sent to summon me. 'Straight away, mama. Straight away.'

When the Khatib wants to see me, he uses Alisha as his messenger. I took my time, brushing my hair, fastening my necklace. No point in pretending any longer to be a good wife. Better this way, I thought, my heart thudding. Better for him to cast me out than for me to slip away, shuddering, wondering all the time if I am to be discovered. And Udo Schiller will have to help me now, he cannot go back on his promise.

I entered his study. He was by the window, his back to me, looking down on the garden. Without turning, he asked, 'Are you well?'

This politeness must be a trick to lull me before he should vent his rage. 'Yes sir, I am in good health.' (A lie: I felt sick.)

He sighed. 'Then God be thanked. You will need your strength soon.' At last he turned from the window and gazed at me, and I could have sworn it was a look of pity. 'You must leave here today.' (He knew? Why, then, so gentle?) 'You must go to the Mission. They will look after you there. You must stay until the Abbé says it is safe for you to leave.'

'Safe from what?' Fear gave way to surprise, but only for an instant, because even as I asked the question, dimly I began to know the answer. The Khatib had a glint in his eyes, as if he were – excited? 'There will be bloodshed here,' he said. 'Bloodshed.'

Then my fear came rushing back, lifting and bearing down inside me like a wave.

'I can't go to the Mission.'

'You must. Take Alisha with you.'

'Let me stay. Please!' I would run to the boma, beat on that door with my fists, beg Schiller to take me away. 'I must stay. Let me stay. I ... I mustn't leave you now, if we are in danger – '

'You will be a hindrance if you stay here. Go to the Mission, Lucy. Take your maid. Save her, if you will not save yourself.'

'Do you care so much about Alisha?'

'*You* care.'

He was right. I don't want Alisha to die. The Khatib might die. I have imagined myself widowed before.

'Very well, I shall go to the Mission this evening.'

'Go now. Alisha is packing.'

So he had already spoken to her. 'Before I go, sir, I must ask you this. Is Bushiri confident? Is victory possible?' In speaking Bushiri's name, I spoke also of the rifles in the chest, and of my own duplicity, and it was too late, now, for dissembling. I had to know what kind of existence to expect, if I should fail to meet Schiller this evening. If Schiller should fail me.

'Bushiri?' The Khatib seemed surprised. 'Bushiri is in Pangani.' He moved back to the window. 'By the way,' he added absently, 'a very sad thing: a child died last night. The little daughter of one of our visitors. This morning they have buried her. To risk their own lives in coming here: that is their choice. But their children's lives? How can they be so foolish?'

I left him then, full of dread, wondering if Schiller would, after all, honour his promise, and wondering whether I should ever see the Khatib alive again. Those were my first thoughts, and only then did I think of the little girl with hair as fine and white as a dandelion clock, whom I once heard singing behind the thick limestone walls of the boma.

Alisha would not look at me as she moved swiftly around the room, folding clothes, my clothes and hers, laying them in the same basket. I believe she knew it all: my meetings

214

with Schiller, how I planned to abandon her – and Bushiri's plans too, and Schiller's dead child. I was tearful; she ignored my tears. I raged and vowed I would not go to the Mission; she said merely, 'You must look after yourself now, mama.'

Perhaps we should meet Schiller on our way there. Perhaps he had given the packet to some other officer to deliver. Perhaps, in the depths of grief, he would nobly fulfil his promise.

What a fool I was.

While Alisha fastened our bundles and baskets, I stood on the balcony, craning down the street, squinting against the sun for a glimpse of khaki. But there were no soldiers to be seen, only a hurrying stream of Swahili people, each with a burden on his head, even the infants on their mothers' backs clutching a wooden spoon or a coconut grater.

Who ordered this exodus?

This time the wave of fear almost felled me. Tottering against the window frame I wondered what might be about to happen, for people to run from our town like ants from a jug of scalding water.

Alisha chivvied me down the stairs, as she did once long ago, that night on Zanzibar. I stumbled into the street. Everyone leaving, everyone hurrying. My best pupil Juma, a fishtrap on his head, grinning, walking backwards as he sang, 'Welcome to the Mission, mother!' as if we were on our way to a party.

Alisha thrust a canvas bag into my hands. 'Sorry mama, I can't carry everything.'

'What about the other servants?'

'Still at home.'

'Shall they be safe?'

'They will follow when Master permits them to leave.'

If he permits them, I thought. Juma chattered on and on. I glanced this way and that, desperate to see a khaki uniform, a proffered hand. But the Germans were waiting inside their boma, their blockhouses, unseen, observing our departure.

The oxcart was the only vehicle going south. An African held the reins. Schiller and his wife were slumped in the back, leaving Sinamani, leaving their little girl in that cemetery by the shore. Dumbly I turned to watch as the oxcart jolted past. He saw me. For a few seconds misery faded from his face, displaced by something else – regret? Concern? Then it was gone, and his expression became an echo of his wife's, and I knew no German officer would beckon to me through the crowds in the market place, or murmur 'Godspeed,' as he pressed a packet into my hand.

Alisha grabbed my wrist. 'Please mama, hurry.' We half-walked, half-ran towards the grim, distant beacon of the church tower.

As long as I live, I shall remember how the Mission welcomed us: this ragged crowd, this brown tide, swilling down the avenue of sweet young mango trees with fish traps and bundles and baskets and goats, pouring through the Mission gates. There were the pristine blue Sisters, gathered in a semi-circle, singing hymns, and the Brothers coming to greet us, diverting the stream of humankind this way and that, men to the church, women and children to the Sisters' house. I longed to see Felicien, but could not find him in the crowds. The Abbé took my hand. 'You are safe now,' he said. I wanted to ask why he should help me. I could have fallen to my knees, there in front of them all, and confessed my mendacity.

'This way, mama.' Alisha, drawing me towards the Sisters' house. I am not used to being so close to other people. But I managed to thank the Sisters who showed me to a corner of the long dormitory, a high, bright room with

216

sixteen beds and on the wall a crucifix, the Christ's eyes distant, dreaming of somewhere else.

We stowed our bags and bundles under a bed, which they gave me because I am a mzungu. Most of the women must sleep on the floor. I was very hungry. 'Later there will be some soup,' Alisha promised. Africans think nothing of going for a whole day without food. I have never acquired that hardiness. The dormitory swarmed with native women, unfolding mats, giggling, chiding their children, whose shrill voices pierced me as they scampered up and down the central aisle. I needed air. There was no privacy. Only one corner was curtained off, for a woman in labour – a woman who sells oil in the marketplace. Alisha went behind the curtain. I don't know how Alisha knows about these things. The woman was roaring like a bull, a bloodcurdling sound. 'Why is she making that dreadful noise?' I asked the other women, but they just smiled. 'She can't help it, mama.'

I have come outside to breathe. Old men will sleep in the church, young men and boys under the stars. It would be almost festive, but for the Brothers swinging shut the great gates with an awful finality. Father Francis steps forward, in his hands an iron chain, thick as a cobra, which he winds around and around the central bars of the gates, binding the two together, and he fastens the chain with a padlock. A cheer goes up.

Is this sanctuary?

Felicien stands at my side. 'That'll see 'em off,' he says. I shiver. He is as serene as ever. The first time I have seen him by moonlight. He looks younger, nobler. If I were a Catholic, I would beg him to hear my confession. But surely it is enough that I am here, with them all, sharing their peril? Felicien senses my distress, lays his hand on my arm. 'Don't worry,' he murmurs. 'Your husband won't come to any harm.' I don't know what he means – an invocation of

217

faith, perhaps. Or maybe the Spiritans have some secret insight into Bushiri's plans.

That first night, the children were too excited to sleep, running up and down the dormitory, making a racket. At five in the morning the woman gave birth, with a scream that made me leap up in my bed – 'Is she dead?' I cried. The women did not bother to hide their amusement. 'We don't know,' was the sanguine answer, but a minute later Sister Magdalena emerged from behind the curtain and announced a healthy boy. 'Call him Bushiri,' somebody said, and I wondered how they could all laugh.

Then Alisha came to tell me about the baby: how perfect and beautiful he was; such tiny fingers and toes. 'Lovely,' I said, 'but I haven't slept a wink all night.'

'Neither have I, mama. Neither have I.'

And we have been here a week now, and the children are quieter, no longer thrilled by this strange, transient existence at the Mission. I complained to Felicien. 'It's not healthy, breathing in each other's air like that. The stench tells me it isn't healthy.'

'Better you catch some illness in here than a bullet out there, Lucy,' he laughed – with an edge that warned me not to complain again. Which is a problem, because truly I feel unwell.

Alisha's behaviour is odd. As a rule when I am ill she fusses and cossets me, but today, whenever the sickness came she did nothing, just looked thoughtful.

It is because of my treachery. She knows, and she is punishing me.

Of course there must be disease here where there are so many people. Maybe fear is our disease. Last night the gunfire was the worst yet. Nobody dares leave the compound, not even Felicien. We do not know what is happening. Whether Bushiri is alive or dead, or how many may have died with him.

Nobody talks of what will happen when we run out of food. Tonight there was no soup, only plain porridge which we ate outside, shivering under the stars. Alisha wrapped her blanket around my shoulders. The Sisters served me first, to my shame. Here am I, the traitor in their midst, drinking their water, eating their food. 'You won't starve,' said Alisha.

They have found a space for me here, these people whose shacks I have strolled past with my nose fastidiously in the air, whose children I turned away from my school.

I go to pray. The church is dark, hushed. Where once Livingstone's body lay, now the cool floor is paved with bodies craving sleep.

Something is happening to me. Is this to be a long death? Is this my punishment, at last? I can hardly move my limbs for fatigue. But move I must, because I cannot bear the humiliation of emptying my bowels and my bladder and my stomach here in the dormitory in front of them all.

The Mission latrines stink. I retch all the way up the path; the meaty stench hits me before I open the door. Vomit splatters my feet; feeble, watery vomit that feels as if I have turned myself inside out. And then I squat over the black hole, and it is like being scoured by razor blades. Flies brush against my mouth. I deserve this.

I crawl to the dispensary, where Sister Magdalena, the young African nun with the brilliant eyes, washes me and makes me lie down on her couch. She asks me intimate questions and I am hot with shame. She seeks answers to questions I never ask myself. When did my husband last come in to me? What shape was the moon when he came in? And the time before that? And for how long has there been this sensation of fire in my urine? I cannot look at her. I hang my head to ask, 'Shall I die?' and thus I have no warning from her face when she replies, 'You are not going to die, mama. You are going to have a child.'

When she sees my astonishment she does not smile, but inclines her head slightly, and begins to tell me what I must do: the infusion of herbs I must drink to avoid this sickness that is turning me inside out, as if she were advising me of a cure for blackwater fever. Her gaze shifts to the door of the dispensary where people are waiting. I stand up, a little unsteady, scared to move, as if by walking I should dislodge the child in my belly. I thank her and she nods, her expression neutral, and I make my way back to the Sisters' house, seeing the high walls around the compound, the huge gates, the padlock, hearing the hubbub of voices, and beyond, like the sea, like the roar of blood in my ears, cannon fire.

Alisha knew.

'Lie down.' She pressed me gently onto the bed. 'Sleep a little, if you can.'

But I could not sleep for the noise of children chattering and women gossiping, and for astonishment, and, like a rose slowly opening in the sun, this prospect of a new life. Perhaps I could be happy in Sinamani after all.

Felicien reports there are German warships, three grey vessels, skulking far out at sea. Soon, he says, the war will be over.

I climbed to the top of the church tower while Alisha stood at the bottom and scolded me. I was breathless, but I had to see them with my own eyes. At first I thought, there is Zanzibar. Then I realised it was the ships, distorting the horizon.

Like sea monsters they creep nearer and nearer, freighted with guns to blow us all to smithereens.

Sister Magdalena says it has been inside me for five months.

It moves. An anxious flip. A quelled sneeze. A drumbeat.

Especially it moves after dark, when I am confined to the dormitory. Alisha says I must not catch malaria now.

Last night I woke to a terrible churning, and I screamed, thinking the baby had forced its way out, but why should everyone else be screaming too, the women and children and even the Sisters? Because cannons were firing at Sinamani. I lay with my hands over my stomach, and Alisha placed her hands over my hands and so we held the baby safe. We remained, holding fast, long after the cannon fire had stopped, and dark silence hung over us all. I held my belly, repeating Felicien's promise: *your husband will be alright.*

This morning the Abbé summoned us all, and we gathered outside the church, in its shadow. He told us the war is over: Sinamani remains under German control. Soon, says the Abbé, we must return to our homes and continue with our daily duties. God has saved us.

He didn't mention those whom God has surely not saved, those whose bodies must now litter the streets of Sinamani, unless the thin dogs have already eaten them. A brave voice spoke up: What about Bushiri?

Captured, said the Abbé. Sentenced to hang.

The crowd began to disperse, women going to their husbands, children clustering around their mothers. The Sisters strode past, their arms heaped high with linen to launder. The woman with the newborn baby sat under a tree, suckling it. I watched her for a while.

In the afternoon I put a bottle of water and three mangoes into my bag. Alisha forbade me to leave. It was an order: 'Don't go,' not 'I beg you not to go.' She nagged me about my obligations to my unborn child, and the Khatib. I said the Khatib might be dead, and then she began to cry. I didn't tell her I was convinced he was safe.

Doubtless Felicien would have accompanied me, but I preferred to go alone. It was strange to be outside the Mission walls, walking, tentatively, towards the sea. The sun was high, its rays bombarding the water – *dart! stab! vanish!*

An uneasy flutter inside me. Fear? Or my unborn child? Maybe it sensed my anxiety.

At the end of the mango avenue I turned right. From a distance, the pattern of trees was the first sign that a terrible change had taken place. There used to be a thick fringe of palms on the northern outskirts of Sinamani. Now, only a few remained, branches splayed against the white sky like drowning swimmers reaching vainly for help.

I hastened on. The scant screen of trees could not hide the misery. Here was India street – but no street remained. A waste of rubble, tattered fragments of woven leaves hanging lopsided from jagged walls; strange debris: a cheap, tarnished necklace, a tin of jam, a child's toy doll, fashioned from twigs with a face made from a ball of rags. This was Sewa Haji's shop.

No more streets, just piles of crumbled earth and battered branches. Once, these were native dwellings. To my surprise, I felt sorry for their destruction. I came to the ruins of Arab houses. Spars of wood, sticking up from the destruction like broken limbs. A wall with a perfect, circular hole through it, looking out onto nothing. Like the port-holes on the *SS Madura* all those years ago, when I gazed for hours at the sullen sea, failing to imagine Africa.

Was I afraid of what I should find at the tembe? No. When at last I came upon my home, I picked my way through the ruins with a light heart, not flinching even when I found the cage, its bars wrenched out of shape, a gap big enough for Kasuku to escape through. For the briefest moment, again I was sorry. Then my mind began racing ahead, beyond the chaos, picturing a palace in

Muscat where I and my child and my maid should live in peace and comfort for the rest of our days. This was how I should leave Sinamani. My husband must take me away. He would not countenance his child growing up in a town that had been so humiliated.

Scavengers moved slowly through the rubble, pausing now and then to scrutinize some artefact, some broken object, wondering whether it could be useful. They paid no attention to me. I salvaged nothing. With a glad heart, I turned back towards the Mission, its black tower a constant marker against this strange white sky. I followed the sea path. The further away from the town I went, the more trees there were, unharmed by cannon fire. I wove amongst these survivors, closer and closer to the shore. Seeing a boat bobbing in shallow waters I thought, what spirit! Already the people have begun to fish again. Of course, they must eat...

But the boat was too big. Nobody was dragging nets across the beach. Nobody was singing. My fishermen had whips and sticks, and were driving a file of people, yoked together, along a gangplank. Some stumbled. Some wept. Some raged.

Once you know what you are witnessing, you become part of it.

I have seen it before, many times, from a distance. This time, instead of drifting away, I walked towards the boat. I walked as far as I dared, then hid amongst the trees, coarse grass prickling my ankles.

A little way ahead, a man was observing the uproar. He seemed distracted, every now and then gazing up at the pale sky. On his face was a slight frown, which would have gone unnoticed by anyone who didn't know him well.

Inside me the baby moved, kicking and squirming as if it were trying to escape. I could not move. I did not want to see, but I saw everything.

One sight I will record. A child, a girl of around eleven years, digging her heels into the sand, leaning backwards, straining with all her might against the rope that bound her.

And the noise. The shouts, the screams, the long wails. I heard words in a strange language, and knew those words were prayers and curses. I heard men laugh as they beat the people with sticks, and I heard them snarl at those who resisted. I heard the Khatib say mildly, 'Hurry up, will you?'

He didn't lay a finger on any of them. He glanced at them only when he was not gazing up at the sky.

I walked on. At any moment he might have turned and seen me, but he did not. Maybe he didn't need to turn.

I don't know why he sent me to the Mission that day. I don't know whether he knew about Schiller's promise to me, and if so, whether the little girl's death meant I'd lost my only chance of escape. I don't know why the Khatib wanted me to live, or whether Alisha had told him about the baby.

But I think he knows why I have never been able to ask him for my passage home.

I went back to the Mission and confessed everything to the Abbé, not on my knees through a grille but standing, face to face.

He was kind, but I didn't want kindness. Gentle, but his gentleness hurt me more than any condemnation. He told me that people must survive as best they can; did I realise the Germans had already drawn up plans for the rebuilding of Sinamani? Did I know the people were returning to their old lives, full of hope for the trade which the Germans will revive?

He said the Sisters would help me with the baby. He said that we must stay here until Sinamani is fit for habitation again.

I told him through his frowns and little reproaches and assurances of a healthy delivery that I did not deserve to be buried in this holy ground. I made him promise that when I die, I shall not be buried here, but in some place that makes it clear I was an Englishwoman through and through.

I told Felicien about this promise and he was very angry in the way that only Felicien can be. 'Lucy,' he said. 'You can't talk to the Abbé like that. Who do you think you are?'

Who indeed?

1890

This morning, very early, I crept away while Alisha was asleep. Poor Alisha; she had tried to stay awake for me all night, urging me to breathe, breathe, let it pass ... 'They say it sometimes helps, mama, to walk around,' she murmured, rubbing her eyes, and she dozed off and I tucked her in tenderly, knowing she would not wake.

It was easy to leave the compound, since the gates are no longer locked. There was a light in the church. I would have liked to say goodbye to Felicien.

It was easy to walk down the mango avenue, easy, easy. I kept telling myself: just get to the next tree, and the next, and the next, before the pain comes back –

and then a gasp and a shudder and I was calm again, and telling myself: just get to the next tree ...

I mounted the shallow bank, spiny with seagrass, and caught my breath for pain and joy –

For it was dawn, and before me a chessboard of molten pewter, the squares merged to one shining expanse, all the pieces gone, down into the depths, knights and pawns, kings and queens, vanished in a swirl of silt at the bottom of the ocean.

My opponent invisible, somewhere in the distance where sea and sky intersect.

And between us, nothing but water, and what is water if not the element of unborn children? So I began to walk, and walk, and did not falter. Pain tried to detain me but I did not falter. And the drops of blood sank into the sand and vanished like rubies in a fairytale. I should have been cold, wearing only my petticoat, but the pain when it came… the pain crushed me out of existence…

And it was getting worse and worse, so I tried to think of openness, opalescence… sky reflected in sand… great shining veils to be ripped asunder…

So much harder now there were no trees to encourage me. Only the sea. As the first strong light of day came scything through me, I went down like an animal – but I did not turn back – and then I was myself again and got up and stumbled onward, always onward, to the sea, and I did not fear it now, that vast finality I have been brooding on these last few months.

selfish

the life inside me blameless   vengeful

– shouts and screams on the beach, far away, yet very clear

The sea came powering down upon me, and I was crushed and fell in the foam and the searing cold, everything gone, gone, except for the clarity of pain. Wet brown sand spattering the gravid mass of me. I staggered up – but my legs were trembling with pain and it was so much harder, so much harder to walk through water.

What if I couldn't walk far enough?

panic   screaming for Alisha   on my knees

An echoing scream, further down the beach.

Not a boat in sight.

I sat in the swirling foam and dragged myself round.

Two figures, black, tearing down the beach towards me. A giant black flapping bird of a soutane. A black headscarf, streaming undone.

A storm cloud of black hair.

Two voices, dearly loved, calling *come back, come back*

Mama God

2000

The kid on first base was called Baraka, which means 'blessing'. His talent was obvious, right from the very first day of my Little League, that scrawny bunch who always knew when I was about to visit Karatu to monitor their water system; who would mob the Toyota with its Water for Life logo (child, spurting pump, mama), and who just couldn't get enough of baseball. It had to be better than studying, three kids poring over one book, or herding goats, or weeding maize, or picking coffee, or sweeping their school yard to make the beautiful, pointless fans of dust which appear for five minutes every morning in every school yard across Tanzania.

Baraka was a natural, the most gifted kid I ever saw. Best of all, he knew how to contain himself: how to balance his desire to win with the need to stay calm, and respond calmly and constructively to defeat. So when, that Friday afternoon, I called an end to the game with the score against his side, he didn't moan or jeer but instead trotted from base to makeshift base, picking up sweaters and returning them to their owners, helping me carry the crate of sodas from the back of the Toyota. Then, while I handed out to all the other kids the Sprites, Fantas and Cokes which were the highlight of their afternoon, Baraka asked shyly, 'Mr. Sasha, when will you come again?'

And I had to tell him I wouldn't be back for at least three months. His face showed his disappointment, yet somehow he still managed to look polite and bright and keen. I could have given him my bat there and then, but I didn't, because I knew he'd already made himself one by whittling a branch and sanding it to the right shape. I didn't tell Baraka that one day I would adopt him, take him back to the US where he'd immediately be spotted by the Scouts and signed, because that was just stupid. Instead, I waved them all a cheery goodbye and drove away right on schedule, at 4.30 p.m.

This was what I loved: in the late afternoon to travel along the dust-red road, higher and higher as the sun descended, through a paradise of hill upon hill upon swooping hill. After the rains, the curves and swells of the land are lush with crops: rippling, shimmering masses of maize, coffee trees in neat lines like braids on a woman's head, fragile spires of sisal rising from their spiky nests. Tiny homesteads tucked in the folds and valleys, every now and then a distant gleam of a tin roof. Far away, the soft blue line of the Ngorongoro forest.

The first time I made this journey, it marked the start of my double life: the engineer with a proper job to do – and the luckster, the Lazarus who hardly dared believe he was here again. Nobody had told me about this place; nobody had warned me it would be so beautiful. It was too much, I had to pull over. There was barely a sound. Birdsong. Wind flickering through the crops. Somewhere, a goat bleating. I stood on the roadside above a crumbling red gully of eroded soil, with the rise and fall of hills everywhere, gilded in the late afternoon sun. Everywhere was radiant, and I cried with relief, because I had done it. I had come back.

I descended the Rift Valley escarpment, carefully, brakes on, engine growling, looking out for little kids with buckets of water on their heads. It seemed like the hills would go on for ever, but the road plunged and arched and suddenly I was looking down on Lake Manyara, a sheet of liquid silver, with a strawberry ice cream float of flamingos. Far below in the valley, miniature elephants were going about their business. I knew there would be other animals down there too, but I couldn't see them.

At six I arrived in Mto wa Mbu where I picked up a sack of charcoal, bought several bunches of the obscene pink bananas which taste so much sweeter than yellow ones, and drank chai. Then on, across the savannah for miles and miles as the darkness gathered. A left turn: suddenly the road became tarmac, and it was an easy, tedious drive the rest of the way to Arusha. I delivered the charcoal to one very happy nun, then spent the night in the Sisters' guesthouse, a house so clean you could lick the floor and your tongue would come away cleaner than it was before.

The next day I set off early for the twelve hour drive to Dar Es Salaam. Water for Life safety policy forbade drivers to give lifts, but my colleagues ignored this all the time. I did not.

Towards evening, the Morogoro road took me through the outskirts of the city. Familiar billboards flanked the roads, advertising Vodaphone, Blueband margarine ('Your family is well fed / With Blueband on bread!') and the one that always made me wince: Sportsman cigarettes. A nice easy glide down United Nations Avenue, left onto the Old Bagamoyo Road and I was nearly home.

Kunduchi was the area where junior diplomats lived, and middle-grade aid workers. Expats, like me. There were wire fences everywhere. I didn't much like living there, but the head of HR wouldn't agree for me to live anywhere else, not with that expensive Toyota. My plan was to wait another year, then, once I'd proved how useful I was, persuade her to let me rent a place in town. Most Water for Life employees moved on after their two-year contracts, which was inconvenient for the charity. But I had no intention of moving on.

Salim and Agostino, the askaris, came out from their hut to swing open the gates and wave me in. They were bleary-eyed. I grinned to myself and wound down the window to engage them in a few minutes of greetings and news, which they mumbled their way through. Then I parked the Toyota with all the other vehicles, went inside my bungalow, showered and fell asleep.

At four a.m. it was their turn to wake me, knocking on the bedroom window. 'Sasha! Sasha! Wake up!'

Next to the bungalow there was a chicken shed with a tin roof, three concrete walls and a fourth that was wire mesh. I'd got as far as cleaning out the chicken shit, which the previous Water for Life guy had kindly left for me, then I left the shed empty for a while, and then took to using it for storage. At the moment it contained three huge canisters of blue paint, which I'd promised to buy for a primary school in Singida and deliver on my next safari.

Salim was excited. 'We have caught a thief! He was trying to steal your paint!'

I hugged my pillow and groaned. 'How'd he get in?'

'He was cunning. He was waiting outside until we opened the gates for you, and he crawled in, like a snake. Then he hid. He thought we would go to sleep. But he was wrong! We were more cunning than he was! He went to cut the wire, and we caught him.'

'Where is he now?'

'Agostino has him in our hut. Should we beat him up?'

'No, don't.' I pulled on underpants and sandals and followed Salim out to the hut. The thief was just a kid, a teenager. He wore cut-off jeans, black rubber flip-flops, no shirt. He was shivering. 'That's him,' said Salim, and shone his torch in the kid's eyes, making him flinch.

Agostino showed me some wire cutters, which must have been worth more than the paint. 'Says his dad's a teacher, but I don't believe him.' He gave the boy a shove 'You! If your old man's really a teacher, how come you need to steal?'

But to me the kid looked hungry, ribs carved out above a concave belly, his face more angry than afraid. I said, 'Thanks. You can leave him to me now.'

'Shall we come with you to the police station?'

'No, it's OK. I'll take care of that.'

'We'll open the gates for you.'

'I'm going to talk to him first, inside.'

'Best we come too, in case he attacks you.'

'That's not very likely, Salim.'

The kid was watching us, his face wary, his body braced. 'Come on,' I said, and gripped his elbow to steer him into the bungalow. His arm felt brittle. Inside, I thought I saw at last a flicker of fear in his eyes. He was still shivering. 'Sit down. Go on, sit.'

He sat on one of the armchairs, placing his hands carefully on his knees.

'What's your name?'

The question startled him; he answered before he could think better of it. 'Gabriel.'

'Well, Gabriel. Is this the first time you tried to steal from anyone?'

No answer. He must be stupid to break into a fenced expat compound, policed by contented, well-paid askaris, eager for bonuses. Stupid or desperate.

'Where'd you get the wire cutters from?'

'A person gave them to me.'

'The same person that sent you out to steal for him? Is he paying you? Or does he just give you food and somewhere to sleep?'

No answer. Perhaps, I thought, he's been coerced into thieving. 'Is it true your dad's a teacher?'

'Yes.'

'So why are you doing this? Why do you need to steal? Listen, the best thing is, I take you home.'

For the first time he looked directly at me, puzzled. 'Aren't you going to take me to the police?'

'No, I'm taking you right back to your parents, wherever they are.'

'I don't want to go.'

'Why not? Because you don't want them to know what you've been up to? I guess they'll be ashamed of you, won't they?'

He looked away, scowling.

'Come on, tell me where they live.'

A muttered word. I heard him the first time, but I needed him to say it again.

'*Where?*'

'Sinamani.'

And then I realised this was John Simba's son.

There was a moment when I nearly told him to forget it, to piss off back to his Dar Es Salaam slum. Instead I said, 'We'll go to Sinamani tomorrow. I know your father. He's John Simba, Head of Sinamani Sec.' The kid looked startled, then hung his head, totally wretched. Of course, he didn't remember me.

All the bungalows in the Water for Life compound had bars on the windows to keep burglars out. Or in. I hesitated about locking him in the spare bedroom. What if he tore the mosquito net into strips and hanged himself from the wire loop in the ceiling? I decided to risk it, and told him I was locking the door. He shrugged. I left him standing in the room looking resentful and a bit confused. I went back to bed, but slept badly.

Tanzania is a country where everybody *needs* to know everybody else: a nationwide network of some 40 million people, delivering sacks of grain, lending fifty shillings here, a thousand shillings there, hoisting buckets onto heads, giving each other lifts in pickups, on the crossbars of Chinese bicycles, even on shoulders. Sooner or later I was bound to run into someone I'd known before, even though Dar was three hours down the coast from Sinamani.

Except now, in the new millennium with tarmac on the road, the journey time was halved. When I saw the Mission tower against the sky I was confused for a moment – how could we be here so soon? – but then I began to notice half-remembered places: the police station, the German cemetery, a particular group of trees on the sea path, and then I realised Sinamani had grown, whole blocks of houses with tin roofs where before there had just been sandy wasteland; a brand new Post Office, bigger than the old one; a bright pink National Microfinance Bank. A whitewashed wall snaked smartly along the sea front and beyond it were the neatly thatched, perfectly conical roofs of tourist accommodation. 'Is that a new hotel?' I asked Gabriel. He nodded. 'And that?' There was a gleaming white and plate glass building further ahead.

'Yes. These days they're always building hotels in Sinamani.'

It was the only information he'd volunteered all through the journey. I hadn't wanted to talk to him much. My guts were twisting at the prospect of seeing John and Eluminata again. Maybe I could just drop Gabriel and drive off. But no. I needed to make sure this sulky, hopeless kid got home safely.

I was about to turn right towards the school when Gabriel said, 'They don't live there anymore. Keep going.' We continued along the main road by the sea. Perhaps this was a plot, a heist. Perhaps Gabriel had concealed a cell-phone in his ragged shorts and called ahead to his thieving friends, who'd be waiting for me in some lonely spot with their machetes to slice me into little pieces.

'Stop here,' he said as we approached a mud house where hens were scratching in the dirt. Gabriel got out. Eluminata came from behind the house, wiping her hands on her kanga. She froze for a second, then her hands flew to her face, then she ran to him. Tanzanians rarely embrace in public. She held on to that wretched kid, crushing him in her arms as if she meant to take him back into her own body, crying over and over, 'My child! My child!' And he just stood there with his arms hanging down by his sides, and I wanted to hit him. I got out of the Toyota but she didn't look at me. John Simba came out of the house, scowling. He was just as I remembered, except his hair had a dusting of grey. 'You!' he growled at his son. 'I'm going to thrash you!' Then he saw me, and his eyes seemed to kindle with disbelief, and something else. 'Sasha? Can it be?'

And Eluminata, one arm around her boy, was clasping my hand and John Simba gripped my other hand in both of his, so we all stood there, joined to each other, laughing, exclaiming, asking questions –

'Have you brought our son back to us?'

'We thought he was dead, thank you, thank you!'

'I'm sorry I haven't – '

'Are you here now? In Tanzania?'

'We didn't know where he was!'

'I would have come before, but – '

'I can't believe it's you!'

'I've thought about you so many times.'

Only Gabriel said nothing.

They urged me inside, and I accepted, because you can't refuse hospitality in Tanzania. It's worse than rude. This house was much smaller than the old headmaster's house; humbler, the walls wattle and daub with a thin, cool plastering of mud.

'Where did you find him?' Eluminata asked me. There was a moment when I might have told the truth. But she was so happy, and I couldn't bear to spoil it.

'I was driving down Samora Avenue, and he was hitching a lift. Weren't you, Gabriel?'

'Yes,' he muttered. The little shit could have looked more grateful. Then a tiny girl, about three years old, ran in

234

and at last he broke into a smile as he swept her up and swung her round.

'My last born,' John Simba said, smiling too.

There was to be no getting away from them. Eluminata said, 'You will eat with us.' John produced the photo albums and I was glad to flick through the pages while I answered his curious questions. Yes, I was a water engineer now; yes, Water for Life was an excellent charity. Yes, I'd taken an intensive Swahili course in the States before departure and, thank you, I was making reasonable progress. Yes, the engineering degree had been long and hard work and yes, it cost a lot, a phenomenal amount, of money. I didn't tell him exactly how much, nor that my injury insurance had more than covered it. And it was a relief not to have to explain myself, as I'd done so many, many times back home – 'But Sasha, why engineering? You always looked so good on TV, you could have been a great commentator... Gee, you would have made a bomb through endorsements. That girl you were seeing, didn't she go to Africa? You're going to be a what? A water engineer? Don't you have to be good at math?'

Only my brother Carl knew what had happened in Tanzania. Carl was the only one I could tell what it's like, when a woman hoists a bucket onto another woman's head, the biting of the lip, the trembling of the neck muscles. The weight of it – and how they do this every day, like eating or sleeping – and he said, OK, I get it, and never questioned me again about my decision to go back to college. But he did ask: 'Why there? Why Tanzania again?'

Golden morning light. The sun setting and the moon coming up like an apricot. The space. No take-out coffee. No multimedia crap. No houses stuffed with a million trivial objects. The meandering jangle of Afropop, looping on and on and on from some ancient tape machine powered by exhausted batteries. The psychedelic birds whose names I always meant to look up and never did.

Woodsmoke. Frangipani. Jacaranda trees like blue spirits. The way you greet a friend by clasping their hand and they don't let go.

'I get all that,' Carl said. 'But why Tanzania? Why not somewhere else in Africa?'

I told him how I longed to do something useful. I didn't say that my previous existence: those years of bringing the crowd to an orgasmic peak of triumph, or driving them crazy with frustration, seemed like a wasted life.

'Sasha. Why there?'

I said nothing.

My brother, the physician, looked at me hard. 'You can't put those kids right. The little girl on Zanzibar died because she was dehydrated. And those babies, you know, they might have died anyway, even if you had made it to the hospital.'

'It's not that. I don't think.'

'Sasha, if you want to do something useful, there are any number of ways… Why don't you just stay right here, teach crack-head teenagers to play baseball and get them off our streets?'

But in John Simba's house I was a water engineer, and that was all.

Bolder by the minute, I asked whether Juliet was still at the hospital. John couldn't remember her; I had to prompt him. No, he said, she went back to… Germany, was it? England? 'Now they have no wazungu doctors at the hospital, only Tanzanians.'

'That's good,' I said cautiously.

He pursed his lips. 'If they are up to the job.' About his own work he was sketchier. He'd resigned from being headmaster because he was fed up with complaints from his staff, complaints from the students, everyone blaming him for everything. Better just to teach chemistry, ya.

Something wasn't being said. I sensed things had not gone well for John and his family. Eluminata served up rice and beans, and once we'd finished eating I felt I could leave, but they made me promise I'd come again soon. 'You won't recognise Sinamani,' John said. 'You'll be amazed by what they're doing to this town.'

Outside, as Eluminata called her little girl to say goodbye, Gabriel sidled up to me and muttered, 'Thank you?' – meaning, was I really going to keep my mouth shut. I told him he was lucky, that he should go to school, work hard and obey his parents. He nodded, relieved, and managed a half-smile and a wave as I pulled away.

It had been so easy to come back, to face them again, that now I felt dazed, and a little ashamed. Well, time to make up for being such a wuss. Time to see off a few more ghosts. Although from what John had said, those ghosts had gone anyway, back to Europe.

I left the Land Cruiser outside the post office and went down the wide, cobbled path that led to the old Customs house and the sea. In front of me a boy was carrying a sack of rice on his head. Chickens scrabbled for grains leaking from a hole in the hessian. For a while I stood by the Customs house, to my left, the grid of stone pillars topped with metal dishes, as baffling as ever. Men leaned against them, chatting, staring idly at the sea that shifted like a restless sleeper. A distant haze might have been Zanzibar.

I wandered back towards the town. Several old buildings – the boma, the block house, some of the grander Arab houses – were surrounded by miniature white picket fences, no more than two feet high, which a child could have stepped over. Each had its own signboard, announcing that the Ministry for Antiquities was supervising this and that restoration project, gratefully acknowledging the assistance of NORAD or DANEDA or DFID or some other acronym. Looking at the blockhouse, I wondered how they would turn a wedge of mouldy limestone into a tourist attraction. More to the point, *why*?

I went into a bar, and from habit and the need to practise my Swahili tuned into the conversations around me. Two guys were planning a journey: who might give them a lift, where they'd stop along the way, how much it would cost and how they should split it. The barman was complaining that someone had failed to deliver ten kilos of onions. A tall young woman with a pair of glasses clipped to the breast pocket of her white blouse was ticking him off: you should never have trusted that guy, you were an idiot – but it was only a joke, I guessed from his reaction. Other men were laughing. He begged her to leave him alone, and I thought I heard him call her 'Mama God.' After a while she stopped teasing him, strolled over to the open door and stood there, fiddling with the glasses in her pocket, watching everyone who passed by.

On my way back to the Land Cruiser I noticed a bright yellow building in a grove of banana trees. I didn't remember seeing it first time round. Like Gulliver, I stepped over the low fence and read the sign board, which told me the Ministry for Antiquities was rebuilding the Caravanserai with the help of the Danish government. The Caravanserai was where the slave porters rested at the end of their long journey. Porters who were slaves themselves? Or porters who, somewhere in 'the interior', had trapped and captured their fellow human beings and forced them all the way to the coast?

There was a neat pile of trash in the dust: embers, a greasy, crumpled sheet of newspaper, chicken bones, a coke bottle with dregs in the bottom. This was very recent trash, before the dogs had had a chance to get it. And who would drop a valuable bottle, when you couldn't buy a soda without giving an empty bottle in exchange? Maybe a tourist.

But there wasn't a lot for tourists to see; just this long, two-storey building with spaces for the windows and door. I stepped over the threshold. There was a strong smell of paint, the grey cement floor spattered with yellow like smashed eggs. In America there would have been an entrance foyer and gift shop, headsets with commentaries in fifteen different languages; probably some life-size, fibreglass slaves.

Upstairs, at the far end of the landing a window showed a stark view: white sky, dark ocean. There were two rooms off the landing. I was just about to go through the doorway into the first room, when I saw it had no floor. My stomach turned over. In the next room they had begun to lay the crossbeams. Another window, another ocean view.

'What are you doing here without permission?'

I jumped. It was the woman from the café. 'Sorry,' I said in English. 'I don't understand Swahili.'

She laughed. 'You liar, Sasha! I heard you speaking to the barman.'

Where had I seen that smile before?

'Excuse me?' I said. 'Do we know each other?'

She unhooked the glasses from her pocket and put them on.

'*Grace?*'

Grace, Juliet's sidekick. Helpful, kind Grace with the soothing hands. Grace, my only comforter as I lay on that narrow hospital bed. Grace, who had tried to persuade me not to leave Tanzania.

We stood grinning at each other, exchanged brief resumés. She was still at the hospital – 'I'm a doctor now.' I figured this meant she was a medical assistant, doing more or less the work of a GP. Grace nodded approvingly when I told her about Water for Life. Again, I didn't have to explain myself, defend the radical career change. She was more interested in my Swahili – how long had I been learning? A year? How come I was so good, after such a short time?

Flattery and the smell of paint and wet plaster were making me light headed. 'Are you really supposed to get permission to come here?' I asked. 'It doesn't look like there's so much to see.'

'You know, our government loves history, because they can make money out of it. They hope lots of tourists will come to Sinamani – but they haven't planned what to do with them when they get here, so right now they're trying to make themselves very important with all these rules and regulations.' To prove how little she cared for the rules, she moved past me, into the doorway. 'This room has a very nice view, I think.'

She stepped onto one of the bare wooden joists.

'Grace – that's probably not safe – I wouldn't ...'

She began to walk along the joist, steadily, and she did not stop until she reached the window. 'Ah yes,' she said. 'There's Zanzibar. Looks like cloud. But you better not follow me; these planks might not bear your weight. Our leaders don't have money for good materials.'

Then she turned neatly on her heel to face me, and leant back against the sill. I was sweating. If she tripped, she might fall across the beams, or she might drop down between them, straight down to the cement floor several feet below. 'Grace,' I bleated, 'please be careful.' She smiled, that lovely, dancing smile, and walked towards me. She was almost home. Then it happened as quick as this: her foot slipped, she lurched, I lunged forward, grabbed her round the waist, she cried out. I gripped her. I was afraid I might be hurting her with my thumbs jabbing into her ribcage. Her heart was beating rapidly. We stood there until she regained her balance. At last I stepped back, wincing at the pain in my knee, and pulled her towards me, onto solid ground. I loosened my grip a fraction but kept my hands around her.

She laughed, shakily. 'Goodness. You've saved my life, Sasha.'

Through the windows, the white light seemed to tremble too. I gulped a breath, inhaled that dragging fume of paint. 'You looked after me once, Grace. I've never forgotten how kind you were.'

'You were very sick. Malaria, as well as that terrible accident. And then you left us. How long did it take you to recover?'

'A long time. Until I came back here, I guess. I couldn't get over it, Grace. Those babies…' My throat was tightening. This wasn't how I wanted it to be.

She laid her hand on my arm. 'You had very bad luck. Today it wouldn't happen; there are so many more people with cars. And we have ambulances, yes, even here in Sinamani. But then, you had no choice. You did what you thought was best.'

For eight years I had been waiting to hear those words, and now I had to turn my face away. Gently, she pressed her fingers against my forearm, and I wanted her to stop because I was afraid I might cry, but at the same time I wanted her to carry on.

She asked me if I was staying at one of the beach hotels, and seemed only a little disappointed when I told her I was going back to Dar.

'So when will you come to visit me at the hospital?'

Perhaps she understood nothing; perhaps she had no idea how much it would cost me to make that particular journey again. Or perhaps she understood me very well. 'Wait.' She produced a cellphone from her skirt pocket. 'Here is my number.'

The paint fumes were threatening to make me pass out, but I put her number in my phone, and I gave her mine.

Outside, amongst the airy green fringes of the banana trees, I felt better. 'Listen,' I said, 'let's go somewhere and eat, shall we?'

'I would like to, but I have to get home to my little kid. He's only seven. You call me when you want to visit, OK?'

She walked away, a slim, pale figure in the dusk. At the fence she turned. 'You won't forget to call?'

'Of course not,' I said, wondering who the little kid's father was.

Normally during a break between Water for Life safaris I would chill out: swim in Oyster Bay, lounge around the bungalow surfing the Net, go shopping in the ex-pat stores of Dar Es Salaam for apples that tasted like damp cottonwool. But this week, after debriefing at the office, I made sure to keep busy. I swam every day, and every day on the beach I coached my Dar baseball team who had no talent and drove me crazy with their cheating and grumbling. I took the Toyota to the garage for maintenance, and walked all round the city, looking up friends, looking up people I hardly knew: geologists, businessmen, a missionary from Ohio, Peace Corps trainees, beautiful Swedish girls, and I begged them to come out with me for a beer or a meal. It was clear some of them were wondering why this engineer guy, who had a reputation for keeping himself to himself, should suddenly become so friendly. I'm sorry to say the missionary thought I was hitting on her.

If nobody could be persuaded to keep me company, I sat at home firing off emails to everyone and blue airmail letters to Grandma who was not on-line. I didn't tell a soul, not even Carl, that I had been back to Sinamani.

I did not call Grace, did not call, did not call, but thought of her the whole time. At last, when I was on the beach, my cellphone rang. 'Why didn't you call?' she said. 'You promised me. Are you a liar, Sasha?' Then I felt bad. Once we had negotiated my safaris and her duty rota, we agreed that I would visit on a Saturday.

I set off early, so I could see John Simba and his family first. This time there were more children at home, and they all seemed delighted to see me, all except Gabriel, who slouched away muttering, 'Shikamo.'

'How's he doing?' I asked Eluminata. Her face went tight. 'Gabriel's back at school, but he won't study. His father says he's lazy. I don't know... Sasha, do you think Gabriel's intelligent? Are we wasting our money on sending him to school?'

I blustered about qualifications, remembering my own barely contained schooldays. Eluminata looked worried. 'That's what his father says: if you study, you have more chances in life. Me, I think it would be better if Gabriel had a job. He loves money. But there are no jobs. There is no money.'

Gabriel's problems gave me something else to think about as I drove to the hospital. It was just a road, a dusty, sun-hardened road. The bridge had been widened, its walls raised. Because of me? Don't be so arrogant. I took the bridge a fraction too fast, and as the Toyota sailed over the hump my stomach lifted and I thought, 'You've done it. Now forget it.'

The hospital still didn't look like a hospital, with its few, low, whitewashed buildings and orange marigolds planted all along the front verandah. More signboards, this time from the Ministry of Health. Thank you to the Norwegians, for helping us build another ward. By 1998 (two years ago) the maternity ward will be completed.

I drove through the compound gates, parked as close to the main building as I could. There was a smell of food: people with baskets for their sick relatives. One guy carried a plasma bag full of blood – he was in a hurry. A nurse told me how to get to Grace's house, some way behind the hospital buildings. It crossed my mind she might have inherited Juliet's bungalow, but no, hers was much smaller.

Of course. The house stood in a sunny clearing amongst the trees. Women were pottering in and out of what I guessed was the communal kitchen: an ugly grey concrete cube. The trees and bushes were draped with drying laundry.

A girl, maybe twelve or thirteen years old, was kneeling at Grace's front door with a bowl of brown water, scrubbing the step. When she saw me she jumped up, wiped her hands on her kanga and came forward shyly, offering the back of her hand. 'Shikamo mzungu. Doctor is working.'

I hoped, a fierce, angry hope, that there had not been some misunderstanding, or emergency, or any situation that would stop me from seeing Grace today – then the girl chirruped, 'Welcome inside to wait for Doctor,' and everything was fine again.

There was a couch under the window, and two wooden armchairs. The blue seat pads were draped with lacy knitted purple mats, the type that made you twitchy about sitting down in case you dislodged them. Against the wall was a sideboard with a large English dictionary and some medical reference books on top, also a stack of glasses with gold rims, a red thermos flask and a cellphone charger. Placed carefully on another purple mat, the fragile corpse of a butterfly. Above the cupboard there was a picture of the Virgin Mary, holding out her hands and gazing down as if to say, 'Just look at all this mess!'

Through a doorway hung with a bead curtain I glimpsed the corner of a bed, the mosquito net bundled up overhead in its wire ceiling loop. A trunk with a massive padlock was pushed against the wall. Everything was angular and neat.

'Mzungu, have some tea!' The girl poured sweet, black, scalding tea from the thermos and told me her name was Martina.

'Are you the doctor's ndugu?'

'Yes!' She didn't have any tea herself, but went outside and came back with a bowl of fresh soapy water and a sopping brown rag. Then she started to clean the floor, not on all fours but bending from the waist with her butt in the air, shoving the rag energetically from side to side. 'Every day I do this for Doctor. Doctor works very hard. She's coming home soon.' I lifted my huge feet for her to clean beneath, and settled down for a long wait.

At two, I heard children's voices. School was out. A small boy sidled in, and eyeballed me. 'Shikamo mzungu.' Then he said in English, 'How are you?'

'I'm fine, thank you,' I said obediently. 'How are you?'

'Fine, thank you.' Big grin.

'What is your name?'

'My name is Godlisten. What is your name?'

'Sasha. How was school today?'

'Good.' He hesitated, and reverted to Swahili. 'We played soccer.'

He showed me a ball made from scrunched-up plastic bags tied with string. I offered him a game. That was how Grace found us, some time later, kicking the ball around amongst the trees. She walked slowly, her white coat hanging open, and when I saw her I felt a huge rush of relief and uncertainty. She was tired, with that faraway look of someone who has been up all night. But she smiled, and held out her hand to me, apologising for having to work late because her boss, Dr. Hamisi, was away.

'No problem.' Nothing was a problem. I wanted her to sit and rest; Martina begged her to sit and rest, but Grace would not; she and Martina disappeared into the kitchen and after a while came out with a pot full of pilau. We sat outside to eat, Godlisten perched on a stone, Martina cross-legged on a mat, Grace and I on chairs either side of her front door. The afternoon sun was golden; the pilau perfect: tender goat meat, delicate, fragrant rice. We drank more tea. 'Let's go for a walk to my shamba,' she said. She was tired, I protested – but I didn't protest much. Grace wrapped a red and gold kanga round her hips and tucked it in at the waist. Over her hair she tied a black scarf fringed with gold beads. 'The dust is terrible.'

Clouds of dust flared around our ankles as we walked down the path beyond the compound, across open land. Everything was exposed: a thorn tree, a single house, a tiny child herding goats. I had to ask. 'Where is Baba Godlisten?'

'He died,' she said serenely.

'I'm sorry.' It was a lie.

'That's OK. He ran away before Godlisten was born. Godi never knew him. It's a pity he died,' – she shrugged – 'but I have a nice kid. That's all I ever wanted.'

Not so good. For a while we walked in silence. Then I asked about her shamba; she described her two acres that came with the job and a third she'd saved to buy and paid a boy to cultivate; how she juggled the cost of the land and cultivation with the profit she might make, and how it all depended, always, on the weather. This year the weather had been kind; the rains had come and gone at the right time. Ahead of us was a fortress of crops: a thick, solid mass of green. We came closer, into its shadow. Then we slipped between the rows of maize, the tough stalks flapping with long, dark leaves, the cobs swathed in a paler, milky green. It felt secret, almost as if we were underground, breathing the rich smell of baked earth and a sweet hint of what was hidden inside those parcelled cobs. Grace tugged one off the stalk and stripped away its silky sheath of fibres to show the packed nuggets. 'A present for you,' she said. 'This year we won't go hungry.' I ran my fingers along the cool, nubbly grains.

Something rustled. Grace stilled me with her hand. A few feet away, crouching among the lowest leaves was a digdig, a tiny creature part dog, part fawn. It quivered as it held our gaze, then kicked up its heels and fled.

We walked on along the rows, deeper and deeper. 'How will you harvest all this?'

'Everyone must help; Martina, Godi, Juma who drives the ambulance – he's a strong young man and very kind to us. Even I, whenever I'm not on duty I will come here and harvest maize, maize, maize. Then I'll store it until it's dry and then I'll hire a machine and thresh it.' She glanced at me, her eyes full of mischief. 'Maybe you can help too?'

'Of course!' I burbled. 'I'd love to, please let me know when you need me. Any time, honestly. Any time when I'm not working, just give me a call and I'll be right here.'

I'm sure she knew, even then, how often I had to work away; she must have realised how desperate I was to please her. She changed the conversation. Was Water for Life a good employer? How much did I earn? (People asked me that question all the time.) And, 'You weren't with Water for Life before, were you? How come you work for them now?'

So I described what I'd seen eight years ago: the girl walking with the bucket on her head, the bucket rocking and toppling, the drenching, the anger, the wretched waste. How I'd felt bad ever since, because where I came from, nobody had to walk for water.

Plus, I told her, I needed to do something with my life. Something with a meaning.

She nodded. Then she asked another familiar question. 'What about your wife? Where is she?'

'I don't have a wife.'

Another rustle, another digdig – or maybe it was the same one. We waited until it had the courage to run away. 'Too small to eat,' said Grace. 'Not enough meat on it.' I didn't know whether she was joking.

We began to walk back through the maize. 'Why did you become a doctor?' I asked. 'All that training.' (And all that expense, I wanted to say, but I didn't want her to confirm my guess that Juliet had paid.)

'To be a doctor is good, especially for a woman. I have status. Not much money, but status. So I can get things on credit at the market. Don't worry, Mama Godi, they say, pay me for those tomatoes another day. I can send money home to my mother, to help her. I pay my little sister's school fees, and I'll be able to send Godi to secondary school too. I don't need to rely on anyone.'

Here she was, living Nyerere's dream of self-reliance. I was touched. Then, as we came out into the sunlight she said, 'I don't need a man to look after me.'

Back at the staff quarters, Martina and Godlisten came running down the path to meet us. They looked agitated. 'The old man is angry,' Martina piped. 'He's angry with the mzungu.'

'What old man?' said Grace, and then, 'Aah.'

A strange figure was stumping towards us through the trees. He wore a long white kanzu and a kofia, and a peevish look on his face.

'Shikamo, mzee,' Grace said lightly.

He glared. 'This one' – jerking his head at me – 'has parked his car in the ambulance space.'

I didn't like his tone, but I said, 'Sorry, I didn't know. There wasn't a sign. I'll move it right now.'

'You shouldn't have left it there.' As I walked away I thought I heard him say, 'The mzungu says he didn't know, but he's lying.' Or maybe that was just my Swahili letting me down.

It was evening, time for me to return to Dar, but I didn't want to leave like this, hassled by some grouchy schmuck, so I moved the Toyota and went back to the bungalow. Grace was wandering from bush to bush, gathering up the dry laundry. Martina squatted by a small charcoal stove, coaxing heat from the embers ready to cook a stack of

248

chapattis. Godlisten was singing throatily as he cleaned his shoes. I wanted to stay.

They insisted I had more chai and chapattis before I left. 'Who was that bad-tempered man?' I asked.

'Mzee Abdallah?' Grace was placid. 'He guards the compound.'

'Is he always so sour?'

'He just likes to do his job well.'

'I'm not scared of Mzee Abdallah,' said Godlisten, but Grace and Martina turned on him. 'You! You should show respect to your elders! Don't say you're not scared of him or he might give you something to be scared about!'

'Sorry Mama,' he said sweetly.

Later, when their attention was elsewhere, he murmured to me, very low, 'I'm not scared of that old man.'

Grace didn't offer to walk back with me through the compound; maybe she was already aware of how much gossip my visit would stir up, and didn't want to expose herself to any more than necessary. So she said, 'Martina will see you to your car,' and 'When will you come again?' which was enough for me.

For a couple of months we carried on: brief phone calls, longer emails, and I tried to figure out what these chatty, newsy conversations meant, but I was never much good at reading between the lines, and besides, I wanted to take Grace for just what she appeared to be: a kind, intelligent, hardworking Tanzanian woman, who liked me for the same reasons I liked her. In between work safaris I managed three more visits to Sinamani. On none of these trips did I call on John Simba, which I felt bad about, especially when I saw Gabriel lurking around the market place in his school uniform. But I needed to spend as much time as possible with Grace, or at least making myself useful around Grace's house, chopping wood or lugging sacks of beans from the communal storeroom, since despite our efforts to coordinate our schedules, more often than not Grace would be required to assist at an emergency operation or attend to some patient or other. At first I suspected her boss Dr. Hamisi of overworking her, but when I met him I liked him: dapper, bearded, energetic and from the way he talked, very much in his awe of his wife. So he was no rival.

Then we arranged a fourth visit, for the whole weekend. 'You can stay at my place,' she said, not looking at me.

It was Saturday morning. Before I set out from Dar, Grace had called to say she had a meeting in town with her bank manager; could I wait for her. Now I had a few hours to kill in Sinamani. I felt jittery. At the Agip station a battered pickup with the Pwani diocese logo was parked on the forecourt. A mzungu squatted at the rear left wheel, tightening a nut. As he stood up we glanced at each other, as white people do, and then we did a double-take. It was Sid.

'I heard you were back,' he said, and I felt bad for not looking him up. 'John Simba told me how you found Gabriel. So now you're a water engineer?'

'Long story. And you're still the pilot.'

'Still the pilot.'

'And still in that house with the ocean view?'

He laughed. 'My view disappeared a long time ago. They've built a hotel on the beach.'

'Do you mind?'

'Not at all,' he said, mildly. 'I could move if I wanted. Tourism will be the saving of Sinamani, as Kurt here will tell you.'

Another man got out of the pickup: a huge man, bigger than me, with long ginger hair and a dark red beard. Sid said, 'This is Kurt the Dane.'

We shook hands and walked across to the Alpha Motel for a drink. Kurt was a builder, an expert in limestone restoration. He described the finicky, inch-by-inch care

250

needed to remove cryptogamic growth: the mould that stippled the fort, the boma and the blockhouse. 'Little did Von Wissmann know, when he holed himself up in that chunk of stone, he'd be creating a job opportunity for some *kijana* in the next Millennium.'

'What kind of *kijana*?'

'The kind that needs to be kept out of trouble. The kind that hangs around the market place smoking dope and stirring up gossip.'

That gave me an idea, but I stayed quiet about it.

'Are you working on the Caravanserai? I already went in there. Guess I wasn't supposed to.'

Kurt groaned. 'No watchman? These guys! But it's not such an issue there. The Caravanserai is a reconstruction, not a restoration. What did you think of it?'

'It seemed kind of … new.'

'And soulless, I know. But the original didn't survive the Bushiri war, and the Ministry wanted us to rebuild it.'

'Wouldn't they rather forget about that time?'

'Sasha,' said Sid, 'you can't say that. That's sacrilege.'

Kurt shrugged. 'Most people outside of East Africa have no idea about the East African slave trade. I didn't, before Daneda offered me this posting. Maybe you have a point, Sasha, but on the other hand, if tourists come to Sinamani to lie on the beach and take snaps of each other grinning outside historic buildings, well, Foreign Exchange is Foreign Exchange. They're going to make the Caravanserai into a museum, so it will once again be at the hub of the town, but this time for two good reasons: ensuring nobody forgets the slave trade and raking in the dollars. And there'll be plenty more jobs: guides, ticket collectors, someone to sell postcards. It could be the salvation of Sinamani.' Kurt rubbed his hands together, his eyes twinkling – but I sensed some misgivings about this whole tourism thing. He was keeping his doubts to himself and I admired him for that. I'd heard too many wazungu

251

aid workers bellyaching about mischannelled funds, harebrained schemes, lack of Tanzanian forethought, their sorrowful exasperation failing to disguise a smugness that set my teeth on edge.

We finished our drinks. Kurt, in his perfect, idiomatic English, invited me to visit one of the projects some time. 'We're going to start on the chessboard next, and it'll be the devil's own work trying to stop people from walking all over it. You're welcome to come and have a look, if ever you're passing through Sinamani.'

I couldn't help myself. 'I come as often as I can, to see Grace.'

'Your girlfriend?'

I hesitated. 'Kind of my girlfriend, yes.' Kurt laughed, sympathetically. Sid didn't say anything, and I wished he would.

As Sid and I walked back to the Agip station, on impulse I produced my idea. 'Let me run this past you. John Simba's boy Gabriel needs a job – his mother's scared he's going to quit school again. Do you think Kurt could fix up something for him in one of those tourist places?'

'Gabriel? He's a dodgy little kid.'

'Not so little now.'

'And intelligent. Too intelligent, that's the problem. I don't think John could afford for him to go to college, even if he wanted to.'

'Then could we get him a job? It might just put him on the right track; a salary, some responsibility. Would Kurt give him a chance?'

'Kurt would give anyone a chance.'

So I was feeling cock-a-hoop when I went to collect Grace from her meeting with the bank manager. She was sitting on a low wall in front of the bank, fanning herself with a newspaper.

'Was your meeting OK?'

'We've come to an agreement.' She stood up. 'Let's go and eat.'

She took me, I noticed, not to the café where we usually went, but to a smaller place with a smaller, cheaper menu. We ate omelette and chips and I told her my great plan for Gabriel.

'He's lucky,' she said. Her tone was sharper than usual.

'Don't you think it's a good idea?'

'There are others who deserve a chance more than he does.'

I was surprised at her lack of enthusiasm, and I admit it, indignant. How come she was pouring cold water on my brilliant idea? 'He's very young, Grace, he's just a kid who needs... a bit of guidance, that's all. Sid said it would be good for him.'

'Sid is soft-hearted. Like all wazungu.' She saw I was hurt and patted my arm, which didn't help. 'Sasha, it's not *bad* to give Gabriel a job – but his father's a teacher, his mother has her chickens, which he could help her with. There are so many ways to make a living. It's a struggle for all of us.'

I wanted to say: then why not let me pay for our lunch? Why fret about Godi's school fees when I could take care of everything for you?

Things got worse. We went back to the Land Cruiser and as I turned the key in the ignition Grace said, 'You're not wearing your seatbelt.'

Still annoyed I said, 'I'll put it on if it makes you happy.'

'No, put it on to keep yourself safe, and keep your passenger safe too.'

I had a flashback: John and Eluminata and me, upside down in a ditch. I jabbed my foot down and revved the engine.

'OK,' she said, 'I'll walk.' She opened the door and jumped out.

I did a U-turn, drove off down the main road to Dar.

I drove for five minutes, feeling like I had a rock in my throat. Angry with Grace for talking down to me. Angry with myself for being upset that my brilliant idea had been rubbished by Grace. Furious for being afraid that Grace only wanted me because I was a mzungu who would give her lifts and help her do errands. There, I'd admitted it. Sad, above all, for wanting so desperately to fit in. What came first: my own pathetic keenness to belong here, or the genuine desire to help?

When I played baseball, had I wanted to win because I loved winning, because I needed to please other people, or because it had never occurred to me that you could play not to win, and one day you might not be able to play at all?

And there was more. I was angry with myself because I'd seen it in others: the arrogance of white people who didn't like being told they were in the wrong – who'd made all this effort to come to Tanzania and 'live like *this*' – the deprivation, the lousy roads, the absence of fast food, the constant guilt – when we could so easily have turned our backs, and yet still 'these people' weren't grateful enough.

Driving fast along the coast road, I gulped that lump of anger until it melted down to a sadness deep in my belly. Then I did another U-turn and drove back to Sinamani.

I slowed to a stop at the sight of her tall figure ahead of me on the road to the hospital. She didn't look round, marching on with her chin up. I got down and ran after her. 'Grace, that was a stupid, stupid argument.'

She kept on marching. I danced in front of her, blocking her way. She stopped. It could have been that she was figuring out how to get past without us touching.

'Please, Grace, I'm sorry. Please forgive me.'

I was speaking English. It made me sound weak and dumb. I didn't care. Perhaps that was what made her relent. She seemed to sigh as she came towards me, and kept on

254

coming, until she was close enough to embrace. A bittersweet kiss, all muddled up with regret and concern, but there was relief at the end of it.

Back in our seats, I fastened my belt and said, 'Why was I such an idiot? Forgive me. You were right.'

'Hamna maneno,' she replied, which in Tanzania is a polite waving aside of an apology: *you have no need to say anything*. Truer than she knew. Our rambling conversations, me with my inadequate Swahili, my hilarious errors, all that was just a diversion from the real work of love, which is trying to understand how the other person thinks; to second-guess their happiness and their loneliness.

All the rest of that Saturday I made myself useful around her house, fixing the kitchen roof, chopping wood, and when Grace got summoned to the hospital I prayed: please don't let her have to work tonight, please let her come home soon.

She returned at seven. We ate, we went for a walk. When we came back, Martina and Godi were asleep. This was how she had planned it. So I enfolded her weary limbs in mine, on that narrow couch under the window, moonlight exposing every dark thread in the thin cotton kanga pinned over the glass. I had often wondered how couples in Tanzania found privacy. Now I knew. And we were at ease with each other, maybe because she was so tired after her long shift, too tired to be on edge, and I was still dazed from the great good luck of having my stupidity forgiven and my audacious hopes fulfilled.

Tracing her belly with my finger I found the jagged, rosy seam of a scar. 'Ah yes,' Grace murmured. 'There it is.'

'What happened?'

'Godi did not want to come out,' she said serenely. 'We both nearly died. You know, Africans say a pregnant woman has one foot in the grave. But we were lucky, God heard my prayers. That is why I called my child Godlisten.'

I stroked the scar. She laid her hand over mine, pressed it against her.

Next morning Godlisten said 'Shikamo' to his mama and then to me, and Martina ladled out four bowls of maize porridge and we all ate breakfast together. My leg didn't hurt. The sky was molten blue, and I felt I had never been so happy in my life.

How much time did we spend together, that year? Between my safaris and her shifts, not much – but enough for it to become known that I was Grace's lover. We were an item of interest; people seemed pleased to see us around Sinamani, hailing Grace as 'Mama Doctor,' or 'Mama God,' and me as 'Bwana Maji' – 'Mister Water'. I was suspicious at first, looking out for signs of jealousy, resentment, anything that might make life difficult for Grace. But there was nothing. Just the weary politeness of women on their way to draw water, or trudging back from the fields; or the passing muttered greetings of men walking, walking, walking, some of them skinny as skeletons, their faces so hollow you could see the outline of their skulls, who had more serious things to worry about than the good lady doctor and the oversized mzungu.

The only blight on our happiness was Mzee Abdallah, the watchman with that yellowish, reptilian face that seemed about to collapse in on itself, the leathery wattles, the darting, malicious eyes.

I know it shouldn't matter what he looked like.

He took against me from the start. If I parked in front of the hospital, that was where the ambulance should go. If I parked to the side, I was taking up the ambulance's turning space. If I parked behind the buildings, the Toyota was out of his line of sight and therefore he couldn't be blamed if anyone stole it. One night, when Grace and I had been out visiting friends, we came back late and he snapped at us through the iron bars, 'The gates are closed at eleven.'

'That's right,' I said, 'and it's your job to open them.'

Grace laid her hand on my arm. 'No problem, Sasha.'

'There *is* a problem. There's a problem if he makes out we're doing something wrong when we're not. Plus, does he have a go at you when you come back late on your own? No, I thought not.'

I'd never seen Grace so mild. 'Mzee, we beg forgiveness. We shan't offend again.' Perhaps that was just me, struggling to translate her Swahili. But I don't think so. He wouldn't make eye contact, muttered to himself as he opened the gates, managed to spoil the end of our evening.

And I swear I didn't do it to provoke him, but I took to travelling to Sinamani late at night, after work, just so Grace and I could have more time together. I always had to pass Mzee Abdallah first and he'd keep me waiting; ten, fifteen minutes before he came trudging along with his torch and his bunch of keys; or sometimes he wouldn't come at all, forcing me to shout and rattle the gates. 'Don't wake the sick people,' he'd snarl. Or, if I'd waited patiently like a good boy, 'How come you're just standing there? You're supposed to call me.'

To be honest, I minded that Grace wouldn't side with me, didn't seem to get that what he was doing was outrageous. Racist, even. Once, when he'd bawled me out in front of Grace and a crowd of hospital visitors for driving 'too close' to the gatepost, she said, 'Sasha, leave him, he's a stupid old man,' which comforted me – until some time later, when I realised my Swahili had let me down again, and I'd confused *mjinga* (stupid) with *mjanja* (cunning) which was what she'd actually said.

I groused to Carl, who emailed straight back, 'Why are you getting so wound up about some totally powerless menial guy? You should just enjoy what you've got. Be happy, Sasha. At long last.'

He was right; everything else was going well. The rhythm of my working days: hard physical work, grappling with pipes, connections, pumps, to achieve that final precious spurt of clean water. The hours I spent on the road did not seem lonely when I knew I would soon see Grace again. I relished the new energy in Sinamani too: the spruced-up buildings, the hotels along the beach, gleaming slabs of concrete and plate glass, or, for the more daring tourist, picturesque huts that were so far from the reality of a Tanzanian round house, swirling with smoke and the thick stench of cattle dung. All the talk around town was of Foreign Exchange and development. Maybe a leisure industry servicing the needs of white tourists wasn't the self-reliance Nyerere had in mind back at Independence, but it seemed to be effective. Already, tourists roamed the streets, zooming in on a carved lotus flower, patting the heads of small children. And this was before any of the historic buildings were officially open, although I saw some whites on tiptoe, trying to peer in through the slit window of the blockhouse. What did they expect to find in there? They would have had more fun playing chess on the giant chequerboard, but that was impossible because Kurt had fenced it off. 'We're going to polish up that marble, make it look real smart,' he said crisply. 'By the way, I put in a word for your young friend. He starts English lessons next week, ready for his job at reception.'

'You got him a job? Where?'

'At the Caravanserai, just as soon as we persuade those Mission guys to part with their archive.'

It seemed the White Fathers weren't so keen on handing over whatever it was they had stashed away at the Mission, although, Kurt said, there were a couple of young dude monks who couldn't wait to be rid of the historic junk and use the space for a youth club. I'd never seen the stuff and didn't feel inclined to. Grace said she hadn't either, even though she went to Mass at the Mission every Sunday. Privately, I still thought the tourists would be happiest on the beach.

One night I ran into John Simba, drinking in town. 'Ah, my friend! Thank you for helping that kid of mine. Ya, let's hope he rises to the challenge.'

'I'm sure he will,' I said. 'He's bright. He'll enjoy earning a salary.'

John sighed. 'If he can accept it's enough.'

Again, I felt miffed. But he had a point: most Tanzanian salaries were so low, they barely made any difference.

As I spent more and more time in Sinamani I took pleasure in losing my ex-pat connections in Dar. Those placid Dutch guys who used to drink beer with me by the pool at the Kilimanjaro Hotel; the cute Swedish girls with their ponytails and bubbly conversation – for a while I'd enjoyed hanging out with them, but now I hardly saw them. I lost interest in what was happening back home. Bush got elected? So what? I even, finally, stopped following the baseball, although I took a respectful interest in whatever golf tournament Tiger Woods was winning. More often than not my laptop, that sleek little box of tricks, remained unopened at the Dar bungalow, and instead I'd hang out at Sinamani's only Internet café, check my emails, fire one off to Carl. He, in his deadpan way, kept me up to speed with the rest of the family, and that was all the contact I needed.

Grace, though, asked constant questions about my relatives, and loved to pore over photos of them. For a long time I didn't tell her that Carl was gay, making excuses to myself about it being Carl's business and his alone, until in the end she asked me if he had an mpenzi, a sweetheart, and then, hesitantly, I told her the truth about Carl and Graham. 'Oh,' she said. Then, 'In America, that's legal, isn't it?'

She asked me why didn't I make friends with Frank, the new Peace Corps veterinarian who had been given a bungalow on the hospital compound. I said it was because I preferred to spend my free time with her, and besides, I didn't like animals. She clicked her tongue, as she did whenever Godlisten committed some minor misdemeanour. 'Liar, Sasha! You love your dog, that you left in America.' (Grace had been baffled to find a photo of Flo in the album, in between a snap of Grandma and a cousin's wedding.)

'Grace, you got me.'

'But this Frank. He's one of your tribe.'

And there she really had me, because, no matter how hard I tried, I never understood this tribe thing: how Grace could be living here in Sinamani, miles from her birthplace, her family, and yet still feel close, sisterly, to a hospital patient, or some woman who sat next to her on the bus, or some seemingly random person we met while strolling along the beach, just because they were a Chagga. I marvelled how she could strike up a conversation and within seconds identify some shared knowledge, usually something practical, like the acreage of a shamba, or what money-making project they did alongside their day job – 'Is he still hiring out his bicycle? He's made a lot of money from that bike…' Her manner with these Chagga strangers was the same as a person living with their family day in, day out: slightly bored, slightly nosy; an unspoken sense that you had to look out for this person, whether you liked them or not.

The nearest I ever got to a tribe was my team, and now I'd lost all that. I'd walked away from my tribe, and looking at skinny Frank I was afraid, very afraid, he might turn out to be a Red Sox fan. 'Hey Sasha, didn't I see you before, some place…?'

For all she loved me, Grace would never be able to understand that fear.

It was Sunday morning. Grace had taken Godlisten to church. I was lazing on the couch under the window with the cat on my stomach, flicking through the crime and scandal stories in the Daily News and pulling ticks off the cat's neck. Over in the kitchen Martina was washing rice and singing to herself in her reedy little voice, a funny, mumbly song that went round and round in circles, lulling me into a doze.

Martina's voice changed, became gruff. 'Fuck,' she was saying. It wasn't like Martina to swear, or to speak English. The window went dark. Someone was staring down at me. I leapt off the couch, sent the cat skittering across the room. There was an old man, scowling, fingertips splayed against the glass like suckers on some weird sea creature. Damp dirt clotted the lines of his face; his hair was a filthy halo. Despite the heat, he wore a bulky, ragged brown coat, fastened by a woman's stocking tied around his waist. He watched me as I stood for a moment, shaking.

'Mzee, can I help you?'

'Fuck, fuck, fuck,' he mumbled, and let rip a rasping fart. So, he was a madman. Or did he just think the mzungu was fair game? Then he shuffled across to the door and said, 'I would like a glass of water, please.'

'OK,' I said. 'Wait a moment.' He didn't move so I had to squeeze past him, gagging at the smell, to reach the communal kitchen. I shut Grace's door behind me which was rude, but I didn't want to risk him helping himself to her possessions or settling his backside on one of her immaculate chairs.

'Martina, there's an old man outside who speaks English. He wants water.'

Martina's face brightened. 'A mzungu?' But when she saw him she was disappointed. 'It's only Mister Jambijambi.'

It was weird, that English *Mister*. 'Who is he?'

'He's a crazy old man,' Martina said. 'Completely crazy. All the little children are scared of him.'

'How come he speaks English?'

She shrugged. 'I don't know. Perhaps because he's crazy.'

I found the chipped glass that we all avoided using, filled it with water and gave it to the old man. He gulped it down steadily almost to the end, then, in the Tanzanian way, tipped the last few drops onto the ground. 'Thank you,' he said, and wiped his mouth on his filthy sleeve. For some reason I felt ashamed. He wandered away, past all the kids who were peeping from behind trees, clutching each other, trying to shove each other into his path and squealing with laughter, except for one little girl who screamed and burst into tears when she saw him.

When Grace came back from church I told her about the visitor. 'Oh really?' she said. 'He's been round here a lot, lately.'

'Who is he?'

'He's a crazy person.'

'You don't say. How come he's called *Mister*?'

Martina was keen to explain. ' Everyone calls him Mister Jambijambi, because he does this all the time – ' she stuck out her butt, pointed to it and blew a loud raspberry. Godlisten fell on the floor laughing. Martina wagged her finger at him. 'You won't laugh, Godi, when Mister Jambijambi comes to get you in the middle of the night.'

'Don't frighten the child,' said Grace.

'Did I do the right thing, giving him water?'

She looked puzzled. 'What do you mean, the right thing? Why shouldn't you give him water?'

I was too ashamed to say I hadn't trusted him; that he made me want to puke. Grace went on, 'It's sad. He used to live in the ruins of the old Caravanserai, until the Danes came to develop it. I don't know where he lives now. He just wanders around begging. People say he fought in the Second World War, so that's probably when he learned English. He must have been OK in those days.'

I'd seen mentally ill Tanzanians before: a skeletal man running across the plain in Singida, clawing at his face and screaming, 'Mama! Mama!' The poor, stark naked girl who used to follow me to the post office in Kunduchi, imploring me to give her my letters. There were others, less extreme but just as pitiful. I remembered how people treated them with good humour and compassion, or at the very least, indifference. I wished I'd been nicer to Mister Jambijambi, until I met him again a few weeks later.

We were at the market, shopping for fruit and vegetables at Grace's favourite stall, piled with tomatoes, onions, swollen papaya, bundles of dark green leaves. The stallholder was full of schmooze: 'For you, doctor, only the finest tomatoes! These onions will help you cure many many patients,' etcetera, and Grace was lapping it up, but acting terse with him. I half-listened to the banter, thinking maybe I'd exercise a little muscle and insist that Martina should let me cook our meal tonight – how I'd buy the best joint of goat meat I could find, marinade it for a few hours in papaya flesh to make it tender, add some pilipili …

'Why don't you buy potatoes for your bwana?' the stallholder said to Grace.

'Feed me up, Mama,' I smirked at Grace, and then wondered if I'd said something wrong, as the stallholder's face changed, became wary. He murmured, 'Look behind you.'

Hoarse muttering, and a smell worse than chickenshit told me who it was, even before Jambijambi laid his hand, his filthy, stinking hand, on my arm and said, slowly and precisely, 'Stop fucking the English whore.'

Grace, paying for her vegetables, didn't seem to have heard. She drifted along to the next stall. The stallholder made himself very busy counting the cash. I couldn't move. My face was burning. I was flexing my fists and sweat oozed through my clenched fingers. Mister Jambijambi took hold of my chin and nudged it a little, so I had to look him in the eye. He said in Swahili, very low and gentle, 'Why haven't you greeted me?'

I replied like a schoolboy. 'Forgive me, mzee. Shikamo.'

'Marahaba,' he replied graciously, and shuffled away, farting.

It had all happened in a few seconds, not long enough for anybody else to get interested. If anyone had heard what he said, probably they wouldn't have understood. Or maybe they would. Some words travel the world. I forced my face into what I hoped was a breezy expression, said I'd like to buy some onions. The stallholder pointed out that Mama Godi had already bought onions. I said, 'Don't you want my money?' Took two knobbly handfuls, stuffed them into my pockets. Now the stallholder looked sorry for me. 'Here, Bwana Maji, your discount' – and he gave me a huge, overripe papaya, which I'd forgotten I needed.

But I didn't get to make my marinade that day, didn't even get as far as the butcher's. I'd caught up with Grace, admiring some new kangas just-in-from-China draped all over her pal Mama Bettina's stall, when Juma, the young driver from the hospital, came running over. He was too agitated to greet us. 'There's a very sick man, but the ambulance is in the garage and the mechanic says it won't be ready for another two hours. I think the man will die if we don't get him to hospital.' He was looking at me, not at Grace. 'Mr Sasha, could I take the patient and Mama God in your Toyota? And you could bring the ambulance back later?'

If the wrong person saw Juma behind the wheel of a Water for Life vehicle, it could cost me my job. People watched as I dug in my pocket, sending onions tumbling all over the dusty ground, and gave him the keys. He and Grace ran.

I picked up Grace's shopping basket and went to the garage to speak to the mechanic. As usual he had a posse of hangers-on, kids who had nothing better to do all day than skulk around the oil drums and the litter of spare parts, inventing errands for themselves or smoking dope. Today,

Gabriel was among them. 'Shikamo, mzungu,' he murmured, and that got my back up: the little shit knew my name, so why didn't he use it?

Then, when I explained what had happened, the mechanic shook his head. 'I can't let you drive the ambulance. Nobody is allowed to drive the ambulance except Juma.'

'Yes, I know; Juma says it's OK. This is an emergency.'

Even as I was saying those corny words, I could see how the guy had the upper hand, and how he was enjoying it. He shook his head sorrowfully. 'I can't. I have the keys and if I give them to you I might lose my job. I'm already very poor. How can I feed my kids if I lose my job?'

'Look, you have to let me take the ambulance back as soon as it's ready, because somebody else might need it, OK? Do you want to get the blame if somebody dies?'

He shrugged. 'I'm very poor.'

It dawned on me that he wanted a bribe.

People would have you believe this happens all the time: Tanzanians calculating how much they can screw out of the rich mzungu; Tanzanians refusing the simplest request unless money changes hands. Well, it never happened to me before that day, and it's never happened since. Even so, I was furious. For one wild moment I considered punching him in the face; then Gabriel stood up. 'Let me help,' he said. He turned to the mechanic and spoke to him in a low voice, too fast for me to catch everything, although I thought I heard him say, *the mzungu knows my dad.*

The mechanic glanced at me. Then he said, into the air, 'OK. It's up to Juma. Maybe Juma and Mama God will lose their jobs as well; I don't know. Come back at five.'

'Thank you,' I muttered to Gabriel.

With a strange half-smile he said, 'I owed you a favour.'

I wanted to say, Gabriel, you owe me absolutely nothing. I wanted him to recognise that as soon as you start dealing

265

in favours, you lose anything of value, anything that might possibly have real meaning.

Instead I said, 'When do you start your job?'

'When Bwana Kurt says the Caravanserai is ready for the tourists.'

Pointedly I looked around the garage, at the dead-eyed teenagers. 'The sooner the better, eh?'

'Yes,' he agreed, all innocence.

I went to kill time at the Alpha Motel, where I found Kurt and Sid. 'How are you?' they said.

Creeped out by a madman, touched for a bribe, patronized by a teenager. I've had better days. Oh, and I've given away the Toyota and I might lose my job if word gets back to Dar Es Salaam, which it probably will.

With a great effort I managed to shuck off my discontent and, missing out Jambijambi, I told them what had happened. A new worry was nagging me: one I should have considered before. 'Grace won't get any hassle for this, will she?'

'Hamisi's reasonable,' said Sid, 'and he knows which side his bread's buttered. Grace has propped him up for as long as I can remember. I'm not saying he isn't a good doctor, but really she works just as hard as him, for less money.'

'Grace can't say no to anyone, that's her problem.' As soon as the words were out, I hated myself.

Above his cartoon pirate beard Sid's eyes were a cool appraising blue. 'Grace is wonderful.' A slow flush spread over his face.

'You don't have to tell me that,' I said, and Kurt, who hadn't missed any of this, said, 'Sure she is. Sasha, don't worry. Let me get you a beer — or maybe a soda would be better?'

We sat together, they with their bottles of Safari Lager, I with my lukewarm Fanta, and Kurt told me the Caravanserai was nearly finished, they were just waiting for some glass cases to display the archive from the Mission, then they could open to the public and 'my kid' Gabriel could start earning a few honest shillings. From time to time I spouted ex-pat buzzwords: sustainability and donor involvement and all that crap, but my heart wasn't in it because my head was full of sour thoughts. The bribe. The smirk on Gabriel's face. Whether the Toyota was at this moment upside down in a ditch. Jambijambi.

If Sid had doubts about the Caravanserai, about this whole regeneration thing, he kept them to himself – but when Kurt said the opening would be celebrated with 'one hell of a party,' and would we like to come, he accepted, and so did I.

When I arrived at the hospital gates behind the wheel of the ambulance, Mzee Abdallah said nothing. Didn't even look at me. Grace, Martina told me, was still with the patient. Hamisi had gone to visit his aged mother in Morogoro and wouldn't be back until late. We ate ugali and beans. I went to bed. At some point in the middle of the night, the firm warmth of Grace's body pressed into mine, and I murmured, 'What happened?'

'He's OK,' she said. 'He had peritonitis but he's OK.'

Grace, wonderful doctor Grace, saintly heroine Grace had saved his life, and I went back to sleep happily, knowing she'd saved mine too.

The next morning a child brought a message. 'Mama God and Bwana Maji, you are wanted by Dr. Hamisi in his office.'

Expecting gratitude, what we got was an embarrassed Hamisi sitting behind his desk like my high school principal, sucking the tips of his fingers, unable to make eye contact. 'Sasha, I have been told you were driving the ambulance without permission.'

Grace gasped.

Unbelievable. The whole compound knew what had happened the day before, but I knew just which reptile had spotted an opportunity to stir up some shit.

My voice shook. 'Oh. *You have been told.* This is Abdallah, right?'

'I'm not at liberty to disclose my sources,' Hamisi said primly. I slammed my fist onto the desk and they jumped.

'You have *no idea*' – spit frothed at my lips – 'absolutely *no idea* what happened, yet you choose to believe that asshole! Bring him here. Bring the old man here, right now.'

'I can't do that,' Hamisi said.

A thousand times, at work, on the streets, even in Grace herself, I'd seen this calm Tanzanian refusal to react, and every time it wound me up until I felt myself in danger of turning into somebody I hated: the irate mzungu spewing out vicious, resentful criticism of Africans, their stubbornness, their laziness, their self-defeating passivity.

But Grace *was* reacting. 'What can he do to us? Sasha, what can he do?' and yet again I misunderstood her and began to quieten down, reflecting that, OK, she had a point: Mzee Abdallah was just some guy who opened the gates; how could he possibly harm us? And already Grace was explaining to Hamisi what had really happened, and I let the mellow Swahili stream lull me into silence, so by the time Hamisi turned to me and said in English, 'Sasha, I am so sorry,' it was a relief to say, 'No problem, doctor. These mistakes happen.' And when, a few hours later, I left the compound to drive to Dar, the gates were open and there was no sign of Abdallah.

But I had apologized to Grace for losing my temper, and maybe it was her concern for my soul that made her sidle up to me, a few weeks later, and murmur, 'Come to Mass with us tomorrow.'

*

Grace would slip Jesus into the conversation as easily as she'd mention Godlisten or Martina or Hamisi. That cheesy picture of the Virgin Mary in her living room was her most treasured possession, the thing she'd save if the house burnt down. She was tetchy if she had to work on a Sunday and missed church. She always knelt to say her prayers last thing at night – yes, even when I was lying on the couch waiting for her to wrap her body around mine. Religion was part of Grace's life, as it seemed to be part of everyone's life here, whether they were Catholic, Muslim or Seventh Day Adventist.

Unfortunately for me, Grace was Catholic. Her priest, Paulo Migire, was a lousy driver and had overturned his Suzuki jeep four times in the last year, his survival without a scratch seen as proof that he was truly a man of God. Each accident was caused by a pothole, absolutely nothing to do with speed or alcohol. When he wasn't terrorising the roads, he organised compulsory soccer games for unemployed youths and told people off in public if they didn't look after their elderly relatives. He also ran a one-man crusade against witches, regularly denouncing them in church although never actually naming names. 'Wouldn't it be easier,' I said to Grace, 'if he tried to convince people there's no such thing as witchcraft?'

'No, they'll be more impressed if he gets the witches to give up their bad magic.'

I didn't want to ask, but I had to. 'Do *you* believe in witchcraft?'

She snorted. 'Are you crazy? Of course I don't.'

Whenever people asked me about my faith I'd give a fuzzy answer, saying I'd been brought up Episcopalian. Ah yes, they nodded. Very good. Grace and I never discussed my beliefs – probably, she didn't want to go there. But I did once challenge her to defend the God who let children starve while fat rich white people grew fatter and richer.

'Has God been cruel to you?' she said.

My leg. Eluminata's twins.

'Not really, no, but …'

'You've been blessed, Sasha. That's how you should know that God is good.'

I tried a different tack. Didn't it make her mad, all her patients with AIDS who hadn't used condoms because the priest told them not to? Yes, she said, it made her angry, and also all the women who get infected by their adulterous husbands. 'The world is full of bad people, Sasha.'

Grace always had an answer. Now she was upping the ante, inviting me, no, pressurising me – to come to church with her. I told her the truth about my reluctance. It was OK us hanging out at the compound together, or in the town bars, or strolling along the beach. But the pair of us in church would be a very big statement. It would be like we were married, or something…

And what's wrong with that? I wanted her to say. Instead she snapped, 'For goodness sake, it's only church. I'd love you to come, but nobody else is going to bother whether you're there or not.'

'OK,' I said, 'but we'll go on foot. If we take the Toyota everyone will want a lift.'

After breakfast on Sunday morning Godlisten disappeared, and by the time we'd found him pestering Juma in the workshop, we were late. Grace, who never ran anywhere if she could help it, made us sprint the shadowy green length of the mango avenue. At the gates she panted, 'Wait a moment!' – smoothed her skirt and drew her kanga over her head. Then she spat on a corner of the kanga and wiped some porridge off Godlisten's chin.

After the shade of the mango avenue, the Mission compound was sunny and calm. Father Migire was standing at the church door. I hoped he wasn't going to make any funny comments. 'Mr. Sasha, at last we see you in church!'

He shook my hand vigorously. 'You are very welcome! This is a happy, happy day!'

Inside, the church was light, plain, spotless. Probably Migire had a gang of nuns scrubbing the place before every service. At the far end, there was an altar made from a wooden crucifix on a table covered with a red and yellow cloth, and three arched windows where birds swooped across a blue sky. All the pews were full, but some women at the back squeezed up to make room for us. Everyone sat still, waiting for the service to start. Even the kids were quiet. Godlisten sat on Grace's lap, picking his nose until she noticed and slapped his hand. I glanced around and realised she'd been right – nobody was looking at me. She shifted a little on the hard wooden pew, our thighs rubbing, and she slid her hand over mine, just for a moment. Then Father Migire came striding up the aisle, followed by two bearded White Fathers, and people stood and began to sing. No hymnbooks; everyone knew the words and the harmonies. The music melted my worries away.

When I was a boy, religion was a problem in our home, since dad preferred to spend his Sunday mornings on the golf course and our mother resented being left with the responsibility for our souls on top of everything else. Aged twelve, Carl stopped coming to church with us. I cornered him drinking Jim Beam in the cellar. He said he didn't believe in God, that was why he didn't do church any more. For a day or two I stumbled around full of dread, convinced Carl would burn in hell, or at the very least, that we wouldn't see each other after death. Then I thought some more and decided it was easier to believe that none of us would see each other, and none of us would burn. It was a relief. For years afterwards I hardly gave God a thought, just once in a while muttering as I stepped up to the plate, 'Please let this one be a homer' – it seemed to work if I said 'please'. But when that ligament at the back of my knee ripped, I didn't blame God and I didn't pray for a miracle.

So how come the people in this sunny room made me feel like I was missing something?

I knew the bars of Sinamani were full of drunken Muslims. I knew there were Catholic priests with kids in every village from here to the Masai Mara. I knew, because Grace had told me, there were people in this congregation who believed if you filled a bowl with the blood of an animal and stared at your own reflection in it, you would turn into a leopard. But somehow, I still felt I was an outsider, and that baffled me, since I was so happy with Grace, happier than I had ever been in my life. When the time came for people to go up for the bread and the wine I whispered to Grace, 'I'll stay here,' and the sunlight glinted off her glasses as she hissed back, 'You're coming with us,' and pulled me to my feet and made me go in front of her, with Godlisten. 'Oh Grace, don't ever leave me,' I thought, a kind of prayer, as the three of us knelt together below the blue arched windows.

We came out of church to an unpleasant smell. Dogshit? Rancid butter?

Jambijambi sidled round the porch and took my hand. He was not wearing his Sunday best. I greeted him and hoped that would be enough, but he wouldn't let go. Grace drifted away, chatting with her friends as if nothing was happening. Some people hung around to watch, hoping for a scene. Only Godlisten and the other kids seemed to feel like I did; they made themselves scarce. Father Migire was laughing loudly, surrounded by attractive young women. How come he wasn't helping me out here? What about when the old man starts cursing?

Jambijambi was calm and perfectly civil; he just wouldn't let go my hand. My smile was beginning to quiver. He said, 'Please help me.'

So that was it. From my pocket I pulled out a fifty shilling note – pathetic. People leant forward to see better. I thought I heard someone say, 'The mzungu doesn't want to part with his money.' Flustered, I dug in again and tucked the whole wad into his crusty palm. 'No problem, mzee,' I bluffed, but nobody was fooled, least of all him. He looked at me from under his woolly brows, then thumbed through the notes, took out the original fifty, which wouldn't buy him so much as a bottle of coke, and gave me back the rest. 'You're welcome,' I said. 'Goodbye.'

He took my hand again. 'Let's go for a little walk.'

'I can't. Sorry, we have to go home now to eat. Grace, don't we have lunch waiting for us at home? Sorry mzee, another day, perhaps.'

'It's OK,' said Grace. 'We'll keep some food for you.'

'Grace?' I yelped.

'Go on,' she said quietly. 'Go with the old man.'

So there was nothing I could do, but let Jambijambi lead me through the gates, away from the Mission, all the way down the mango avenue, kids peeping and shrieking at us through the trees, and for an old guy he could really move: it wasn't long before we'd left them all far behind, so by the time we reached the marble cross and the sea path I was beginning to feel more uneasy than embarrassed. He was big, my height. And bulky. Beneath those layers and layers of reeking clothes, he might be strong. He breathed heavily and noisily as he strode along, the stocking around his waist swinging with each step, reminding me of an elephant. Harmless until provoked. To this day it freaks me out: the way elephants always look like they're smiling, even when they're about to stampede.

I tried to talk. Where do you live? Your English is so good. I heard you learned it in the war. He didn't answer and I didn't say what I really wanted to say: Why are you doing this to me? I contented myself with planning how pissed off I'd be with Grace when I got back. *I didn't appreciate that, Grace. It's not like we get much time together; I'd rather have been with you.* But then I imagined her surprised, wide-open face, her hurt feelings. So I changed the plan: I'd say carelessly, *yeah, we had a nice walk, it's good to hang out with the elders,* and she'd be pleased with me for doing what wazungu are supposed to do and integrating. Surely you can't get more integrated than taking a stroll with the local lunatic?

As we reached town there were more people, who stared at us, delighted, and called their friends over to have a look. We absolutely made their Sunday morning. Jambijambi walked me down Main Street and at the Sewa Haji school took a sharp right towards the crossroads and Von Wissmann's blockhouse, recently restored to sparkling white limestone. Hand in hand we marched towards it, straight towards the dinky fence that warned off trespassers. 'Mzee, I think we have to stop here ...' But he wasn't stopping; stepped right on over, dragging me with him until we were up against that white wall, warm in the sun. The old man stooped to look through the slit of a window. 'It's very small,' he said. 'The Germans must have been very uncomfortable. Look.' Obediently I peered into the dark space and could see nothing. I expected at any moment some Ministry official to come along and scream at us.

Things got worse. Jambijambi, still gripping my hand, wandered away. 'There's the school,' he said, 'for the children. That's where I went to school when I was a little boy.' It was painful to imagine. 'And here is where we used to play. Why won't the wazungu let the children play here any more?' It struck me how old he must be, if Grace was right and he fought in the Second World War. Incredibly old, by Tanzanian standards. A survivor. He took another elephantine stride over the fence around the chequerboard – Kurt's precious chequerboard with the newly polished marble squares. 'Mzee, they're trying to keep it clean for the tourists,' I pleaded, cringing at the prissy whine in my own voice – useless; he was already up there, and so was I. Quite a crowd had gathered now, to watch the mzungu and the madman; it felt like we were on stage. Jambijambi obliged his audience by letting rip with a tremendous fart; they roared and gave each other hi-fives. Gabriel was there with some of his doped-up friends. The sight of him made me angry – I wanted to snarl, 'Where are your family?' because I knew John and Eluminata went to the Lutheran church every Sunday. But the anger pumped me up enough to say, 'Let's go, *mzee*,' and I gently tugged him away from the chequerboard, and then, desperate to be away from that crowd, allowed him to wander with me down towards the sea.

I'd had no reason to go back to the German cemetery since that time with Juliet. The place was even shabbier than I remembered, the gate hanging off one hinge, crumbling gaps in the low wall. Perhaps people had stolen the bricks. The Danes with their regeneration plans hadn't come here yet.

He stood aside for me to go in first, then held out his hand towards the graves like a priest giving a blessing. 'They all died,' he said. I laughed, couldn't help it, a nervous splutter. He ignored me, shuffling along the overgrown paths, pausing now and then to peer at headstones, trail his fingers over the hair of a stone angel. We walked the length of the cemetery until we reached the end, and he stopped in front of a faint rectangle amongst the weeds and the long grass. 'Read it,' he said.

My voice came out hoarse and anxious. 'Lucy Hemmings. Born England, died Sinamani 1890.' Then, angry again, I said, 'Why are we standing here?'

He gave a low, wheezing chuckle, pointed to the grave. 'Like you.'

I sighed. 'You know, I'm not English. I'm American. A lot of people make that mistake.'

'Like you. *Mgeni.*'

Stranger, visitor, foreigner, guest. So much truth in that one word. But only an hour ago I'd been in church, the music soothing my soul, Grace warm and alive at my side. I was a lucky man. Jambijambi wasn't going to spoil all that.

'Come on now, mzee. Time to go.'

His moist old eyes were distant, scanning the sea. 'It makes us sad.'

I said gently, 'She died way, way back, you know. Before you were born.' That's what you're supposed to do when you talk to people who are mentally ill; remind them of reality as kindly as you can. He took my hand again and this time I gripped it, and meant it, and didn't mind that he squeezed his filthy palm into mine all the way back through town until we reached the crossroads where he let go, only to lean in close and whisper, 'Please could I have a little bit of money? For tea?' I gave him five hundred shillings and he thanked me and wandered off to a café, just like a sane person.

Wishing I'd brought the Toyota after all, I began the long trek back to Grace's. There was plenty of time to brood on what the old man had said. The more I tried to reassure myself he was crazy and not worth worrying about, the more of a liar I felt, until there was a small war inside my head which made me feel perhaps I was the crazy one, for never pausing to ask myself: How long do you think you can carry on living here?

On that long, hot walk I said goodbye to the illusion that I'd found myself, reinvented myself, in Tanzania. All I'd found was Grace. And nothing would really be OK until we were married.

When I reached the hospital, tired and footsore, something was wrong: it had all, as they say in Swahili, gone *shaghalabaghala*: angry mamas with hands on hips, Abdallah scurrying around like a lizard, Hamisi dashing past in his sharp suit too preoccupied even to greet me, some pumped-up macho young guys who seemed to be searching for something. People visiting their sick relatives looked bewildered. There'd been a burglary, a sack of rice stolen in broad daylight from the store-room where all the hospital workers kept their food. Hamisi suspected an inside job and was conducting a house-to-house search. 'Why not just wait for the police?' I asked Grace.

'Hamisi wants to catch the thief before the people get there first and kill him.' I knew it could happen: thieves beaten to death by a mob. But on a hospital compound?

Martina was fussing and flapping around her pot of water on the stove. 'Does Hamisi think I did it?' she squeaked, opening a bag of flour. 'I was here all by myself while everyone else was at church.'

'Maybe there's a ghost in the store,' said Godlisten.

I remembered how much I needed to wash my hands, so I cadged a ladleful of Martina's hot water, tipped it into a plastic bowl, went inside the bathroom, hunkered down with a stick of slimy grey laundry soap and although the water was too hot, I scoured every speck of dirt, every flake of the old man's skin from mine. Then I tipped the scum down the pit latrine.

Mzee Abdallah was coming out of our neighbour's house, scowling. I braced myself for him to come to us next, because he'd sure as hell find a way of pinning the theft on me – but he stumped over to a house further away, and Mrs. Mhilu told us Abdallah was in deep shit because Hamisi caught him asleep on the job. This pleased me so much, I hoped he *would* be sent to search us so we could ask him a few innocent questions about his future.

But it was Juma who came, and he was tender and tactful, holding up his hands to Grace: 'Forgive me, Mama God,' before he went to rummage in the trunk where she kept her clothes and her sanitary pads. Grace, coolly indifferent, sat on her chair just outside the front door, murmuring to Godlisten in Swahili, too fast for me to follow. When Juma had finished his search she invited him to share our ugali and beans; he refused, with just a little self-importance, because Hamisi had entrusted him with this 'special duty,' and would be disappointed if he, Juma, did not fulfil it to the best of his ability. 'Is anyone going to search Abdallah's house?' I asked.

'Oh yes! All of us searchers must search each other's houses. Even Dr. Hamisi's place.'

Fifteen minutes later Juma was back. They'd found the sack amongst the trees, split open where it had snagged on a thorn, and the thief frantically scrabbling grains of rice from the dust. 'He was just an mshamba kid.' A hick, a country bumpkin.

'What did you do to him?'

'Nothing. We could see he was starving, so we just beat him up and sent him on his way.'

Grace said, 'Did you save all the rice?'

'Not yet. It's everywhere; that stupid kid had been trying to run with the sack.'

'OK then, Godi, you take this bowl and you go to help. Every single grain, mind!'

And away they all went, Godi to pick up rice, Juma to the workshop, Martina to rest on her mat, the neighbours to gossip, Hamisi to cure the sick as best he could, Abdallah to sulk. Grace and I had one precious hour alone together before her shift began and I went back to Dar. I could have asked her to marry me then, but I didn't. After everything that had happened, it seemed the wrong time. That morning at the Mission I felt like I had the day in my hands; now, it had fallen away. So we wasted that hour listening to music, snuggling together on her couch, and it should have been sweet, but it wasn't, because I knew I couldn't live the rest of my life in Tanzania, where I would always be the *mgeni*, and yet the only alternative was to wrench our lives around to make Grace the *mgeni* instead. How could I do that to her? Take her thousands of miles to a place where she'd be stranger, visitor, foreigner, guest to everyone else and *mgeni* to herself? How could I do that to Godlisten, who never whined for toys or candy, who kicked a ball made from plastic bags and string, who was learning to write his name with a stick in the dirt? Who picked up grains of rice to please his mama and loved her just as much as I did?

'We won't see each other now,' I said to Grace, 'until after I get back from Karatu. Three weeks.' That was how I presented it to her, hoping she'd be upset and say she wished I didn't have to go. Or at least give a sigh of regret.

'Three weeks,' said Grace, frowning slightly as if she were doing mental arithmetic. 'Three weeks, but you will be back in time for the party at the Caravanserai, won't you? It would be nice if we could go together. Wait – ' and she went to the sideboard to find the invitation. 'The fifteenth. When are you coming back?'

'I'll be in Dar on the fourteenth.' I had my fingers crossed.

'Oh good,' she said, and I was so desperate, I told myself that meant she really loved me.

They say the great rift that runs down Africa is creeping wider and wider all the time, until one day the land mass will split completely, and turn into two separate continents. I thought of this whenever I drove up the Rift valley escarpment to Karatu; played the sick game of imagining how it would be if the earth cracked open and took me down with it. And there were a few times in Tanzania when I felt the earth quake for real, just tremors, so slight and sly that each time it happened I thought, not, 'What was that?' but '*Who* was that?'

But this time, when the ground shifted beneath my feet, I hadn't even left Dar Es Salaam.

It was Monday. That morning I'd been to the office, checked arrangements for the big safari, and now I was back home, planning a day of paperwork and emails, looking forward to a late afternoon swim. There was a knock at my front door. The windows were open; I hadn't heard the watchmen talking to anyone at the gate; nobody called 'hodi?' So I knew my visitor had to be a mzungu.

I opened the door and saw Lou.

In that first moment of shock, I thought, 'She's got the wrong house.'

'Hi Sasha. My goodness, you lost weight.'

From his sentinel hut, Agostino glanced across, then looked away again and settled himself in his chair, to stare at the row of Land Cruisers and jeeps, their flanks gleaming white in the sun.

Lou didn't fool me; she was nervous. Somewhere in all my confusion, my helpless anger, I registered it must have taken guts for her to come here. But that didn't mean I was going to make it easy for her.

'How did you know where I was?'

She glanced away. 'I heard you were working for Water for Life. I couldn't believe it at first, I thought, it has to be another Sasha Greene, but – the person who told me said you were American, very tall, teaching kids how to play baseball…' She shrugged, grinned, and still wasn't convincing.

'OK, Lou, next question. What do you want?'

'Well … We never finished things properly, did we? It was such a mess, the way it ended.'

I began to laugh. 'You want *closure*, Lou?'

'If you choose to call it that.'

'After nine years?'

'So you've been counting too.'

Sunlight ricocheted off the Land Cruisers, gleamed in the tiny dots of sweat on her face. A heavy voice inside me said, she'll cause trouble, whether she means to or not.

'Alright,' I said. 'Let's do it.'

*

280

She stood, incredibly, in my living-room, smiling a tight smile. She had lost weight too, a lot more than I had. The skin was taut on the big bones of her face, and her hair, her beautiful auburn hair which used to ripple in thick, sexy waves, was lighter, gingery, pulled into a frizz at the nape of her neck. The denim dress was her favourite shade of sludgy blue, but it fitted neatly round her breasts and waist, nothing like the loose clothes she used to wear.

My hands trembled as I made coffee. We talked, through an invisible block of ice, about our families, our half-forgotten mutual friends. Then I said, 'So are you still on Zanzibar, after all these years?' and she snapped, 'What the fuck is that supposed to mean?'

'Sorry. I didn't mean anything.'

She sank back again into her chair. 'So. You didn't go straight home? You travelled around first?'

'Not exactly.'

'Where did you go?'

'Lou, I don't want to talk about that time.'

'Yeah, but I do.'

She was still tough, still said whatever she liked. I used to love her for that. I forced myself to remember the funeral, and the wake afterwards.

'OK Lou, if that's the way you want it, then we need to talk about why I left. I think we both know I should never have come to Zanzibar.' *Although thank God I did.* 'It was already over, wasn't it?'

'Maybe so.' She wasn't looking at me now. Funny how, in all this time, I'd never thrashed out what it was that had made her turn away from me – whether the accident that left me blubbering and raging in my hospital bed, or her decision, just weeks later, to go ahead and catch that plane to Zanzibar, or my limping, tongue-tied arrival on the island, or something deeper, that had always been hiding inside one or both of us, waiting for its moment.

But none of that mattered. All I wanted was that she should get back out of my life, quick. So I started to lie.

'I'm sorry I left the way I did, without saying goodbye. I was mad, but you know, looking back, it was cowardly. I shouldn't have done it, and I'm sorry. There you are. Is there really anything else you want to hear from me?'

Her mouth was twitching. And her freckled, tan face was reddening and twisting, and then, for only the second time ever, I saw Lou cry. It was a shock. What the hell was she up to? But you can't sit and watch a woman cry and do nothing. 'Wait there,' I said, and rushed to the bathroom. 'Sorry it's not Kleenex.' I gave her the roll of scratchy pink toilet paper. The Lou I knew was gone; who was this quivering, out of control wreck, her face all smeared with tears and snot? I went to lay my hand on her shoulder, but then the thought of Grace came to me, Grace who also did not cry, and I went back to my chair the other side of the room from Lou. For a long while she didn't look at me, didn't even try to speak. Once, she hiccupped and took a deep breath and it seemed like she'd stopped – but at the peak of the breath she gasped and plunged into sobs. The window was open. The whole compound must have heard.

At last, she went quiet.

'You want some water?' She nodded. I poured a glass, gave it to her, felt like it was dangerous to be kind. She took a few sips, then fixed her eyes on me.

'I'm stuck on Zanzibar. I finished the PhD ages ago and I can't get a job back home, leastways, not any place that's any good. I have emailed hundreds of applications. Nobody needs Africa people now, it's all about the goddamn Middle East. Plus, I'm thirty-seven. Why would anyone give me tenure over some blonde with a doctorate and legs all the way up to her tits? The whole system stinks. It's all who you know and I don't know anyone any more. So yes, I'm still on that shitty island, after all this time. I went home but I couldn't bear it, and I came back to

Zanzibar. I went into business for a while with – with a friend. We started to build a hotel over at Nungwe, like, this dream hotel on the beach, and I really felt, there could be more to life than being an academic. We were all set to employ at least twenty people, how cool would that have been? But it all fell through, the way things do here. My partner let me down. And now the Immigration guys are after me. You want to know how I eat? I tutor kids who need help with their English, and their parents pay me with food. Another year of this and I'll be invisible. Me!' She laughed.

I just wanted her to shut up, my mind scrambling to take in what she'd said. 'Well, maybe you have to find a job at some college that isn't so hot.'

'I tried.'

'Then go home anyway and stay with friends while you look for something else. Anything.'

'Nine years, Sasha. My friends all got married and had babies, remember?'

'How about your folks?'

'It would kill me to go to them.'

'Well, that's what I did, for a bit. It's not so bad.'

She glared. 'Yeah, but you managed to go on and reinvent yourself, you of all people. That's why I'm here, Sasha. I need to know how you did it.'

'You make it sound like some kind of conjuring trick,' I said coldly. 'It took years. I had to study hard. I failed exams and sat them again and then I looked for jobs.'

She sat forward, leaning towards me. For the first time, this did not look like pretence. 'But how did you know what you wanted?'

How did I know? The memory of a girl, a bucket tipping, a shimmering arc of water vanishing into the dust.

'Well, Lou, it sounds like maybe that's just your problem. Sounds like you're not so keen on being a Professor any more. Do you know what you really want?' I asked her as gently as I could, which was the worst thing to do, because it set her off crying again.

'I want – I want to feel like everything won't stop with *me*. I want to have a *baybeeeee*.' She howled the word, while my mouth hung open.

Then I thought, 'Of course' – and then I got a sick feeling in my guts, as I realised whoever had told Lou about me would have told her about Grace as well. Next thing, she'd be asking me if Grace and I were going to have kids. I mustn't let her ask that question.

'So, Lou, is there anyone …?'

She shook her head.

'Then maybe that's another reason why you should go home … go find someone?'

'And waste another ten years? No. Sasha, I don't mean I have nobody to sleep with. You know what? Maybe I should just go right ahead and get pregnant before I leave Zanzibar. I might just do that.'

You and all those others, I thought. I'd heard of women getting their little Tanzanian baby stashed away inside them before they went back to the States or Europe. A win-win situation, was what people usually said. White people.

Again, uneasily, I thought of Grace. Grace and Godlisten, who was 'enough' for her; who was, perhaps, all she'd ever wanted.

Lou stood up. 'You're very lucky, Sasha. I'm happy for you, really I am. I'm glad you found another career. But it's different for women, it always has been. So I'll try and get me a baby before I slink home with my tail between my legs, and I hope everything works out for you here, really I do.'

I wanted to say, 'Are you satisfied now? Have I given you enough to keep you out of the rest of my life?' but I could not bring myself to ask. I wished she hadn't come. I wished I didn't ever have to see anyone from my own country again. So I opened the front door. Lou said, 'Thanks for hearing me.' She held out her hand, and to touch her, after all that time, was like a snakebite.

For the next few weeks in the northern highlands I tried to put Lou out of my mind while I worked like a maniac, all that hands-on, right-on stuff, laying pipes, sinking drills, the low-tech Lotus pumps my employers loved, and I cleaned filters with my bare hands, gouging out lumps of crud, transferring the mud from the wire mesh to my finger nails. I sat docile and benevolent in meetings while village elders lamented the laziness of those youths who should have kept the filters clean. I inspected pipes that had been trampled and broken by elephants in the night; elephants who left footprints like half moons in the earth, those gentle, heavy beasts who could kill a man, and who could easily have been kept at bay if only the night watchmen had stayed awake. I said nothing. In my head I prepared the lie I'd tell my boss: how the watchmen had run out, waving their weapons, but the herd was too angry, too volatile.

I gave a lift to a pregnant woman. I didn't know she was pregnant until she was sitting in the cabin beside me, and I saw how her kanga was stretched over her belly. I kept on driving. We reached her village and she thanked me and got out. Nothing bad happened.

When I first drove into Karatu town my Little League mobbed the Toyota; after that evening they became gradually less enthusiastic, patchier in their attendance at practice sessions. New kids showed up who had no idea of the rules and weren't much interested in finding out; they just wanted to whack the ball so hard it went sailing into the corn fields over and over again. Baraka didn't come. When I asked where he was, the kids said, 'He is studying,' or 'He is helping his father,' or 'We think he has gone on a journey.' Then, one night, I was sitting at the bar of the Safari Inn, and he slid onto the stool next to me, murmuring, 'Shikamo, coach.' He looked older, the beginnings of a moustache above his lip. He used to be exuberant; now he was self-conscious. We talked about the weather, his school work. I asked, 'What next for you?' So I think I must have already abandoned that stupid dream of Baraka in the Major League, and it was no surprise to me, no surprise at all, when he looked me in the eye and said quietly, urgently, 'I want to train to be a carpenter. I have money to go to college, but no money to buy the tools. Please, can you help?'

'Of course I can help,' I said. Relief poured off both of us like sweat. Relief mingled with regret. Baraka began to thank me, to promise he would pay me back as soon as he started earning, how he would make all the furniture I wanted for my house in Dar Es Salaam. I told him not to pay me back, I would rather it was a gift. Then he thanked me even more, and I could see he didn't know how to bring the conversation to a close, and neither did I.

All this time I was dreading my return to Sinamani. Soon it would be decision day, truth day, the day when I'd have to say to Grace, 'Will you marry me and come away with me?' and the day when she might say, 'No.' And in my head it was all tangled up with two things: the opening party at the Caravanserai, and Lou. I dreaded seeing the Caravanserai all finished and bland and reinvented for tourists. I dreaded anybody finding out that Lou had visited me in Dar, because I didn't want all that to be brought up again, that other life which had gone wrong. That life was over. But I knew the only way to keep it in its place, buried, was to tell Grace, not have any secrets.

It seemed like a reprieve when my colleague came to me one morning in Karatu and told me we needed spare parts for the drill, spare parts that could only be obtained by driving to Arusha and, probably, hanging around there for a morning or maybe even a whole day. For once, the delay delighted me. And it was even a relief that whenever I tried to call Grace, her cellphone was off. Maybe she was busy covering for Hamisi.

But when, at last, I drove through the hospital gates in the early evening, with enough time to wash, change and go to that Caravanserai party, Hamisi's jeep was in its usual place, and it was Juma, not Abdallah, who came running out to meet me. He looked agitated. For one bad moment I thought he was going to ask to borrow the Toyota again.

'You know Bwana Frank, the vet? From your country? He needs your help with Mama Anna's dog.'

Mama Anna was a Finnish missionary who had left a few months earlier, along with her husband and their two blonde daughters. I didn't recall any dog.

'Why does Frank need me?'

'The dog has gone crazy.'

'So?'

'Bwana Frank says we must help him sedate this dog.' I was already shaking my head. 'Please, Sasha. I'm afraid if we don't help, Bwana Frank may be badly injured.'

At the staff quarters, Mzee Abdallah was perched balefully on a wall, his long feet sticking out beneath the hem of his white kanzu. Several women and kids were gathered near him. In front of the missionaries' empty bungalow was a post. Tethered to this, by a long chain and a short length of frayed rope, a creature. Frank crouched just beyond its reach, speaking in a gentle, coaxing voice. A mist of flies hung in the air, and a thick stench of shit. The dog was repulsive. It was a filthy ochre brown, with dank, matted hairs up its legs. Its ribs stuck out and its head looked ragged, the mouth pulled back over yellow teeth and a flailing, foaming tongue.

I'd seen Frank in town a few times, practising his Swahili in the bars. Already he had that slightly battered, stringy Peace Corps look; he wore shorts, had an eager face, a grown-out haircut and glasses. We'd nodded to each other, and that was all.

Now, though, he couldn't wait to speak to me, but he was so choked with anger he could hardly get the words out. 'I gotta have at least three people help me sedate her. This is disgraceful. You don't take off half way around the world leaving your dog tied to a fucking post. Did you know these idiots?'

It felt like an accusation. 'No. No, I didn't know them. They were always busy visiting patients, all that kind of stuff. I can't believe they'd do this on purpose.'

With its whole body the dog strained at the rope and yanked itself towards us. 'He's not too friendly, is he?'

'She.' Frank was gripping a grey hospital blanket. 'We have to get her under this.'

'Frank, I just drove two hundred miles, my girlfriend was expecting me back yesterday, we have to go out soon, to the Caravanserai – '

'You want her to starve to death in her own shit?'

Our audience watched with interest. How come Grace wasn't here? It seemed like everybody else was – and along came Hamisi, lean and dapper in a blue short-sleeved shirt. OK, so Grace must be on duty.

'Good evening, gentlemen,' Hamisi said. 'This is an appalling business. Frank, if I had known, I would have called you in before. Now what can we do to help?' And Frank was explaining his trick with the blanket, and the doctor was looking shrewdly at the dog, nodding, measuring distances with his eyes.

The four of us each took a corner of the blanket and hovered as if we were waiting for someone to jump from a high building. 'You look stupid,' Mzee Abdallah called.

'Easy does it,' Frank breathed. She was braced and growling. 'Nice and slow … a little closer…'

She leapt at me and the crowd gasped as I dodged. The rope was taut, its frayed fibres twisting convulsively. 'You OK?' Frank grunted. 'Think you can handle this?'

I gritted my teeth. 'I'm fine. Come on.'

She went for each of us in turn. Once, we managed to drop the blanket on her, but she just shook it off and came back madder than ever, and Hamisi had to pull Juma away when she got her teeth into his shoe. Mzee Abdallah was having a field day. 'Let her starve! That would shut her up.'

'That's enough, Mzee,' Juma said lightly, his eyes still on the dog.

Abdallah carried on. 'If I had a gun, I'd shoot her.'

'Mzee, if *I* had a gun I'd shoot *you*,' Frank roared, and got a laugh from the crowd. I had to admire his Swahili.

After several humiliating minutes, Hamisi suggested that Juma, the youngest and quickest, should provoke her while the rest of us stood ready to one side. When she hurled herself at him we got her. Under the blanket she became pathetic: a desperate, writhing mass of grey wool, the bulge of her skull thrashing around, her scrawny legs splayed. 'Keep it tight!' Frank yelled, holding on with one hand so he could get the syringe from his pocket. 'Keep the blanket tight!' As soon as he let go, she reared up but Juma flung himself across her, and I thought how terrible it would be if, after all this, she was crushed to death. Then Frank flipped the blanket off her flank and plunged the needle in. She twitched, gave a long, slow shudder, fell still. The crowd sighed.

'Have you killed her?' Mzee Abdallah's voice floated over. 'How come it took you so long?'

Even though Frank was cradling her in his arms, I tensed as he uncovered her head, and pushed back the lids of her beautiful, blank, chocolate brown eyes. Perhaps it was my concern about Grace that made me say sourly, 'What the hell are you going to do when she wakes up?'

I walked away from them all, trembling. It was the safari, I told myself, that long, long drive and then all this adrenalin. There had once been a time when I could seize fear and disable it with self-belief. But those days were, apparently, gone.

The dark was coming down fast. I thought I saw Martina's red dress through the trees; maybe she was on her way to fetch water. Some kids were playing. Godlisten wasn't among them.

The door to Grace's bungalow was open. I stood on the threshold and called, 'Hodi?' A lamp was burning. I walked inside and through to the bedroom.

Grace was sitting on the bed. She was wearing her white coat. She didn't move. Her face was like wood.

'Hi.' I reached out to her.

'Don't touch me.'

'What's the matter?'

'Stay away from me.'

'Are you angry because I'm late? I tried to call you.'

'You're a liar.'

'Grace, what do you mean? I haven't lied to you about anything.'

'You lied that first time we met, in the Caravanserai. You lied that you couldn't understand Swahili.'

I laughed, a stupid, frightened laugh. 'But Grace, that was nothing at all – Grace, forgive me if I've done something wrong, but I really, really don't understand what this is about – please, tell me what's the matter.'

I knew what it was, even as she whispered, 'You've been deceiving me. With that mzungu.'

'No! No, I have not! Who told you that? It was Abdallah, wasn't it?'

'It doesn't matter. It's the truth. You've been with her.'

I knew, straight away, it was Abdallah. But I knew, also, there'd have been a web of others, starting with my askari Agostino, passing the message on, spreading it: 'The mzungu had a visitor, a woman, she was crying, he took her inside, she stayed for hours, she stayed the night …' I could understand why people might enjoy a bit of mischief; why they might want to make trouble for me, the rich white mzungu, just because they could. But it was unbearable to realise that those same people might not care about hurting Grace as well.

'Grace, you've got to believe me. Yes, Lou came to visit; yes, she was my girlfriend years ago. But I never asked her to come, and I got rid of her as soon as I could. Nothing is happening between me and Lou. Nothing. Nothing at all.'

She stared at me, her face hard.

And then a voice called, 'Hodi?' and Grace replied mechanically, 'Karibu,' and Hamisi appeared in the doorway, in his best suit and tie. 'Let's go,' he said doubtfully, looking at Grace's grubby white coat.

'I'm not going. I'm sick.'

There was an embarrassed silence. I turned to Hamisi. 'I should stay with Grace. Juma could drive you.' Hamisi was already backing off, but Grace said, 'No, I don't want you to stay.'

In a panic, I went to the bathroom where there was a bowl with a few inches of grey water. I washed the grime from my face and hands, put on a clean shirt, swore I'd come up with some way of convincing Grace; some brilliant idea which would make her see the truth.

Hamisi was sitting on a tree stump, looking thoughtful. As we walked through the compound he talked about the dog and about Frank, how Frank was a brave and determined young man 'of great principle'. It felt like Hamisi was really making some kind of comment on me. And once we were on the road into town, he said, 'So, Sasha. I hear congratulations are in order.'

'Excuse me?'

'I'm told there is to be a happy event. You and a certain American lady.'

Trying to keep my voice calm, I said, 'Doctor, you have made a mistake. I'm going to marry Grace.'

'Oh.' Hamisi sat back in his seat. Then he said, 'So what about the baby she's expecting?'

I slammed on the brakes. 'Grace is *pregnant*?' How stupid I was, how vulnerable to that astonishing moment of hope.

But Hamisi was looking ruffled now, and the spark vanished as he said, 'Well, I heard the American lady was carrying your child…'

Then I saw how it was to be: the story unfolding, how this imaginary white baby would live on and on, perhaps on Zanzibar, perhaps in the US, and how I'd never be able to prove to Grace that it didn't exist.

I put my head in my hands. 'Who told you that?'

He hesitated. 'The old man. Mzee Abdallah. Has he made a mistake?'

'Yes. No, he's done all this on purpose. You have to fire him, Hamisi. You have to fire him because he is malignant and he'll just lie and lie until he's ruined everything.'

'I'm sorry you're upset,' Hamisi said, not believing me.

Perhaps I should have turned back then. Perhaps I should have politely asked Hamisi to walk the rest of the way and pass on my apologies to Kurt and everyone else at the Caravanserai. If I had gone back to Grace and begged her to believe me, things might have been different – but the truth was, I was scared to face her, in case the lie was too powerful, too overwhelming. I decided to carry on, give myself some time to think what to do for the best.

At the Caravanserai lights blazed from every window. Yellow paint gleamed through the dark fringes of banana leaves. The newly carved wooden door was wide open, and flower garlands were draped over it. Just inside the door was a low desk, presumably Gabriel's 'Reception', and Gabriel himself was hovering nearby, in a very clean white shirt. He murmured greetings, smiled the half smile that wound me up. Ahead of us, long neon strips lit the main exhibition room, which surely would once have been shadowy with lanterns. A crowd blocked the entrance, paunchy business men and their fat wives in brilliant print dresses: pink, yellow, electric blue. Then Father Migire said, 'There is a bottleneck at the first exhibit,' grabbed my hand and dragged me through the crowd to a neglected display case, which contained a photograph, or rather a Xerox of a photograph, of 'the last slave' – a blurry grey image: an old woman, mouth set in a line, gazing away from the camera as if it disgusted her.

'Do you believe this is really the last slave?' Migire asked.
'No.'

He nodded. 'You are quite right. Slavery continues.'

The crowd shunted us into the next room, where food was set out on long tables against one wall, opposite a low platform. A man was turning people away from the stack of plates, telling them they must wait until after the speeches. There were groans – 'Who's speaking? We won't eat until midnight! The meat will go cold. How come the women are too early with the food?'

'Let me just check my speech,' Father Migire murmured, unfolding a wad of closely typed sheets. Other men were doing the same.

First up was the District Officer, whose speech was as long as his belly was large. It could have been written for any occasion where Africans and wazungu were gathered: 'Welcome to our friends from Denmark, we are very grateful for your help, we are a very poor country and you are very rich so we couldn't have restored this building without you, we hope many tourists will come and bring us lots of foreign exchange…' No mention of what the Caravanserai once used to be – but who was I to feel indignant? Kurt made a decently short response, thanking everyone and hoping everyone would pull together to make this project a success.

Father Migire was a surprise hit. With a sweet smile he declared, 'This is our culture!' and held his arms high. 'This is our history! Let us never forget the terrible things that

293

happened here, and let us never forget how blessed we are to be alive in the twenty-first century.'

Next, John Simba, swaying a little as he also spoke of history and culture, and teaching our children and the children of the world about the slave trade. I remembered what he had said to me years ago. 'Sinamani is a backwater.' Would it still be true ten years from now? For me, Sinamani was already the centre of my universe.

People were fidgeting, gazing pointedly at the table of food, drinking too much beer as John Simba rambled on and on. There was a commotion in the doorway. A familiar figure was ignoring officials who were trying to explain entry was by invitation only. In America they would have gripped his elbows and marched him out, or forced him down on the floor to search for drugs or weapons. Here, everyone murmured, 'Shikamoo Mzee,' as he made his way through the room, and onto the platform. John Simba looked surprised. 'Come and sit down, Mzee.' Yes, there were a few sniggers, and if I had not been so on edge I might have smiled at the sight of him, standing up there in his filthy brown coat with the stocking belt. But he spoke, and whether or not he raised his voice above the beery hum I don't know; I just know that everyone fell silent as he said, 'Welcome to my house, and to my mother's house, and to my grandmother's house.'

This was so weird, even by his standards, that I cringed with pity for him. A woman nearby murmured, 'He was living here for a while, before the Danes came.' And there was something so sad about the way everyone listened to him harder than they had listened to all those other speeches. It was enough to make my own sadness brim over: his bulk, the electric hair, the brown eyes, the calm voice, sweet as honey, explaining that the district council had done very badly to make him leave his grandmother's house, and they must please allow him to live here again.

'Enough!' barked the District Officer.

The crowd shivered. The old man looked round at everyone in shock. 'Forgive me,' he said, and some men helped him down from the platform and steered him towards the exit. Quickly, the noise level swelled to a roar as everyone headed for beer and food. I could not bear to see him wander off, lost, confused. So I followed, and caught up with him in the foyer, where some kind soul had seated him at Gabriel's table with a plate of pilau. Gabriel was hanging about at the door. I approached the old man.

'Mzee,' I said.

'Mzungu!' His face was radiant. 'You were there, at the celebration? I didn't see you. Forgive me.'

There were two hundred dollars in my wallet. 'Take this money to the Bahari,' I said. 'Say you want a room. Speak to Edison, tell him I'm asking him to get you a room. Edison will help you. I'll visit as soon as I can.'

He fanned out the notes and studied them. 'American dollars.'

'Yes. You should be able to stay there for a fortnight.'

'God bless you.' He squeezed my hand, one last time, then shuffled away.

I felt calm. Outside, the night was warm, starbright. Gabriel leaned against the wall, looking bored.

'Do you have to stay out here all evening?'

'Yes.'

'Then I'll bring you some food.'

He leapt up as if the wall had burned him. 'They will bring me food later.'

I laughed. 'There won't be any left. It's no problem, Gabriel, wait here and I'll get you some.'

It took me maybe ten minutes to stand in a line, elbow my way towards the table and load two plates. I thought about bringing him a beer as well, but didn't.

When I returned to the foyer Sid was there, reading a leaflet, but there was no sign of Gabriel. I frowned. Surely he wouldn't be stupid enough to screw up this job?

'Where is the little fucker?'

'Trust him,' said Sid. 'Maybe he went outside to take a slash. Just trust him.'

I wanted to say, 'I've learned the hard way not to trust anyone here.' But that would have been ridiculous. And racist. The problem wasn't *here*.

'Sid, has anyone said anything about me recently?'

He smiled. 'That's kind of a Tanzanian way of asking a question.'

'OK. Has anyone told you about my non-existent pregnant American girlfriend?'

'Yeah. I heard that story in the Alpha, a couple of times.'

'And what did you say?'

He looked directly at me. 'I told them it was bullshit, and that I paid no attention to gossip. And that's what you should do, Sasha.'

I felt tired. All the anger, all the tension of the day had seeped away. 'But Grace believes it.'

'Maybe she's scared.' It was the last word I'd connect with Grace. 'Scared of losing you. Show her it isn't true. Sasha, it will be OK. This place is always crawling with rumours. Just prove to her it isn't true.'

Hamisi, very drunk, told me he didn't need a lift home; he'd stay in town. That was a relief. I said goodbye to Father Migire and left. Gabriel's food lay untouched on the desk. It didn't matter; I'd given him this chance, now it was up to him to decide what to make of his life. As I walked away from the Caravanserai the warm night air and the sound of the ocean tempted me towards the beach. Palm trees leaned into the sky, resisting an invisible force. But I didn't go for a walk along the beach. Instead, I drove back to the hospital. When the skinny white figure of Abdallah appeared at the gates I braced myself for his rant, but nothing came. He swung the gate open and I thanked him and drove into the compound.

Grace's front door was locked. I made up a bed in the kitchen from a rush mat and a few old kangas, and lay, going over and over how I could persuade Grace that nothing mattered except us and Godi. How I would wait, and wait, and come to her time and time again until she would accept me back. How these rumours might hound us for the rest of our lives, because she was a poor black African and I was a rich white American.

Morning. Martina's high, carefree song at the kitchen door. She squealed when I sat up, then reproached me for not waking them in the night. Grace had already gone to work; she'd be working all day, I guessed, while Hamisi nursed his hangover.

For the whole day I kept busy: chopping firewood, scouring pans, weeding the shamba, fixing a neighbour's bike. I kept away from Godlisten, not wanting Grace to think I was using him to bring her round. In the late afternoon I saw her coming through the trees in her blue dress and my heart began to beat faster. Would she walk past without a word? Or get mad at me for not leaving her in peace?

Grace sat on the tree stump and watched, for a long time, as I mended that puncture. Martina brought us a thermos of tea, and I wished she would go away. Martina said, 'Doctor, please may I go to the shop?' Grace gave permission. What didn't she want Martina to hear?

The patch was on the tube. I tested it with water, then turned the bike the right way up.

She said, 'I have made a terrible mistake.'

I had to ask, get it over with. 'What kind of mistake?'

'I should have believed you before, when you said you wanted to stay here in Sinamani. Not go home to America. You must love me, if that's what you want.'

'Yes, that *is* what I want, really I do. Of course I love you.' My voice felt thick in my throat. Was this all it took?

'And also ... ' She hesitated. 'That American woman came here. That Lou.'

'She came here? When?'

'Today. They called me from the ward to see her. She was very angry.' Grace looked impressed. 'She told me she used to be your girlfriend once, but it finished many years ago. She said, *do I look pregnant?* Then she pulled up her blouse and showed me her belly.'

'How – how did Lou know about all this?'

'Some relation of Abdallah's on Zanzibar. Gossiping. That's how she heard. She said, *I caught the very next boat.* And then she asked me to take her to Abdallah.'

'And did you?'

'Yes.'

'Grace, what happened?'

'She was very, very angry.'

'Sure, but what did she say?'

'She said – ' Grace paused, then spoke carefully. '*Listen to me, motherfucker. Tell any more lies and I will strangle you.* Yes, I think that's what she said. *I will strangle you.* But she was shouting in English, so the mzee couldn't understand. But it didn't matter, he ran away from her. He's not there now, Hamisi told Juma to watch the gate, and Juma is not pleased about that.'

Grace folded her hands in her lap. 'So that is what she said, your friend Lou. I invited her to come in for a cup of tea, but she said she had a lift waiting for her. She sent you her greetings.'

We sat for a while, in a silence that wasn't hostile, but which didn't yet feel as if we were back to our old, easy understanding. Both of us, maybe, still shocked at Lou, hurtling through our lives: for Grace, a total surprise; for me, the Lou I had once known so well, who didn't care what anyone thought, who had always dared to walk the line between cruelty and courage.

It was four in the afternoon. There were still some hours of light. 'Shall we go for a walk now?' I asked. 'Are you too tired?'

'I am tired, but I'd like to walk.'

'Where shall we go?'

'The beach.'

We didn't talk much as we drove into town. Grace asked how the party had been. I didn't say anything about Jambijambi's speech. We left the Toyota by the old post office and walked down the cobbled path.

Sinamani was creeping nearer and nearer to the sea. There were hotels enough for an army of tourists; bland, concrete blocks all along the beach, windows flashing in the sun. We passed their perimeter walls, whitewashed and topped with fancy bricks to avoid looking like prisons. We passed the Bahari, valiantly staying open for its aid workers and back packers and Saturday night discos.

Clouds were gathering, the bulging bruise-grey clouds that might roll away over the sea, or burst open above us. Grace wrapped her kanga around her shoulders. We held hands as we walked towards the boma, its arched windows stark and black in the white limestone. Debris from the sea and the building work lay scattered all around. Vicious spikes of grass poked up through the sand. Nearby, the hull of a half-built boat, a lattice of caulked timbers. A brown heap, propped against the dark hull, slumped to one side.

We stood still. 'What's that?'

'It's a person.' She began to walk towards the boat. Then she ran. The old man was lying with his face in the sand. A mess of blood and sand and hair. One eye was closed, the other a gleaming slit.

'He must still be alive. He moved, so he must be alive.' I was gabbling. She was checking his pulse, her slim, clean fingers pressed against the filthy skin, the caked blood.

'Mzee,' I sobbed. 'Who did this to you?'

'Bring your car, bring it right onto the beach.'

I ran back the way we'd come, crying and shouting for help. Two men outside the post office stared, but when I said a man was dying on the beach they got into the Toyota with me.

Grace was cradling his head on her lap. Between us we lifted him in. 'We must go to the Mission, it'll be quicker. Try not to hit any potholes.'

I thought if I veered off the road and drove across country it would be faster still – but I couldn't risk the bumpy ground. Even so, once we reached the mango avenue I put my foot down, zoomed past an astonished white priest, sent children and goats scattering.

The nuns were very distressed. 'Was it an accident?' they kept asking. 'Did a car hit him?'

Grace was murmuring to the senior Sister, and shaking her head.

'We'll look after him,' the nuns said. 'Have you told the police yet?'

That was the worst of all, the drive back to the police station, knowing what I would have to say. But when I got there, I didn't need to say anything because John Simba was already there, sitting on a bench with his head in his hands. He told me that Gabriel was in the interview room. 'I know he has done something terrible,' said John, 'because he had two hundred dollars and his shirt is covered in blood.'

I never understood whether Gabriel had meant to confess to his mother or just change his clothes before hitching a lift to Dar. John found him cowering behind their chicken shed. Maybe the kid didn't know what to do, now he'd laid hands on more money than he'd ever seen in his life.

I stayed with John in the police station all night, until an officer came out and said, 'He admits it.'

Crazy from lack of sleep, but not so crazy as to drive, I walked in the blue morning air to the Mission, where the nuns told me the old man was still alive, but very weak.

At first I thought they had brought me to the wrong room. His hair had been washed and shorn, leaving only a grey fuzz on his scalp. The dirt and blood had been sponged from his face. His skin was like old copper.

I sat by his bed and laid my hand on his. 'It's Sasha,' I said. 'The mzungu. Mzee, I'm sorry.'

The fingers twitched a little under mine. His eyes were almost closed, only a sliver of white showing beneath his eyelids, as if he lacked the strength to close them completely. 'Thank you,' he whispered. And, 'Go now.'

So I leant forward and kissed him, and left, stumbling past the nuns, who tried to detain me with sympathy and offers of tea.

July 2001

Dar Es Salaam: that strange haven of chaos and sunlit concrete, clapped-out Peugeots, officials with rubber stamps and all the time in the world, the scent of rotting mangoes, diesel fumes, the roar of raging buses, bellowed destinations, endless Afropop bubbling from every cassette player on every street corner. I always loved Dar for harbouring me, and I love it still. In those final months, when I wasn't at work I pounded the pale grey streets of Dar, walking, walking, walking. The long rains were over. I had a marriage to arrange, and an adoption. Stranger, visitor, foreigner, guest: which would I choose? I chose

Grace and Godlisten, and they chose me. At least we would never be *mgeni* to each other.

One day, while I sat drinking soda in the Salamander café, my cellphone rang and Grace's quiet voice said, 'The old man has passed away.'

He took two months to die. The lawyer said he would argue it could never be proven that death had been caused by the blow to the back of the head with a lump of limestone. I told Gabriel's parents this, and Eluminata cried: tears of relief and anguish. But I couldn't cry.

I walked the streets some more, and on leafy, tranquil Shabaan Robert I found the National Museum, a place I should have visited a long time ago. There were no other tourists. I mooched around, peered into display cases at the fussy copperplate of 19th century wazungu, describing their impressions of Zanzibar.

The basement had a 'Pre-History' exhibit – a cave, a glass-fronted box. 'Press the switch to see Man of the Past and Man Today.' I pressed the switch; the box lit up to show the face of a friendly hominid. I pressed again and the light went out. So what happened to Man Today? Then I saw my own reflection, lost in the dark glass.

Outside in a courtyard garden, a tangled metal sculpture commemorated those who lost their lives in 1998, when Al-Quaeda bombed the US embassy. Twelve people died, all of them Tanzanian nationals.

For one last time I went back to Sinamani, which seemed to have grown even more, new breeze-block houses clustering either side of the main road. From inside the Sewa Haji school came the joyful chanting of multiplication tables. Three wazungu were taking turns to peek through the blockhouse window. On the chessboard a man lay in a deep and peaceful sleep.

I walked down the wide path to the Customs House. Amongst the grid of stone pillars topped with crosses, men leaned, arms folded, gazing out to sea. Why do people stare for so long at the ocean? That flicker of light on water, those distant platinum waves so bright they hurt your eyes?

I could have visited the German cemetery where, at his own request, he lay buried – but I did not. Instead I drove straight to Grace's house and was moved when I saw Grace's packed-up possessions: a small metal trunk, a woven basket with a wooden spoon sticking out, a plastic bag stuffed with clothes. That was all. She and Godlisten were sitting on the trunk, next to somebody with their head completely covered in a kanga, sobbing noisily. 'Stop crying, Martina,' said Grace. 'You'll be very happy working for Mama Mhilu. She has so many chickens! You'll eat eggs every week.'

Godlisten was excited. 'Is it time to go on the aeroplane?'

'Not today, but soon. How do you feel?' I asked Grace tenderly. 'Are you very sad to be leaving?'

'No,' she said. 'This was never my home. The village is my home. When we go to Kilimanjaro and say goodbye to mama, that's when I'll be sad.'

The plane remained on the tarmac at Kilimanjaro airport for some time after we had boarded. It was early evening. Godi had the window seat and was engrossed in the controls of the screen in front of him. Between us sat Grace, frozen, her tears long since dried. But her family were on the viewing platform above the departure lounge; they would stay, surely, until our plane took off, and then maybe Grace would cry again. From my aisle seat I glanced out to check they were still waiting – and there, like a miracle, was the mountain, no longer hidden by mist. It took my breath away, the size of it, the vast cone etched on the sky, and as I stared, the summit was lit up by the sunset.

In that moment when the snowcap turned pink, orange, flame, I knew how much it mattered that Grace and Godlisten must see this. But I don't remember which language I used as I told them both to look.